ALSO BY TATE JAMES

MADISON KATE
Hate
Liar
Fake
Kate

HADES
7th Circle
Anarchy
Club 22
Timber

TIMBER

TATE JAMES

Bloom books

This book is dedicated to survivors.
You're the real heroines.

Published by Bloom Books, an imprint of Sourcebooks
P.O. Box 4410, Naperville, Illinois 60567-4410
(630) 961-3900
sourcebooks.com

Originally self-published in 2021 by Tate James.

Cataloging-in-Publication data is on file with the Library of Congress.

Printed and bound in the United States of America.
LSC 10 9 8 7 6 5 4 3 2 1

CONTENT WARNING

Dear Reader,

If you're here, then you're already up to speed on Hades's journey so far. You know what kind of life she's led and what kind of person that's shaped her into.

Knowing that, I think you're probably able to use your own good judgment on whether you'll find the scenes and content in this book triggering or upsetting.

Please remember that every person processes and deals with trauma in their own unique ways; no *one* way is correct. This is Hades's story. Her methods and mechanisms to survive and thrive are her own. I hope you will read through the tough parts and trust that Hades will get her happy ending, made all the brighter for the darkness she endures along the way.

CHAPTER 1
ZED

The dull ache in my hand sparked hot as I flexed and released my fist. Years of split knuckles had built up enough scar tissue that they hadn't busted this time, but goddamn, I'd have liked them to. I'd have liked to slam my fist into that smug bastard's head about seventy-five more times until both my fist and his face were nothing but hamburger.

One punch was all I got, though—after he clapped me on the shoulder, oozing victory as he called me *old friend*. Like I'd been colluding with him this whole goddamn time. My stomach flipped at the idea, but I knew damn well how it looked. Even so, I couldn't stop myself from swinging that punch.

"You should have fucking killed him," Lucas announced, his arms folded over his chest and his expression stricken. I paused briefly, surprised to see him still inside Timber. Then again, the Gumdrop was made of tougher stuff than I'd originally given him credit for. It'd take more than one omission of truth for him to give up on our girl. Shit. *His* girl. She wasn't mine anymore. Not after the way that shit had just gone down.

"The fuck are you still doing here, Lucas?" I asked with a weary groan. "Shouldn't you be pouring your feelings out into a diary or some shit?"

He gave me a baffled expression as I reached over the bar and grabbed a bottle of Maker's Mark straight out of the speed rail. "What?"

I just shrugged. Wasn't that what teenagers did? Fuck if I knew; I'd never gotten to be one. Neither had Dare.

Lucas's jaw clenched as he stepped closer, his eyes darting to the door, then back to me. We were alone inside Timber, the FBI crew all gone now that they'd picked up their mark. After I'd punched Chase, they'd pulled guns on me. But he'd waved them off with a laugh and all but taunted me into hitting him again. No doubt he'd have happily taken the opportunity to have me shot, so I'd backed off.

"Look, I'm still here," Lucas snapped, raking a hand through his hair in exasperation, "because I *know* this isn't what it looks like. You're not seriously going to act like that was all true."

I cracked the wax seal on the cap with my teeth, then tugged the stopper out and spat it aside. No way in hell was I putting the bottle down before it was empty. "Wake up and smell the betrayal, Gumdrop," I muttered, then took a long pull on the bourbon. "Sometimes if it quacks like a duck and shits like a duck, it's a fucking duck."

Lucas stared at the side of my head for a long time, but I kept my dead eyes fixed on the bar that was supposed to be the crown jewel in the Copper Wolf empire. The bar Dare and I had worked our asses off to build into something worthy of the new Timberwolves. Something to finally erase the ghosts of her father's reign. Fuck.

"You're so full of shit I'm basically choking on it," Lucas told me in a quiet voice as he leaned in close. "No way in hell would you betray her like this. You might have *Chase* fooled. You might even have Hayden fooled. But I can see right fucking through you." He gave a disgusted shake of his head and backed off a bit. "You know where to find me when you're done sulking. In the meantime, I'll start working on a plan to get our girl released from

FBI custody. Fuck knows I don't trust whatever Chase has up his sleeve now that she's separated from us."

He started to walk away, and I turned to scowl at his back. "That's it?"

"What else is there, Zed?" he asked, pausing to shrug at me. "You can save your excuses and apologies for Hayden. God knows you'll need them."

Fucking kid had me speechless. I'd expected him to punch me in the face or something. I sure as fuck hadn't expected this *trust* that I hadn't just screwed over the love of my life.

"Oh, actually, now that you mention it." Lucas snapped his fingers like I'd just reminded him of something. Then he strode back over to where I sat on one of the brand-new barstools and slammed me with a viper-fast right hook. The force of the blow knocked me clean off my stool, and my head smacked into the parquetry floor as Lucas stood over me with a hard look on his face. "That was for the look on Hayden's face when she realized you'd been lying to her. You *ever* make her feel like that again—no matter how noble your intentions—I'll fucking kill you. We clear?"

I groaned, touching my fingers to my throbbing cheek. "Yeah," I spat out. "Clear."

Lucas just nodded and stormed out of the bar, leaving me to lick my wounds all alone. How fitting.

The front door of Timber slammed behind Lucas, and I rolled to my feet with a heavy sigh. I'd known this day was coming; I'd *known* all the secrets would bite me in the ass. Yet I'd kept my mouth shut. Over and over during the last few months, I'd wanted to tell her. And over and over I'd lost my nerve. At first, I'd worried she'd shoot me. Then I'd worried she'd stop loving me. And goddamn if I wasn't willing to do *anything* for even one more day inside her heart. Even knowing this would be the sorry outcome of it all.

I righted my stool and sat back on it with a muttered curse, grabbing for my bourbon that had thankfully remained upright.

Karma was kicking the shit out of me today, though, so I barely managed three swallows of bourbon before the hollow sound of footsteps echoed through the empty club behind me.

A familiar perfume reached my nose, betraying my visitor's identity before she slid onto the stool beside me.

"Can I have some of that?" she asked, giving me a watery smile and nodding to the bottle in my hand.

I leveled a scathing glare in her direction and took a long, deliberate sip directly from the bottle. "Get fucked," I replied with a wince after I'd swallowed.

Her mouth tightened with anger, and one brow lifted. "That's no way to speak to your mother, Zayden."

I snorted a humorless laugh. "My mother is dead."

She gave an exasperated sigh and folded her hands together on the bar top in front of her. "Fine. Then it's no way to speak to your handler, Agent De Rosa. You knew—"

Fuck that. She'd just poured gasoline on the smoldering burn of my anger, and I exploded before she could get any more words out.

"I knew *what?*" I roared, shoving my stool back from the bar and kicking it aside when it fell. "I knew that you were setting us up? That you were working with that revolting piece of *shit* Chase Lockhart this entire fucking time? Mom, you *promised* me she was safe. You fucking *swore* to me that this would all *keep her safe.*" My voice broke over that, and I knew she heard it. Her eyes tightened like I'd just fired shots. "You told me that if I did this, Dare would be untouchable."

I was begging her now, with my eyes, with my very being. This whole shit show had gone against *everything* she'd promised. I wanted her to explain, and I lacked the maturity and faith in her that Lucas had just shown in me. Call me crazy, but I'd been burned by my mother's lies before. Somehow, I knew this hadn't been done to help me *or* Dare.

My beautiful mother, the former Veronica De Rosa, just drew a deep breath and cocked her head as she blinked at me unapologetically. "I lied."

Those two words had me seeing red, and before I even registered what I was doing, I had my gun to her head. Only then did I see any kind of guilt cross her face.

"Are you going to shoot me, Zayden? Your own mother?"

I scoffed. "Give me *one* reason why I shouldn't."

She wet her lips, her eyes wide and unblinking as I held the gun to her forehead. "Because I love you, son. I would never do anything to hurt you."

Tension stiffened my trigger finger, and I gave a bitter laugh. "You don't even know what love is, *Veronica.*" Swallowing the bile in my throat, I withdrew my gun and averted my gaze. "You're not worth the cleanup fee."

Her posture slumped ever so slightly in relief, and it made me furious all over again. I should have killed her the moment she walked back into my life five years ago.

"Zayden," she said softly, "I know you don't understand—"

"That's an understatement. Are you going to explain it to me?" I swung my gaze back to hers, meeting cool blue eyes that were a mirror image of my own. I already knew the answer, though. It was written all over her face. "Of course not. Get the fuck out of my venue, Agent Laurence." She'd never used her real name when she'd been married to my father, and when she'd resurfaced to recruit me that day after the Timberwolf massacre, she'd reintroduced herself to me as Agent Rebecca Laurence.

Her mouth tight, she drew another long breath, then gave a short nod and stood up. "This isn't finished between us, Zayden," she told me quietly.

I sneered. "Oh, it really is. Consider this my resignation."

She stiffened, and tension radiated through her face. "Don't be stupid, son. This wasn't a voluntary position."

"No, it wasn't," I agreed with a bitter laugh. "But you just destroyed the only leverage you had against me. So, with all *due* respect, Mother? Go fuck yourself."

She stared at me for a long moment, then gave a frustrated sigh. "We'll discuss this further when you're less emotional." Spinning on her heel, she started to leave the bar per my request, but I let out a low, irritated growl as a thought sparked in my mind.

"Wait," I snapped. She paused, turning back to look at me with a cocked brow. "How long?" I asked. "How long has *he* been involved with the FBI? That simpering fool outside called him the director, but you and I both know that's not true." One of the backup agents had said it right after I'd punched Chase. He'd smirked, too.

My mother wrinkled her nose in disgust. "Of course he's not the FBI director. But he *has* been lobbying for an elevated position, and somehow—lord knows how—he's charmed a lot of the lower-level agents into supporting him. They call him 'the new director' when no one is around to hear their disrespect of the current director."

I shook my head in disbelief. "I don't get it. Chase Lockhart. He's clinically insane. How the fuck did this happen? Why did you never tell me?"

She huffed a short, angry sigh. "I only found out a few weeks ago. He's using another name, of course. And in case you forgot, the number of people left within the bureau who could identify him as Chase Lockhart are pretty damn limited." She held two fingers up. "You and me."

I scowled. "That still doesn't explain how the fuck he even got in. I'm missing a piece of the puzzle here, Mom. Fill me in."

Her gaze darted to the ceiling like she was debating whether to tell me the truth or lie. Then she touched a hand to her hair in an anxious gesture. "I don't have the full story," she admitted quietly. "It's above my pay grade. But I do know he was a protégé of a former director. Brant retired a couple of years ago—medical reasons—but still had a lot of connections, political and otherwise in DC."

I had nothing to say to that, so I remained silent as she glared at me.

"Is that all?" my mother asked. "Because if there is something else you want to know—"

"Who gave them that recording?" I demanded. "Was it you?"

She wet her lips, then nodded. "I know you care for her, Zayden. But she's one of *them*. She's a criminal."

I exploded, smacking the bottle of bourbon off the bar to smash on the floor. "So am I!" I roared back at her. It was an old argument, though, and I knew better than to try to change her mind. "Get out before I shoot you, Agent Laurence. We're done here."

She was smart enough not to hang around this time, quickly exiting the bar and closing the door carefully after herself.

Once again, I was alone. But this time I felt like I'd been repeatedly kicked while I was down. Hanging my head, I let myself crumple to the floor. Brant Wilson. Why had that name not registered when we first saw it in the file Dallas delivered? All the redactions should have been the first fucking tip-off, but for fuck's sake, I *knew* him. Or at least I knew *of* him. When I'd first been coerced into the FBI, I'd done my research. Brant Wilson was an associate director within the FBI and not connected enough to the Shadow Grove area for me to have paid much attention. Still, I should have remembered.

I'd never met him, of course, and hadn't recognized him when he was caught snooping around. But when I saw his name, it *should* have reminded me. There were no excuses. I'd fucked up royally.

Now I was paying the ultimate price. I'd lost the only person I'd ever truly loved. She'd never forgive me for this, and I didn't even blame her.

CHAPTER 2
HADES

The sharp taste of chemicals in my mouth made my stomach churn. I gagged as bile rose in my throat. No way in hell was I vomiting, though. Not when I couldn't move my body.

I blinked my heavy lids, trying to bring the room around me into focus, but it was to no avail. Everything remained dark and hazy, and just that small amount of effort wiped me out. I backslid into unconsciousness once more.

The next time I woke, I could have easily been inside a nightmare. Chase's leering, one-eyed face loomed over me. He spoke to me in low, quiet words that I couldn't make out over the deafening rush of my pulse inside my head. But it was enough to spark the memory of how I'd ended up where I was.

The arrest.

Jeanette stopping her car about half an hour out of Cloudcroft and getting out to meet with a dark-suited man. Jeanette getting shot in the head. The back door being opened and the stinging bite of a tranquilizer dart in my neck as I tried to fight back.

Zed's betrayal.

Zed's *goddamn fucking betrayal.*

How could he? I trusted him more than *anyone*.

This time when the blackness of drugged sleep reeled me back in, I went willingly. Anything was better than reliving the pain of Zed's lie. With just one flippant comment from Jeanette—*Agent De Rosa*—he'd achieved the one thing Chase had failed at for so many years. He'd broken me.

Pain became my constant companion from that point on. As the drug dripped through the IV Chase had hooked me up to and coursed through my veins like fire, the agony of my best friend's treachery scorched holes in my soul. He'd set me up. All the years we'd worked together, all the people we'd killed…and *this* was what he pinned me for? A crime I didn't even commit—*would* never commit. Not her.

Poor Maxine. Now whoever had really killed her would walk free, and for the first time in a long time, I was powerless to change that.

She deserved better.

I deserved better.

Or…maybe I didn't. Maybe karma was finally catching up with me, doling out punishment for all my crimes in the form of Chase motherfucking Lockhart. What had that crazy bitch Jeanette said? He was an FBI director now?

No. Wait, she elaborated while on the road. He wasn't *actually* a director. Not yet. How the fuck he'd even managed to cover his crazy long enough to get into the bureau in the first place…who fucking knew. Everything had a price, I supposed.

Dimly my body registered motion, but no matter how hard I tried, I couldn't shake myself out of the drugged haze. Not that it even mattered. Chase had won.

In a way, he'd done me a favor by keeping me so heavily sedated while he transported me to god knows where. It gave me a place to hide, a reason to close my eyes to the atom bomb Zed had just dropped on our lives.

I was being weak. I knew that. But I was so utterly exhausted, sick to death of being strong all the time. I simply had nothing left. No motivation to fight. No will to continue. Not when my heart hurt so much.

More drugs burned through my veins, and I surrendered to the dark abyss. Nothingness was the best I could have hoped for. Much better than the hopelessness and heartbreak of my semiconscious but paralyzed state.

Time lost all meaning as I drifted endlessly through the blackness of my own medicated sleep, but at some point, the motion stopped. At some point, the drugs began to fade from my system, and the gut-wrenching agony of awareness gripped me once more.

"Wakey, wakey, Sleeping Beauty," Chase's leering voice sang, grating across my mind like a rusty razor blade.

As badly as I wanted to ignore him, I'd rather channel my anger than wallow in it. So I forced my lids to open and my eyes to focus on my psychotic ex-fiancé.

"Aw, there she is," he cooed, stroking the side of my face. "I was worried for a moment that I'd hit you a bit hard with the sedatives. You always had such a good tolerance for the hard shit, though. Didn't you, Darling?"

I drew a breath and tried to say his name, but no sound came out. His brows hitched slightly, and he shifted away to reach for something. That small movement gave me a quick glimpse of the room. Calling it a room was generous, though. More of a prison cell, complete with a steel-reinforced door and a metal toilet in the corner.

"Here, you must be thirsty," Chase murmured, pushing a thin ice cube between my lips with forceful fingers. I tasted copper and dirt on his skin and resisted the urge to dry-retch. He was right; my mouth was as dry as the Sahara. I needed that ice cube.

"Chase," I croaked when I felt more confident in my voice.

He smiled down at me like a loving partner. "Yes, my sweet?"

I needed to swallow a few more times before I could muster

the energy to get the rest of my words out. Thankfully, he leaned in closer so I didn't need to do anything more than whisper.

"Go fuck yourself."

He jerked back and glared death at me, then as if a light switch was flicked, he started laughing.

"Oh, Darling. Sweet, pretty Darling." He chuckled, tapping something on his knee. As far as I could tell, I was bound hand and foot to the small prison cot. I couldn't tilt my head far enough to see what he was holding. "You've gained so much spark since we last spent quality time together. I greatly look forward to snuffing it out."

If I had any saliva to spare, I'd have spat at him. But as it was, I could do nothing but sneer and offer a lame retort from my vulnerable position. "I'd like to see you try."

Chase clicked his tongue, then lifted his hand to show me the dagger he held. "Well, that's the whole reason why I brought you here, my sweet." He brought the tip of the knife to my throat, and for the briefest moment I really believed he would end it all. Right then and there. Drive that blade home through my carotid artery and finish our sick game of cat and mouse once and for all.

For a moment, I hoped he would.

But this was Chase, and nothing was ever so simple. He turned the knife over and carefully, methodically, sliced away my clothing. Piece by piece, he tossed scraps of torn fabric over his shoulder, grinning like a crocodile when he discovered my lack of underwear. Yet another knife in the back from Zed.

Had he known when he took my panties? Had he known I was about to be arrested? I was going to fucking kill him. If I got free… *when* I got free…he was fucking dead.

"As much as I'd like to think you dressed just for me," Chase murmured, his breathing heavy as his hands gripped my thighs, "you had *no* clue what was waiting for you, did you?"

I couldn't stop myself from jerking with shock as his fingers pushed inside me, rough and demanding. My stomach knotted, and an acidic wave of old fear washed through me. For a second, all I could feel was pure hopelessness like I was right back where I'd been as a teenager. Totally and completely at Chase Lockhart's mercy.

But that feeling only lasted a second before anger and outrage washed it away. I *wasn't* that girl anymore. I'd fought tooth and nail to put her so firmly in my past that I'd be damned if I let Chase's assault erase all my hard work. I wasn't his Darling. I was *Hades*.

Forcing my lips to curl in a cold smile, I gave a hard laugh. "You're disgusting," I spat out. "Some things never change."

Chase's jaw tightened, and he shoved his fingers deeper in retaliation. But when I gave no reaction this time, he pulled them out and slapped me hard across the face, hard enough to make my head spin and my ears ring, but I'd happily take a thousand slaps over the alternative.

"You think you're so tough now, huh?" he sneered, swiping his fingers across my lips and leaving the taste of myself behind. "You think you're so untouchable. Well, Darling, I have news for you." He leaned down close, his lips brushing the side of my face as he lowered his voice to a whisper. "I've broken you before, I'll do it again. And there's *nothing* you can do to stop me."

Instead of the maniacal laughter I might have expected to follow that statement, he gripped my face with his hand and crushed his lips to mine. The shock of it gave him the upper hand, but it barely took me a second to regain my wits and bite the hell out of his lip as he tried to kiss me deeper.

Blood filled my mouth, and I released his lip. But he didn't pull away completely, just gave a throaty chuckle and licked a long, bloody line up the side of my face.

"Oh yeah," he groaned. "This is better than I'd imagined."

His hands trailed down my body, groping every damn inch of me before he made a satisfied sound and stood up. "Don't worry, my sweet demon, I'll get you nice and warmed up before we start the real fun." He reached into his pocket and pulled out a preloaded syringe. Staring down at me with a deranged smile, he plucked the safety cap off the needle, then bent over my arm. I was bound so securely, at wrist *and* above my elbow, that there was no chance of wriggling free as he found a vein and slid the needle home.

"Chase," I gasped, unable to help myself as fear washed through my whole damn body. "Please. Don't..."

It was pointless, though. He'd already pushed his thumb down on the syringe, and the fire of drugs burned up my arm. No sweet darkness of sleep claimed me this time. Nope, he removed the needle and smirked his victory as the familiar, dreaded high hit my brain.

"I'll be back to play soon," he assured me. "Let's leave that to sink in a bit first."

Terror gripped me, even as my hold on reality started to slide. "Chase, please, don't do this."

"Aw, begging so soon? Nah, that doesn't sound desperate enough. Don't worry, though. We'll get there. Sweet dreams, Darling." With a snicker, he shut the lights off, plunging the room into darkness. The door opened briefly, just long enough for him to slip out then slam it behind him.

The loud scrape and clang of the heavy bolt on the other side echoed through my pitch-black cell in a way that rattled me right to the core. Shame filled me as a few hot tears rolled down my cheeks, but I quickly swallowed it back.

It was too soon. Chase had barely even started, and if I knew him like I thought I did, there would be a long road to go yet. I needed to get control. He'd done so much worse to me in the past. I'd endured such horrific abuse over the years at his hands, yet I'd survived it all. I'd survived it then, just like I would now.

Besides, one dose of PCP wasn't going to kill me. I'd endured way more and lived to tell the tale. Still...the blackness of the room was suffocating me, and I squeezed my eyes shut. Better to keep them closed than see things that weren't really there.

Yeah. Like that would stop it.

The clang of the door jerked my head up. I opened my eyes automatically, refusing to be helpless when Chase walked back in. All I found, however, was unrelenting darkness. It clawed at my naked skin. Icy hands pinched and groped. Was it even real? Was it Chase fucking with me? The drugs messing with my head?

The drag of blunted nails over my breasts barely registered.

He'd done worse.

I kept my mouth closed and my jaw tight.

"What do you think, old friend?" Chase's voice was right in my ear, and I swore even the darkness recoiled as though it didn't want to be close to him. My shoulders could barely move and there was no slack on my wrists and arms; still, I leaned away. I'd rather rip my fucking arms off than let him breathe on me.

"I think you suck at this." Zed.

Fuck me.

Tears flooded my eyes. That voice was right there. Right next to me. As familiar to me as my own heartbeat.

"You've never understood how to break her."

"Oh, I know her better than you think. I know you both better than you think." Chase let go with another nasally laugh. This time he was right in front of me, and he gripped my face again. The darkness peeled back, and his vicious skull was right in my face. The flesh melted away leaving only the mangled skull and the black eye patch.

"You're an ugly fucking pirate."

He chuckled. "Am I? Well, look at what Zed brought you."

I wouldn't look. I didn't want to see Zed. I couldn't. Not after all of this. Not when my fucking heart leapt just to hear him. His betrayal was still an open, festering wound.

Not that Chase gave a damn; he dug his fingers into my face, wrenching my head to the side. It didn't hurt, but I couldn't stop myself from seeing.

Zed stood there, a stone-faced sentinel with Lucas at his feet.

"How do you think you'll like your dancer with one eye?" Chase asked. "What do you think, Zed my old friend, should we take the eye or the cock?"

"Does it matter?" Zed sounded almost bored. "Just put a bullet in him. You want to hurt her, don't you? She loves this pathetic bastard so much, it'll decay her soul knowing he died because of her."

No.

I opened my mouth but no sound came out, and the darkness rushed in, stealing my voice. They were laughing. In the dark.

The flash of a muzzle.

Smothering in the blackness, I choked on my screams.

Water dripped somewhere. The plopping fell like a metronome. The continuous sound raked over my every nerve. I swore they were on fire. Maybe that was where he'd burned me. Had he burned me? Wait...

"Dare," Seph whispered into the darkness, and I jerked my head up. I fought to look past the water running over my eyes, but they stung when I blinked. No, she wasn't here. Seph wasn't here.

Exhaustion pulled my head back down.

"Oh, for fuck's sake, Dare, you think you're such a badass you can ignore me now? I'm not a child, you know."

I squinted through the darkness. Only it wasn't dark. It was bright. Too bright. The light hit me from every angle, and I held up a hand to block it out before it burned my retinas. The moisture gathering in the corners of my eyes spilled down my cheeks.

"What the hell are you wearing?"

Instead of her uniform or even jeans and a T-shirt, Seph was dressed in the skimpiest piece of lingerie. It was pitch-black and set off her pale skin perfectly. Even her red hair looked lustrous, a bright flame amid the porcelain and onyx. "Do you like it?"

She did a little shimmy walk like she was on a runway—in my Louboutin stilettos. Confusion and irritation vied for control.

"Daddy got it for me."

A fist in my hair dragged me upward, and I stared into the empty eye sockets of my father. His face had rotted like something out of a zombie movie. This wasn't real. It couldn't be real.

"Daddy and Chase are going to have a party that's just for me." Seph all but skipped over to me and then pressed a kiss on our father's rotting cheek. "Daddy still loves me." The happiness she radiated flooded my mouth with bile. The innocence. "Don't worry, we found the others. They're coming too."

She held out her hand, and Diana took it. Diana wore the same skimpy, awful outfit and it looked even worse on her child body.

"Virginity gets quite the high price," my father whispered in my ear, the rough sound like a thousand insects clicking and crawling. They were falling off of him and onto me. I wanted to shrug them off. But this wasn't real.

"This isn't real," I said. "Not real."

"You're such a selfish bitch," Seph complained. "Even now, you have to have everything *your* way. Well, it's not. Hades is dead. Long live Persephone, the new queen of the underworld."

Our father's corpse laughed, and black ichor sprayed like flecks over my skin. "You never asked her what she wanted, did you?"

My heart was in so many pieces, shattered on the rocks. The lighthouse was gone. Cass…Cass…

I swallowed.

"She didn't," Seph protested and suddenly her hair was up in a pair of pigtails, and she twirled around. "She never asks me anything. She didn't even bother to see if I wanted to be sold. The man who would pay for me would want me. And I know just who my high bidder is gonna be."

A shudder of revulsion went through me. This wasn't Seph. A hand closed over my throat, and I was slammed against a wall.

Once. Twice. On the third slam, I cut open my eyes to see Chase leering down at me.

"If you beg me to fuck you, I'll keep her safe for you. That's all you wanted, isn't it, Dare? For your baby sister to be an ungrateful little bitch, sheltered from the world?" I really didn't care what he did with me. "I can make that happen for you, Dare. What other man in your life could do that for you?"

I licked my lips. They were so dry. The dripping was still there. My mouth tasted like copper.

Belatedly the dripping made sense. I was melting. Chipped. Split. Cracked. Broken. Bleeding away. Good. Then I wouldn't feel this for much longer. The emptiness in my soul, the gouged-out place where my heart used to be.

I slammed my head forward into Chase's.

The next time I opened my eyes, I was alone. The lights were on. Chains hung from the ceiling. I tried not to focus on anything for too long. The walls were melting—no, they were bleeding. I pushed my hands down against the floor and shoved myself upward.

Blood crusted my nails. The skin over my knuckles was littered with bruises and scrapes. My panting breaths came in faster, shallower gulps. I had to slow it down. Calm down. I peeked at the bleeding walls again—yeah, still bleeding.

Slowly, because my stomach lurched at the idea of moving, I turned in a circle.

Alone.

Good.

Now...door.

If I put one foot in front of the other, I could get to the door.

Then I could figure out how to open it.

One problem at a time.

"You're so pathetic," a voice as familiar as my own said

in an almost bored tone. "How the fuck did you take over the Timberwolves again?"

Head turning, I fought against my reaction. The woman leaning against the far wall was me. Her expression was cool, remote, unapproachable. Every inch Hades. The woman Cass had been so reluctant to even touch.

"This is sad." She motioned to me. "Why are you sniveling?"

"I'm not," I argued, even as my voice cracked and a sob tried to escape.

"I just think it's sad." Daria Wolff shook her head. She wasn't alone. Hannah stood at her side taking notes. "You had so much potential. But look where you ended up."

"Right back where you started," Hayden decried. "How the hell did you fuck up what we spent years dreaming of?"

"Because she let the boys into her bed and into her heart." Dare's voice cut worst of all. "Zed rejected us before, but did we remember that? Nah. Not when he fucked us until we needed a damn ice pack. And now where is he? Off sucking Chase's dick or something? You should give that man an Oscar. It only took them twelve years, but they finally beat you."

"They haven't beaten me."

"No?" Hades snorted. "From where I'm standing...you're done. You're finished. The Timberwolves are going to scatter unless Zed takes the mantle. They might follow him, you know. He knows where all the bodies are buried. He even helped you bury a few."

And dig some up—even bodies that weren't there.

A slap caught me across the cheek and knocked my head to the side. I spat blood and looked back at myself.

"Zed. Zed. Zed. What the fuck has Zed ever done for you? Really? He couldn't even bring himself to touch you until he thought he was losing you again. How many times did he make a point of fucking women in front of you?"

"It doesn't matter."

"How can you say that?" Dare demanded. "He could have saved us, and he didn't."

"It doesn't matter."

"She's a lost cause," Daria stated. "This woman has no head for business. She's just a mess of chaotic emotions and drugs."

"We had Lucas," Hayden whispered. "Remember that."

"We don't need him." Hades sliced a hand through the air. "And we don't need you."

She hit me again.

Then again.

I welcomed the blows.

One after another until my eyes ached and my jaw didn't quite work right and all I could taste was blood.

"You done?" I asked in a voice hoarse from choking. I didn't wait for her answer. I went for her. "I'm Hades."

"I always was your better half, Darling," Chase mocked as Hades melted into him and the others vanished. He caught my next fist, but not my knee. I didn't care what I tore or broke. I was taking him to hell with me.

CHAPTER 3

When the scene finally faded, my sobs echoed hauntingly through the dark. But no one came. Not when the walls started dripping with burning lava. Not when the ceiling started closing down on me and spikes shot up from the floor.

Thankfully, the drugs in my system allowed me to detach from my own body. I couldn't feel the bite of the leather straps restraining me. The chill in the room had no meaning to me. My body was not my own. I had no physical form anymore. Yet my mind remained tethered to that bed. To that cell of horrors. To the heartbreaking, soul-crushing delusions I was helpless to escape.

The cell door slammed open, deafening, and the harsh light flared to life above me, blinding. So I barely even registered Chase looming over me until he spoke.

"Are we having fun yet, sweet little demon?" He swiped his tongue over his lower lip, and his presence was more tangible this time.

My gaze ducked past him, seeking the patch of floor where Lucas had knelt. Where he'd stared back at me with accusation and betrayal in his eyes as Zed held a gun to his head. It was spotless, though, the floor. Not a single droplet of blood.

I'd imagined it. Of course I had. I should have known my hallucinations would be so much more vivid, more real and painful now. Because unlike the last time I'd been at Chase's mercy, now I had so much more to lose. Lucas, Cass, Seph...*Zed*. But I didn't need drugs to make me feel the acidic burn of Zed's betrayal. He'd done that all on his own *before* I'd landed in Chase's dirty clutches.

That clarity alone told me the drugs were wearing off. How long had it been since Chase injected me?

Humming a happy sound, he groped my body again, making me stiffen with revulsion. The drugs were wearing off, and I was back inside my body. Able to *feel* once again.

Chase smirked as he twisted my nipple, and I clenched my jaw tight to swallow the scream of pain. "Oh good, I timed this beautifully," he murmured. The same knife he'd used to cut my clothes was in his hand once more, and the mattress dipped as he placed a knee on the side of the bed.

Holding my gaze, he climbed on top of me, straddling my bare stomach and barely bothering to hold his own weight as he leaned in close. His nose trailed a line down the side of my neck as I turned my face away, and the tip of his knife scraped over my ribs, taunting me.

"I wanted to wait until that first high wore off a bit," he confessed in a low murmur. "I'd hate for you to *not* feel anything when I do this..." Sitting up again, he raised his knife, then slammed it down.

A scream tore from my throat as agony blazed through my shoulder, but Chase just shushed me with his finger over my lips. He left the blade buried in my flesh, right below my collarbone, and unbuckled his pants.

Licking his lips, he gripped his hard dick and started stroking it right there on top of me. I flinched, bile rising in my throat at the sight of his erection. But I'd known it was coming from the second he captured me. He'd taken *such* delight in abusing my body when we'd been together; why the fuck would he pull his punches now? After all these years of festering, plotting, obsessing… Nah, I'd known full fucking well that given half a chance, Chase would rape me.

Gritting my teeth, I focused on the pain in my shoulder. I ignored the weight of Chase sitting across my torso, ignored his harsh, heavy breathing as he jerked himself off. But that wasn't good enough for him. He raised a hand and cracked it across my face hard enough to make me see stars and jostle the knife.

Fuck *me*, that hurt.

"Look at me!" he demanded, more than an edge of madness in his voice.

Reluctantly, I brought my gaze back to his face, resolutely ignoring his hard dick and pumping hand. Cruelty flashed in his single eye, and his lips curled in a snarl as I hardened my own expression.

"Stubborn bitch," he spat out, grasping the handle of the knife and jerking it out abruptly.

I screamed again, and he came. Hot, wet semen splattered my chest, my neck, my face, and blood streamed from the stab wound. Chase just grunted his satisfaction and smeared the mixture all over my tits with his dick. Then he jammed a finger into my bleeding shoulder wound to make me scream again.

"That's the sweetest sound in the world," he groaned, then pulled his finger out once more and brought it to his mouth.

My whole body quaked with pain and shock, and I couldn't drag my eyes away as he licked my blood from his hand. Then he climbed off the bed as casually as if nothing had happened.

"Let's try something new," he announced, picking up a tray from the floor. I hadn't seen him bring it in, but it was laid out with three syringes. "This is a really special cocktail. Created *just* for you, Darling girl."

He gave me a smirk, tapping the crook of my arm to bring up

my veins. One after another, he injected the drugs while I tried my hardest not to slip into a panic attack.

I wanted to ask what the hell he'd just shot me up with, but it didn't matter. All asking would do was show my fear. And *fuck that*. So I kept my lips shut tight and my jaw clenched as he placed the empty syringes back on the tray and scooped up his knife from where he'd tossed it.

"Wouldn't want to leave this lying around, would I?" He chuckled, waving the knife at me tauntingly. "Don't look so worried, pretty Darling. I won't leave you alone so long this time. I want to *fully* experience this mix for myself."

With that ominous promise, he gave a mocking salute and slammed the cell door shut behind him. He'd left the lights on, though, which was a small mercy.

Dizziness swept through my head as the mystery concoction of drugs kicked in, and I let out a strangled groan. There was PCP in there for sure, but it wasn't as strong as the last dose. Or if it was, whatever else I'd been given was counteracting the numbness and dissociation. My body flushed with heat, and I steadily grew painfully aware of every inch of my skin—total opposite of how angel dust usually made me feel.

Wave on wave of warmth washed over me, making my breathing harsh and my chest heave. The tight leather straps holding me to the bed scraped my limbs distractingly, the sensation more intense with every passing second until it was all I could focus on.

Sweat dripped down my forehead, stinging my eyes, and I tugged against my restraints. Fear of the unknown was spiking my paranoia worse than usual while high. Not knowing what Chase had injected me with...

The door opened sometime later, and I groaned with frustration. What *now*?

"What did you give me?" I muttered, unable to hold my

tongue. "I feel…weird." I rolled my head to the side, only to gasp in shock when my eyes focused.

"Shh," Zed whispered, holding a finger to his lips.

"Zed?" I croaked, then instantly remembered him telling Chase to shoot Lucas. But shit. No, that was a delusion; it hadn't really happened. "What—"

"Dare," he breathed, coming closer with an intense look in his eyes. "You've got to be quiet. I'm getting you out." He held up a key, pointing to my restraints.

I swallowed, searching his face. Was this real? Or just another hallucination? It felt real. But what did that count for? "Zed, you set me up," I murmured, shaking my head as much as I could. "You set me up. You were working with him all along. Why?"

"No, baby." He sighed as he quickly unlocked the small padlocks on each of the leather restraints. "No, I would *never* betray you. I love you, Dare. That was all Chase. He set it all up to make you think I'd stabbed you in the back."

Zed reached across to unlock my other arm but brushed my hard nipples as he did so. A low moan escaped my throat without my permission, and he paused.

"This isn't real," I mumbled. "This is just another psychotic episode. Chase drugged me, and this…this isn't real. You betrayed me. Nothing can change that."

Zed shook his head, looking upset, but continued unlocking my restraints. Still, I couldn't help arching my back and writhing when his movements brushed my skin. What the hell was wrong with me? I was like a cat in heat. Every damn touch, every *glance*…

"This isn't a delusion, Dare," he told me in a rough voice when I was fully unbuckled from my bonds. "Please, trust me. I'm trying to get you out of here before Chase comes back." He held out a hand, offering to help me up. But the underlying message was clear. He wouldn't force me. I needed to accept his help willingly.

"Please, *trust* me. I never betrayed you, Dare. I love you." His face was so full of sincerity, so honest and open… I couldn't fight it. I lifted a heavy arm and placed my hand in his.

The second our fingers touched it was like a match had just been dropped on gasoline. I threw myself into his arms, my mouth finding his like a homing beacon. Our lips locked, and I gasped into the kiss as his tongue plunged deep, tangling with mine and damn near swallowing me whole.

My skin was still on fire, my heart racing like it was about to explode, and all of a sudden I couldn't focus on anything except sex. I wanted him *so* bad.

"Zed," I moaned as his lips moved to my neck and I bucked my hips in his lap. "Zed, I need you."

"We can't," he groaned, reluctantly pushing me away. "Dare, we can't risk it. I don't know how long Chase will be gone. It's more important to get you out of here."

I knew that. I *knew* he was right. But I just…couldn't focus. My breathing was rough and my nipples harder than diamonds as I pulled myself back against him. "Please, Zed. I need you so bad it hurts."

No. It was my shoulder that hurt. Fuck, it was *agony*. Dimly I registered the fresh blood flowing from the wound Chase had inflicted, but that was dull compared to the ache between my thighs.

Zed gave a pained groan as I kissed him again, and his hand skated down my body, finding my throbbing core. "Fuck," he hissed as his fingers delved into me, "you're *drenched*. You really want this, huh?"

Words failed me as I rode his hand. All coherent thoughts fled my brain. All the fear, the panic, the urgency of the situation… gone. The only thing I could focus on was the intense orgasm building from Zed's rough fingering.

"Zed," I groaned again, more insistently. He knew what I wanted; he was just teasing me.

He chuckled a couple of curses, then pushed me back down on the bed. "Okay, Dare. But we gotta be quick. I'd hate for Chase to come back and catch us like this." He unzipped his pants, pulling out his cock and showing me that he wanted it just as badly. "Lie back, baby, spread those legs for me."

I moaned, doing as he said. He hovered over me, his hands at my neck for a moment, but I wasn't paying attention. All I wanted was him to sink inside me. Fill me up. Fuck me until the crazy, insane, uncontrollable need was sated.

"Come on," I all but screamed. The heat was painful now. Like my skin was about to blister.

Zed hooked his hands under my thighs, pushing my legs wider as he lined up. Then he pushed inside, and I convulsed with tremors as I screamed.

Sweat coated every inch of me as he thrust in and out, and my eyes rolled back in my head. What if it killed me? Whatever drugs were filling my veins, pumping through my heart...what if they killed me? It felt possible. I thought I was okay with it, too. I'd lost everything. Why would I want to continue? Not now. Everyone hated me. The look on Lucas's face as they'd cuffed me had been pure torture. Cass would be better off if I weren't around. Even Seph...I did nothing but make her life hard.

A hard and fast orgasm hit me, and I shrieked, writhing and bucking under Zed. But he didn't slow. He just fucked me harder and faster, grunting and sweating as he bit his bruised lower lip.

When had that happened? It looked like teeth marks in his lip. Like someone had bitten him.

"Come for me again, Darling," he snarled, reaching a hand down between us and violently pinching my clit. My body responded, though, crashing me headlong into another orgasm that left me seeing stars and hoarse from screaming.

Still, he kept going, fucking me so hard the bed rocked and smacked the concrete wall behind us.

So much sweat poured from my body, and my heart thumped so hard I was sure I must only be a second away from cardiac arrest. Fuck. Why couldn't I focus my eyes?

Reaching up with a heavy hand, I swiped the sweat from my eyes and blinked a couple of times to clear them. Then screamed when I refocused on Zed.

Except it wasn't Zed at all.

A wide grin of triumph curved Chase's lips as he pumped harder. His hands pinned my wrists against the bed, holding me with all his strength as I thrashed and fought, desperately trying to push him away.

It was no use, though. A moment later he grunted his climax with a handful of slamming thrusts. The second he finished, he climbed off and stepped back from the bed with a delirious grin on his face.

"Oh, sweet Darling," he purred, "that cocktail worked like a *treat*. You really believed I was *him*, didn't you?"

He just stood there, pants around his thighs and his dick out, slick with my own arousal. How could I have done that? How could I have *seriously* believed…

Unable to stop myself, I rolled to the side and vomited straight onto the floor. He'd released my bonds. I wasn't trapped. I could make a run for it.

Gathering every inch of my strength, I coiled my weak muscles and lurched forward. I had no plan, just desperation. It was all for nothing, though. I barely got within a foot of Chase before something jerked me back by the neck.

Chase cackled with glee, shaking his head at me as I collapsed at his feet. "You didn't really think I'd let you go, did you?" He clicked his tongue. "Silly girl. This was fun. Let's do it again. Soon."

This time when the cell door closed and the bolt shot home, I gave in to hopelessness. To despair. I huddled there on the floor, shaking and crying, wishing I was dead.

27

CHAPTER 4

Unknowingly, Chase had given me some small mercy in the cocktail of drugs he'd shot me up with. The one he'd used to erase my inhibitions had also wiped a good chunk of my memory. When I woke, naked and aching on the floor of my cell, I had only the faintest memory of how I'd gotten there. Echoes. Like it'd happened in a movie I'd watched or that I'd dreamed it all.

Only the collar around my neck—chained to the wall—and the raw ache between my legs confirmed that it'd been real.

Vague or not, the knowledge of what he'd done...of what *I'd* done...cracked something deep inside me. Something, I suspected, that could never be repaired.

I lost track of days as Chase escalated his torture. Half the time he seemed content to just shoot me up and let my mind deteriorate into psychosis. The other half, he preferred to be hands-on. He grew relentless in his obsession with my fear, each encounter subtly pushing me closer to death.

But to my disappointment, he always seemed to know when to stop. When to pull my head up from the trough of water he'd been drowning me in. Or when to turn the voltage down on his cattle prod.

I also lost track of how many times he mixed those three fucking drugs in my veins, then reaped the benefits of my mindless, drugged state. PCP for delusions, of course. GHB for erasing inhibitions—and memory. Lastly, a modified version of bremelanotide, which increased arousal and sexual desire.

Any idiot with half a brain could say that mixing drugs like that could result in death, but Chase didn't seem to care. Neither did I. Every time my heart beat so hard it hurt, I prayed for it to just...stop.

But then later, when Chase was gone and the drugs faded, I revived myself with the burning fire of anger and determination. Thoughts and dreams of what I'd do to Chase if I ever got free were the only things that kept me going.

Yet every time I started to fall asleep, I was plagued by one gut-churning, heartbreaking thought.

Why had no one come for me?

Surely, even as mad as Lucas had to be, he'd have called Cass. Or Demi. Or hell, even Gen. Was anyone looking for me? Did anyone care?

It was so damn easy to sink into depression and despair.

Time was passing—it had to be—because every time I woke up, I was weaker. Chase barely fed me, just enough to keep me alive but not enough to give me strength. Water was the only thing maintaining me, and half of that came from his torture. There was something particularly terrifying about having a wet towel wrapped over your face for extended periods of assault.

He didn't bother to treat the wound in my shoulder, and it soon grew red and puffy around the crusty edges. When I woke up trembling uncontrollably, coated in cool sweat, I knew infection had set in, either there or in one of the many other injuries—flesh wounds and burns only—that Chase had inflicted on me.

I said nothing about it when he entered the room, but I should have known he wouldn't let me out so easily.

29

"Good thing I have antibiotics here, hmm?" he commented, pressing his thumb into the edge of my infected wound. Putrid, yellow-green pus seeped out. "Don't go anywhere, Darling. I'll have you back to fighting fun in no time." Whistling a tune, he left my cell and left the door open as he went to fetch the medication.

It was another damn mind game. I couldn't run. Not with my collar tethered to the wall and fever raging through my body. He was just mocking me.

When he returned, he made quick work of locking my wrists back into the leather restraints on the bed. I said nothing about it, too sick and too weak to give a fuck how he was getting his rocks off today, but he seemed to feel the need to explain.

"I'll need to leave the IV hooked up for a bit," he told me, squeezing my breasts as he spoke. "Can't risk you trying to kill yourself with the needle, now, can I?"

I managed a weak scoff. "I'd rather kill you with it," I mumbled.

He grinned. "That too." He made quick work of hooking up an IV of antibiotics, well practiced at finding my veins already, then checked the time on his watch. "As much as I'd dearly love to stay and play, I have a call to make."

He left my cell door open again, laughing to himself as his footsteps faded away. It was just more bullshit power games. He knew full fucking well I was too weak to free myself now. Too sick and frail. Broken.

But he'd underestimated me. My body might be his to play with, damage, starve, and weaken…but he didn't have my mind. Not yet. Damn it, he was close though. If I wanted any hope of getting away with even a shred of sanity, I needed to act soon. Act fast. And if I died in the process, then so fucking be it.

Lucas and Cass would take care of Seph, I knew that. Even if I was dead, they'd continue to protect her just as fiercely as I knew they were now.

Zed…shit. I didn't know what to think. At face value it seemed a whole lot like he'd stabbed me in the back, totally betrayed me and our friendship. But I wasn't so stupid as to take things at face value. There *had* to be an explanation. But if there wasn't and he really had betrayed me? Well...karma could take care of him.

I'd rather die trying to escape than live under Chase's control for one more day.

He hadn't shot me up with any other drugs through the IV, thank fuck, and it gave me an opportunity to use my brain without the noises of paranoia and delusion. Based on how feverish I felt and how infected my shoulder was, I'd need more than one bag of IV antibiotics. That meant I had some time to plan and to regain some strength if Chase was inclined to feed me while I was hooked to the medicine.

I'd vomited so damn much since he started his abuse. The mixture of drugs seemed to have me constantly nauseated—not to mention my own disgust at the things he'd done to my body. I knew I was malnourished, but I wasn't hanging around to try to regain any weight. The second I saw my opening, I was gone. No matter what condition I was in.

Except sometimes, no matter how determined the mind was, the body simply wouldn't—or couldn't—cooperate.

So I closed my eyes and slowly, deliberately put myself through the mental exercises I'd learned all those years ago. The careful compartmentalizing that had allowed me to survive the first round of abuse I'd suffered at Chase's hands. The same coping mechanisms that'd seen me forge my path of blood and bodies as the leader of the Timberwolves without totally succumbing to insanity. It'd kept me safe then, and it was keeping me safe now. Just.

Piece by piece, I took all the recent torture and abuse—no matter how patchy the memories—and tucked them into a box. Then I locked the box, wrapped it in chains, and dipped it in molten steel. *Crack that, motherfucker.*

I had plenty of those same boxes littered through the infinite darkness of my mind, each neatly labeled with the damage they contained. But sooner or later, I knew they'd become too heavy to hold.

With that mental exercise complete, I could breathe easier. My pulse slowed back to normal, and the hurt in my body eased. It was an illusion, but I was okay with that. Any reprieve was welcome, and this one allowed me to slip into a restorative sleep. One unsullied with chemicals and blissfully dream-free.

It was the fullest sleep I'd had since being arrested by stupid fucking Jeanette. FBI my ass, there was no way that woman had passed any kind of psych evaluation. Or if she had, they'd left her undercover *way* too freaking long and she'd cracked.

I wondered what had happened to that yappy little dog she had. The one that peed when it was excited. Damn, I'd laugh if that was the future of their K-9 unit.

A couple of times I roused when Chase returned to my cell, but surprisingly, he didn't touch me. He just changed the IV bag, then sat there beside my bed, staring down at me for *ages*. Then he'd check his watch and leave without a word. Psychological warfare was basically his middle name.

At some stage my fever broke, and the whole-body chills and aches subsided, allowing me to rest easier between Chase's visits. But as was inevitable, after maybe the fifth or sixth dose of antibiotics, his patience seemed to run out.

I woke from a deep sleep with the suffocating knowledge that he was back, and I blinked my eyes open, then stiffened when I registered how close he was. How close his knife blade was to my eye.

"How easy it would be," he murmured, his single eye glittering with madness, "to carve out this pretty blue eye of yours. Even the score a little. An eye for an eye." The knife in his hand didn't waver, his grip strong. I barely dared to breathe, it was so close to taking my sight—even partially. But I also refused to blink.

For a long moment, neither of us spoke. Chase remained frozen there, his blade point a millimeter from my pupil and his breathing rough. Then he licked his lips and gave a low chuckle, withdrawing the threat. For now.

"Nah, we'll save that for later. I like you being fully aware of everything happening." His knife tip scraped the skin of my throat, and I swallowed back my disappointment. Maybe if he'd been weaker, if he'd given in to his urge and stabbed me through the eye…maybe he'd have gotten carried away and pushed too deep. That'd end it all.

"You're looking so much healthier, Darling," he murmured as he continued dragging the knife tip over my flesh, circling my nipple and pushing hard enough that it broke the skin. Hot blood trickled down my side, but I clenched my teeth to ignore the sting. "I gave you a little boost in the drip. You're more fun when you can fight back a bit, and lately I'm thinking you just aren't trying hard enough."

I said nothing but couldn't hold back a small grunt of pain when his knife bit into the skin over my ribs. Ever so slowly, he dragged the tip through my flesh, slicing me open in a shallow cut. It was intended to *hurt*, not maim or kill.

"See what I mean?" he muttered. "Nothing."

He sat back, tapping the bloody knife tip on his cheek as he pondered his next move. Me? I might as well have been a statue. He wanted a reaction? Well, fuck that.

But then…goddamn it.

"Did you give me fluids?" I croaked out, my voice rough from a whole lot of involuntary screaming under his care.

Chase arched a brow at me in question, then smirked. "You need to pee, Darling? How uncomfortable."

I scoffed. "You say that like I won't just pee myself right here. I don't give a fuck, Chase. It's *you* who will either need to clean it up or suffer the smell."

He scowled like he wanted to call my bluff. But I guess urine wasn't one of his kinks, because he put the knife down and started unhooking my IV line. The attached bag was almost empty, anyway.

As unhurried as he was in removing the IV equipment, I was damn close to peeing the bed by the time he returned to unstrap my wrists. He left one wrist cuff on me but removed it from the bed frame and hooked it to the wall chain instead.

"Can't be too careful," he told me with a smirk as I eyed the wrist tether. Did he expect me to protest it or something? Fuck if I knew. He'd literally had me collared and chained up like a dog for fuck knew how long. Days, certainly. Weeks? Maybe.

"You gonna watch, Chasey?" I murmured with my rough, abused voice as I struggled to push myself upright. Holy shit, I was a mess. Blood coated my side, sticky and wet, but the cuts themselves were only seeping, not deep enough to really even acknowledge.

He didn't answer me, just stood with his arms folded over his chest, watching as I forced my limbs to move and make my way over to the toilet in the corner. I wasn't fucking around with false modesty, so the second my butt hit the cold metal seat, I let go.

There was a lot to be said for the relief of a good pee, and I needed to bite my own cheek to keep from groaning out loud as my bladder emptied. Goddamn, it was good, though.

When I was done, I wiped with the scratchy toilet paper Chase had provided—what a prince—then returned to my cot. With a yawn, I lay back down in exactly the same position I'd been in for… however long I'd been on the IV.

"What the fuck are you doing?" Chase demanded, his scowl tugging his eye patch slightly askew and revealing thicker scars. It warmed me inside to know I'd put those there.

I gave him a dead stare and said nothing.

His jaw tightened, and his fists clenched at his sides. "This isn't a game you can win, Darling. Whatever you think you're doing… *stop it.*" He spat those last two words with enough frustration to completely contradict the statement. It was definitely working.

Furious, his attention jerked away from me, and he checked his watch. "I'll be back soon. And you'd better be ready to play, or I swear to god, Darling, I'll drag your pretty little sister in here and make you watch while I fuck her to death. Am I *clear*?"

I gave him a serene smile that was totally at odds with the panic flooding through me. "Crystal."

He glared at me again, but when his watch beeped, he growled a curse and stormed out of my cell. He flipped the lights off and slammed the door behind him, but it bounced slightly against the frame and didn't click shut.

I stared, wide-eyed, at the small crack of light from the hallway, holding my breath in anticipation. He didn't come back and lock it, though. Angry footsteps faded from earshot, and I slowly, silently, pushed myself back to sitting. All the while, my eyes remained locked on the unlatched door.

Was this the opportunity I'd been waiting for? Or just another game?

Fuck. Could I really afford to waste the chance if it *wasn't* intentional? Hell no. I'd just made a promise to myself to escape by any means possible, and after that threat about Seph? I needed to act now. And act fast. Even if it was a trap…well, anything was better than just giving up.

I made it a couple of steps across the room before my wrist tugged on the chain, reminding me that I was still tethered. Small hurdles, but at least it was only one wrist.

Moving back to the wall I searched with my hands until I found the anchor point and tested it for weaknesses. Totally futile, of course. The fucking thing was cemented into the wall, and I was sadly lacking in super strength.

I groaned to myself and collapsed back onto the bed. Just another fucking tease. Something scraped when I moved my foot, though, and I froze. It'd sounded metallic… And the legs of the bed were bolted to the floor; they couldn't have made that noise.

Holding my breath, I stood up once more, then crouched down to pat around the floor under the bed. Concrete and more concrete. Great. Maybe Chase had dosed me up and I was starting to hallucinate *again*. Maybe this whole damn time was just one big delusion and none of it was—

There!

"Get the fuck out of town," I muttered, my fingers closing around the handle of Chase's knife, the same one he'd just used to slice my skin open. It must have gotten knocked under the bed when I got up to pee.

I pulled it out, bringing it up in front of my face and squinting. The tiny crack of light from the door still wasn't enough to see shit, but a light touch with my finger confirmed it *was* the same knife and not some dummy, fake one.

"This is definitely a trap," I whispered into the darkness. "There's no fucking way he dropped this without knowing. No *fucking* way."

But the darkness didn't reply, and somehow that made me more anxious than if it had. I was that familiar with my own crazy by now.

"It's a trap," I said again, like I was trying to convince myself. No hallucinations of myself appeared to tell me otherwise, or agree, but I could hear the voice of my own various identities as clear as day inside my head. Their message was unanimous.

Who fucking cared if it was a trap. A slim chance was better than no chance, and stuck in the cell? Strapped to the bed while Chase raped me, burned me, drowned me, choked me? There was *no* chance there. So…screw it. Escape or die trying.

Swallowing hard, I used touch to bring the knife point to the leather strap around my wrist. Chase hadn't used traditional handcuffs—he'd probably seen me escape from the last set he cuffed me with—and hadn't used zip ties either, probably knowing I could get out of those, too. No, these were thick leather cuffs locked with an actual padlock. On one hand, impossible to slip free of. On the other...*not* impossible to cut through.

Just really freaking hard. Especially when I was using my non-dominant hand to do the cutting, it was pitch-black, I was weak, dizzy, panicked, and rushing, and the shoulder on that side was screaming in agony every time I moved.

Several times the blade slipped and bit into my flesh, but I ground my teeth together and kept going. If this was my one and only chance of escape, I wasn't quitting thanks to a few scratches.

I had no idea how long it took me to saw through the leather, but by the time it finally dropped away, my whole wrist was wet. I could only hope it was sweat...but the second I cracked the door open further, I sucked in a breath at the blood coating my hands. Crap.

Peeking out into the hall, I confirmed Chase wasn't just standing there waiting for me. Then I used the light from the hall to rush back to the bed and tear a strip of cloth from it to bind around my bleeding wrist. One of those *slips* must have gone deeper than I'd realized.

Too damn bad. I was *out of here.*

As silently as I could, I made my way down the short corridor and crept up the staircase at the end. Not a single stair creaked, and I made it to the top with nothing but the sound of my own pulse rushing in my ears. Chase's voice trickled out from further inside the house, and I stiffened, listening.

His words were muffled as he spoke to someone, too muffled for me to make out. Instead of going in the opposite direction, I crept closer to where his voice was coming from. Call it an instinct, but I silently sought out the room where his voice was loudest. The door was open because why the fuck would he need to close it? Especially if he really *hadn't* intended for me to break free just now.

I paused outside the room, resting my head against the wall. My fingers clutched the hilt of the knife tight, and I held my bleeding wrist to my chest as I listened. He was on a conference call, and I stood there for way longer than I should have. About ten times longer than any sane escaped captive really should. But goddamn, it would pay off if I really did walk away from this. Six names I committed to memory. Six men who were colluding with my psychotic torturer.

Satisfied with that much, I silently padded back through the house. It was a lavish, show-home-style property, all white furniture and impersonal crap. My blood dotted the alabaster floors like a neon sign, and I mentally cursed myself.

If I was going to go, I needed to do it *now*.

Luckily, the house was laid out in a semi-logical way, and I found the front door within moments. Not stupid, I grabbed a coat from the hook and picked up a pair of men's boots with numb fingers. They'd be too big to allow for a speedy escape, but at some stage they might come in handy if my feet got all torn up.

The door handle turned soundlessly, and I slipped out into the crystal-clear night. Instantly I saw why Chase was unconcerned with security. There was no driveway, no road...just a helipad. And a helicopter, but goddamn it, my driving skills did *not* stretch that far.

Past the helipad there was nothing but forest for as far as I could see.

Running blindly into that with no clothes, no shoes, no freaking clue where I was... It was suicide. But I'd never been known for taking safe choices to begin with, so I barely hesitated a second before rushing past the dormant helicopter and delving into the tree line.

My heart was in my throat the whole damn time, but I didn't look back, just kept my focus on freedom. Who knew how long my meager strength would hold? I just needed... Fuck, I had no idea. I just needed to *not* be in that room of horrors any longer.

But the further I stumbled into the forest, the tighter my stomach clenched with fear.

It'd been so easy.

Too damn easy.

There was no longer any doubt in my mind. I'd played right into a trap. But he still had to catch me, and it was about damn time Chase Lockhart realized I wouldn't go down easy.

CHAPTER 5

My absolute confidence that this was all part of a sick game for Chase didn't slow me down as I plunged into the darkness of the forest. It was cold enough to make me shiver, despite being May. Or…I thought we were still in May. Maybe June? Time had lost all meaning.

Thoughts and plans turned over and over in my brain as I forced my feet to keep moving, one step after another. I'd tucked the knife into the pocket of the coat I'd taken, and the boots were still clutched under my arm. But they were growing heavy, and I'd need to drop them soon.

My feet were too small to wear them. I'd just trip over shit and break my neck. I'd grabbed them on a whim, thinking they might save me if my feet got damaged, but they were just slowing me down.

Gritting my teeth, I dropped the boots, then forced myself to lay a false trail through soft earth, leaving obvious footprints as I went. I could hear water running somewhere in the distance, but I needed to cover myself. If Chase was following—and he would be—then I couldn't just run blindly in a line and hope he was too dumb not to see the signs of my clumsy passage.

So after a couple of minutes, I dug *deep* for strength and slowly pulled myself up into a tree. Fuck *me* dead, it hurt. Way more than I'd anticipated, and I found myself clinging to the first branch and praying I wouldn't pass the fuck out.

Berating myself mentally for being so damn weak, I took deep breaths and forced some calm while the blood returned to my head and the fuzziness cleared. Then I refocused on my goal. Getting *free*.

The process of climbing the tree was agony and took so long that I could swear Chase would find me any second. But he didn't, even after I made the reckless crossover to the next tree. Then the next. Then the next. I was so damn slow. Time still held no real meaning, though. It could have been hours since I'd escaped his house or just minutes. Based on how slow my movements were, I'd hedge my bets on hours.

When I'd made it only about fifty yards away from where my trail had ended, I had to admit defeat and drop back to the forest floor where the going was considerably easier. I'd have to hope that gap would be enough to lose him, at least temporarily.

"Shit," I breathed to myself as I checked my wrist. The fabric I'd cut from the bed was soaked through, and blood was running down my arm as I held it to my chest. If I didn't make it to medical attention soon, this whole escape plan would be for nothing. I was bleeding out.

My feet burned as I stumbled through the forest with no real direction. I was weak enough, injured enough, that my coordination was severely impaired. I kept tripping on shit and bumping into trees. My sole focus was on following the sound of running water because that was my best bet at hiding my trail.

Then a sound behind me made me drop behind a boulder like a puppet with cut strings. I held my breath, my ears straining.

Just when I thought I'd imagined it, the sound echoed through the darkness again. Breaking twigs.

I swallowed hard and frantically tried to calm my racing heart. I was in no condition to outrun him, and I sure as fuck wasn't winning in a fight. My absolute best bet was to lie low. Hold still and silent and pray that the darkness would conceal me until he passed right by.

"Come out, come out, little rabbit," he called out in a singsong voice. "I know you're close. I can practically *smell* your fear."

More slow, deliberate footsteps and crunching twigs. He was so goddamn close I was surprised he couldn't hear my racing heartbeat.

"I knew you couldn't resist the lure of freedom." He chuckled, stepping closer still. By my guess he was only twenty or thirty feet away. Far too close for me to make a run for it. "I have to say, Darling, you got out a whole lot faster than I expected. I'm *impressed*." He clapped slowly, and I stiffened against the shudder that ran through me. Sick fuck *had* wanted me to run.

I kept my mouth shut, though. Not a single sound left my lips as I huddled behind the boulder. Silently I prayed to gods I didn't believe in, begging for Chase to keep going and pass me by.

For the longest time, there was total silence in the forest. Total, eerie silence. Then the unmistakable slide and clunk of a shotgun being loaded.

"You wanna do this the hard way, huh?" Chase called out into the night. "So be it! I'm going to shoot your sexy legs out from under you, then fuck your ass raw while you bleed out in the dirt."

He fired off a shot, and I flinched. The sound of it was damn near deafening, but I didn't move from my hiding place. His shot hadn't hit anywhere near me, anyway, so *hopefully* he was looking in the wrong direction.

The running water that I'd been following sounded so close; I must almost be there. If I could only get a moment's distraction... just enough to sneak away and hide my trail in the water...

"What the fuck?" Chase muttered the comment under his

breath, sounding like he was almost on top of me. He was confused about something.

It took me a few moments longer, but then I heard it too. The faint whirring of an engine in the distance. But there were no roads leading to Chase's house. Were there? Maybe I'd just overlooked one…except Chase clearly wasn't expecting visitors.

He grunted another curse and took a few strides away from my hiding place—enough that I risked peeking around the boulder, still hoping the darkness of the night would conceal me from his gaze.

Chase was about fifteen feet away, his shotgun resting on his shoulder as he scowled down at his phone screen. The light from his device illuminated his face, which told me that whatever that sound was, it was wrinkling his plans.

Good.

The sound grew louder, and Chase looked up to the sky. I did the same, realizing it wasn't a vehicle approaching. It was a helicopter.

"What the *fuck*?" Chase hissed again, still with his head tilted up to the sky.

That was my opportunity. I knew it. He was distracted, there was noise… If that wasn't my chance to escape, I didn't know what else I was waiting for.

Biting down on my cheek to steel myself against the pain, I pushed to a crouch, then as quietly as I could, started moving away from Chase.

My pulse raced so hard I couldn't tell the sound of the helicopter nearing from my own heart, but a few steps later, my nerve snapped and I broke into a run. The motion or maybe the sound alerted Chase, and a shot rang out to my right. Splinters of tree bark sprayed at me as I ran, but I didn't slow. Now, more than ever, I was running for my life.

Strength wasn't on my side, though. No matter how badly I

wanted to survive, I was still only human. Barefoot, basically naked, malnourished, weak, drug-damaged, and bleeding, I was no fucking match for Chase and he knew it. His laughter echoed through the night as he pursued me at a leisurely pace.

I stumbled my way through the darkness, my heart in my throat, bracing against a flinch with every shot he fired off. He wasn't trying to hit me—yet. He just wanted to scare me. Right as the river came into view, I tripped on a tree root and ate dirt as I crashed to the ground.

Chase didn't pounce on me. He just casually strolled closer as I scrambled to find my feet. But it was like they no longer wanted to obey me. Like the second I'd hit the ground my whole body had shut down, every last ounce of strength depleted.

Nope. No way. I was *not* going out like this.

A pained, primal scream wrenched from my throat as I dug deeper. I staggered to my feet, threw myself forward, and used gravity to my advantage as I continued toward the rushing river. It wasn't even all that wide and probably not overly deep, so what the fuck was my plan once I got there? I didn't have one. But the alternative was to roll over and give up.

Hell no.

Chase increased his pace, closed the gap between us, and reached out to snag the back of my stolen coat. I'd anticipated it, though, and slithered free of the fabric. The sudden lack of a person inside the garment made Chase jerk off-balance and fall on his ass, but I just pushed on. When I reached the edge of the river, I simply collapsed into the water and let the current carry me for a moment, weightless.

My cold fingers still clutched the knife, having managed to keep hold of it when I lost the coat. So when a strong hand gripped my hair and yanked me out of the water, I lashed out.

As the blade sliced through the flesh of his side, Chase gave a shout, releasing me in surprise, and I instantly plunged back into the water. Not out of choice, but simply because my legs had stopped working.

The current pulled me, finding no resistance, and swept me quickly out of Chase's reach while I fought to simply stay conscious and hold my damn breath. Imagine if I escaped all Chase's torture and drowned after the fact.

Every time the river tossed me, pushing my face above the water, I gasped another breath. Otherwise, I just let myself go limp and free, allowing the river to take me wherever the fuck it pleased. Far too soon, though, the water pulled me to a point of the river where it was too shallow for me to keep being carried, and I reluctantly pushed myself to hands and knees in the sand.

"Did you have a nice swim, Darling?" Chase called out, his voice booming through the night air and sending a wave of terror down my exhausted spine.

I swept my soaking hair from my face with a trembling hand and spotted him on the far bank of the river. He must have kept pace as the water carried me, but now it was too deep in the center, and too wide, and too strong for him to risk crossing it right then and there.

It wouldn't hold him for long, though. We both knew it. So with weak, jellylike limbs, I staggered out of the water, flipped Chase my middle finger, and hauled ass into the trees before he changed his mind and decided to shoot me.

The cold from the water had given a welcome numbness to all the aches of my body, and I could barely feel the cuts in my wrist anymore. Which, a fuzzy part of my brain told me, was probably not a good thing. But it was also not a good thing to be caught and dragged back to Chase's little cell of torture. I bit my cheek and lifted my bleeding wrist back to my chest as I continued aimlessly through the forest.

It was only a few minutes later—I think—that my vision danced with black spots and my knees gave out midstride. I crumpled, but didn't hit the ground.

Strong arms caught me, crushing me tight against a hard body and making me cry out in pain. It was enough to shock me back awake, though, so I wasn't totally mad about it.

"Quiet," my savior hissed, clapping a hand over my mouth as he lifted me in his arms and started *running*, a hundred times faster than I'd managed since breaking free. The world whipped past my face as I inhaled the smoky, rich smell of man sweat, gunpowder, and *Zed*.

Zed. He'd come for me.

Tears heated my eyes, sliding down my face as waves upon waves of relief, anger, fear, frustration, and heartbreak racked through me.

I twisted my head, pushing his hand away from my mouth. But before I could do something stupid, like tell him to take his lying, treacherous hands the fuck off me, he grunted in pain and stumbled. His grip on me didn't falter, though, holding me tight to his chest as he regained his balance and pushed on. Shouts echoed after us, but I couldn't make out the words. All I could focus on was the pounding of Zed's feet on the forest floor, the rough panting of his breath, and the steady, comforting thump of his heart under my cheek.

Zed had come for me.

"Fuck," he cursed when more shouts followed us. Chase. How the hell had he caught up? He must have found a point to cross the river. The fact that he wasn't shooting suggested he'd had to ditch his shotgun to swim across, so that was something.

"Dare, baby," Zed muttered between breaths, "I'm going to put you down, and I need you to *run*. Do you understand me? You need to fucking *run* until you're safe. Clear?"

No. Not clear. Not even close to clear. But he gave me no time to disagree, swinging me down out of his arms and placing my damaged feet on the ground.

"Run!" he barked, spinning back around and catching Chase off guard with a vicious right hook.

I couldn't run, but I did my best. Staggering and stumbling, I pushed myself forward in the direction Zed had urged me. My blood rushed so hard in my head it deafened me, muting the sounds of fighting behind me and making it hard to focus on anything.

Then I realized it wasn't in my head. The deafening sound was from the helicopter hovering above us. As I stared up, dumbstruck, a rope uncoiled from the hovering chopper. Bright spotlights lit the forest floor where the rope extended, and I pushed myself harder to get there. Surely this was the safety Zed was talking about. If not... well, that'd be some *shitty* luck.

Just thirty feet to go.

One foot after another.

Left. Right. Left. Right.

Stumble.

Stinging pain zapped up my leg as my knee hit a rock, and I gasped.

"Come *on!*" I yelled at myself.

Twenty feet.

Fifteen.

Ten.

My foot snagged on a root, and I tumbled forward with a cry of desperation.

Zed caught me again, his sprinting momentum sweeping me up in his arms as he threw himself at the rescue sling that the helicopter had dropped.

The strap hit me in the diaphragm, knocking all breath clean out of my lungs as Zed's body blanketed me. Protecting me.

Then...nothing but darkness.

CHAPTER 6

Fragments of shouting voices filtered through my consciousness, but they were muffled and static-filled. Roaring white noise filled my whole head, and no matter how hard I tried, I couldn't open my eyes. I couldn't raise a hand or even move. Fuck. *Fuck.* I was strapped down to something.

Panic clawed at my throat, but before I could scream, I slipped back into unconsciousness.

The next time I woke, I sat up with a gasp, that same panic still coursing through my veins.

"Hayden," a soft voice exclaimed. That wasn't Chase. Wait. Was that...

"Lucas?" I croaked, rubbing my eyes and squinting in the dark room. Several things became clear immediately. One, I was in a bed. Unrestrained. Two, while it was dark, it wasn't the oppressive, suffocating darkness of my cell. Light filtered in from the ajar door to the hall, and the curtains were open to allow moonlight in.

Three, Lucas was here with me.

"Yeah, babe, it's me," he murmured, reaching out for me. Without meaning to, I flinched away before his hands could reach me, and he froze. "Shit. I'm sorry, I shouldn't have..." He swept his hand through his hair, the movement just visible in the moonlight.

"Can you turn a light on?" I asked, hating how small and weak I sounded. How *scared* I sounded, even to my own ears.

Lucas didn't question me, though. He just reached over and flicked on the small bedside lamp closest to where he sat beside the bed. Then he clasped his hands on the mattress in front of him and bit the edge of his lip, his eyes drinking me in. Every visible cut, scrape, bruise, and burn seemed to be cataloged as he stared silently, and I ducked my eyes away from the intensity of his expression.

That was when I noticed the IV line hooked to my other arm.

Terror spiked, and I drew a sharp breath through my nose, my eyes darting up to the bags I was hooked to.

"What are you giving me?" I demanded, panic flooding my voice. One of the bags was almost empty, and what remained was an ominous, dark-colored fluid.

"Blood," Lucas replied quickly, spreading his hands flat on the mattress like he was fighting his need to touch me. "Mostly blood. We've also given you a dose of antibiotics and attached you to a morphine drip."

I said nothing in response, too busy fighting with my inner trauma to speak. It took everything I had not to rip the IV line out of my arm in sheer terror, believing there was more. Maybe this was another PCP-induced delusion.

"Who's 'we'?" I asked in a thick voice when I managed to tear my panic-stricken eyes from the needle piercing my arm. "Why blood? I'm…" I gave a small shake of my head. It was fuzzy, but I had no pain. That must be the morphine at play. Despite knowing I needed to steer well clear of narcotics right now, the break from constant pain was a welcome relief. I could detox when I'd regained some strength. Unless this wasn't real…

Lucas was talking, but I hadn't been listening. "Not sure how long you'd been bleeding. Figured we didn't want to take the risk.

49

Hayden, you're in really bad shape." His voice cracked slightly, and my heart ached.

The last time I'd seen him, I was being arrested by stupid, tits-for-brains Jeanette, and Lucas was finding out just what a shitty excuse for a girlfriend I was.

"Lucas," I whispered, sagging back into the pillows. I simply lacked the strength to stay upright any longer. "I'm so sorry."

His brows hitched in surprise. "For what? You didn't ask for any of this. If—"

"No, not... I'm sorry for not telling you that I killed your father. That was a shitty thing for me to hide." My voice was rough and scratchy. Unsurprising, given how badly abused my vocal cords must be.

Lucas stared at me in shock for a moment, then swiped a hand over his face and gave a small laugh of disbelief. "Hayden...that man wasn't my father. I was raised by a single mom, and she's the *only* parent I've ever had. Brant Wilson was little more than a mysterious sperm donor, and if you killed him, then I'm sure he deserved it. I don't give two fucks about that. I was just hurt that you hadn't *told* me about it."

Ugh. He had a valid point. It'd been a dick move on my part not telling him the second I'd connected the dots. I was just *so* used to taking care of everything myself and not trusting anyone other than Zed.

And look where that'd gotten me.

I blinked slowly, trying to gather my thoughts.

"Where are we?" I mumbled, looking at the room again. It was well decorated, comfortable, but somewhat impersonal, like it was a vacation house or something. A long yawn filled my lungs, and my eyelids drooped.

Lucas leaned in close but didn't touch me. He just laid his head on his hands and gazed at me with worried eyes. "We're safe, Hayden. Doc and Maria are on their way back with Cass now. They'll want to check you out properly, so just rest until they get here."

Confusion swept through me, and I frowned. "Doc's not here? Who hooked all this up?"

Lucas flashed a grin. "I did. With some video-call guidance from him. Most of the supplies were in the medical kit Cass tossed in the helicopter, which was lucky."

I gave a vague nod, my body demanding more sleep. But something was nagging at my mind now that I'd realized we weren't in a hospital.

"The blood?" I mumbled. "You had O negative in the supply kit?"

The look on Lucas's face slipped to something more troubled as he shook his head. "We weren't that prepared. Luckily, though—"

"Zed," I mumbled, already knowing what he was going to say. Zed and I were both O negative, and while we could *donate* to anyone, we could only *receive* O negative blood. We always joked that it might come in handy one day.

My eyes drifted shut. I didn't have the energy to unpack all my feelings surrounding Zed right now. Giving me a pint of blood was probably the *least* he could do.

"Yeah," Lucas whispered. "Fucking idiot probably should have told us he had a knife lodged in his side before I took his blood, though." My lids snapped open once more, but Lucas just shook his head. "Don't worry, he's fine. Alive, anyway. Go to sleep, Hayden. I'm not going anywhere."

With that reassurance, I let my eyes drift closed once more. As sleep pulled me back under, Lucas's soft whispers of safety lulled me into a sense of peacefulness that I'd never known existed.

I slept heavily, waking only to the low murmur of voices near my bed. The morphine was fogging up my head, though, and it took me some time to really wake up.

"Fucking lights on?" someone was asking.

"Because she asked for light," Lucas replied in a low voice. "You didn't hear how scared she was when she woke up in the dark, Cass. I'm not risking that again."

My grumpy cat just grunted a sound of reluctant understanding, and I cracked my lids open to double-check that it *was* him and not a figment of my imagination. Again. I'd had plenty of delusions of him in the time Chase held me, but this felt different. The safety and calm that I felt in Lucas's presence wasn't something that any drugs could imitate, so I wanted to know...

"Saint," I breathed, my eyes locking on his scowling face above the bed. "You're here."

His brow furrowed deeper at my words, and he crouched down. "Where the fuck else would I be?" he grumbled. "I only left to get Doc. Otherwise the hounds of hell couldn't have made me leave."

My lips tugged with the faintest hint of a smile, but it was an uncomfortable feeling and I quickly let it slip. Now that he'd mentioned it, I shifted my gaze past Cass to spot our one and only trusted doctor waiting patiently near the door.

I swallowed a lump of anxiety in my throat and gave Doc a small nod before refocusing on Cass and Lucas.

"Thank you," I murmured. "You saved me."

Lucas gave a small scoff. "You were doing a pretty good job of saving yourself, Hayden. Just when I thought you couldn't get any more badass." He gave a disbelieving shake of his head.

"Doc wants to check you for broken ribs," Cass rumbled. "And whatever else. Lucas stitched up your wrist but probably made a mess of it."

"Fuck you, dick," Lucas muttered. "I stitch like a damn sewing machine."

Drawing a breath, I tried to give him a grateful smile. It just came out as a grimace, though, so I gave up with a sigh. "Can you give us some privacy?" I asked, my voice weak. Both Lucas and

Cass looked surprised by that request and didn't make any move to leave the room.

"You heard her," Doc's wife, Maria, snapped, pushing her way into the room with a stern, no-nonsense scowl. "Hades gave you an order. Get out."

A shudder ran through me at her words, but I kept my mouth shut as Lucas and Cass reluctantly left the room. When they were gone, Maria closed the door firmly behind them and crossed over to my bed with a warm smile.

"Sir," she greeted me with a sigh. "You've definitely looked better."

For some reason, that amused the hell out of me, and a startled laugh escaped my chest. But it was quickly followed by a flare of pain, and I groaned.

"You probably need to use the bathroom," Doc commented as he checked my IV line, and then he hummed under his breath. He disconnected the line from the cannula and gently peeled my blankets away. "I knew we were only a couple of hours away and didn't want Lucas fumbling around with a catheter."

"And I appreciate that," I replied quietly, internally flinching at the thought of having *anyone* between my legs. I was dressed in a pair of unisex sweatpants and a loose T-shirt, so *someone* had handled me, and that was enough.

Doc offered me a hand to help me up, but when I pointedly *didn't* take his offer, Maria pushed him aside and offered me her arm instead. Smart woman, she knew what she was doing. I gave her a tight nod of appreciation as she helped me ever so slowly to my feet, not rushing me when I needed to pause and let my head clear.

Eventually I made it to the attached bathroom to pee—rehydrated now, thanks to the saline drip—and back to bed once more.

In the meantime, Doc had set up all the equipment he needed to fully check me over. I gritted my teeth, knowing full well how invasive this was all going to be but also understanding it was necessary.

"I'm going to get this done as quickly as possible, Hades," he told me in a low murmur, "and Maria can do the rest, okay?"

I jerked a nod and blew out the breath I was holding. "Hit me with your best shot, Doc. I can take it."

He gave a soft snort of laughter, indicating for me to lie back down on the bed. "That, I don't doubt."

With his wife's help, he ran through a physical check from head to toe. He thoroughly cleaned the nasty mess of my shoulder and muttered some comments about needing surgery to repair the AC joint that Chase had fucked up. The damage was where the collarbone met the shoulder blade. It didn't sound like an urgent thing, though, so I said nothing and let him continue.

I winced a couple of times as Doc tested my ribs, so he used the portable X-ray machine he'd set up to check for breaks. Sure enough, three ribs on the left and two on the right were fractured but not at risk of puncturing anything.

It was impossible not to notice how careful Doc was about limiting the physical contact between us, and I appreciated the fuck out of him for it.

When he was satisfied with everything he wanted to check, he packed up his things and gave me a tight smile. "I'll leave you with Maria and pop back when she's done. Are you feeling hungry at all?"

Was I? I didn't even fucking know. My stomach was a mass of knots and anxiety; I doubted I'd keep any food down even if I tried. But my logical brain told me that I *needed* food in order to recover, so I nodded to acknowledge him.

"I'll tell Lucas to get you something easy," Doc told me, then gave Maria a nod before leaving the room. Before he closed the door fully, I heard the rumble of voices in the hall. Clearly Cass and Lucas hadn't been willing to go any farther than *right* outside the room.

54

Maria opened up her own medical bag on the chair beside the bed and gave me a long look. "Do you want to talk?" she offered after an extended silence. I arched one brow in response, and she bobbed her head. "Fair enough. The offer is on the table if you change your mind."

From her bag she pulled out a small packet and popped a tiny white pill out into her palm. Without a word, she handed it to me, and I damn near choked with how fast I swallowed it down.

That done, she pulled on a pair of gloves and got to work on her part of my physical.

"How long ago did you get your IUD?" she murmured as she took the swabs necessary for testing. "I should have checked your file, but everything was a bit of a rush."

I swallowed past the tension in my throat before I could reply. "Only a year ago." And they lasted for five. The pill she'd given me was just an extra precaution, and one I was more than happy to take.

She finished up and helped me back under the covers before sitting down with a sigh. "Hades…"

I tensed. As weak as I was, as damaged, abused, and fragile as I was, I didn't feel like Hades anymore. She was strong and unshakable. I was nothing but an empty shell of that woman.

"You need to talk to someone," Maria said quietly.

I shook my head—not just to deny her statement but to shake away the painfully depressing thought that had just filled my head. Where the fuck had that even come from? I wasn't an *empty shell.* I was a goddamn survivor.

"Boss, believe me when I say I won't breathe a word of this to anyone," Maria continued. "I'm not stupid. But for your own well-being, I want you to seriously consider therapy."

I gave a bitter laugh, meeting her sad eyes. "I was way past the point of help even before this happened, Maria." That statement didn't reassure her, though. If anything, it just made her more worried. "I have coping mechanisms," I offered, as though that was sufficient.

She pursed her lips, frowning, but gave another nod and sigh before standing up. "We're all done. From what Gerry was muttering, I understand you're going to be on antibiotics for a while for that shoulder. I'll let him back in here to give you his final assessment, though. Unless there's anything more you want to talk about with me?"

I shook my head. "I'm alive, Maria. That's the only thing that counts."

She huffed a sound like she disagreed but moved over to the door to let Doc back in. He slipped in and quickly shut the door again, blocking anyone else from pushing in after him.

Maria gave him a rundown of everything in quick, clinical terms, and to Doc's credit, he didn't give me any pitying glances. After all, he'd patched me up before, so none of this should really come as any great shock.

"Okay, Boss," he announced, sitting down in the chair to give me a stern look. "Here's the plan. I've got you back on antibiotics and have given Lucas clear instructions on how and when to dose that. You *will* need surgery to regain full range of motion in that shoulder, but I can appreciate that's maybe not on the top of your priority list right now."

"You'd be right about that," I agreed. If it wasn't life-threatening, it could wait. Besides, it was my left shoulder, and I was right-handed. So long as I could still fire a gun, I would be fine.

Doc nodded. "I'll make an appointment for you to see a friend of mine in Toronto when you're well enough to make the trip. He's the best in the business, and I wouldn't send you to anyone less." He ran a hand over his tired eyes. I had no clue what time it was but could imagine he had been dragged out of his bed to be here. "I know you told me earlier, but remind me again. Roughly how often were you injected with those drugs?"

I'd given him the pertinent facts of my abuse while he'd checked me over, filling him in on the drugs when I asked to be taken off the morphine.

"I couldn't say accurately," I admitted. "Too fucking often. But it must be at least twenty-four hours since the last dose. Or longer. Time was…fluid."

Maria made a sound under her breath, and the expression on her face said she'd like to get her own hands on my captor.

"That's good," Doc murmured. "You don't seem to be withdrawing too badly, but the next few days might be a bit rough. Time will tell."

It wasn't anything I hadn't mentally prepared for starting from the first moment Chase injected me. "I'll be fine," I assured him. "Nothing I haven't done before."

It was only the PCP and GHB that would give me a nasty drying-out period, anyway. And I suspected I'd suffered through a bit of that while feverish from my infection. Small wins.

Doc grimaced. "Well, it's going to be a slow recovery anyway. We're talking weeks, not days."

I gritted my teeth but didn't argue with him. It was pointless when he was simply giving me an expert opinion. I could have that argument with my own body after he was gone.

"We'll make sure Lucas is up to speed with all the medications and care instructions," Doc continued. "He impressed me with his work before I got here; I think you'll be in good hands."

That comment made me crack a smile as the two of them packed up the last of their things and made for the door. Maria paused after her husband left and gave me a long look.

"Do you want me to send these boys in to sit with you?"

I thought about her question for a moment, closing my tired eyes. Then I shook my head. "No. I just need to be alone."

Maria gave a small sigh. "No, you don't. But I'll tell them to give you space for now. Call me any time, Hades. Or Nadia, even. We're here for you."

That statement almost brought me to tears, and I bit down hard on my cheek to hold them inside. I just gave her a small, brittle smile of acknowledgment and sank back into my pillows as she left the room.

The door clicked shut, and I counted to one hundred inside my head, waiting for the door to open again. Only after reaching one hundred did I let the tension seep out of my body and the breath rush out of my lungs.

Then, only then, did I let myself fall to pieces.

I'd held so damn strong, stoic, and calm for the entire time Doc and Maria had been here, but I had nothing left. My walls turned to dust, and a silent scream racked my chest. When the tears finally rolled free, I knew there would be no stopping them. So as carefully as I could, I curled into a ball and sobbed into my pillow, letting the emotions flow. But I stayed silent. Always silent and alone.

But I wasn't alone. Just when I felt like my soul was shredded beyond repair and my mind splintered like a broken mirror, the muffled sound of voices cut through my agony.

Cass and Lucas...and *Zed*. They were in a heated argument outside my room, but they were *here*. I wasn't alone. I'd never truly be alone again, and that knowledge calmed me enough to finally sleep.

CHAPTER 7

"You didn't think you could escape me that easily, did you, Darling?" Chase's cruel words taunted me, mocking as I jerked awake. I was back in his cell. It was all just a goddamn delusion. All of it.

Tears pricked at my eyes, but I swallowed them back. It'd been the most real one yet, and I was struggling to separate reality from fiction. Even now, with Chase's leering, eye-patched face hovering over me, I could still feel the warmth of the blankets. The softness of the pillows.

"Ready to play?" my psychotic captor asked rhetorically. He grabbed a handful of my hair, using it to pull me upright out of the bed, and dragged me across to the deep bucket of water he'd prepared.

I struggled against his hold, clawing at his hand to try to loosen his grip, but I knew it was pointless. It was *always* pointless. Nothing I did would stop him when he had set his mind to something. Especially this.

"Deep breath in, my sweet," he purred, forcing me to my knees in front of the water. I did as I was told, having learned the hard way that I wouldn't get another chance. A moment later, my face was covered in a cloth bag.

I stole one more quick breath, then my head was forced down into the bucket of water. Chase's grip on the back of my neck was like steel, totally unrelenting as the cloth of the bag soaked through and my lungs burned. As always, I counted in my head, but it was never the same length of time that he held me under.

Right as panic flooded through me and my body screamed at me to take a breath, he hauled me back up, and I reached out blindly to steady myself. It was impossible to draw a full breath, though. The saturated fabric stuck to my face like a second skin, suffocating me as he kicked my legs apart and knelt behind me.

"That's it," he purred as I choked and gasped, desperately trying to get enough oxygen before he pushed me back down again. "Beautiful."

I jerked away as his hand smoothed down my back, aware of what was coming next.

But all of a sudden his hand was back on my shoulder, shaking me. What the fuck was he doing now? Whatever, it didn't matter. If it delayed him pushing my face back into the water for even a moment, I'd take it.

He shook me harder, his words muffled by the rushing in my ears. Oxygen deprivation. I'd probably pass out soon, and he'd finish himself in my unconscious body.

He slapped my face, his warm palm striking my wet cheek with an audible smack, nowhere *near* as hard as he usually hit me. But. Wait. His *palm* struck my face. How? There was a wet bag over my head.

Wasn't there?

"Hayden!" the voice shouted, shaking my shoulder again. That wasn't Chase. Chase had never in his life called me Hayden.

Forcing my way through the mental minefield, I pried my eyelids open and locked eyes with Lucas.

Lucas.

Not Chase.

60

"Hey, hi," he breathed, stroking my clammy hair away from my face with gentle fingers. "I'm here, babe. I'm here. It was just a dream. You're safe."

My heart was still racing with fear, sweat coated my skin, and I needed to swallow a couple of times as his words sank in. I was safe. It'd been a dream.

"Just a dream," I whispered in a scratchy voice. If only that were the truth.

"We good?" Cass rumbled, and I twisted my head to find him hovering at the other side of the bed, his tough face etched with worry. Behind him, another figure lurked in the open doorway, and my mouth went dry as Zed met my gaze.

For a moment, I froze. For a moment, all I felt when I looked at him was sheer relief. Like my heart was whole again.

But all too quickly, the memory of his betrayal resurfaced in my damaged mind, and I flicked my gaze away from him. From the corner of my eye, I caught the way his shoulders drooped. He took it as the dismissal I'd intended it to be and disappeared once more.

"Yeah," I answered Cass's question finally. "Yeah. Just…just a dream." Or a memory. Whatever.

Cass held my eyes, searching, then scrubbed a hand over his face. "Want me to punch Gumdrop for you, Red?" I blinked at him in confusion, but he just arched a brow back at me. "He slapped you, Angel. You look as weak as a kitten right now, but I'm more than happy to act as your fist."

My lips rounded in surprise, and I flicked my gaze back to Lucas. Now that Cass had said it, my cheek was a bit warm.

"I'm so sorry," Lucas groaned. "I didn't know what else to do. You weren't waking up, and I panicked."

Despite myself, my lips curled in a slight smile. "It's fine," I told him quietly. "I'm glad you did it. That…" I swallowed. "That dream wasn't one I wanted to stay in."

He gave me a sad smile back, squeezing my hand. Only then

did I realize that he was touching me, and I wasn't turning into a raving madwoman. Maybe Chase hadn't fucked me up as bad as I'd thought. Maybe I could find my way back to me after all.

"Well, now that you're awake," Lucas said with a slight cringe, "I should change that dressing on your shoulder. I might have bumped it a bit hard when I was trying to wake you up."

"Oh." I looked down at the shoulder in question. I was still wearing the plain, loose-fitting T-shirt I'd woken up in, and now that he mentioned it, the wound was aching. Nothing I couldn't handle, though. Hopefully, that meant it was healing. "Actually...I need to shower. Can I do that first?" I should have done it while Maria was here to help, but I'd been so fucking tired and so tightly wound up to maintain my composure. There was no way I could have held on to that facade long enough to get through a shower.

"Absolutely, yes," Lucas agreed. "Cass, can you get the water running?"

The big guy silently did as he was asked while Lucas released my hand and disconnected the IV line from my cannula. Working quickly and confidently, Lucas applied plastic shower shields over my cannula site and all my wounds. He wasn't taking any chances with further infection from them getting wet and soapy. Smart.

"Do you need help?" he offered hesitantly when he was done and I struggled to get up. Groaning, I held my ribs. Doc hadn't been able to do anything for them except offer painkillers. Which, knowing how many drugs my body had processed lately, I was reluctant to take.

"No," I grunted. "I'm fine."

I wasn't fine.

Lucas knew it, too, because despite what I said, I leaned in to him when he put an arm out for support. My feet were purple with bruising, and just walking across the carpet to the bathroom felt like I was walking on broken glass. But eventually I made it, and Lucas sat me down on the closed toilet.

Cass had his hand under the water, testing the temperature, but when he saw me sitting there, he scowled once more. No doubt I looked like something the cat had dragged in. Then shit on.

"Back in a minute," he muttered, exiting the bathroom and leaving me alone with Lucas.

I blinked a couple of times after Cass, then looked at Lucas. "I've got it from here."

He bit the side of his lip, giving me a look that said he didn't believe I really *did* have it. I needed to regain some of my mental fortitude, though. I needed to stand on my own two feet, even if that was metaphorically and not physically.

"Please, Lucas," I whispered. "I need a minute. I'll stay sitting."

His frown dipped low, his eyes searching my face. Then he sighed and ruffled his fingers through his hair. "Okay. I'll wait outside. If you need me, just yell. Please don't try getting in the shower alone, though. If you fall, Cass will skin me alive."

I assured him I would behave, then just sat there for a moment in silence after he'd gone. Cass had said he'd be back in a minute, which implied he was fetching something. But when he didn't return, I figured I needed to get on with things.

My ribs ached as I carefully tried to pull my T-shirt off, but my shoulder wasn't messing around. The moment I tried to lift my arm to take the garment off normally, sharp, hot agony lanced through me. I cried out before I could stop myself, and the door immediately popped open.

Cass was right there in the doorway with a stool in his hands and a panicked look on his face.

"What happened?" he demanded, his eyes sweeping the bathroom like he was searching for an attacker.

I rolled my eyes. "Nothing fucking happened," I muttered. "I just got stuck."

His brow dipped low, and his piercing gaze ran over me. I had one arm out of the T-shirt but the other was still trapped in the

63

sleeve. How the hell had Lucas just accessed my wound to apply that shower guard? Oh wait, he'd pulled the loose neckline down.

Cass moved past me, placed the stool inside the shower for me, then reached for the hem of my shirt. I flinched back and slapped his hands away harder than necessary.

He froze, scowling. "Red, you need help."

"Fuck off," I growled. "I can do it myself."

One of his brows twitched with something bordering on amusement, and it just pissed me off. Vaguely I acknowledged the fact that I wasn't *afraid* of him. His huge, strong frame didn't shoot fear through me. No part of me thought he would hurt me in any way, but…my body just didn't want to be touched.

"You're being an asshole, Red," he drawled, crouching down in front of me but not trying to force the situation. "You *need* help, and you damn well know it."

My temper flared, but better that than to be a cowering mess. "I'm being an asshole?" I hissed back at him. "*You're* being an asshole. I'm not a fucking invalid. I can get myself undressed just *fine*."

Cass glared hard, then shifted his gaze to Lucas, who hovered in the doorway. Seeking backup, no doubt.

Lucas just shrugged back at him. "If she doesn't want your help, that's her choice."

The wave of frustrated anger that rolled through Cass was obvious as he squared his shoulders and narrowed his eyes at Lucas. "You can't be serious," he rumbled. "She's been in that sick fuck's hands, beaten, tortured, stabbed, drugged, starved, and *fuck knows* what else, for twelve goddamn days, Lucas." He shifted his furious glare back to me. "You *are* an invalid, Red. Suck it the fuck up and accept some help."

My mouth had dropped open in surprise, though, as I processed his words.

"Twelve days?" I croaked, feeling my stomach clench and twist with nausea.

Cass's eyes softened in a flash, all traces of frustration gone and replaced with sympathy. I hated it.

Lucas was the one who answered me, though, his voice soft as he stuffed his hands into his pockets. "Twelve days, four hours, and fifteen minutes. That's how long he had you."

I blinked up at him in shock. "It felt like longer," I finally whispered.

"It was twelve days, four hours, and fifteen fucking minutes too long," Cass growled. His hand was balled into a fist as his side, and I could see the violence etched across his whole body. Without a doubt, he would hunt Chase down and kill him with his bare hands if they found out even a fraction of the details.

Which was why I would tell them *nothing*. I had my own revenge plot already in the works, and I refused to be cheated out of that.

"We know you're not an invalid, Hayden," Lucas soothed, shooting Cass a warning glare. "But you *are* hurt. Let us help you. Please?"

I gritted my teeth and shook my head.

Cass blew out a frustrated breath, pushing back up to his feet. "You're so goddamn stubborn," he snapped.

"Screw you, Saint," I snarled back. "I just need space. Help me get this arm out of my T-shirt, then back the fuck off."

I could practically hear his teeth grinding together from where I sat on the toilet lid, but after a breath he sank back to his knees and gently reached for my T-shirt once more.

Holding my breath, I braced for the pain. But he stretched the T-shirt fabric out enough that my body barely needed to move to get free. The only touch between our skin was the accidental brush of his knuckles when he maneuvered the shirt over my head, but then it was gone.

"Thank you," I whispered as I instinctively held the fabric to my chest.

His dark eyes took in the defensive gesture, and his jaw tightened. "Any time, Angel," he murmured in a husky voice, his focus locked on my wrist. My right one was bandaged heavily from where I'd cut it, but my left showed all the clear signs of my restraints: scabs and bruises in a near perfect band, the same width as the straps that had held me immobile. Without looking, I knew my ankles would show the same marks.

When I said nothing more, he shook himself and surged back to his feet.

"Don't fucking leave this room," he ordered Lucas. "If she slips—"

"Yeah, I know," Lucas cut him off. "Spare me the threats. I've got this handled."

Cass shot me a warning look, then disappeared out of the bathroom once more. As much as I loved him, I also felt like I could breathe easier with fewer people in my personal space.

Lucas came closer and offered me his hand. "I'll just put you on the stool," he said softly, nodding to the seat Cass had placed inside the shower, "and you can tell me what you need help with. What you're comfortable with. Deal?"

I nodded, swallowing my own refusals because contrary to what Cass might think, I wasn't a total idiot. I could recognize when I needed *some* help. So I took Lucas's hand, letting him pull me to my feet once more.

Not meeting his eyes, I dropped the T-shirt, then wiggled out of the sweatpants. He'd already seen all my injuries, the physical ones, anyway. So there was nothing to hide from him as he guided me into the shower stall, yet I still kept my gaze locked on the tiles.

"Thanks," I breathed as my butt reached the stool. Cass had put it out of the direct spray, but it'd be easy enough to move the direction of the showerhead.

"Stop thanking us," he murmured back. "There is literally *nothing* we need thanks for here." He straightened up and grabbed the soap, shampoo, and conditioner from the shower caddy, placed them on the floor beside my stool, then sat back on his heels in the open shower doorway. "Can I wash your hair?"

I liked the way he phrased that, like he *wanted* to do it, rather than was offering me help. A faint smile curved my lips because, holy hell, my hair needed washing so freaking bad. It was a tangled, greasy mess. The swim I'd taken in the river during my escape was the only reason it wasn't crusted with blood and semen.

"Sure," I agreed, wrapping my arms over my chest. I didn't need to hide from Lucas, but it was a self-comfort move.

He flashed a reassuring smile back at me, then stepped fully into the cubicle with me. His T-shirt soaked through in an instant, but he made no move to take it off as he reached over to angle the shower spray toward me.

The first warm droplets to hit my skin were soothing, and I shifted on my stool to get my hair wet. The moment it touched my face, though, I was plunged right back into that *dream* Lucas had only just pulled me free of. The sensation of being drowned was so fucking fresh in my mind that all logical thought flew out the window when the shower cascaded over my face.

"Shh, babe." Lucas's soothing voice cut through the rushing in my ears. His hand stroked ever so gently down my arm, and it took me a second to realize my head was between my knees. "Hey, I'm here. Just take it slow, babe. Deep breaths, okay? In and out. Don't rush. We've got all the time in the world."

Panic attack. I'd just had a motherfucking panic attack over a *shower.*

Oh, hell no.

No freaking way was Chase taking *showers* away from me. No way, no how.

"I'm okay," I mumbled, lifting my head ever so slightly. The water was off, and Lucas was on his knees in front of me, totally saturated. "I'm okay."

"You're not," he argued, "and *that's* okay."

I wrinkled my nose. "Nothing about this is okay, Lucas." My voice was hollow and bitter. "But this is something I can and *will* push through. My desire to clean his touch from my skin is stronger than my fear of drowning. Just...stay with me."

A thousand emotions flashed across Lucas's face, but the one that remained at the end was the only one that counted. Admiration. With a small nod, he sighed. "All right. Let's take this slow. Can you turn around?"

Gritting my teeth, I did as he suggested, spinning on the stool until my knees were against the cool tiles of the wall and my back was to Lucas. With a murmur of warning, he turned the water back on.

This time, it didn't touch my face. He kept the pressure gentle and used the handheld attachment instead of the full showerhead. It meant that at any given time, only a small part of me was under the spray, and it helped.

Adding my anxiety to the mass of injuries, I ended up relying on Lucas *a lot* to get clean. He was gentle and respectful as he helped wash me, and bit by bit, the lingering, repulsive sensation of Chase was washed down the drain.

By the time Lucas started washing my hair, my breathing was almost back to normal and my spine no longer as stiff as a board. Lucas's long fingers caressed my scalp, sliding carefully between tangles to work the shampoo in, and I sagged back against him in relief.

"Will you be okay if we leave this conditioner in for a bit?" he murmured in my ear as his hands smoothed the cream through my tangled—but clean—tresses. "It'll be easier if we try and brush it through before rinsing this out."

Words were too freaking hard, so I just mumbled a noise of agreement. He twisted my conditioner-slick hair into a loose knot to marinate. Using a washcloth, he went back to my skin, soaping me up a second time.

I appreciated the hell out of him for it because it would still take a shitload more scrubbing before I truly felt clean. Tired or not, I took the cloth from him to clean my own vagina. *That* would need to be scrubbed with sandpaper and still might not ever be clean enough.

"Hayden," Lucas said softly as I bit my cheek against tears and handed the washcloth back. "Did he..." His question died out, and I knew he'd changed his mind—not because he didn't want to know but because he thought he was crossing a line by asking.

I loved Lucas. Really, honestly loved him like I hadn't known I was capable of, and I knew in my bones that our relationship needed—deserved—total honesty. But I didn't trust him not to do something stupid. Like tell Cass. So I lied.

"No," I murmured back, my eyes locked on the shower wall.

I felt the tension sag out of his body behind me, and his long exhale of relief. It made me feel worse, but I just tightened my jaw and pushed the ugly feeling aside. Some things were more important than honesty. Like my carefully planned revenge. I couldn't risk that all going to shit, not now, not after all I'd suffered at Chase's hands. Now, more than ever, I needed my plan to succeed.

Chase would pay. Dearly. But it'd be on *my* terms and no one else's.

CHAPTER 8

The expedition to the shower had exhausted me more than I liked, but I was powerless to fight the lure of sleep as Lucas laid me back down in bed and started changing my dressings.

He talked to me softly as he worked, about everything and nothing. The words themselves weren't important; it was just the soothing sound of his voice that mattered, and he clearly knew that. At one point I think he told me about his economics exam that Cass had forced him to attend.

But that quiet chat stayed with me as I dozed and kept me free of the darkness lurking behind my eyelids. He'd grounded me and saved me from backsliding the moment I fell asleep.

The alluring scent of food was what woke me again, and I took a moment to wake up as the rumble of Cass's voice joined Lucas's.

"She said he didn't do that," Lucas was saying, his tone determined and defensive. "I asked, and she said no."

Cass gave a humorless snort. "Gumdrop, you believed that? Chase psychotic-fuck Lockhart didn't abduct her and drug her mindless so they could play Monopoly and have pillow fights."

There was a pause while guilt and shame damn near choked me. "She told me he didn't," Lucas said again, quietly and firmly.

"Until she says otherwise, then that's the truth. Clear?" There was a thread of pure steel in his voice that would have filled me with pride under any other circumstance. Lucas was standing up to *Cass*, and Cass was actually listening.

"Sure," he grunted back. "Whatever you say, Gumdrop."

I thought maybe Cass would leave after that, but a moment later he gusted a sigh as it sounded a lot like he'd flopped down into the armchair beside the bed. Deciding it was time to quit eavesdropping, I yawned and let my lids open a crack.

Sure enough, Cass was right there beside the bed, his long legs kicked out and a weary look on his face. His eyes were soft as he gazed back at me, though.

"Angel," he rumbled. "You hungry?"

My stomach howled loudly, answering that question for me. Lucas moved into view, holding one of those little trays with legs.

"That smells so good," I murmured, wincing as I pushed myself to sit more upright. Both of them watched me like damn hawks as I huffed and shifted, but they let me work it out. When I was sitting, Lucas placed the tray on my lap, and I got a good look at the soup and freshly baked bread laid out for me.

My stomach rumbled again, and a wave of nausea made me sweat. But I knew it was hunger making me feel so sick. Hunger, drug withdrawal, exhaustion... Food would help.

I picked up the spoon, then paused before dipping it into the soup.

"Zed's still here," I said out loud. This food had his finger-prints all over it, and neither Lucas nor Cass could bake bread from scratch, as far as I was aware.

Cass dipped his head in confirmation. "He won't leave."

That didn't surprise me. Or it wouldn't have...before. But now? Why the fuck was he hanging around *now*? Was he just here to put me back into custody the second I recovered?

Bitterness swirled through me, and my heart ached inside my chest. He'd fucking *betrayed* me.

"Eat the food," Cass rumbled. "I watched him make it. It's safe."

Lucas scoffed. "Watched? You ate about three bowls of soup and six slices of bread just to *test* it."

Cass gave an unapologetic shrug. "Dead-Man De Rosa is a good cook."

I bit back all the poisonous, sour emotions welling up inside me and dipped my spoon into the soup. If Cass had already eaten it, there was no reason why I shouldn't. My body needed the nutrients, and Zed *was* a great cook.

That first taste almost made me forget how much I now hated my second-in-command. Almost. Wordlessly, I made my way through the bowl—as much of it as I could handle, anyway. Which wasn't much.

I stopped the second my stomach tightened, though. The last thing I wanted to do was vomit it all up again because I'd pushed too hard too fast.

"Do you want to go back to sleep?" Lucas asked as he took the tray away. "Or watch a movie or something? Or—"

"No," I cut him off a little too sharply. "No, sorry. I want you to get me up to speed on everything I missed. What happened after I was arrested?"

I shifted against the pillows, trying to get comfortable. My ribs hurt like a *bitch* now that the harder painkillers had all worn off.

"You're in pain," Cass announced, and I rolled my eyes.

"No shit, Captain Obvious."

Cass glowered and reached for one of the pill bottles beside my bed.

"She won't take those," Lucas murmured, seeing which pills Cass had picked up. "I tried last night."

Cass arched a brow at me, and I just met his stare impassively. Lucas was right, though. Unless I was damn near dying, I wasn't putting any hard drugs back into my system. Not until I was sure

I'd dried out fully from the shit Chase had shot me up with, and that could take *weeks* for all I knew.

"Fine," Cass growled, slamming the pill bottle back down and snatching a different one. He shook four pills out into his huge palm and held them out to me with a glass of water. "It's Tylenol, Red. You need something to take the edge off."

I sighed because he was right. Sulking a little, I took the pills and swallowed them down with a gulp of water.

"Where do you want to start?" Cass asked, sitting back in his chair and looking satisfied that I'd taken the medicine.

I drew a deep breath, looking over to Lucas. "Timber," I told him. "When Jeanette was stuffing me in her car, I saw..." A wave of disgust and stale fear rolled through me. Maybe I wasn't ready to unpack everything that'd happened. Not yet.

"Do you want to hear it from Zed?" Lucas offered carefully, his eyes locked on mine. "He's the best person to explain what happened there."

I shuddered. "No. Fuck no. I'd rather pull my fingernails out with pliers than hear any of Zed's fucking *explanations* right now."

Cass gave a smirk. "That's what I told *him*."

"Then why is he still here?" I snapped back. I was angry...but it wasn't entirely at Zed. I was angry at *myself* for trusting him so completely and for falling so hard in love with him that even now part of me hoped he could explain it all away.

I didn't want to give him that opportunity. Nothing he could say would redeem this level of betrayal. Colluding with *Chase*... after everything we'd been through. After everything Zed *knew* Chase had done to me. No. He was dead to me.

Neither Cass nor Lucas answered my question. They just exchanged a long look, and Lucas raked his hand through his hair as he perched on the end of the bed.

"Where are we?" I asked instead, sensing they were both at a loss for what to tell me.

Cass leaned forward, bracing his forearms on his knees. "We're in the last place on earth Chase Lockhart would ever think to look for us." His eyes twinkled with evil mischief. "We're at Foxglove Manor."

I jerked in shock, then winced as my shoulder throbbed and my ribs screamed. "Saint, I swear I just heard you wrong. Did you say we're at *Foxglove?*"

His smirk spread wider. "What better place to hide out?"

A small laugh bubbled out of me. "I have no words. You bought it?"

He gave a shrug. "After you wiped out the entire Lockhart bloodline, all of their properties went up for auction due to the sole beneficiary being too unwell to maintain them. I bought up as many as I could, hoping to find a safe or lockbox or something."

I nodded my understanding. "Hunting for Nadia's egg."

He inclined his head. "Didn't find it but held onto a few of the properties anyway. Turned out to be a good idea."

How right he was. Foxglove Manor had been in the Lockhart family for several generations, so Cass was right that Chase would be unlikely to *ever* suspect that's where we were. It had originally been built as a luxury hunting cabin and was tucked away up in the mountains near Salt Lake City. One road in, one road out, best accessed by helicopter.

A sharp knock at the door startled me, and Lucas smoothly unfolded from his position to answer it. He barely cracked the door open a couple of inches, blocking the gap with his body as he snapped, "What?"

Zed muttered something in reply, and Lucas shot a quick look at me over his shoulder.

"Back in a minute, babe," he told me with a hard smile, then slipped out of the room. He closed the door firmly behind himself, shutting Zed out there with him, and I tilted my head at Cass in question.

74

"Dunno," he replied. "Don't care, either. You want me to just shoot him and be done with it?"

Did I? It was curious that he hadn't already done it. And that in itself told me Cass wasn't totally convinced of Zed's betrayal. Or maybe he was just keeping him alive for me to deal with personally.

"Lucas mentioned something about Zed donating his blood," I murmured, biting the edge of my lip.

Cass huffed an irritated sound, then dragged his armchair closer so he could lean his elbows on the edge of the bed. Close enough to touch if I wanted to.

"Yeah. Martyr bullshit, trying to earn back some karma points or something." He propped his face on his hands, watching me. "Do you remember much from when we found you?"

It was a valid question. The details of it all were hazy and dark. "Yeah, some of it. I remember Zed picking me up and running full sprint through the forest, then putting me down and screaming at me to run. Then...I don't know. Were you in a helicopter?"

Cass gave a small head tilt. "Yep. When we pulled you both up, you were out cold. Blood fucking *everywhere*. Zed was barking orders at us, and you... Shit, Angel. You looked like you were dead." His voice turned rough over that statement, and my fingers twitched at my side, brushing his elbow in a tiny gesture of comfort.

His gaze darted down to that minuscule touch, and a deep sigh shuddered through him as he closed his eyes.

"Zed told us you have the same blood type, and we didn't fuck around with questions. Lucas got Doc on the phone and had drawn a bag of blood from Zed before we got back here. Neither of us even knew he'd been stabbed until he collapsed on the lawn."

Despite myself, I sucked in a sharp breath.

Cass gave a small headshake, meeting my eyes again. "He's fine now. Stubborn fuck. Lucas stitched him up, and Doc gave him a check-over after he saw you yesterday."

I wet my lips, anxious energy making me jittery. "Lucas sure is getting thrown in the deep end on this medical shit."

Cass huffed. "He loves it. Little shit thrives on the challenge. You should have seen how damn precise he was with those stitches in your wrist."

Smiling, I brought my bandaged wrist to my chest. As messed up as the thought was, I kind of loved that Lucas had stitched my wrist up. It would scar, but now instead of being reminded of cutting myself free of restraints, it'd remind me of Lucas. And how much he loved me. That was a little bit awesome.

"He called you?" I asked in a quiet voice, bringing my fingertips back to where I'd been touching his elbow. "When I was arrested?"

Cass nodded. "Before the car had even taken you away. He called me and left a voicemail, then immediately went to work on planning a jailbreak." A small, proud-older-brother kind of smile crossed his gruff features. "Gumdrop was made for this life."

My pulse raced, a warm, fizzy feeling diluting the anxiety. "He wanted to break me out of FBI custody? Even after hearing how I'd lied to him?"

"You know he did. It'll take more than one lie to shake his faith in you, Red."

He was so right. I didn't deserve Lucas.

"Is Seph safe?" I asked in a thick voice. It was the question I'd been wanting to ask since waking up but had been too scared to hear the answer.

Cass dropped one of his hands from his face, his fingers brushing against mine and linking just the tips together in a soft, gentle gesture. "She's fine. Rex has her under lock and key until we say otherwise."

A long breath of relief gusted out of me. In my mind, I could still hear Chase's threat, telling me that if I wouldn't cooperate, he would take it out on Seph.

"Thank you," I whispered, my eyes hot with unshed tears. I didn't know if I could have handled it if the answer had been worse.

Cass just watched me for a long moment, his fingers barely touching mine yet somehow offering me so much strength and support it was staggering.

"You should rest," he told me quietly. "I'm not going anywhere."

"Actually..." Lucas said, coming back into the room and leaving the door open behind him for once. I didn't see Zed out in the hall, but he was there somewhere. He wouldn't leave. Not until I either heard him out or killed him.

"What now?" Cass growled, his fingers linking further with mine in an almost unconscious movement. Protective. Possessive.

Lucas cringed, giving me a sad look. "Gen's dead. Hannah found her but thinks she was killed a couple of days ago."

Shock stole the breath from my lungs, and my lips moved soundlessly as I processed that. I liked Gen. Sure, maybe I hadn't trusted her implicitly like I had Zed, but she was a valuable member of the Timberwolves.

"How? Why?" I frowned up at Lucas, trying to make sense of it. "Why would she be killed? As far as anyone knows, I'm in FBI custody, right?"

Lucas rubbed a hand over the back of his neck. "Actually, no. When that blond bitch was found with a bullet in her head, you were declared a fugitive. Gen was working around the clock to get the evidence against you thrown out. It was flimsy as shit to begin with, and she was actually getting somewhere on it."

Fuck. That was a lot to process. I was a fugitive? No wonder Cass hadn't taken me back to Shadow Grove.

"Hannah's freaking out," Lucas added. "She doesn't know what to do, and apparently Maurice has been spotted around Shadow Grove."

Irritation swept through me, overtaking all my other damage

while I focused on the threat to my empire. "What the fuck is *he* doing in town without permission?"

"Why are you bringing this to her?" Cass demanded in a threatening growl. "Zed can handle it. Red's in no shape to—"

"I know," Lucas snapped, cutting him off. "But Zed told me I had to take it to Hades. He won't deal with it."

That motherfucker. He was trying to force me to deal with him.

"Shut up, Saint. There's nothing wrong with me." Okay, *that* wasn't true. But I didn't appreciate his attempt to sideline me, no matter how busted up I was. To Lucas, I gave a worried frown. "Give me a minute to think. Can you get me a phone? I need to speak with Hannah directly."

Lucas left the room to do as I'd asked, and Cass made a sound of disagreement.

"Do you trust Hannah?" he asked quietly.

I gave a bitter snort. "I don't fucking trust anyone. Not anymore."

Because if I couldn't trust *Zed*, then my faith in everyone was shaken. I didn't even trust myself anymore. This could *all* still be one big delusion, for all I knew.

Fuck. I really was messed up.

CHAPTER 9

Cass's question played across my mind as Lucas returned to me with his phone, and I tried to decide how in the fuck to handle things. Ordinarily, if I was out of commission, Zed would take over. Failing that, next on the list was Alexi.

Zed wasn't an option. Alexi…he wasn't an option either. Even if he had resurfaced after I was arrested, there were too many questions around him. Like why his GPS had placed him at Timber right before the ambush. Or why he had blood on his cuff after Agent Hanson was murdered.

Cass was still dead; he couldn't go back and run things for me.

"Has anyone spoken to Demi?" I asked, before hitting the call button to Hannah. "Does she know what's going on?"

"Yep," Cass answered. "She was back in Shadow Grove working on your case with Gen."

Crap. That meant she was in danger, too. My aunt was a hell of a lot better at protecting herself, though. But it made my decision easier regarding the interim leadership of both the Timberwolves and Copper Wolf Enterprises.

Instead of calling Hannah, I dialed Demi from memory.

The phone rang a couple of times in my ear before she answered with a professional greeting. Her day job was as a divorce lawyer, but she also used to be chief counsel for all my gang's legal brushes.

"Demi," I said, hearing how rough my voice was still. "It's Hades."

There was a long exhale on the other end. "Thank fuck you're alive."

I quirked a brow at Cass. "No one told you I was?"

"No," she snarled. "Those little shitheads of yours shut down all communication three days ago. Not a fucking squeak out of any of them."

I shot Cass a sharp look but filed that away to deal with it later. "I need your help, Demi."

My aunt snorted. "No shit. I heard about Gen, but they didn't gain anything. I've already had the so-called evidence against you extracted from the FBI servers and filed all the paperwork to have your arrest wiped from the record. It's just a matter of time."

I grimaced. "You're making a target of yourself, Demi."

She gave a low chuckle. "Let them fucking try. I've already been in touch with Rex."

That simple statement made me breathe easier. Rex would protect Demi just as fiercely as he did Seph. Maybe it was time I let bygones be bygones and pulled him from retirement.

"I need your help with running things until I can get back," I told her, wincing. I fucking *hated* asking for help. "Hannah doesn't know what she's doing, and I don't trust Alexi right now. If he's even alive."

There was a pause on her end, then she asked quietly, "Where's Zed?"

I swallowed hard. "Long story. I'm sending Lucas back to help you run things." I met his eyes as I said that, and he jerked in surprise, shaking his head in refusal. "Cass is still supposed to be dead, so Lucas is the only one I..." *Fuck.* Trust. That word was so goddamn tainted I couldn't even get it past my lips.

"All right, you're the boss," Demi replied when I didn't continue my sentence.

I cleared my throat. "I don't want to drag you back into Wolf business, but you know what's what, and Maurice has been spotted around town."

She gave a sigh. "That prick. Of course he's taking advantage of the situation. Don't worry about it, I'll take care of him personally. Just send me that beautiful man of yours, and we'll handle things until you're back." Then she made a thoughtful sound. "How clean do you want me to keep his hands?"

Despite the gravity of the situation, I gave a short laugh. "That's his choice, Demi. But until further notice, Lucas *is* Hades. Clear?"

"Clear," she confirmed, even as Lucas frantically shook his head at me.

Ending the call, I stifled a yawn and looked to Cass. "Any chance you can give Lucas a crash course in how to run a gang?"

Cass scoffed, and Lucas threw his hands in the air.

"Hayden, I'm *not* doing that. Are you kidding? I can't run your gang! More than that, I *won't*. I'm not fucking leaving you. Who's going to take care of you?" He planted his hands on his hips, his jaw set with determination.

That quick conversation with Demi had helped me slide so easily back into my Hades mind, so I wouldn't budge on my decision.

"Lucas, you did an amazing job patching me up, but there's very little to be done for me now. So long as I take my antibiotics and Tylenol when needed, it's just time. I *need* you back in Shadow Grove. If Maurice is lurking, he's planning something. The longer the Wolves go without leadership, the weaker we seem." I gave him a fierce look, unrelenting. "I risked *everything* for the new Timberwolves. I won't lose it all now."

He stared back at me for a long, tense moment. Then he cast

his eyes to Cass like he'd accepted that he couldn't change my mind but wanted backup.

"Don't give me that look, Gumdrop. Hades gave you an order." There was an edge of teasing in his voice, and the corner of his lips had kicked up slightly. "I'm sure I can take care of things here while you're gone."

Lucas glowered, and I stifled a groan. Trust them to turn this into a pissing match.

"I gave you an order too, Saint," I snapped. "Get Lucas up to speed on gang politics, then deliver him back to Shadow Grove to run my empire."

Lucas groaned and scrubbed his hands over his face. "No pressure or anything."

Cass scoffed. "You fucking love it." He shifted his dark gaze back to me. "We'll leave you to rest."

"No." I shook my head. "Stay. I can doze while you talk." *I'd prefer to nap while you talk so I don't slide back into the dark place.*

Lucas snickered, dragging another chair over to the side of the bed where Cass was already seated. "Sounds like she doesn't think you'd properly educate me, Grumpy Cat. The Reapers *were* minor league compared to Timberwolves, right?"

Cass glowered. "Shut the fuck up and turn your listening ears on, Gumdrop. We've got a lot to go through."

Despite his stern tone, his fingers were gentle as he shifted his hand back to mine. As before, only our fingers touched, but it was enough. I flexed mine against his, showing I was okay with the touch, then let my lids fall as the deep rumble of his voice lulled me.

The two of them sat beside my bed for hours, talking quietly and totally unhurriedly as Cass tried his best to explain the power structure and politics of everything the Timberwolves were involved in. At some point, I could have sworn I heard Zed correct him on something, but maybe that was just my imagination.

Eventually I must have slipped into a deeper sleep because when I opened my eyes again, I was alone.

Someone had left the bathroom light on and the door open, giving me more than pitch-blackness in the bedroom, but it was still dark. Too dark. A physical shudder rolled through me, and my hands were sweaty as I gripped the blanket.

Fucking hell. *Now* I could see why Zed had refused to deal with business earlier. Not that I wanted him to, but he hadn't refused simply to be a douchebag.

He'd done it to help me heal. He'd known that the easiest way to slide me back into my strong, emotionless, *safe* personality was to present me with a Hades problem. It'd worked for me for five years; Zed had seen it firsthand.

Now, alone in the dark with nothing but my own decaying thoughts for company, things were different. As badly as I tried to shift my mind to *Hades* and block out all the noise, I couldn't. My heart was already racing, and every time I tried but failed to wrap the safety of detachment around myself, my panic escalated.

A dark shape rushed into the room, and I screamed. I couldn't stop myself.

"Fuck," a voice as familiar as my own cursed; then a switch was flipped and light filled the room. "It's me, Dare. It's just me. I heard you crying and…" Zed trailed off with a grimace, stuffing his hands into the pockets of his hoodie. He looked *rough*.

Pain lanced through my heart as he met my eyes, and I wanted to scream. Just *scream* at him. If I had a gun, I probably would have shot him.

My jaw clenched tight as I tried to control my panic attack, and now that he'd mentioned it, I realized my face *was* wet. Fuck me, I hadn't even known I was crying, let alone making enough noise to alert him like that.

"Where's Cass?" I croaked, and Zed flinched.

His gaze ran over me carefully, though, and his brow was tight with tension. "In the barn, teaching Lucas how to handle higher-caliber weapons. They didn't want to leave until you were awake again." He hesitated, then shook his head, discarding what he'd been about to say. "I'll go get them."

He started to leave the room, and I sucked in a sharp breath of panic. "Wait."

Zed stopped in the doorway, turning to give me a curious, *hopeful* look. Fuck, that wasn't what I meant at all.

"Never mind," I mumbled, lying back into my pillows and closing my eyes. Surely, he could take that hint and get the fuck out of my room. I was nowhere near ready to unpack all the pain and heartbreak he'd caused me. It hurt too damn much, and I'd been through enough. Zed could sweat it out until I was in a more stable headspace.

A moment later, I felt him place something on the bed beside me, then without a word he retreated out of the room and closed the door quietly. He'd left the lights on, and when I cracked an eyelid, I saw what he'd left.

His knife. A deadly sharp bastard, eight inches long and crafted from Damascus steel.

I stared at it for a long moment, then reached over and picked it up. My hand curled around the handle, testing the grip and weight, even as fresh tears poured from my eyes. Then I tucked it under my pillow, just as Zed must have intended. He knew me. He knew what made me tick and what would make me feel safe. Being armed, no matter how secure the house was, would ease my mind.

That display of knowledge... Fuck. I both loved and hated him for it.

I hated *myself* for it.

Because despite how much he'd hurt me, despite his betrayal and everything it had caused, I still fucking loved him with my whole sullied soul.

CHAPTER 10

When I'd made the decision to send Lucas back to Shadow Grove in my place, I hadn't really considered the logistics, like, say, how he was getting from Foxglove Manor back to Shadow Grove. Because, apparently, they hadn't brought any cars to our hideout. Just the helicopter.

"I feel like I'm discovering new shit about you every damn day, Saint," I muttered as he helped me dress after another shower. There could never be too many showers, and I needed to force myself through my sudden fear of drowning.

He'd just informed me that *he'd* been the helicopter pilot. I don't know why I'd expected anything less, though. Cassiel Saint, international man of mystery and drop-dead sexy asshole.

"It's been a few years since I was in a cockpit," he admitted, gently brushing my hands aside and buttoning my shirt up for me. After I'd struggled with the T-shirt yesterday, someone had found me a men's button-down shirt to wear instead—infinitely easier to get on and off, that was for damn sure.

Lucas snorted a laugh from where he was slouched on my bed. "That much was obvious. I thought you were going to crash us straight into the side of a hill when we first took off."

Cass flipped him off with a scowl. "It's like riding a bike," he growled. "But it means you'll be here alone until I can get back."

"She's not alone," Zed snapped, pushing the bedroom door open. "I'm still here." Fucking hell, if that wasn't a loaded statement, I didn't know what was.

Shooting him a death glare, I nodded. "Right, so, worse than alone. Perfect. I'll be sure to keep my back to the wall so no one can stick a knife in it."

Zed winced, and I remembered too late that he'd quite literally taken a knife in his back while rescuing me. "Well, you're sounding more like yourself."

I scowled, a sharp comeback right on the tip of my tongue, but Lucas beat me to it. He hopped up off the bed and shoved Zed back out of the room with a hand to his face, then slammed the door.

Stunned, I gave a short laugh. "That's one way to shut him up. He's probably just lurking in the hallway, though."

Lucas shrugged. "Definitely. He's been sitting out there pretty much twenty-four seven since we got you back."

My brows shot up, but Cass just muttered some shit under his breath about a guilty conscience.

Changing the subject, I refocused on the conversation we'd been having before Zed interrupted. "How long will you be gone?" I asked Cass quietly, hearing the *need* in my voice and cringing at it. "Doesn't matter. However long it takes, I'll be just fine. It's more important to get some leadership back into Shadow Grove. Fucking Maurice has another think coming if he thinks he can take anything that's mine."

Carefully, watching me like a fucking hawk, Cass grazed his knuckles over my cheek. I stiffened slightly but didn't flinch away, so he did it again with a little more purpose.

"I will be back as fast as that helo can fly, Angel," he promised me in a low, husky voice. "Even if it means kicking Gumdrop out before landing."

86

"Dick," Lucas muttered, but my eyes were locked on Cass.

I wanted to kiss him. It would have been as natural as breathing to just lean forward and press my mouth to his. But my mind and body were in disagreement, and I remained locked in place like a fucking statue.

"Don't do anything stupid," I warned him instead. "I can handle Zed."

And by that, I meant I could more than happily stay put in bed with the door *locked* and his dagger gripped in my hand. I'd fallen a hell of a long way from the badass gang leader who could make grown men pee their pants with nothing more than a glare.

"If you decide to kill him, make sure he cooks dinner first," Cass suggested. "I don't want you going hungry if I get delayed."

I snorted a laugh, but knew damn well he was serious. He hovered near but not touching as I climbed back into bed. Lucas had already checked all my dressings and lined up my medication beside the bed, so I was all sorted.

"If you *do* decide to kill him," Lucas added, not bothering to keep his voice down. If Zed really was just outside the door, he'd be able to hear us discussing his death. Good. He fucking deserved it. "Then I hope you will listen to his side of everything first. I'm not saying it will justify *anything*—far fucking from it—but for your own peace of mind, you should have the full story."

That rendered me speechless, and Cass glared at Lucas like he'd just grown six heads and a fucking tail.

"Screw that," Cass muttered. "Just make it hurt. I'll clean up the blood when I get back. You shouldn't be inhaling peroxide right now."

With a laugh, I shook my head at both of them. "You two are too much." Then I paused and forced my way through yet more damage. "I love you, though." My words were so quiet, so rough, I wouldn't be surprised if they hadn't heard me at all.

Cass leaned in close, his short beard brushing my neck. "I

love you more than life itself, Angel. I'll be back before you know it."

He straightened up and left the room with a muttered comment to Lucas on his way out, and I locked my eyes on the wall across the room. Tears heated my face, and if I met Lucas's gaze, I would totally lose it.

Silently, he came around the bed and sank to his knees beside where I lay. Carefully, not wanting to startle me, he reached out and closed his hand over my fist clenched in my lap.

I inhaled at the touch, then relaxed my hand so he could link our fingers.

"Hayden," he murmured. "Words quite literally can't express how much I love you. There is no doubt in my mind: You're it for me. You don't just own my heart, babe, you *are* my heart. Without you, nothing matters. Every minute of the twelve days, four hours, and fifteen minutes you were gone, I was dead inside."

Oh fuck. There was no stopping the tears now, and they only got worse when Lucas tenderly swiped a knuckle under my eye.

"Thank you," I whispered, "for not giving up."

His smile was full of warmth and adoration but tainted by sadness. "It was a team effort." As quick as lightning, he dropped a kiss to the back of my hand, then untangled our fingers and stood up. "I should go before Daddy Cass comes to drag me out of here."

A sob caught in my throat, and I sputtered, "Never call him that again, please."

Lucas grinned wide, proud he'd stopped my tears with humor. "Why not? He's old, for starters, and he oozes dom energy. Daddy Cass just *fits*."

I groaned and scrubbed a hand over my face, swiping the tears away and pulling myself together. "Call me when you get back to Shadow Grove, okay? Lean on Demi in private, but remember when you're in public—"

"I know." He cut me off with a smile. "I'm *Hades* now. Nowhere near as beautiful, but it's only temporary." He gave a shrug, then blew me a kiss on his way out the door.

After he was gone, I lay there staring at the ceiling for ages. It wasn't until the hum and whir of the helicopter faded away in the distance that I decided I needed to do something to keep the dark thoughts at bay. I needed to keep busy.

But with what? I was a fucking fugitive until Demi could get everything squared away with the FBI. More than that, I couldn't risk painting a target on anyone for Chase to take a shot at. Gen was already dead. Who would be next? Hannah? Nadia?

Fuck. If he went after Nadia...

Visions of all the gruesome, bloody, violent acts I'd like to do to Chase filled my mind, playing out with such detail I could almost smell the copper in the air. But as quickly as those fantasies came, they morphed into memories of the things *he'd* done to me. Not just recently, but in our past too. Memories of things I'd long since locked away and had *no* intention of taking out to reexamine. No. Fucking. Thank you.

My eyes snapped back open, and I swiped sweat from my face. I needed to just *not* think for a while.

My eyes lit on the huge flat-screen TV mounted opposite the bed. I'd spent much of the three days since escaping Chase asleep. I'd needed it because every time I woke, I had more energy.

Except now I was too awake to sleep and too hurt and pissed off to leave my room and potentially run into Zed. So I huffed a sigh and grabbed the remote from where Lucas had placed it beside my medication.

Way too quickly, I flipped channels without really paying attention to what was on them. Most of it was reality TV shows, I think, and a handful of soap operas. It was the middle of the day, after all.

With an irritated sigh, I decided on an Israeli soap opera with subtitles, mainly because they were pretty reliable for the worst kinds of unbelievable plotlines. Shit like secret evil twins popping out at the perfect time or total amnesia making people forget their friends and family. I'd even seen one where a woman had *no idea* she'd had a baby until she met the girl eight years later and thought she looked familiar. Shit like that simply didn't happen in real life, so that was the energy I needed. Crap that took suspension of disbelief *way* too far.

Initially I was rolling my eyes every three seconds, but before I knew it, I was *hooked*.

So much so that I didn't hear the door open.

"You're not seriously watching *this*," Zed muttered in disbelief. "There must be something better on."

My eyes had been glued to the damn screen reading the subtitles because my Israeli was about as good as my Chinese. Terrible.

"Fuck off, Zed," I tossed at him, then shifted my eyes back to the screen.

He let out a long, pained sigh. "I figured we could talk."

My answering laugh was pure venom. "You figured *wrong*. Get the hell out of my room."

He didn't move from his position against the doorframe, just folded his arms over his chest and glared back at me. Fuck him for still looking so goddamn gorgeous while being a dirty, poisonous snake in the grass.

"Dare…" he started, but my anger flared hot to hear my nickname on his lying lips. So I hurled the TV remote at his head.

Stupid me, though, I used my left arm to throw, and my injured shoulder shrieked at me in pain. I *should* be wearing the sling that Doc had left for me, but it made me sweaty so I'd been leaving it off more than on.

"Jesus, Dare, what the fuck were you thinking?" Zed barked, coming two steps into the room before I held up my palm to stop him.

"I was thinking I want you to *shut the fuck up!*" I shouted back, still wincing as I cradled my arm to my chest. "Get *out*, Zed. I owe you nothing. I definitely don't owe you the chance to explain. Get. The. Fuck. *Out.* You're *dead* to me."

Every word out of my mouth tore shreds off my heart, but I couldn't hold it back. I wanted him to hurt like he'd hurt me.

His jaw clenched, and he gave a small nod. "You're wrong about that," he murmured, his eyes blazing with determination.

I scoffed. "Oh, am I?"

He nodded again, retreating to the door once more. "If I were dead to you, you'd have thrown the knife, not the remote." With a pointed look, he closed the door behind himself and left me to my crappy TV.

CHAPTER 11

After Zed's little visit, I couldn't get back into my foreign soap opera. Fuck him for ruining it, too. I'd been just about to find out whether the badly burned hero had gotten a total face transplant or not.

Asshole.

Then, to add insult to injury, I realized the remote had landed all the way over near the door after bouncing off his lying face.

Muttering curses to myself, I climbed out of bed and went to fetch it so I could flip the channel over to the news. While I was out of bed, though, I took note of how stiff my muscles were. I was stronger now, thanks to nutritious food, water, and sleep. Doc had boosted me with some medication too. So there was really no reason for me to stay in bed all day.

With a grimace, I tossed the remote back onto the bed and started running my body through some *very* gentle stretches. Only a couple of minutes in, I needed to admit defeat and put my sling on to support my bad shoulder. It was just too hard *not* to use it, despite how badly it hurt.

"Have you taken some painkillers for that?" Zed asked,

appearing in my doorway *again*. Christ, he just couldn't take a hint.

Shooting him a glare, I adjusted the Velcro strap to hold my arm a bit tighter, then flipped him off with my good hand.

"Pretty sure I made myself clear earlier, Zayden. Fuck off."

He gave me a brittle smile. "You did. But no one else is here, so I came to ask what you want for lunch. You've still got to eat."

"I'm well aware," I snapped. Chase hadn't totally starved me for those twelve days, but it was safe to say at least two of the three main meals each day had been pure chemicals injected into my veins. I'd carefully avoided looking at the angry marks on my inner elbow but couldn't escape the way my ribs protruded when I looked in the mirror after a shower. "I don't care, Zed. Just...leave me the hell alone. Simply *looking* at you makes me so goddamn angry I could shoot you."

He dipped his head. "Fair. Good thing I gave you a knife and not a gun, then." He paused, then passed a hand over his short hair. "I'll bring something up in an hour or so. Unless you want to come downstairs and eat with me?"

The look on my face must have said exactly what I thought of that suggestion because he huffed a short, bitter laugh. "Yeah, I thought so. Don't push yourself too hard."

I rolled my eyes. "Don't pretend like you care, *Agent* De Rosa."

Blowing out a breath, he nodded and closed my door again. There was a long pause before his footsteps sounded in the hall, like he'd just stood there for a minute.

Why the fuck he was still here, I had no idea. Maybe he was just waiting for me to shoot him and have it over with. That seemed like his style. He never was one to run and hide.

Fueled by anger, I turned the volume down on the TV so it was little more than background noise and went back to my exercises. Aside from my ribs, nothing else was broken. So there was no reason to let my body soften and weaken any further. If I wanted to get back to my life, to get my *plan* back on track, then I needed to regain my strength. Fast.

Eventually, though, my body forced me to stop and rest. A storm had rolled in while I was stretching, and I hobbled over to the window to pull the curtains open properly. There was something so soothing about the sound of pouring rain, so I opened one of the windows to hear it better.

I retreated back to my bed to rest, but the constant edge of anxiety didn't melt away at all. Despite how calming I usually found rain, my new wariness of water in general was casting a dark shadow. Fucking Chase was ruining *everything*.

My depressing thoughts were interrupted by the sound of the door opening again, and I blinked several times to bring my head back into the present. How long had I been staring out the window like that?

"Lunch," Zed announced rather unnecessarily, as he was carrying a tray of food. I really needed to get my ass downstairs and make my own meals. The idea that I was depending on him for *anything* rubbed me the wrong way.

Rich, mouthwatering smells reached my nose, and my stomach rumbled.

"Lamb ragu with sweet potato mash," he informed me, placing the tray down on the bed beside me and not getting any closer than he needed to.

In fairness, Zed was an incredible cook. His mom had taught him before she'd murdered his father and disappeared—most likely died—leaving Zed an orphan at age fifteen.

"This storm will probably delay Cass getting back," he muttered, rubbing the back of his neck. "Can't fly a helicopter in this weather."

"No shit," I grumbled. I'd thought the same thing when the rain had started, but I was hoping the storm would pass over quickly. It was roughly a two-hour helicopter flight back to Shadow Grove from Foxglove Manor. By the time Cass had dropped Lucas off, collected the supplies Demi was arranging for us, refueled the helicopter, and flown back…

I checked the time on the TV and frowned. "He should already be on his way."

Zed just gave a shrug. "He'll likely wait until the storm passes. Guess you're stuck with me a bit longer." He arched a brow in a clear challenge, and I seethed. Was he deliberately taunting me? Did he *want* me to kill him?

Maybe he did.

Something on the news caught my attention, though, and I gave a startled gasp. Zed was halfway out my door but stiffened when he heard me, spinning around to scan the room with sharp eyes.

"Shut up," I snapped, even though he hadn't spoken. I scrambled for the remote, turning the sound up so I could hear what the reporter was saying—the reporter who stood under an umbrella, grim-faced in front of what seemed to be helicopter wreckage in the field behind her.

"No," I breathed, my chest tight with fear. "No, not possible."

I couldn't make sense of what the reporter was saying. The words just weren't sinking in, drowned out by my own fears and panic. Had Cass crashed? He'd said he was rusty…

"Look at me," Zed's voice cut through the rushing in my head. "Dare, baby, come on, look at me. Listen. It's not Cass."

That cracked through, snapping my eyes away from the TV screen to lock with Zed's gaze just a few inches away. His palms were on my cheeks, and I jerked away with a sharp inhale.

Hurt flashed across his face, but he moved back a little more to give me space.

"It was a light aircraft," he continued, indicating to the TV. "Scenic flight. Not Cass. Look." He held up his phone, showing me a text from someone saved under *Grumpy Fuck*.

The message was short, just saying that he couldn't fly in the storm and to steer clear of Red if Zed valued his skin.

I snatched the phone from his hand, careful not to touch his fingers, and hit the call button. It rang only twice before Cass answered.

"What?" he barked.

"Thank fuck, you're okay," I exclaimed. "Fucking hell, Saint. I just saw something on the news about a crash and thought..."

"I'm fine, Angel," he replied, his voice drastically different from the one he'd answered the call with. The hard fuck-you tone was gone, replaced with concern. "Is everything okay there? Zed still breathing?"

I huffed a short laugh. "For now. No guarantees he'll stay that way." My eyes shifted to Zed, who was listening intently. Nosy prick never did understand boundaries.

Cass gave a low rumble like he was perfectly fine with whatever I wanted to do. "I've been checking the weather reports, and this storm doesn't seem to be stopping anytime soon. I'd hoped to get back before it hit." He sounded irritated as hell, but there wasn't much to be done about it.

"How long are we talking?" I asked quietly, hating how *needy* I felt.

He gusted a sigh. "Days. I'm going to leave the chopper here and drive back. It'll still get me there quicker than if I wait for the rain to stop."

I swallowed hard, but relief had eased some of the tension in my bones already. "Okay, yeah, good plan. Just drive safely."

Cass gave a husky laugh. "To get to you? Always. I'll see you in twelve hours, Angel."

He ended the call, and I reluctantly handed Zed his phone back. He arched a brow at me in question, and I rubbed at my tired eyes.

"He's driving back," I told him.

Zed nodded. "So...do you want to talk now?"

I snorted. "Not fucking likely. Get out of my room. I'm nowhere near ready to deal with your betrayal, Zed." Against my own will, my voice cracked over that statement and my eyes heated with unshed tears. "Seriously. Get out."

He *needed* to leave me alone before I broke down and started crying. He didn't fucking deserve to see my pain. He didn't deserve anything but my anger and an ice-cold shoulder. I should shoot him and get it over with. Yet...I hadn't. Deep down, I knew I could if that was what I really wanted. Zed would have handed me the gun himself if I'd *really* wanted to kill him.

But I didn't. Because goddamn it, I still loved him. And that just made it all a thousand times worse.

"Get out," I whispered again, and this time he listened.

Tears started rolling slowly down my cheeks before the door even clicked shut, and I could do nothing to stop them. Zed had hurt me worse than I'd ever known was possible. Worse than all of Chase's physical abuse. I'd let him into my heart; I'd fallen in love. Stupid, foolish me.

I should have known better. Part of me wanted to spit and hiss, raging about how no one could be trusted anymore. That love brought nothing but pain.

But the other part of me just sat there and pointed to Cass and Lucas, the physical contradictions to all my negative thoughts. The living proof that just because *Zed* had betrayed me, not all love brought pain. Sometimes it made us stronger and better humans.

Brushing the wetness from my cheeks, I made myself a mental promise not to shed any more tears over Zayden De Rosa. Enough was enough, and I needed to take control again. I needed to stop giving other people so much power over me.

It was a promise I already knew I couldn't keep. But the intention alone gave me strength.

Cass would be back in just twelve hours. I could avoid Zed for that time and simply work on *me*. On healing. That was what mattered most.

Just twelve hours. Easy. Right?

CHAPTER 12

"Bad news, Red." Cass looked grim on the video call from inside his car. His eyes were bloodshot and tired, and I knew he'd been driving nonstop since ending his call to me eleven hours earlier.

I groaned. "Don't say that. You're almost back."

"Yeah, unfortunately, *almost* is as good as it gets." His picture went blurry as he popped his car door open and stepped out into the pouring rain. "I got as far as the creek at the base of the mountain, but…look." He flipped the camera direction to show me, and I deflated.

"Where's the bridge?" I asked in a small, hopeful voice. Maybe I was looking at the wrong thing. Maybe he took a wrong turn somewhere.

Cass flipped the camera back to himself. "Good question. Looks like it's been washed out." He swiped a hand over his wet Mohawk, sending water droplets flying. "I dunno how else to get to you. This is the only road up to Foxglove, and the water is way too deep to drive across."

"Fuck," I muttered. There was no way he could even charter a helicopter in this weather. The wind was too strong and the clouds were thick.

"I'm sorry, Red," he said, getting back into his car and out of the rain. "I'm going to head back to the nearest town and try to come up with another plan."

I gave a long exhale, running my fingers through my tangle-free hair. Lucas had saved my ass by combing all that conditioner through it a couple of days ago. I'd have probably just lost my shit and cut it all off.

"No, it's pointless," I replied, trying not to look as devastated as I felt. "You're not going to rebuild a bridge any faster than it takes the rain to subside."

Cass grimaced, but I knew he agreed. "So, what now?"

I chewed the edge of my lip, thinking. It was silly to have him just sitting there in town waiting for the weather to clear. We'd already checked the meteorological maps, and it was likely to be another three to four days of heavy rain.

"Where were you at on your secret mission?" I asked reluctantly. "When you found me, I mean."

Cass quirked a brow. "Uh...I hadn't done a lot more. After Lucas called me, I dropped most of it to help him search for you."

I nodded because it was what I'd thought he would say. "So, get back on that. Now, more than ever, I want all those pieces to fall together. But I think our timeline needs to move up, and..." I sighed. "I don't know how much of the plan Zed has spilled. It might all be for nothing."

Cass scowled. "It better fucking not be."

Maybe I *did* need to talk to Zed after all, even if it was just to get an idea of how badly he'd sold me out. If Chase already knew what I'd had Cass doing...if Chase knew Cass was still alive...we could be screwed no matter what.

"Head back to Seattle," I told him reluctantly. "Finish your task as quickly as possible, then come back to me."

"You're the boss," he murmured, his eyes looking troubled on the video screen. "Are you going to be okay there?"

I gave a short, forced laugh. "I have to be, given we're trapped for the foreseeable future." My eyes flicked to the door, where Zed was likely to be lurking and listening. Or maybe not. Maybe I was being self-important in thinking he had nothing better to do than stare at my closed door. "I'll survive, Cass. I always do."

His mouth tightened, and his brow dipped low. "I'll be back the second the weather clears. I love you, Angel."

Ah fuck, he had to go hitting me right in the feels while I was already fragile. "I love you too, Saint," I whispered back, then ended the call before I could fall to pieces. Goddamn, I needed to get a grip.

I knew just the way to do it, too.

Climbing out of bed, I tied my sweatpants so they weren't falling off my ass. Then I left the room for the first time since I'd arrived four days ago.

I'd barely made it two steps into the hall before tripping over Zed. Literally. He was sitting slumped against the wall opposite my door, fast asleep, and my foot caught on his outstretched leg as I tried to pass by unnoticed.

Epic fail. Especially when I stumbled, cursed, and caught myself against the wall with a loud *thump*.

Zed—still half asleep—leapt to his feet like someone was attacking.

"Dare," he exclaimed, seeing me standing there with my hand braced against the wall. "What happened?"

I scowled. "I almost died tripping over your stupid fucking leg, that's what happened. What the hell are you doing out here, anyway? Don't tell me there's not a single other empty bedroom in this house."

Foxglove Manor, from what I knew, was a massive estate that had been added to multiple times over the years to accommodate the increased wealth of the Lockhart family. I didn't blame Cass for thinking it was the kind of property Channing Lockhart might have kept a vault within.

Zed just stared back at me, not rising to the bait I'd dangled. Dammit. I could have used a good verbal sparring match to shake me back into my Hades mindset.

"Cass can't get back," I finally told him. "The bridge at the bottom of the mountain is washed out. We're trapped until the rain eases." Zed's brow arched, and I glowered. "At least *pretend* to look unhappy about it."

He just shrugged. "Why would I be unhappy? We're trapped. Which means sooner or later, you're going to be bored enough to hear me out."

I scoffed. "Or I'll use that knife of yours to cut restitution from your flesh."

"Whatever works," he shot back, unconcerned. Motherfucker thought I was joking.

With a growl of frustration, I turned my back on him and headed down the hall away from my bedroom.

"Where are you going?" he called after me, but I just responded with a middle finger over my shoulder.

"Bite me," I muttered under my breath, taking my time heading down the stairs. My feet had mostly healed up, but the muscles all through my legs were still aching, so my speed was roughly that of an arthritic tortoise.

Zed didn't crowd me, but I could feel his eyes on me as I moved through the enormous house, eyeing the god-awful hunting decor. I doubted Cass had touched it since he'd taken possession, aside from searching for a vault. The huge mounted stag heads and bear-skin rugs definitely didn't feel like his idea of interior decorating.

I didn't really have a plan in mind, just knew I was losing my damn mind cooped up in that bedroom. If Zed and I were stuck here alone another few days, I needed to find something *else* to do. Especially because Lucas and Demi refused to involve me in business, citing some crap about me needing to rest and recover.

"What are you looking for?" Zed asked after shadowing me

through the kitchen, the formal dining room, and the casual lounge areas.

"Good fucking question," I muttered under my breath, but didn't raise my voice to offer an actual answer. Truthfully, I had no idea. I just wanted to explore a bit. I *wanted* to focus on something productive, but with the rain pouring down outside, I was stuck with whatever was inside the house.

"If you're bored, we can sit down and have that talk that's long overdue," Zed offered when I returned to the kitchen and stared blankly inside the fridge. At least there was plenty of food in there, so we shouldn't starve while trapped.

"Pretty sure that boat sailed about two weeks ago," I snarled back, grabbing a bottle of soda and slamming the fridge shut again. "Or, shit, maybe it sailed years ago. Either way, it's long fucking gone—hit a storm, capsized, then been smashed against jagged rocks. We're done, Zed. There's nothing left to discuss."

Zed snapped, his hand slamming down on the polished wooden counter. "Bullshit!" he barked, a flash of frustrated anger crossing his face. "You're punishing me, and I *get it.* I fucking deserve it. But you and I both know *that boat* is still happily afloat out on the ocean. Ignore me, ice me out, make me grovel, but don't fucking lie to yourself, Dare. You're better than that."

Indignation and outrage swept through me, and I stalked toward him. I put my soda down, ready to punch him with my good hand—since I still wore my sling—but at the last second, I reeled it in and gave a bitter laugh.

"Cute," I spat out. "You think you can push my buttons that easily? Think again. I'm not *mad* at you, Zed. I feel *nothing*. The only reason you're still alive is that you might prove useful when I bring Chase to his knees. Don't read too much into it."

With a serene smile that lacked even the tiniest bit of sincerity, I grabbed my drink and brushed past him. Maybe I was better off in my room after all.

When Zed didn't follow me onto the stairs, I glanced over my shoulder. He seemed frozen at the edge of the counter where I'd left him. His hand was balled into a fist against the wood, but he remained motionless.

Cursing myself silently for even turning to look, I continued up and shut myself back in the little haven of safety that my bedroom had become. My TV was still on, turned down low like I'd kept it almost every minute since Cass and Lucas had left, and *High School Musical* was playing.

Fucking Zac Efron bouncing around in his red singlet just made me snarl—the last time I'd seen that movie was one of my favorite memories with Zed. So instead of throwing the remote at the screen, I took the mature option and flicked the TV off.

I'd missed a call from Lucas while I was on my little wander around the house, so I climbed back into bed to call him back and fill him in on Cass's situation.

"Ah shit, Hayden," he groaned when I explained the bridge being washed out. "I'm so sorry I'm not there."

I smiled. "I'm not. You're doing a hell of a lot better being there. Is anyone giving you a hard time?"

Lucas gave a low chuckle, the sort that warmed me all the way to my toes. "Nah, nothing I can't handle with a little help from Demi and Rex. He's a barrel of fun, by the way. You didn't warn me."

I wrinkled my nose. "Fucking Rex. I knew he'd take this as an invitation to slink back into the Timberwolves."

"I don't know your history there—Demi said to ask you another day—but he seems like an asset." Lucas sounded curious but was also respecting Demi's advice not to ask for all the history just yet.

I huffed a sigh. "I guess. Are his boys keeping their dirty fucking hands off Seph?"

"They're getting along *all right*, according to Rex. I'll stop by and see her tomorrow if you want."

My chest ached, and I rubbed the heel of my hand across my breastbone. "Yeah, that'd be good if you could. She's probably worried. Or, I dunno. Maybe she's not." The last time I'd spoken with her, it'd been an argument. Maybe she was glad to have me gone and out of her life. I hadn't called her myself, partly because I didn't want to put her in danger—Chase would *expect* me to reach out to my sister. Partly...I didn't want my fears confirmed that she was better off without me.

"I'll visit tomorrow," Lucas assured me. "After my meeting with Vega."

I hummed a thoughtful sound under my breath. "Vega is a good ally. Hopefully, that hasn't changed and he can help with this Maurice bullshit. Steer clear of Ezekiel though. He's...a slippery fuck."

"I know," Lucas replied, patient as a damn saint. "I've got this, babe. You don't need to worry. Just take care of yourself. Have you been remembering your antibiotics?"

"Of course," I murmured, reaching out for the pills as I spoke. I was only an hour or two late.

There was a pause on the phone before he asked his next question. "Have you and Zed talked?"

I grunted an annoyed sound as I swallowed the pills. "Talked in general? Yes."

I could practically feel Lucas's deadpan glare over the phone. "Hayden..."

"Why do you care?" I rebutted. "Do you truly think what he did can be explained away? You must if you're pushing me to hear him out."

"I'm not..." He gave a frustrated sigh. "Look, I won't ever make you do something you're not comfortable with. And no, I *don't* think it can be explained away. But I also don't believe for a fucking second that he set you up like it seemed. He loves you, Hayden. And I know how that feels. He would do *anything* for you…even at the risk of his own happiness. Just think about it. There're two sides to every story."

When I said nothing in response because words were failing me, he changed the subject.

"Are you going to be okay showering without Grumpy Cat to help out?" His concern was evident, and I couldn't help smiling. It was absurd, really.

"I'm sure I can handle it," I replied with a short laugh, "so long as I take it easy and don't use my shoulder. Better that than marinate in my own stink until Cass gets back. Besides, I told him to head back out to Seattle, so it could be longer than expected."

Lucas hummed a thoughtful sound. "Well…you can always call me. I can't be there to help, but I could chat with you. Distract you a bit."

I knew what he meant. He wasn't worried about me hurting myself so much as sliding into another panic attack if the water hit my face. Fucking Chase, it was like he deliberately chose torture techniques that would mess me up in the deepest ways.

"Thank you," I murmured, meaning it. "I'll work it out, though. I can't shower with you for the rest of my life."

"Why not?" Lucas replied, and I could almost hear his grin. "I'm not complaining. It's kind of nice being able to take care of you for once." Then he gave a small groan. "I didn't mean… Ugh, sorry, that came out wrong. Obviously, I don't think—"

"You're fine, Lucas," I said, cutting his panicked ramble off. "I know what you meant. I promise, you can wash my hair for me anytime you want. You do a *really* good job of it." He actually did—hairdresser standard of clean—and the way his long fingers massaged my skull would have been downright sexual if I wasn't such a broken mess.

He gave a happy hum. "I'll hold you to that, babe. I'd better go, though. Demi is tapping her watch at me."

I smiled. "Say hi for me."

"I will," he promised. "I love you, Hayden. Think about what I said."

My only response to that was a grumpy huff and a muttered "I love you back, Gumdrop."

Despite him pushing me to talk with Zed, I ended the call with a warm, happy glow inside. Talking to Lucas always seemed to leave me feeling like that, like I could shed a ton of emotional baggage in just one conversation with him. Damn kid was a wizard. Fuck, I was lucky to have him.

CHAPTER 13

Stupid me, I should have grabbed breakfast while I was wandering aimlessly downstairs. Only a few moments after ending my call with Lucas, my stomach was rumbling. I *badly* didn't want to deal with Zed again so soon, though, so I just drank my bottle of soda and hauled my ass through to the bathroom.

After discussing it with Lucas, I knew I needed to push through and shower alone sooner rather than later.

"Come on, you big wuss," I scolded myself as I stood there staring at the dry shower cubicle. "It's a fucking shower. You're alone. No way to drown."

Except logic and trauma occupy two totally separate areas of the brain, and no, they don't talk. No matter how calm and rational I got myself, when I reached out to turn the shower on, the trauma side slammed front and center.

"Fuck *off*," I snarled at the irrational fear flooding my body when the shower spray soaked my wrist before I could pull it out.

Leaving the water running, I turned back to face myself in the mirror.

Slowly, I undressed and muttered motivational verbal abuse at my reflection, pepping myself up for taking this next step in busting through my damage. Ultimately, though, I decided that I was just making myself *more* anxious.

So, I drew a deep breath and got into the shower.

The stool was still in there, but I was strong enough now to stand on my own feet. I bit my cheek and let the water cascade down my back. Not so bad. It was just like when I was in there with Lucas, minus his soothing voice and gentle hands.

I gave myself a small, mocking laugh as I relaxed. I'd gotten so worked up in my head about it, and it wasn't even a problem at all. This was *fine*. That panic attack on the first day must have just been because I'd *just* woken from a flashback about being drowned.

Buoyed with that confidence, I shifted further under the water, tipping my head back to get my hair wet. Then a stream of water sluiced over my face, and I instantly regretted my choice.

Flashbacks hit me hard and fast, speeding between one another in a jumble of fear, suffocation, and pain. Not just contained to the drownings, this time I was treated to a whole tangled-up montage of the torture highlights, and for one desperate moment I wondered if this was the breaking point. One quick flash of clarity, of *knowing* how badly my mind was spiraling out of my control, and I wondered if maybe there was no coming back this time.

Strong hands grasped my wrists, and I fought back, screaming and thrashing, but it was no use. I was too weak, too damaged. I was no match for Chase's superior strength, and he picked me entirely up off the floor, crushing me to his chest as he walked.

But his touch wasn't rough or cruel.

Chase...fuck. No. It wasn't Chase. I'd *escaped* that psychotic fuck. I'd gotten free.

"Zed," I gasped between harsh breaths. It was a question more than a statement, and he must have heard that in my voice.

"Yeah, baby, it's me. You're safe. Just take some slow breaths, okay? Can you do that?" His words were low and calm, soothing.

Damn him straight to hell, all I felt for him in that moment was relief. Love. My arms were banded around his neck, my shoulder injury forgotten as I held him close and trembled through the fading memories.

He didn't push me away, either. One of his arms was tucked securely around my waist, holding me against him as the other rubbed circles on my back. He just held me and gently talked me down, helping me regain my sanity piece by piece. Just like he'd done countless times before.

I'd once said to Lucas that without Zed, I doubted I'd have kept even a shred of my humanity. And it was true. He'd kept me grounded while I massacred my father's gang and my fiancé's family. He'd tethered me to humanity throughout five years of ruthless killings and violence. And now here he was, pulling me from the brink of total despair. Again.

Yet this time, it was tainted with the ache of his betrayal.

As soon as I felt like I was back in control of my own mind, I pushed out of his lap. We were sitting on the edge of my bed, and I pulled a sheet up to cover myself as I cast my gaze away from his prying eyes.

"Sorry," I croaked, having seen the bloody scratches on his cheek and forearms. "I'm fine now."

Zed gave a vexed sound and didn't move from his position. We were still close enough that my bare leg pressed against his thigh, but I was too physically exhausted to move.

"You're the furthest thing from fine, Dare." There was an edge of something in his tone that boiled my blood. Pity.

Instantly furious, I snapped my gaze back to glare death at him. "What the fuck would you know? You're the one who handed me over to him all wrapped up in a nice, neat bow. Everything that happened to me? Is *your* fault, Zed. *You* did this to me just as much as he did." I was so mad I was shaking. "How dare you look at me with pity. Shouldn't you be off somewhere with your old friend, toasting your successes? Why are you even still here? Or is this part of the game? Save me, just to bask in how utterly *fucked up* he left me?"

Zed didn't try to defend himself. He didn't even look *shocked* by my accusations. Just…resigned.

Then after a tense moment, he gave a short nod and left the room.

I blinked at the open door in confusion, wondering what fresh hell he was playing at now. Then he came storming back in with a Glock 19 in his hand, and I stiffened with fear.

He didn't aim it at me, though. He just came back around to the side of the bed where I sat and held the gun out butt first.

"Take it," he told me in a clipped tone.

I stared down at the gun, then back up at him with suspicion. "Excuse me?"

"Take it!" he shouted, and curse it all to hell, I did. My fingers wrapped around the grip like I was reuniting with an old friend, and Zed released his hold on it to take a step back. "Now. Shoot me."

My brows hiked. "Excuse me?" I was repeating myself, but that's how thoroughly off-balance he'd left me.

"You heard me, Hades. Shoot me." He stretched his hands wide, his chin tilted up in stubborn defiance. "You're *Hades*. You don't suffer betrayals or insubordination from fucking anyone. If you truly believe everything you just said to me, this should be easy. Shoot. Me."

The breath caught in my chest and my fingers tightened around the gun. He was absolutely right; I *should* just shoot him. It's what I'd have done to anyone else, wasn't it? So why hadn't I done it?

"You can't do it, can you?" he taunted, his gaze steady and confident as I stared back at him. "You can't do it because you *know* that's not what happened. You fucking *know* how much I love you, Dare." His voice cracked, and raw pain shone through his eyes. "You know I will spend every damn second for the rest of my life regretting the choices that got us here and desperately trying to make this up to you. But you *need* to hear me out."

I swallowed the hard lump of emotion trapped in my throat and shook my head. "I don't need to do shit for you, Zed."

His jaw clenched and his eyes flashed with determination. "You're not doing it for me, Dare. You're doing it for you. Get all the facts, then if you still don't believe me, you pull the damn trigger."

My pulse was still racing from my panic attack in the shower and my shoulder ached from being used, but my hand was steady on the gun. If there was one way to make me feel more like myself, it was to put a gun in my hands. Zed was no idiot; he knew what he was doing.

"Or pull it now," he pushed. "But this ends now. I've given you time and space, but you're hurting yourself now. That's where I draw the damn line."

My brow creased. "What the fuck are you talking about?"

Zed nodded to my shoulder, and I gave it a lightning-fast glance, just long enough to see blood seeping up through the dressing. *Shit.* How badly had I been flailing when he pulled me from the shower?

Drawing a deep breath, I let it sweep through me in a weak attempt to calm my mind. It worked...sort of.

"Fine," I snapped, tightening my jaw. "So be it."

I squeezed the trigger.

The shot was deafening in such a confined space, making my ears ring and my weakened arm kick ever so slightly on the recoil. Damn it, I needed to get back into a gym sooner rather than later.

"What the fuck was that?" Zed exclaimed, eyeing the destroyed TV. A perfect bullet hole pierced the center of the screen, a spider-web of fractures radiating from it.

I shrugged and placed the gun down on the bedside table with my medication. "Checking if you were bluffing."

His brows hitched. "You thought I would give you blanks?"

"I don't know what to fucking think anymore, Zed," I admitted with a tired sigh. "Grab my shirt from the bathroom. I'm not having this conversation sitting here naked."

He went to do as I asked but muttered something about it being dirty. Instead, he tossed me a towel to dry off and disappeared out of the room. He returned a minute later with an almost identical button-down shirt in a soft shade of gray that he held out to me.

"I should have fucking known that was your shirt," I mumbled, tugging it onto my good arm, then wincing as I wrestled my shitty one through the sleeve. "Neither Cass nor Lucas would own Hugo Boss."

I buttoned just a few buttons, leaving the neck open and nodding to the stack of dressings Lucas had left for me. "Pass me one of those."

Zed picked up a dressing from the pile as I carefully peeled the old one off. But instead of passing it to me, he batted my hand aside and applied it himself. Thankfully, it was one with adhesive sides, so it was a quick and easy process.

"Are you ready to shut up and listen now?" he asked when he was done.

His face was only inches away, his broad frame leaning over me in an imposing yet unthreatening way. I clenched my teeth, prepared to be hit with an onslaught of memories of my own delusions starring Zed. But they didn't come, and I slowly released my breath.

"Fine," I whispered. "Start from the beginning."

He gave a small nod, shifting away to sit on the edge of my bed, close enough to touch if I wanted to. Not that I did.

"All right," he agreed, rubbing a hand over his short-cropped hair. "So we start on the night of the massacre."

Somehow, this didn't surprise me in the least. Deep down, I'd known that was where this story began. The Timberwolf massacre.

CHAPTER 14

Zed didn't immediately start spilling his story. Instead, he sat there for several moments, staring out the window like he was trying to collect his thoughts. Then he gave a weary sigh and let his shoulders slump.

"Do you remember what happened after that night?" he asked softly.

I frowned. "Of course I do. How could I not?"

He arched a brow at me like he wasn't so sure of that. "You remember how badly messed up I was? How Chase had stabbed me sixteen times with my own fucking knife and you saved my ass? Then after you shot him, you dragged me out of the cursed Lockhart mansion like I weighed nothing. Like you had a sixth sense that the whole place was about to go up in flames."

I shook my head. "I didn't. I just knew I needed to get you help. You were half-dead when I got you out to the lawn." I pinched the bridge of my nose, recalling memories I'd long since buried. "You said some shit about it all being worth it, then you choked on your own fucking blood and I thought that was the end."

He flashed me a grin. "Nah, can't take me down that easy." He paused, his smile slipping as his eyes turned serious. "Do you know what the last thing I heard was? Before I woke up in the hospital?"

I wet my lips. "I can guess."

His eyes held mine captive, a lifetime of shared history passing between us. "Did you mean it?"

It was the first time I'd ever told Zed that I loved him.

"You know I did," I whispered, feeling my heart breaking all over again. How could he have betrayed my trust after everything we'd been through together?

Zed closed his eyes for a moment, a long exhale shuddering through him. Then when he opened his eyes again, it was with a certain measure of calm restored.

"When I woke up in the hospital, you weren't there," he continued.

Guilt twisted my stomach, even though we were talking about an incident from more than five years ago. "I had to finish our plan. Gather up the remaining Timberwolves and offer them the choice to stay or go, just like we'd agreed."

He nodded. "I'm glad you did. I wouldn't have had it any other way. But while you weren't there, someone else was. Someone who had evidence of everything we'd done and was threatening to use it if I didn't cooperate." He swiped a hand over his face, cringing. "Turned out the FBI had been heavily involved with the Lockharts. They had an inside man placed somewhere in the family's security team, and his surveillance caught everything from the moment we entered the Lockhart compound."

I stared at him with a frown of disbelief. "So you just...rolled over?"

Zed gave a sharp, harsh laugh. "Hell no. I told them where to shove their *evidence* and threatened to come for the little douchebag trying to extort me as soon as I was able. I was pretty confident we could find a way to erase their tapes if we put our minds to it."

Now? Yes, we could. Back then? I doubted it. Maybe if we'd

physically broken in and stolen the recordings, but we'd definitely lacked the IT department that the Timberwolves currently employed.

"So what changed?" I prompted. Despite everything, I was eager to hear the whole story. To understand how we'd gone so far off the rails.

Zed gave me a tired look. "The next day a different agent came to me with an upgraded offer. Work undercover for them and provide evidence on *other* gangs, and they'd offer immunity."

My eyes widened, and my lips parted in shock. "You sold us out to save your own ass? Jesus, Zed—"

"Not for me, dipshit. For you. They told me that if I took the job, that *you* and *only you* would be off-limits. The case against you that had been started would be tossed out, and you'd be safe." His eyes implored me to see the truth in his words. That he had wholeheartedly believed he was protecting me. "All I could hear in my head was you telling me that you loved me, Dare. They offered me a chance to protect you not just against the crimes we'd just committed, but against everything we hadn't yet done. I couldn't say no to that."

My mind reeled, struggling to process the choice he'd made. "And...you just believed them?" I whispered. "No FBI agent could make that promise. Not against future crimes. How could you seriously have just taken them at their word?"

He gave a self-deprecating laugh, swiping a hand over his face. "Because the offer came from the one person who knew how to manipulate me better than anyone on earth." He hissed a breath through his teeth, shaking his head. "My mom."

"What?"

"Yeah." He grimaced. "I know. So much for being dead, huh? Turns out she'd been working for the FBI the whole damn time. Dad blew her cover, so she shot him and 'disappeared' so she could go back to her real life—without the fake name, fake crime family, fake *son.*" His voice was so sharp it could cut glass, and against all my better instincts, I reached out to place my hand on his.

"Zed...I don't even know what to say." I frowned, chewing the edge of my lip. "You should have told me. The second you found out, you should have *told* me. We could have worked shit out together."

His sad gaze dropped from my face down to our hands. "I know," he admitted, turning his hand over beneath mine so we were palm to palm. "I fucked up, and my only excuse was that I trusted her. I trusted, even though she'd abandoned me, that she would protect you. Above all else, Dare, I *only* wanted to protect you."

As badly as I was hurting, I believed him when he said that.

Because wouldn't I do the same for him? If the shoe had been on the other foot and they'd approached me with an offer to protect Zed...yeah, I'd have taken it in a heartbeat.

"This is a lot," I murmured, retracting my hand from his. "Can I just get a minute to process?"

He gave a swift nod, standing up from the edge of the bed. "Of course. I'll...I'll just be downstairs...whenever you're ready to hear the rest."

When he was gone, I allowed myself a moment to flop back against the pillows and blink up at the ceiling. I didn't know *what* exactly I'd thought his explanation would be...but his mom being alive *and* the one who'd coerced him into the FBI? That I hadn't expected.

It hurt that he hadn't immediately told me. But given the situation at the time...We'd just executed dozens of people we'd known our whole lives, Zed had been stabbed sixteen times by his best friend, and he would have been heavily dosed up on painkillers in the hospital. Yeah, I could understand why he'd made a shitty choice under those conditions.

It wasn't even a shitty choice to accept the deal with the FBI.

I'd have done the same for him, a hundred times over. But he *should* have told me about it.

He'd been dealing with so much, with his mom… Fucking hell, I just wished I could have been there to support him through that. Where had I been? Why hadn't I *noticed* something was wrong?

I cast my mind back to that time, recalling long-buried details. In the aftermath of that bloody night, so many things had happened *so* damn quickly. Archer, Kody, and Steele had bought their freedom from the Reapers with blood and fear, and I'd provided the insurance they needed by handing Archer half of the black-market trade routes for Shadow Grove. I'd gone headfirst down the rabbit hole of my new life, eating, sleeping, and breathing *Hades*. I'd shut off my humanity as much as possible just to survive the awful things I'd done.

And Zed? He'd been in hospital recovering from what should have been multiple death sentences. When I'd finally made it in to see him almost a week after the massacre, he'd been grim when he told me about some possible long-term damage from an injury to the nerves in his arm.

He'd been discharged not long after and immediately slipped into his role as my second-in-command. Together, we were unstoppable. We'd planned it all down to every detail, and it ran flawlessly. Within two months, we had fully secured our seat of power. The Timberwolves, for public knowledge, were extinct. And we were well on track to building up our empire in the shadows.

Then Zed had gone for surgery on his damaged nerves, followed by a three-month stint in a rehab facility in New York.

Taking a harsh breath, I strapped on my sling, because my shoulder was killing me, and left my room in search of Zed. I needed *way* more answers than I currently possessed.

I found him downstairs in the living room, a crystal tumbler in his hand and an open bottle of scotch on the table near his foot.

"Good thinking," I muttered, pouring myself a healthy triple in the empty glass beside the bottle. I hadn't taken anything for pain in close to twelve hours, and my ribs were making it known.

Zed arched a brow as I sat down on the leather sofa beside him and took a large mouthful of liquor. I was steering clear of opioids, not joining a convent.

"You're not taking the painkillers, huh?" He murmured the observation under his breath, even though he already knew the answer. He also knew the reason.

I clicked my tongue, then swallowed the rest of my drink in one huge mouthful. Cringing at the alcohol burn, I held my empty glass out, and he refilled it without complaint.

"Rehab," I croaked, dabbing my lips on the sleeve of my shirt.

Zed knew what I meant and nodded. "Yep."

I drew a long breath, letting it swell my lungs, and winced at the press on my ribs. "They put you through some kind of crash course in how to be a snake in the grass or something?" My words dripped with bitterness, but Zed didn't shy away from it. "Three months isn't long enough for standard FBI training."

"Something like that, yeah. Special exemptions or some shit, I figured, seeing as I wasn't being trained to *be* an agent, just to do one specific job." He gulped his own scotch and refilled it. "Hindsight tells me the whole thing was completely unauthorized, but at the time"—he shrugged—"I guess I turned a blind eye to it. I convinced myself I was doing the only thing that could keep you safe."

I scoffed at that. "Don't act like that was all *for me*, Zed. Nothing involving Chase could ever be for my benefit, and you damn well know it. I don't know what else you were getting out of this, but—"

"Nothing," he snapped, cutting me off. "There was *nothing* else to be gained. I didn't even barter for my own immunity, but my mom offered it up unprompted. Turns out her word isn't worth the oxygen in her breath."

I bit the inside of my cheek, forcing myself to hold back the cutting remarks that I already knew were totally false. We wouldn't get anywhere if I just hurled insults, and I really wanted the whole picture.

Zed took another gulp of scotch. "Let's hit the important points," he muttered. "Then we can circle back for details when you need them."

I arched a brow. "Suits me. Tell me how you got tied up with Chase. Was it before or after you saw those tapes? Did you partner up with him already knowing how badly he'd abused me?" Because I doubted I could ever come back from that if he had. If he'd knowingly joined my enemy with full knowledge of what he'd done to me in my darkest hours...

"I didn't," he huffed. "The first time I suspected he was even still alive was at the same time as you did, when we dug up his empty grave."

I frowned, confusion pausing my fury and outrage. "Huh?"

Zed gave me a pointed look. "Dare, I *never* colluded with Chase. I *would* never. If your car hadn't pulled away when it did, you'd have seen me deck him, then almost get shot for it. That sick fuck was playing us all, but I swear to you, I had no clue he was FBI until that moment."

That made me stiffen in surprise. In all the possible scenarios I'd played out in my head, none of them had considered the possibility that Zed honestly had no clue he was working with Chase. But... that was exactly Chase's MO, wasn't it? Head games. Constant head games. What utter delight he must have taken in knowing Zed had no clue he was actually working for the villain himself.

"The second I walked back into Timber, Lucas fucking basically told me to stop being a little bitch and to come help him plan your jailbreak." Zed gave a small smile, like he couldn't help being proud. "I was well into the depths of despair, though, thinking about that look on your face when that nutty bitch Jeanette outed me. Fuck me, that chick had totally cracked undercover."

That was something we could agree on. "Did you know about her?"

Zed shook his head. "I *really* wasn't an agent. The only contact I had with the FBI was through my mom. She was my handler. Sure, they slapped the title on my name for the paperwork, but I was little more than an informant. And a bad one at that. More often than not, I turned the wires off and conveniently forgot to turn them back on again."

"They let you do that?" I frowned.

He shrugged. "Like I said, it was an arrangement as dodgy as they come. I would be surprised if anyone even knew what was going on. In the last few months, something changed, though. My mom became more demanding that I turn in *something*, like her own ass was on the line if I couldn't deliver. So I gave them little pieces here and there. Things that wouldn't impact us. Innocent conversations that would lead them nowhere."

I sipped my drink and the alcohol buzzed in my veins. Mixing it with antibiotics wasn't strictly the best idea, but given everything else my body had been through, it was far from the worst.

"That's how they got that recording? Of me talking to Maxine?"

Zed nodded. "My mom admitted to that. After Maxine was attacked, she pulled that sound bite and submitted it. For a promotion, can you believe it? When I confronted her, she wasn't even sorry. All those years, thinking I was protecting you...and she never intended to keep her word."

Well, shit. I'd only met Zed's mom a couple of times before she "disappeared," but she hadn't seemed like the cold, calculating bitch type. Then again, she also hadn't seemed like the deep-cover FBI agent type.

"Why didn't they get me sooner?" I asked, gritting my teeth against all the heartbreak. "I've done a hundred things worse than that weak link to Maxine's attack. Why were none of those used?"

Zed gave me a pointed look. "I never gave them any of that.

I guess I always had a suspicion that there was more going on, so I just…deleted everything. Anytime you and I were directly involved, I deleted the files before she got them. This was the closest she had to dirt, and she took it and ran."

I blew out a long breath. "What a bitch."

Zed barked a sharp laugh. "Understatement."

"Why didn't you tell me, Zed?" I asked softly, my eyes on my drink. I didn't want to see whatever emotions were on his face, since he'd apparently stopped shielding them from me. "I get why you didn't at the time—there was so much going on. But…it's been five years. Surely there was at least *one* opportunity to tell me."

He was quiet for a long moment before responding. "You're right. I had a thousand opportunities to tell you, but I didn't. Then it was like the longer I went without telling you, the more I convinced myself you'd never forgive me. I got it into my head that so long as I was protecting you, then you never needed to know. I couldn't…" His voice trailed off, his words drying up. Taking a swallow of his drink, he leaned his head back on the sofa to look at the ceiling for strength or something. "I was scared, Dare."

That admission was a rough, heartfelt whisper, and it struck a chord deep inside me.

"You're not scared of anything, Zayden," I muttered back.

He grunted and shook his head. "Not true. I was scared I would lose you. I watched you harden after that night—the way you closed yourself off from the world, from your own emotions. You did everything you needed to do to survive your new role. But I was scared that it meant you wouldn't forgive me for lying. For deceiving you. For being the fox in the henhouse. I was so fucking scared that if I told you, that'd be the end of us. So I convinced myself the only thing to do was keep my mouth shut and…keep going as I was."

I said nothing. What the hell could I even say back to that?

"I didn't give a crap if you shot me," he continued, his voice low and quiet. "I just couldn't stand the thought of...not being *us*. I didn't want to lose *us*, because even though you'd seemed to have forgotten what you'd said to me that night when I was bleeding out and heading toward the light, I never had. I was just biding my time, waiting until you were ready to let your walls down again."

Somehow, I got the feeling I knew where he was heading. "And then I met Lucas."

He gave me a lopsided smile. "You know, I started to tell you everything so many times after you met Gumdrop that I lost count. But every damn time, I came up against the exact same problem. You were letting your walls down, so I *needed* to confess everything. But..."

I groaned. "But I thought you were trying to confess *feelings* and totally derailed everything, didn't I?"

Zed wrinkled his nose. "A little bit. Because then I could see a future for us that rivaled even my most far-fetched fantasies, and I had an even stronger desire to never fuck it up."

"Until you did."

His shoulders sagged, and he swirled his drink in his glass. "Yep."

We sat in silence for a while, drinking our scotch. After Zed refilled our glasses again and with the haze of intoxication seeping into my brain, I decided I needed to hear more.

"What happened after I was arrested?"

Zed scrubbed his hand over his head. "Uh, let's see. I stood there in shock as Jeanette pushed you into her car, then Chase slithered up to me all smug as fuck. I turned around and decked him, had four agents pull their guns on me..." He was ticking off the points in the air, then rolled his eyes. "Apparently Chase has been spreading his unique brand of poison in his division of the feds for a while. They defer to him as a director, even though he's not."

My stomach churned, remembering how I'd felt in that

moment when Jeanette had called him *director* and stupid, shell-shocked me had actually believed her.

"Lucas gave me a dressing-down and told me he didn't believe I'd really sold you out and that we needed to get to work on breaking you out. Oh, and he punched me pretty damn hard, too." That proud smirk was back, and I rolled my eyes. Only Zed would be proud of someone punching him in the face.

"Good," I muttered. "I hope it hurt."

"It did," he confirmed. "Then I had an unpleasant interaction with my mother where I told her I was done being her puppet and threatened to shoot her in the head if she didn't fuck off."

My brows shot up in surprise. But also…relief.

"Anyway. After I drank a whole bottle of bourbon and trashed Timber, I passed out. Then got woken up with a bucket of ice water dumped over my head and Cass snarling in my face." Another hint of a smile. Zed liked Cass way more than he ever admitted. "Turns out, even as pissed as they were, they didn't give a fuck about the how or why, they just wanted me to help get you back. So…that's what we did."

I peered into my glass, a niggling question on my mind. "How *did* you find me? Twelve days is a long time. The trail must have been cold."

"Stone cold," he confirmed. "Chase had put a lot of planning into that abduction. I'm guessing he drugged you right from the back of Jeanette's car?"

I cringed, badly not wanting to examine what had happened to me. Zed took the hint and continued talking without waiting for me to reply.

"Well, we tracked you as far as the Montana border. Then you just…disappeared. We figured he had to have a hideout somewhere in that area, so we stayed close and searched extensively. There's a *whole* lot of wilderness for him to hide in, though."

I took a huge mouthful of scotch, needing to do *something* to distract myself, despite the way I could already feel my hand shaking. "You tracked me?" I repeated, shooting Zed a puzzled look. "How?"

His eyes widened, and he looked uncomfortable for the first time since we'd started talking. "Uh, I thought you knew. Wow. Cass implanted a GPS tracker under your skin."

I choked on my drink, and scotch sprayed everywhere.

"What?" I shrieked between coughing fits. Lungs really don't like scotch, in case anyone was wondering.

Zed reached out and patted me on the back as I spluttered and cringed. "Dare, I honestly thought you knew. He never said you didn't, and I couldn't imagine that was something he'd done against your will…but look, it was a fucking good thing he did. We spent all that time searching the wilderness of Montana and coming up blank, then all of a sudden you were back on the tracker. We piled into the helicopter. Cass almost killed us a couple of times flying too close to trees, and then when we got close to your location, he dropped me down to try and find you on foot."

I slammed my glass down on the table and covered my mouth with my palm, stunned. Cass had *chipped* me. When? How?

"Holy shit," I murmured. "I'm gonna kill him." But the timeline clicked in my brain. "Chase must have had a blocker on his house. Or on the cell, anyway. He's so fucking paranoid he would have done it just to protect himself. If he'd known there was a chip on *me*, he never would have let me out."

Zed arched a brow. "He *let* you out?"

A deep shudder rolled through me, and cold sweat broke out on my palms. "I don't want to talk about it."

"Fair enough," he murmured. "Anyway…I think that's all."

Leaning forward, he topped up our drinks and handed mine back to me while I sat in stunned silence for a while.

"Did you kill Agent Hanson?" I asked after a while, looking up at him through my lashes. "When she called to warn me that there was a mole in my organization, you weren't answering your phone."

Zed frowned, shaking his head. "No. I was at Club 22, beating the ever-loving shit out of those pricks that tried to threaten Max. Rodney witnessed it all if you need to check my alibi."

A small sigh of relief slipped out of me. I didn't even *like* Agent Hanson, but the thought of Zed killing her had been eating away at me.

"What about Alexi?" I asked. "Is he a fed?"

Zed shrugged. "If he is, I never knew about it. My instincts say he's not…but I guess no one is above corruption these days."

"Did you…did you tell anyone what I'm planning for Chase?" This one question made my pulse race harder than ever.

"Not a soul," he replied, his tone rough with sincerity.

This time when I exhaled, a huge chunk of anxiety flowed out of my body, leaving me lighter. I nodded, intensely relieved, then unfolded myself from the couch. The booze hit me hard, and I wobbled a bit, but waved Zed away when he reached out to steady me.

"I'm fine," I mumbled. "Just need to go lie down for a while."

"Not a bad idea," he agreed with a lopsided smile.

I started to leave the living room, but he called out after me, making me pause and look back.

"I hope you know how sorry I am," he told me, his eyes shining with emotion. "If you let me, I'll spend every day for the rest of our lives apologizing for this fuckup. If I could go back and do it all again…" His voice trailed off, his expression tightening.

"If you could go back in time, you would still take the deal," I finished for him, my tone neutral and nonjudgmental. He gave a slow nod, anguish creasing his features. But I just shrugged. "So would I, Zed. I'd have done the exact same thing for you."

Swallowing hard as the room swam, I made my exit back up to the illusion of safety in my bedroom. But I meant what I'd said.

How could I judge his actions knowing I wouldn't have done anything differently?

Right down to keeping it all a secret. Faced with the same choice...I'd have kept my mouth shut too. His love meant that much to me.

CHAPTER 15

I slept off the worst of the alcohol and woke up feeling dusty enough that I took the Tylenol beside my bed. There was also a glass of water and a freshly baked banana muffin on a plate waiting for me. Fucking Zed still managed to create mouthwatering food while half-drunk.

I inhaled the muffin, then went hunting for some pants. Earlier, when I'd gone downstairs to talk with Zed, I hadn't bothered. His shirt was long enough on me that my ass was covered, but if I wanted to exercise, then I probably needed pants.

Except the ones I'd left in the bathroom were the ones I'd been wearing for several days, and I had no desire to put them back on.

Shrugging to myself, I left the bedroom dressed in just Zed's shirt and my sling once again. It was midafternoon, and I was hungry enough that I needed a proper meal.

Apparently, I wasn't the only one with that idea. I followed my nose and the scent of frying bacon into the kitchen where Zed was plating up a couple of gourmet burgers with all the trimmings.

"You're awake," he commented.

Suddenly uncomfortable, I wrapped my free arm around myself and shifted my weight. "Yeah."

I hadn't really thought things through since our conversation. I hadn't even taken a minute to consider where the fuck the two of us stood with each other. Was I still holding a grudge? Probably. I lacked the emotional maturity that Lucas seemed to have in spades and didn't find it so easy to let bygones be bygones.

But…what the fuck was I waiting for? He'd already called my bluff on shooting him. So, were we okay again? Friends? More than friends? Or just people who used to be so crazy in love that it physically hurt?

Who was I kidding? That love hadn't faded. Not even a little bit. It was just clouded by heartache, betrayal, and confusion. Most of all by anger. Anger which had all but fizzled out with the clarity of context and open communication.

To think so much could have been avoided if Zed and I had worked harder on our relationship years ago.

That didn't mean I was ready to forgive and forget, though. Just because I could understand why he'd done what he'd done didn't make it okay. At the end of the day, he *had* done it. And now he needed to kiss my ass until the end of time if he wanted to have any hope of redemption.

Starting after I got that burger in my belly.

Without speaking, I parked my ass on one of the barstools, and Zed slid one of the plates in front of me. Then he grabbed a couple of cold waters from the fridge and pulled up a stool beside me to eat his own burger.

Not a single word passed between us while we ate our lunch and let the food soak up the last of this morning's breakfast scotch. It wasn't even uncomfortable. Just…different.

Zed finished before me—it was hard to eat a burger one-handed—but just hung out in silence while I navigated my meal. When I was done, he cleared up the plates, then turned to me with an arched brow.

"Coffee?" he offered, an edge of hope clear in his voice.

Despite my need for caffeine, I shook my head. Things weren't automatically back to normal now that he'd given an admittedly good explanation for his betrayal. And lingering for coffee would definitely send the wrong signal.

So I slid off my stool and cleared my throat. "Thanks for the burger." Then I left the kitchen to head back up to my bedroom. I needed to stretch out my muscles, find some clean pants, tackle the shower. Crap, how was I going to tackle the shower?

It was a problem for later. First, I needed pants.

Rather than asking Zed, I decided to use my own initiative and go looking. It was Cass's property, after all, so not like I was snooping around a stranger's house. Surely, if the guys had some clothes here, there would be at least *one* pair of pants left behind.

Except I didn't anticipate the sheer number of empty guest rooms I'd need to look through. On the third empty, dust-filled room, I gave up and sent a message to Lucas on my new phone. It was a burner phone that Cass had kept in one of the supply bags, but it was helping me feel a little more connected to the world outside Foxglove Manor.

He replied quickly, saying that there should be a bag of my own clothes somewhere.

Sure enough, back in my own bedroom I found a small overnight bag tucked into the closet. It hadn't even occurred to me to check there first.

I shot him a quick thanks, then pulled out some panties and a pair of yoga pants. Perfect. There was no way in hell I could wrestle my arm into a sports bra, so I'd leave Zed's shirt on for now, but at least my bum was covered.

Without my TV, I had to listen to the sound of my own dark thoughts as I started to stretch out my muscles. Which was a crappy idea, to say the least. After the third time I had to haul my mind out of the black fog, I gave up and went in search of the gym.

No way in hell did a mansion like this *not* have a gym.

One step out of my room, I pulled up short, though.

"What are you doing?" I demanded, eyeing Zed on the floor opposite my door.

He held up the book in his hands. "Reading Homer's *Odyssey*. What are you doing?"

I scowled. "What are you doing *here*, outside my—" I cut myself off with a shake of my head. I already knew the answer to that. "Forget it. Where's the gym?"

Zed arched a brow, but pushed up from the floor and tucked his book under his arm. "This way."

He led the way through the enormous Foxglove Manor and held the gym door open for me when we arrived. Sure enough, it was almost big enough to be a commercial setup, and most of the equipment was coated in dust. A couple of the machines had been wiped clean, though. I wasn't the only one with the urge to work out while trapped here.

I sent Zed a level glare as I entered, and he just smiled back at me before leaving.

Weirdo.

With a sigh, I headed over to one of the few pieces of equipment I could safely use with my arm in a sling. The treadmill. I didn't even have shoes, but too bad. I had to get my strength back, and that wasn't going to happen lying around and drinking whiskey.

Not wanting to be an idiot and kill myself just yet, I set the machine to a walking pace. It took me a second to find my balance on the belt—I didn't realize how much I used *both* my arms in everyday life. But after a minute I was walking with a confident pace.

The gym door opened again as I set the video screen to show me a path through the Cotswolds—it was better than staring at the wall—and Zed came back in wearing sneakers and a loose tank top.

I narrowed my eyes at him as he made his way over to the

rowing machine, but he didn't speak, so neither did I. Instead, I refocused on the Cotswolds and picked up my walking pace a bit.

There was no doubt in my mind what Zed was doing. He was keeping an eye on me, probably worried I was going to fall off the deep end again. He didn't know what my damage was with the shower, though. He didn't know about the drownings or what had sent me spiraling. So he was just watching me *constantly*.

And for some reason, I didn't feel the urge to fill him in. I kind of liked his presence, even if we were at odds. Having him there, his eyes on my back as I walked the virtual paths of England, kept my mind clear. It gave me something to focus on, and that prevented me from wallowing in self-pity.

Eventually, though, my body tired, and I reluctantly shut the machine off.

"Done?" Zed's voice cut through the silence of the gym, startling me.

"Uh, yeah," I confirmed, swiping at my face. I'd worked up a light sweat, which was probably great for my body to shed more toxins.

But it meant I couldn't put off my shower any longer. Despite everything else on my mind, I constantly felt the need to scrub my skin with scalding water. Add sweat? Yeah, I needed to brave the shower.

"Are you seriously going to follow me everywhere?" I blurted out as Zed shadowed me up to my room.

His face was deadpan when I spun around to glare. "Yup."

Narrowing my eyes, I seethed. "Fine. Make yourself useful, then." I stomped over to where Lucas had left the shower shields and held out a pile to Zed. "Help me cover all my dressings so I can wash."

He looked surprised but took the waterproof dressing covers without an argument. When my fingers fumbled at the straps of my sling, he gave a small sigh and took over.

I flicked the buttons of the shirt open and shrugged out of the sleeves before I could second-guess myself. Zed had seen me naked plenty of times before; this was nothing new. If anything, this was just clinical. I needed his help to cover my wounds, or I risked them getting infected again. No, thank you.

He needed no guidance as he carefully peeled the backing from the first shower shield and stretched it over the dressing on my shoulder. His fingers were firm as he smoothed the sticky edges down, and I found myself unconsciously leaning in to him.

The second I realized what I was doing, I stiffened my spine, but I wasn't dumb enough to think he hadn't noticed.

Still, he kept silent as he repeated the process on my wrist and my ribs.

"Is that all?" he murmured in a low, husky voice that sent a shiver through me.

Shit, maybe this wasn't as clinical as I thought. Too fucking late now, though. I was done backing down. From anything. It was about damn time to nut up and stand strong, even in the face of my own damage.

So I tightened my jaw and wiggled my yoga pants off to show him the only other injury that required a shower shield: two small burns on my inner thigh, courtesy of Chase's electric cattle prod.

Zed's shoulders bunched with tension, but he knelt to carefully apply one more shower shield for me.

"Thanks," I muttered when he was done. Stepping back from his touch on my thigh, I made my way into the bathroom and eyed my nemesis. "Fuck you, shower," I whispered under my breath as I psyched myself up. "You don't get to win this one."

Still, I couldn't *quite* bring myself to reach in and twist the handle. The memory of my meltdown early this morning was still fresh in my mind.

Zed's gentle touch on my waist shifted me aside, and he reached in to turn the water on for me, then glanced back with a thoughtful frown.

"Would a bath be easier?"

I shuddered. "Fuck no." The only reason I was making any progress was because the shower didn't hold large quantities of water. A bath would just be a bigger version of that bucket Chase had held my head under in. Hard pass.

Zed just nodded and kept his hand under the water to check the temperature. When it was warm, he stepped back to give me space.

Briefly, I considered telling him to fuck off, that I had it handled from here. We'd have both known that was total bullshit, though, so I just gritted my teeth and avoided eye contact as I wiggled out of my panties.

Carefully, I collected my lady-balls and stepped into the shower cubicle. I turned my back to the spray and closed my eyes as I leaned into the warm, cascading water.

A rustle of movement made me crack my eyes open again, and I caught Zed tossing his clothes aside. A small, startled sound squeaked out of me, but he didn't hesitate before stepping into the shower with me, leaving his boxer-briefs on.

"Zed—" I started to protest as he got wet.

"Shut up," he muttered back, his voice dark. "Close your eyes and pretend I'm Lucas or something."

I almost laughed at that. As if I could *ever* mistake Zed for Lucas. But when his hands rested gently on my hips and guided me further into the water, I didn't resist.

Zed didn't speak as he carefully glided the soapy sponge over my back, sweeping my hair out of the way as he worked. There was no way I could pretend he was Lucas, but the tension seeped out of my body nonetheless. With every slow, deliberate sweep of the sponge, I let a little more anxiety wash away.

When he was done with the soap, he angled my body to rinse

it all off, and his fingertip traced the swirling marks of the tattoo running down my spine.

"Do you still believe this?" he murmured softly, following the elegant, looping characters. It was a quote written in Tibetan, a tattoo I'd had done after a trip we'd taken when I was fifteen. Chase had been stuck in Cloudcroft for some family business, so only Zed and I had gone. We'd trekked to Mount Everest base camp on what was supposed to be endurance training.

A small smile curved my lips, and I sighed as his fingers traced the tattoo again. "Everything happens for a reason." It was a statement that our guide had used *far* too often but also one that resonated with me at that stage in my life. "Yeah, I do. Don't you?"

Zed gave a long exhale but didn't answer. He just threaded his fingers up into my hair and tilted my head so that he could get my hair wet.

I let my eyes close once more, letting him take care of me. Not once did the cold, clammy fear wash over me. Not once did panic seize control of my breathing and let my anxiety take over.

Hell, I was so relaxed that when his lips brushed my wet shoulder, I leaned into the caress. His hands were back at my waist, and when I didn't pull away, he held me tighter. His chest met my back, the warmth of his body blanketing me as he kissed the bend of my neck more deliberately.

For a blissful moment, I let myself sink into his embrace as his strong fingers stroked my sides. For a second, I let myself slip back into the Dare of three weeks ago, before Chase had clawed his sticky fingers back into my mind and set fire to my emotional stability.

"Zed..." I sighed his name with regret as his chest rose and fell against my back.

"I know," he whispered back, his voice husky. With a shuddering inhale, he moved away, creating space between us as he shut the shower off.

I wrapped my arms around myself as the water drained away, and Zed stepped out to grab a towel. Instantly, I wanted to call him back, to take things further like my heart was begging for.

No words passed my lips, though.

Zed held out a towel for me, and I stepped into it with bitter disappointment choking me. He just wrapped the towel around me, hugging me through the thick fabric.

"I'm not going anywhere," he whispered in my ear. "No matter how long it takes, I love you, Dare. That will never change, and I'll never stop waiting for you."

We both ignored the silent tears tracking down my cheeks after that.

CHAPTER 16

The next morning when I woke up, things were different. For one thing, there were fresh coffee and a homemade croissant beside the bed for me...making my mouth water as I scrambled to sit up and eat it. I *loved* Zed's homemade croissants, and he knew it.

Underneath the plate, I found a small stack of printer paper, and on closer inspection—with a mouthful of buttery pastry—I found printed photocopies of the *Shadow Grove Gazette*. More specifically, of the obituaries.

Shit. Zed really was pulling out all the stops.

Finally, after finishing my croissant *way* too fast, I realized what else was different. The rain had stopped.

Licking pastry flakes from my fingers, I slid out of bed and grabbed my coffee to take with me on my way downstairs. Surprisingly, I didn't find Zed parked in his usual spot opposite my door, so I continued down to his second-favorite location. The kitchen.

He wasn't there, either. But I soon found him standing out on the lawn, staring up at the gray sky with his phone to his ear. When he saw me approaching, a smile curved his lips. It was the kind of smile that didn't quite touch his eyes, and I frowned as he ended the call.

"What was that about?" I asked, suspicious.

"Cass," he replied. "There's a prediction for high winds this afternoon in this area. He doesn't think he can get back to Shadow Grove and the helicopter with enough time to pick us up."

I nodded slowly. "So we're here a while longer?"

Zed watched me carefully, his expression not giving away what he was thinking. "Is that okay?"

Wrinkling my nose, I shrugged. "Makes no difference, does it? I'm still a fugitive, so until Demi can sort out all that paperwork, I can't go home."

Zed grimaced. "Yeah, that too. But if you're desperate to leave, I can call in a friend who is closer than Cass. He might be able to get us out before the wind picks up."

"I'm okay here." Strangely, I was. "Are you?"

Zed held my gaze for a moment, unblinking. Then he gave a small nod. "Yeah, I'm happy to stay a few more days."

Well, that felt like a loaded statement—on both our parts.

"Tell Cass to just focus on his job," I said, taking a sip of my coffee. "We can hang out here until Demi gives us the okay to come home. In the meantime, I think Lucas has things handled."

Zed shot me a quick smile. "Yes, Boss." He jerked his head in the direction of the kitchen. "There're more croissants keeping warm in the oven."

"Yum," I murmured and took my coffee back indoors with me. I needed to call Lucas and let him know what we were doing, but it could definitely wait until I'd eaten some more.

Zed found me a few minutes later as I coated a hot croissant in strawberry jam, and gave me a grin. "I thought you'd like those." He watched me with dark eyes as I crunched into the flaky pastry and savored the buttery goodness. "Cass wanted to talk to you himself."

I quirked one brow. "That's nice." I'd been ignoring his messages since finding out he'd chipped me like a prize bitch.

He huffed a laugh. "Yeah, I figured that was how you felt. Told him to take his licks in person like a big boy."

"Any chance of another coffee?" I peered down into my mug, mournful at how little was left already.

Zed swiped the mug out of my hand and took it over to the coffee machine without complaint. "Do you want to shoot some shit while the rain is holding off?"

My eyes widened, and I needed to swallow my mouthful to reply. "Is that even a question?" He met my eyes, grinning, and butterflies went nuts inside me. "I need to call Lucas first, make sure everything is running smoothly there. If Chase had Gen killed, he'll be gunning for Demi too."

Zed pulled his phone from his pocket and slid it across the counter to me, saving me from going back up to my room to fetch the burner I was using.

I only hesitated for a second before dialing Lucas and putting the call on speaker beside me—partly so I could keep eating. Partly so Zed could participate.

"What do you want, dickhead? I don't have time for bullshit right now," Lucas answered, and I snorted a laugh.

"Um, it's me," I replied, grinning. "Zed gave me his phone to call."

"Fuck, sorry, Hayden," Lucas groaned. "I always have time for you."

"Shithead," Zed muttered, loud enough for Lucas to hear him if the answering chuckle was any indication.

"So he's still alive," Lucas commented. "Cass owes me fifty bucks. How are you doing, Hayden? How's your shoulder?"

Before I could answer, in the background of the call was the sound of shouting men and breaking glass. Lucas gave a frustrated sigh and cursed under his breath.

"I'm so sorry, babe, I need to… I'll call you back, okay?" Lucas didn't sound worried or stressed, just pissed off. There was a note of authority in his voice that swelled my chest with pride. "I love you. Don't forget your meds."

The call ended before I could reply, and I met Zed's eyes across the counter.

"Sounds like they're testing him," he commented, unconcerned.

I bit the edge of my lip, agreeing. On one hand, Lucas getting his hands dirty was the fastest way for him to earn respect in the Timberwolves. But on the other…I really hated being the corruption in his life. He'd been such a *normal* teenager before getting mixed up with me.

"Don't worry about him, Dare," Zed soothed, sensing my turbulent thoughts without a word from me. "He was made for this shit. And I do kind of mean that literally. His family's involvement with the Guild is…creepy. Not to mention Gumdrop's uniquely useful skill set."

I couldn't argue with that. The Guild had always given me the creeps; they were intense in a way no other criminals or gangsters I'd met were. Something about their organization being so ancient and international made them…inhuman.

"You've got a theory?" I was curious to hear his thoughts. I thought about it myself every time Lucas surprised me with a new skill. Everything I'd come up with seemed so far-fetched it might as well have been straight out of a science fiction novel, though, so I'd kept it to myself.

Zed drummed his fingers against the side of his own coffee mug. "Yeah. Brant Wilson."

I frowned. "Lucas's sperm donor?"

"And former FBI associate director, the very same. But *prior* to his time in the FBI, he *was* Guild."

Surprise rippled through me. "Are you sure?"

"Yeah. I asked Danny to see if she recognized his name. She

did." He gave me a pointed look. "Of course, she couldn't confirm that he was one of them but *did* say she was familiar with the name, and that generally means they were either a mercenary or a mark."

I hissed a breath through my teeth, weighing that info in the same way, I had no doubt, Zed had. "With his military training, then going to work for the Feds… Yeah, I see what you mean."

Zed sipped his coffee, then dropped the next bomb. "I think Brant Wilson is more involved in this mess than any of us has really considered. It's been on my mind a lot in the last few weeks. When did all this shit with Chase start up again?"

I frowned, thinking. "The night I met Lucas?"

Zed shook his head. "That's the first *we* found out, but he had to have started his little war on Shadow Grove a couple of weeks before that to have so many people already in his pocket and for those Darling-marked PCP bags to be circulating."

Groaning, I put my mug down and rubbed my forehead. "Like…around the time I killed Brant Wilson, thinking he was no one special?"

He tipped his head, giving a small shrug. "Maybe. I'm taking major leaps here, and none of them are substantiated by much more than instinct. But remember how I said that the FBI had an inside man at the Lockhart estate?" My brows hitched, following his train of thought. "What if that was Brant? Or someone working for him? What if *he* was the one who saved Chase that night?"

My lips parted as that scenario swirled through my brain. We knew *someone* had saved Chase; there was no way he'd pulled himself free before the explosion.

"When I questioned my mother about Chase being an agent, she said something about him being Brant's protégé." Zed held my gaze steadily. "It's adding two and two to equal seven…but I dunno. It's just been running around my head, and that's what I've ended up with."

"I mean…it's not implausible," I agreed. "You think me killing Brant was what triggered Chase?"

Zed ran a hand over his head, grimacing. "Maybe. Maybe Brant was somehow keeping him on a leash, and with him gone there was just no one standing in Chase's crazy-ass fucking way anymore."

I rubbed the bridge of my nose, feeling a headache building. The *last* thing I wanted to do was waste brain space to Chase Lockhart's motivations. But if I really wanted to beat him at his own game, any information could only be useful.

"What about Lucas?" I redirected. "How does he play into all of this? I don't for a second think he deliberately targeted me."

"No, neither do I," Zed agreed, making me sag with relief. "I have no clue. Other than his family being all tied up in the Guild and Brant being his bio dad? Maybe he's not connected. Or maybe Brant was sniffing around because he was looking for Lucas."

That jolted another thought out of the depths of my brain. "Didn't Sandra imply that she had other children? Like, *actual* children, not failed IVF cycles. She said something to Lucas about his uncle Jack hurting her *babies*, plural."

Before Zed could answer, his phone rang again on the bench. I expected it to be Lucas calling back, but the caller ID showed a number I didn't know.

I slid it across to Zed, and he frowned, then answered the call without leaving the kitchen. He brought the phone to his ear but didn't say anything, which told me he also didn't recognize the number.

It only took a second for the tension to fade from his face, though, and he switched the call to speaker. "Yeah, Maria, she's right here."

He placed the phone back down on the counter in front of me, then went to get another croissant out of the warm oven.

"Hades?" Maria's voice filled the room. "Sorry to call from

a burner phone. Gerry told me it was too dangerous to call, but I had to check in and make sure everything was going okay up there."

I smiled at the genuine concern in her voice. She was a lot like Nadia with all the motherly concern but balls of steel. "I'm fine, Maria. Been taking my meds and keeping the wounds dry."

She hummed a sound of approval. "Good. Have you been wearing that sling?"

"I have," I replied, only sort of lying. I wore it a lot, but I also left it off a lot. "It's feeling a lot better already, though."

She clicked her tongue. "Don't get cocky and damage it further. Gerry said he'll take a look when you're back in town and see if you can maybe get away with just physical therapy instead of surgery. It'll be easier to know once the wound heals up."

The phone beeped with another incoming call, and Demi's name flashed on the screen.

"Maria, I'm sorry, I have another call," I told her, eager to see what Demi was calling about. "Thank you for checking in, though."

"Take care, Boss," she replied.

I answered Demi's call before it could drop, letting her know it was me, not Zed.

"Good," she barked back. "You weren't answering the other phone, and I have news."

I exchanged a look with Zed. "Good news?"

Demi gave a low chuckle. "You bet your ass. All charges against you have been dropped. You're good to come home, my little fugitive."

My jaw fell open in shock. I hadn't expected that so soon.

"That's great," Zed spoke up, filling the silence. "How?"

"Well, for one thing, all the evidence including the entire file on Hayden Timber disappeared from the FBI's central database. Permanently. But better than that, a young lady by the name of

Maxine Hazelford verified that it was a man who'd attacked her, not you."

Stunned disbelief washed through me. "Maxine? But...she's dead. Isn't she?"

"Not as recently as an hour ago," Demi replied. "According to my source, her parents pulled her from life support two weeks ago, but she didn't die as expected. Then this morning, she woke up."

Holy. Shit. Maxine was *alive*? I guess miracles did happen.

CHAPTER 17

Due to the high wind and intermittent thunderstorms, it was another three full days before Zed and I could leave Foxglove Manor. The bridge at the base of the mountain had been totally washed out and the river had broken its banks, so there was no access until a helicopter could get in.

It was okay, though. I despised the idea of arriving back into Shadow Grove looking weak. So I spent a good majority of that time running on the treadmill or in the barn testing my accuracy shooting with my arm in a sling.

Ultimately, though, I would need to ditch the sling before we got back. Chase would be watching my every move from the second I stepped back into the game. Worse, my competitors would be watching—all of them like hungry wolves searching for any sign of weakness they could exploit.

Most of those three days, I avoided contact with Zed. I wasn't still holding a grudge or trying to punish him. We'd moved past that, and knowing I wouldn't have done anything differently went a long way toward healing the wounds between us.

But those moments we shared over coffee or in the shower, when I let my tightly wound cage of functioning anxiety soften?

They scared the hell out of me. I'd had enough of being scared to last me seven lifetimes, so I took the mature approach and just avoided the crap out of him when I could.

On the morning of the fourth day, when Zed announced he'd received confirmation of our transport coming within a few hours, I was relieved to see the worst of my cuts and bruises had healed. With a bit of makeup and not moving my left shoulder, no one would be the wiser.

"Help me peel this off?" I asked him absentmindedly, wincing as I tried to reach the dressing on my ribs. The sticky edges had lost their stick, and the cuts were itching like crazy. During a quick chat with Doc over the phone, he'd told me it'd be okay to remove the dressing and let it breathe.

Zed came farther into the room, taking over where I couldn't quite reach, mainly because it was on my right-side ribs and my left shoulder wasn't cooperating to get my arm into that position.

He peeled the dressing off gently, then made a disgusted sound in his throat.

"What?" I asked, frowning. "Is it infected?"

"No," he hurried to say, shaking his head as he stepped back. "No, it's healing up well. Just…have a look."

He had me worried, so I made my way over to the mirror in the bathroom to see what he was talking about. On my ribs there were a couple of long, sharp slashes that had healed to a dark scab, and one curved cut.

"I don't get it," I admitted, dropping my T-shirt into place and coming back out of the bathroom.

Zed grabbed a pen from beside the bed and flipped over one of the printed obituaries I'd been doodling on the night before. Thinking for a moment, he then sketched out a design similar to the *Darling* logo inked on his chest. And on Lucas's too.

"He had me make one for him, too, when I got yours tattooed.

He was going to ask *you* to get it done." He handed me the paper, and I scowled at it.

Now that I knew what it was, I went back to the mirror and inspected the cuts in my side. "That motherfucker was trying to cut his name into me," I murmured. I vaguely recalled he'd been interrupted, so he hadn't finished the pattern.

"Cass can cover it up with something," Zed suggested.

I sighed and let my T-shirt drop again. "Yeah. Doesn't matter, anyway. It's just skin."

"Bullshit," he growled. "It's *your* skin. It fucking matters."

He stormed out of my bedroom, leaving me staring after him in confusion.

Shaking it off, I set about packing up my meager bag of belongings, mostly medications and spare dressings, then headed downstairs. As much as I'd been avoiding Zed the last few days, I wanted his opinion on one of the pressing matters I would be dealing with back in Shadow Grove.

I found him out in the barn packing up all the guns we'd been playing with in our boredom. He looked a whole lot like he'd rather be shooting them, with how aggressively he was moving things around.

"You said the helicopter is still a few hours away, didn't you?" I called out, jerking his attention away from what he was doing.

He scowled. "Yeah. So?"

I shrugged. "So, what's the rush? You look like you could shoot some shit to deal with whatever has your panties in a twist, and I could use the opportunity to redeem myself." To demonstrate my point, I grabbed a handful of glass soda bottles from the pile we'd brought out of the house and carried them down to the far end of the barn where we'd set up our various household shooting targets.

I laid out the three bottles, then went back for three more and placed them in a line as well before returning to Zed.

He arched a brow at me. "How is this going to redeem you?

Those are the easiest targets in the world. We will both hit all three, and no one will win."

Grinning, I waved a hand at the stack of gun cases that he'd just packed up. "Choose your weapon, Zeddy Bear." I took a basic Glock that he hadn't packed yet from the table, and unstrapped my sling so I could load the gun properly.

Zed huffed an impatient sound but took a Glock for himself too—not because that was his weapon of choice but because he was all about keeping a level playing field when we bet on shit.

"What's at stake when I win again?"

I scoffed. "You won't. You sabotaged me last time."

A sly grin spread over his face. "Sore loser. You want *me* to do the strip routine this time?"

"I was going to ask for something else," I admitted with a short laugh, "but yeah, that would be even better. If you lose, you've got to do the same routine in the same costume, *including* the high heels."

Zed cringed. "Fair enough. And if *you* lose—"

"Which I won't," I muttered, giving him a smirk.

"Then I want..." He let his voice trail off, tapping his lips like he was thinking. Then the teasing humor slipped from his expression and his eyes turned serious. "I want you to stop shutting me out."

I stiffened. This was growing heavier than I'd planned.

"I'm not asking for you to forgive and forget, Dare," he continued in a low, husky voice. "I would never ask that of you. I just want a chance to prove to you how sorry I am, how much I still fucking love you. Can I have that chance if I win?"

Finding myself tongue-tied, I just nodded and picked up a spare sweatshirt he'd dropped a couple of days ago.

"Three shots," I announced after clearing my throat, then held up the sweatshirt. "Blindfolded."

Zed's brows hitched, and a grin curled his lips. "What if we both hit all three?"

I pondered a moment. "Then we do it again, but left-handed."

He shot a frown at my near-useless left arm, then gave me a nod. "You're on." He swept out an arm, indicating for me to go. "Ladies first."

I snorted a laugh. I knew full fucking well he would deliberately lose just to spare me from using my left arm. "I don't think so. You won the last bet, so you go first." I indicated for him to spin around, then carefully tied the arms of the rolled-up sweatshirt over his eyes. It was a crappy blindfold tied badly. But it only needed to cover his eyes long enough for three shots.

"Go for it," I told him when I was done. "I'll start planning out your pole dance schedule with Maxine when we get back."

Zed muttered some shit to himself under the sweatshirt blindfold, then brought the gun up in the vague direction of the bottles. For a second, he aimed *way* off target, and I really thought he was going to miss entirely.

But then he squeezed the trigger three times in quick succession, and three corresponding pops of shattering glass answered him.

"Oh hey," he commented, tugging the blindfold off. "What luck, huh?"

Grinning at his smug sarcasm, I switched places with him and waited while he tied the blindfold for me. The fabric covering half my face spiked my anxiety, but I forced myself to take some long, slow breaths to remain calm. The familiar weight of a gun in my hand went a long way to helping that.

"Are you okay?" Zed murmured, his hands lightly brushing over my shoulders.

Far from it. But I let the tension ease with my next exhale, drawing strength from those featherlight touches of Zed's fingers. I'd expected his touch to make my skin crawl and panic to rip through me like a tsunami after the dirty tricks Chase had pulled. But so far, it hadn't happened. The strongest emotion Zed's touch conjured was *safety*.

"Yeah," I replied. "I'm okay."

His warmth radiated against my back like he was only an inch away from hugging me. I didn't move away from him as I raised my gun, steadying it with my left hand and biting back a wince.

Picturing the targets in my mind, I let muscle memory take over as I squeezed the trigger three times. The recoil on my weakened arms made me rock backward, but Zed was right there to balance me. Just like he'd *always* been.

I didn't even hear whether my shots landed or not. I didn't fucking care, because bet or not, Zed deserved that chance to mend things between us. Hell, we both deserved it. Our bond was too tight, our roots too deep to walk away now.

Zed tugged the blindfold off my head as I turned around to face him.

"You don't want to see who won?" he asked in a quiet voice as I tipped my head back to meet his gaze from just inches away. His jaw was dusted in dark stubble, and his eyes were tired. His *two perfectly intact eyes*.

I gave a small headshake, lightly bringing my free hand to his waist. If I had better range of motion in that arm, I'd have looped it around his neck.

"You did, Zed," I replied, softly. "I love you too." Before I could lose the shred of courage I'd grasped onto, I rose up on my toes and pressed my lips to his.

It was a chaste sort of kiss, but when he kissed me back with a small moan, I felt it all the way in my soul.

"We should get these guns up to the house," he whispered, his voice husky and his hand still holding my waist like he didn't want to let go.

I dropped back onto my heels, biting my lip. A huge part of me had wanted to take that kiss further, but even as long as it had lasted, all the fresh trauma of Chase was screaming around my head like a tornado siren.

"Dare," he started as I packed up the Glock into its case, "I want to ask something before we leave here."

I arched a brow at him over my shoulder. "What?"

He hesitated, looking uncertain. "I know Lucas has been playing Hades this week. But when we get back...where do we stand? You and me, I mean."

It was a topic that had been on my mind since the moment Demi had told me it was safe to return to Shadow Grove, and I knew I needed to trust my gut.

"You and me?" I repeated, and he jerked a nod. "We're Hades and Zed. Dynamic Duo." I offered a sly grin. "Same as always, Zeddy Bear. We're the tightest team in crime since Bonnie and Clyde."

A slow smile spread over his face, and relief sagged his shoulders. "Without their tragic ending, please."

"Agreed." I gave a small laugh.

We worked together in silence as we transported all the guns back up to the main house and locked them away in the impressive gun safe, but it was a deeply *comfortable* silence.

Then, because we had some time to kill, we went to work cleaning the kitchen. Based on the dust in the unused rooms, I was willing to guess Cass shared Zed's distrust of staff. And it just wasn't polite to leave our mess when we had no plans to return anytime soon.

"Actually," I said while wiping down the counters. Zed was headfirst in the oven, wiping it all out with some fancy eco-cleaning products. "Now that we're back on the same team, there's an item of business we should strategize. Sooner rather than later."

"Oh yeah?" he replied, his voice echoing inside the oven.

I rinsed my cloth in the sink and squeezed it out. "Cass. Or more specifically, how we're bringing him back to life. We can't keep up the cloak-and-dagger shit much longer, and to be honest, I don't want to. We've got enough to worry about without adding that into the mix."

Zed popped out of the oven, sitting back on his heels to look up at me. "Agreed. What was your plan when you 'killed' him?"

I wrinkled my nose. "Uh, we hadn't planned that far ahead. It was just a loose backup plan at best."

Zed gave me a slow grin, shaking his head. "Fucking hell, Dare. This is why you should have run it past me first. I could have mapped it out."

I gave a one-shouldered shrug, lifting a brow. "Yeah, well, I had a sneaking suspicion you were hiding something from me, and it made me paranoid. Turns out I was right."

He winced. "Fair call."

"Anyway, I'll tell you what I'm thinking, and you can poke holes in it until we come up with something better. Yes?" I tossed my cleaning cloth aside, focusing on Zed.

He gazed up at me with a wide smile, his blue eyes glittering. "Just like always."

CHAPTER 18

Somehow, Zed had thought of everything. I'd told Cass to stay in Seattle to finish his task because I wanted him back in Shadow Grove as soon as possible. So our helicopter pickup was done by a friend of Zed's who simply *screamed* military. I was no fool, though. This was an unsanctioned favor, so I didn't ask unnecessary questions. Even when the grizzled, tattoo-covered old guy handed me a bag on his arrival.

"We can spare twenty minutes," Zed told me, checking his watch. "Hopefully, that's long enough."

Confused, I peeked inside the bag and huffed a laugh. "Twenty minutes. Done."

I hauled ass back inside the house and used the powder room off the foyer to change out of my yoga pants and tank top and into a pair of black figure-hugging jeans, a black push-up bra with decorative straps crossing my chest, and a low-cut sheer blouse. Finished off with my favorite pair of shiny black Louboutins and a heavy coat of makeup, Hades was back.

My appearance was like a layer of armor, and when I headed back out to the waiting helicopter nineteen minutes later, it was with a straighter spine, a higher chin, and a level of confidence I hadn't felt in three weeks.

Zed's gaze heated as he watched me approach the helicopter, but his pilot just gave me a short nod and climbed back into the cockpit.

"Boss," Zed murmured as I stopped in front of him. "You're back."

I shot him a smirk. "Damn right, I am."

The cool wind blew past, making me shiver in my thin top. Without asking, Zed took the bag from my hand and tossed it into the helicopter, then held out his own jacket for me to put on. It was a charcoal-gray sport coat, and I had a feeling it matched my outfit beautifully. Almost like he'd picked it out deliberately.

A moment later we were strapped into our seats and on our way back to Shadow Grove. Zed's hand brushed the outside of my thigh as we watched the endless forest flit past below us, but he didn't push it any further.

Two hours of flying had us landing at the private airstrip outside Shadow Grove just after lunchtime, and I could already see Lucas waiting for us on the tarmac with Zed's cherry-red Mustang.

"Fucking kid has just claimed that as his own, hasn't he," Zed muttered as we landed.

I grinned because he was right. But the car suited Lucas beautifully, so I was all for it. Besides, Zed was much more of a black Ferrari kind of guy.

We climbed out of the helicopter, and our pilot came around to exchange a couple of quiet words with Zed. Then the old guy turned to me with a stern nod.

"Pleasure to meet you, Hades. Give 'em all hell." His gruff advice was accompanied by a strong handshake; then he returned to his seat in the cockpit.

Zed tossed our bags over his shoulder, and I couldn't fight the smile spreading over my lips as we strode toward Lucas, who leaned on the side of the Mustang.

He met me halfway, sweeping me up in a tight hug before cursing and dropping me back to the ground abruptly.

"I'm so sorry," he groaned. "Shit, Hayden, I didn't mean to—"

"It's fine," I cut him off, reassuring him. "I'm okay." Sort of. That full-bodied hug had shocked the shit out of me after spending eight days being so damn careful about casual touches. But I hadn't slipped into panic mode, so that was a win in my book.

Zed wasn't so forgiving, though, clipping Lucas around the head with his hand. "Wake the fuck up, Gumdrop."

"Sorry," Lucas replied, wincing. Then he shifted his gaze to me. "Sorry, Hayden." But he wasn't even trying to hide the smile on his face as he opened the passenger door for me. "It's so damn good to have you back."

I shot him a smile as I slid into the seat. "It's good to be back." In more ways than one.

Zed tossed our bags into the trunk, then grudgingly climbed into the backseat so Lucas could drive. He muttered under his breath about it but shut up quick when I dropped my hand between the seats to touch his knee. He just shifted in his seat and leaned forward to loosely link his fingers through mine instead.

Lucas gave the motion a pointed stare as he drove us out of the airstrip, then shot me a soft look.

"You look incredible, babe. Like you've done a lifetime of healing in the last week." Then his eyes shifted to the rearview mirror. "You both have."

Zed's fingers squeezed mine lightly, and I changed the subject before the thick haze of affection in the car could melt my Hades shell.

"Are we heading straight to see Seph?"

Lucas nodded. "Yeah, Demi and Rex are with her at Club 22 now. Rex said some shit about not wanting to lead people right to his front door by having you go there."

I huffed a laugh, but it made no difference to me about where we met. In fact, it'd be better for me to stick to my own properties for a while—at least until I found my footing within the Timberwolves once more.

"Have you seen her yet?" I asked, glancing over at Lucas. He was dressed sharply in a black button-down and designer jeans as if he'd taken style notes from Zed's casual days. It suited him, making him look much older than he was. But I quietly thought he looked his best in a hoodie and backward cap.

Or, you know, in nothing at all.

"Seph?" he asked. "No, not yet. I left a message, but she didn't call back."

When he'd gone to visit her earlier in the week per my request, she'd refused to see him, and Rex backed her up on it. Some shit about not forcing her to do anything she didn't want to do, which was a load of horseshit from him.

"Probably still sulking about being shipped off to live with Rex," Zed commented. "Seph does sulk like it's an Olympic sport."

Lucas grinned at that, and I couldn't deny it. It was entirely my own fault for sheltering her to the point of stifling her development. But I'd never claimed to be a parent or even a good guardian. All I'd known was that I didn't want Seph to turn into *me*. So I'd done a hard one-eighty on how I was raised and turned her into a spoiled, selfish princess with no sense of self-preservation.

I should have done better by my sister. I should have given her more of my time and attention. I *should* have prepared her for the real world. The horrible, dark, dangerous world we lived in. But I hadn't, and all I could do now was ensure she stayed alive long enough for me to *give* her that time.

"That reminds me," Zed spoke up. "I've had a few calls from Steele."

I shifted in my seat to give him a narrow-eyed look over my shoulder. "What the fuck does he want?"

Zed shrugged. "Testing the waters was my guess. Offering assistance if we need it."

"Fuck that," I muttered, still salty over their failure to keep Seph safe. Of course, it was just as much my own fault, but it was easier to lay the blame at someone else's feet.

Zed chuckled softly. "I'll tell him we're still thinking about it."

I rolled my eyes but wasn't shocked. Zed and Steele had history, with Zed having put Steele through a season of sniper training *years* ago. I knew he had a small soft spot for the former Reaper.

"Has Chase been seen around town?" I asked after a long silence in the car.

Lucas shook his head. "Not a single sighting."

I raised my hand to my mouth, biting the edge of my thumbnail in an old habit. "That almost seems more worrying."

"Agreed," Lucas murmured. "We'll be ready for him, though."

A few minutes later, we pulled into the parking lot of Club 22, and I mentally prepared myself to deal with my little sister. The last time I'd seen her, she was shooting snarky insults at me about my decision to send her to Rex. Now, three weeks later, I couldn't imagine the climate had changed for the better.

My gaze darted around the parking lot as we exited the car, and I spotted increased security in the form of an upgraded camera and a rifle-armed Timberwolf on the roof of the building opposite. When he saw me glance up, he dipped his head in respect.

"Big Sal?" I asked Lucas, thinking I recognized what little I could see of the man.

He shook his head. "Little Sal. Big Sal is apparently all kinds of comfortable on guard duty for my mom." Something in the way he said that, the irritated set of his jaw, told me he wasn't thrilled with that situation.

I made a mental note to pay a visit to Sandra soon. Hopefully, she could answer at least *some* questions about Brant Wilson, and I already knew Lucas hadn't brought it up with her.

"Good work, Gumdrop," Zed commented as he held open the club door for us. "You're a natural." The look he gave me was pointed, and I remembered our conversation about Lucas's Guild ties.

Lucas shot Zed a suspicious glare, then fell into step beside me as I moved inside the club. "I don't ever know when he's being sarcastic," he admitted. "Should I hit him anyway?"

I swallowed a laugh. "If in doubt, always err on the side of violence."

Lucas grinned, then hung back a step to punch Zed on the arm. They were like children some days.

The music was up loud inside Club 22, and I spotted a handful of dancers on the stage in casual clothes as Sabine ran them through choreography. I didn't pay them much attention as we passed by, making our way up to the VIP lounge where Demi usually met me.

We barely made it two steps into the lounge, though, before Seph came shrieking toward me like a banshee.

My whole body locked up on instinct, panic washing over me with such strength I could taste it like acid on my tongue. But Seph didn't pause for even a second, throwing herself at me and wrapping her arms around me in some kind of red-haired teen version of a hungry squid.

It took me a second to realize she was, indeed, *hugging* me and not attacking.

"Seph! Get back!" Zed was shouting, and Lucas was on my other side, his eyes wide as he tried to peel Seph's arm off my neck. He was getting nowhere, though, and Seph was sobbing so loudly into my chest that she probably couldn't even hear Zed snapping at her.

I was okay, though. Once that initial wave of instinctual terror had faded, I realized that I *was* okay with her hugging me. So I gave Lucas a reassuring nod and told him and Zed to back off.

Cautiously, like I was handling a live wire, I hugged my sister back, tucking my face down into her hair.

"Hey, brat," I whispered when she continued clinging and crying. "I thought you would've been happy to get a break from me."

Seph gasped, pulling away from me with a stricken look on her face. "How could you even *think* that? Dare, I thought you were *dead*! Those bastards let me think you were dead for nearly *three weeks*, and the last thing I had said to you was some bitchy crap about how you didn't care about me."

My brows shot up, and I turned an accusing glare to Lucas.

He just shrugged and looked totally unapologetic. "Oops."

CHAPTER 19

No fucking wonder Seph had refused to see Lucas when he stopped by to visit her a couple of days ago. She was *pissed* at him—and had every right to be if they'd neglected to tell her that I was okay.

"Let's all sit down and get a drink, shall we?" Demi smoothly intervened, giving me a warm smile. "We have a lot to catch up on, and I find these discussions go so much more amiably with a martini in hand."

Inclined to agree, I coaxed Seph back to the couch area she and Demi had occupied before we arrived. My sister shot absolute death glares at both Lucas and Zed and sat so close to me that she was practically in my lap.

"I'll put in our orders," Zed suggested, heading over to the vacant bar at the side of the VIP lounge. He used the waitresses' tablet screen to submit an order for all of us, then came back over to sit down. "Where's Rex?"

Demi rolled her eyes dramatically, and Seph cracked a smile for the first time since she'd pounced on me.

"On the stage." My sister chuckled, sniffing away the residue of her tears.

Frowning my confusion, I rose back to my feet and peered

over the railing at where Sabine was clapping a beat for the dancers to block out a new routine. Sure enough, there in the back row, sandwiched between two gorgeous, big-breasted women…was someone who most definitely didn't belong.

"Rex Darenburg," I barked, letting my voice carry over the loud music. His head snapped up toward me, and a huge smile split his face. "Get your sweaty old ass up here right this minute. Leave my dancers alone."

Sabine sent me a bright grin and a wave, then tossed Rex a towel as he climbed down off the stage.

A moment later, he lumbered up the stairs to the VIP lounge as he patted sweat from his brow and grinned wide.

"Hades, baby! My favorite niece!" He spread his arms, showing off dark circles under his armpits, and his breath wheezed.

I leveled him with my ice-cold Hades glare. "Touch me and I'll castrate you, Rex. What the fuck were you doing down there?"

"Hey, what the shit, Uncle Rex?" Seph complained. "She's your favorite? What the hell am I?"

His heavily lined face screwed up, and he gave a shrug. "My *other* favorite niece, of course. I can have two, can't I?" He shifted his attention to Zed and stuck his hand out to shake. "De Rosa. You've grown."

Zed ignored the offered hand and gave me a long look that clearly said *I hope you know what you're doing here.*

Simmering with anger, I hardened my glare. "Rex…"

"I know, I know." He flapped his hand and dropped his solid bulk onto the couch beside Demi. "I was just having a little fun while we waited." He wheezed again, leaning forward with his gut resting on his legs. This time his gaze was a whole lot sharper as he took me in. Calculating.

"Stop it," Demi snapped, smacking his arm with the back of her hand. "Just sit there and keep your trap shut."

Rex shot an amused look at his ex-wife and turned back to

me with a small grin. "It is good to see you, little H." There was an implied statement under his words that said he'd expected me to look a hell of a lot worse than I did. I needed to thank Demi for putting that bag of clothes and makeup together for me because no one else would have done it, even with Zed's guidance.

All of a sudden, Zed had a knife in his hand and was polishing it on his pants.

"Call her that again, Rex," Zed murmured in a dangerously quiet tone. "I dare you."

Rex, thankfully, had sense enough to back down at that threat. He and I were far from loving family members. Hell, we were only related through his former marriage to Demi, and *she* was the only reason he'd survived the Timberwolf massacre. That and the fact that he'd been in prison that night. When he'd been released a year later, he'd had time to plead his case to me by way of Demi.

Ultimately, if Demi hadn't vouched for him, he'd have caught a bullet between the eyes a second after he stepped out of the Cloudcroft penitentiary.

"Apologies, Hades," he grumbled, shooting me a tight smile. "Being around little Persephone these last few weeks got me all nostalgic, and I forgot my place. Won't happen again."

I internally rolled my eyes. Nostalgic? For the days before his incarceration when he'd been the Timberwolf enforcer? Not really happy fuzzy family memories.

Still, he'd done me a service lately, and I needed that to continue.

"I appreciate your help keeping Seph and Demi safe while I was gone," I told him in a cool voice. "I hope there haven't been any incidents?"

Rex shot Demi a pointed look, but my aunt just gave him a hard glare back.

"Nothing we couldn't handle," she told me with a serene expression. "And Seph has been safe around the clock."

My sister's hand found mine, holding on to me like she was a little girl again. "You missed our graduation, Dare," she said in a small voice, "but Uncle Rex took heaps of pictures for you."

Guilt rippled through me, and I sent Lucas a glance. He just shook his head, silently telling me it didn't matter. Fuck, it made me feel awful, though. I'd totally lost track of time.

"I'm so sorry, Seph," I said softly, dipping my head toward her.

She gave me a genuine smile. "I don't care, it was totally lame anyway. And Lucas didn't even show up. But I wanted you to know that I *did* graduate."

"You sure did, squirt," Rex said with a proud nod. "And she's been pulling her weight in the shop too."

That surprised me more than anything. Not that Rex had put her to work in his garage; that part didn't shock me. But that she'd actually done it.

"Well, I'm impressed," I murmured. "Rex, I'd like Seph to stay with you a while longer, if it's not too much trouble. The guys and I have a bit of trash to take out around town, and I have a feeling things might get worse before they get better."

Seph stiffened against my side. I thought she was about to protest staying with Rex any longer, but the frown she gave me was all concern. "You're talking about Chase, right? He's who took you out of that FBI car?"

I stared back at her, slightly at a loss for what to say. I was still adjusting to the fact that she now *knew* what kind of scum Chase was.

"That's right," Zed answered for me. "Until Chase *and* his associates have been handled, we don't feel like you're safe."

Seph's eyes rounded, but she nodded. "Okay. Yeah, I understand. Whatever it takes."

Rodney arrived then with our tray of drinks and placed them down on the low table while everyone waited patiently.

When he was gone, Rex gave me a long look before turning to Seph. "Kiddo, can you give us a minute? I need to chat business with your big sister."

Demi gave a small sigh and grabbed her martini before standing up. "I'll go with you, Seph. This isn't a conversation for me, either."

Surprisingly, Seph went without complaint, and I stared after her in shock. Who the hell was that sweet, understanding girl, and what had she done with my snarling, sarcastic sister?

Rex cleared his throat, pulling my attention back, and I stifled a sigh as I sipped my Manhattan. Yum.

"Name your price, Rex," I murmured, knowing exactly why he wanted to talk away from Seph. He was more than happy to continue protecting her, but not for free.

He gave me a sly smile. "Have I ever told you that you run the Wolves a hundred times better than your papa ever did?"

I rolled my eyes. "Wouldn't be hard. That man never looked at the bigger picture. Too busy indulging his own sick fetishes with the Lockharts. So spare me the pandering, and name your price. You want a second chop shop in Timberwolf territory?"

Running a hand over his bristly chin, Rex gave a husky laugh. "Nah, nothing so expensive. Persephone has really grown on me, you know? She's like the daughter I never had. I'd probably protect her for free."

"But you won't. Not when there's something you want and something I can give. So what is it, Rex?"

His beady eyes glittered with determination. "I want back in."

My brows shot up before I could mask my surprise. "No."

He shook his head slowly. "Come on, Hades. You know I can be useful to the Wolves, and from where I'm sitting it sure looks like you need some fresh blood with total loyalty."

I snorted a laugh, almost choking on my drink. "Total loyalty? You? Is this a joke?"

Rex's smile slipped from his face, and his brow furrowed. "I know we've got our history, but I *am* loyal. Not once broken our deal in four years. You damn well know I protect the women in my life."

That I couldn't argue with. The whole reason he'd gone to prison in the first place had nothing to do with the Timberwolves or his role as enforcer. In fact, it was because of Demi and Stacey, and that was why she'd lobbied so hard for his safety on his release.

Rex and Demi had been a political marriage. Demi was born a Timber, and Rex had been my father's right-hand man. Meanwhile, Demi had been secretly dating pretty, innocent schoolteacher Stacey, and Rex had a whole-ass family with a woman three states away. When Stacey had been attacked by the father of one of her students, Demi had turned to Rex for help.

Rex had helped.

In a twist of fate, though, that man had been a cop, and Rex had gone to prison. Although in hindsight, that had saved his life when I'd gone on my killing spree.

"Why?" I demanded, despite Zed shaking his head at me. "Why do you want back in? You've got a good thing going with the garage."

Rex scoffed. "You know why. I'm not a young man anymore, Hades, and I've got my boys to think of. Only an idiot doesn't seek shelter in a storm, and girl, *you're* the storm. What safer place than in the eye of it?"

I weighed the sincerity of his request, but he was right about one thing. I *needed* more Timberwolves who were beyond reproach, people who would never in a million years flip for Chase Lockhart. Rex, despite his sins, was one of those people.

"Fine," I agreed, ignoring Zed as he ran a frustrated hand over his face. "But only you. Your boys need to earn their places and prove their loyalty, same as any new recruit. Understood?"

Rex nodded quickly, his jowls wobbling. "Understood, Boss. Appreciate it. I'll head on downstairs and let you catch up with Persephone." He hauled himself up off the couch and gave us a broad grin. "Good thing I never got rid of this bastard, eh?" He lifted his sweaty shirt up, showing us his hairy belly and the huge Timberwolf tattoo covering most of his chest.

I bit back a smile. Fucking Rex was too damn jolly for a retired serial killer. "Fuck off with your belly, Rex. You need to take a few more dance classes to trim that up. I expect you to *work* in my Timberwolves."

Barking a laugh, he gave me a salute. "Yes, sir."

When he was gone, Zed gave me a long look. "I hope you know what you're doing there."

I huffed a sigh. "I don't. But I think he will be an asset."

Lucas ruffled his fingers through his hair, his eyes on me. "I don't know the whole story with Rex, but from what I've seen, Demi trusts him. And she doesn't seem to trust real easily."

Zed blew out a long breath. "That's true enough."

Glancing down to the main bar, I spotted Seph and Demi sitting together, giggling about something. It gave me a weird, unfamiliar kind of warmth to watch them together. Circumstances could definitely have been better, but I was glad Seph was spending so much time with Demi.

A wave of exhaustion washed over me, and I covered my mouth as I yawned.

"We should get home," Lucas said, watching me with worried eyes. "Doc said he'll stop by tomorrow to check on you."

I nodded. After a week of day naps, all the activity today had me wrecked. So I finished my drink, then led the way downstairs with Zed and Lucas flanking me like my own personal guardian angels. Or devils.

Seph looked over at me with a wide smile as I approached, and I found I was actually disappointed not to spend more time with her. But it really wouldn't be a good look if I fell asleep somewhere, and my shoulder was *screaming* at me for being out of the sling so long.

"Hey, brat." I grinned back at her. "I need to take off. But I

166

think Lucas grabbed me a new phone, so I'll text you the number later, okay?"

She nodded her understanding. "No worries. We can hang out another day. Maybe just us?" Her eyes widened with hope, and I found myself quickly agreeing.

Another hug stunned me, then Demi gave me a reassuring smile as I left the club. When we stepped out into the parking lot, I was surprised to see the sun setting and quietly patted myself on the back for lasting almost the whole day without napping.

Just before we reached Lucas's car, I spotted a black Dodge Challenger idling farther down the parking lot.

"Just give me a minute," I murmured to Lucas and Zed, continuing past our Mustang toward the Challenger.

The driver rolled his window down as I approached, and I recognized Rex's second-oldest son behind the wheel.

"Little cousin," I purred with cold violence behind my smile. "I'm sure I don't need to spell this out for you, but it'll make me feel so much better if I do."

Rex's son swallowed hard, peering up at me with wide eyes. He was roughly the same age as Lucas, but goddamn, they were just worlds apart. This boy was just that. A *boy*.

"If you or your brothers lay a single finger on my little sister... if you even *look* at her the wrong way...I will personally take a knife to your balls and turn them into a Christmas ornament. Then I'll cut your chest open, reach into the cavity, and rip your heart right out to play tennis with." I flashed another toothy grin. "Clear?"

The boy nodded quickly, looking about six shades paler than he had when I approached.

"Good," I murmured, patting the top of his car. "Nice chatting with you."

As I walked away, a voice crackled from the car speakers.

"Holy shit, was that her? Did Hades just threaten you, bro?" Then

peals of nervous laughter. *"Do you need me to bring you some clean pants or something?"*

"Shut the fuck up," the kid muttered back, rolling his window up and cutting off any further sound. But I'd heard enough.

I returned to Lucas and Zed with a satisfied smile on my face.

CHAPTER 20

Returning to Zed's house sparked a whole mess of conflicting emotions within me—particularly when we passed the entry gate for Chase's house. In the end, though, when I got back up to "my" bedroom, I was relieved to be back. I was *home*.

Zed came up behind me as I stood in the doorway to my room and rested his hands lightly on my hips.

"If you don't feel comfortable here, we can go somewhere else," he told me softly, his lips brushing a kiss across my bare shoulder. I'd taken his jacket off in the car, and my skin pebbled in response to his kiss.

"No," I sighed. "No, this is perfect. It feels familiar. Safe."

I felt Zed's nod, and he kissed my shoulder again. "I'm going to take a quick shower, then get dinner started. Any requests?"

"Pizza," I groaned. "Make me pizza, please?" For all the delicious, nutritious meals he'd made for me at Foxglove, I just badly wanted some greasy cheese.

Zed laughed, his breath warming my skin. "For you? Anything. Give me an hour."

Stepping fully into my bedroom, I yawned again and headed for my closet to find something comfier to change into. I'd barely just kicked my heels off when Lucas arrived with my sling in his hand and a stubborn look on his face.

"I know," I groaned. "Just help me change, and I'll put it on."

Lucas did as I asked, helping me wriggle free of my sheer top and strappy bra. As his hands skated down my bare back, I couldn't stifle a small moan, and he froze.

"Is this okay?" he asked, his hands hovering at the waistband of my jeans. My back was to him, my bad arm pressed to my chest, so he couldn't see how hard my nipples had just gotten at that innocent touch.

"Yeah," I replied. "Sorry, I'm just…tired." *Wow. Lamest explanation ever.*

Lucas must have bought it, though, because he continued undressing me a second later, his long fingers undoing my jeans and helping me wiggle them down my legs.

His hand smoothed down my thigh, almost like a gesture of habit, and for a moment I thought he would push things further. I stiffened with the thought, unsure what my reaction would be if he did. Had Chase robbed me of intimacy without fear? Would I ever know if I didn't try?

But Lucas didn't take things any further. He just reached for the T-shirt I'd grabbed out of my closet and pulled it over my head for me.

"Thanks," I mumbled, threading my arms through the sleeves. I sat on the edge of the bed to put my comfy sweatpants on, then let Lucas strap my sling into place. I sighed at the relief it offered my shoulder, and he gave me a hard look.

"You need to wear this, Hayden," he scolded.

I smiled up at him where he stood between my knees, checking the Velcro of the neck strap. "I *needed* not to show any weakness on my first day back in Shadow Grove."

He heaved a sigh, but I knew he got it.

"Hey." I reached up with my good arm, placing my hand on

his cheek. "I'm getting better, I promise. Every day I feel more like myself."

He turned his face, pressing a soft kiss to my palm. "No one expects you to be the same, babe. However long you need, we'll be here. All three of us."

I pushed to my feet, looping my arm around his neck as my heart thumped hard in my chest. "I know. And I fucking love you for it. But I *need* to regain myself, for my own sanity. I won't let that bastard fuck me up long-term. I refuse."

Understanding shone through his eyes, and he studied my face. "How can I help?"

Pulse racing, I grasped onto my paper-thin courage. "Push me," I urged him. "Challenge my fears, and help me erase them."

A small, worried frown tugged at Lucas's brow, but I knew he wouldn't refuse me. Slowly, so slowly that I had plenty of time to change my mind, he cupped a hand around the back of my neck and dipped his face toward mine.

He hesitated a split second before our lips touched, but I didn't pull away. I *wanted* him to kiss me. So when he closed the gap, I leaned into him, pushing myself to kiss him back.

Ever so softly, he deepened the kiss, his lips coaxing mine to part so his tongue could slip in. A deep shudder ran through me, but I held him tighter when he would have pulled away.

Eventually, though, he gave a low groan and shifted his lips to kiss my cheek. "I have to stop," he confessed in a whisper. "I don't want to push too far or too fast."

I almost told him that was exactly what I wanted. But his hard dick brushed against my body, and my brain short-circuited briefly. And not in a good way.

Lucas saw it instantly and peeled himself away, scrubbing his hand over his face. "Let's... Do you want to head downstairs for dinner? Zed said he'd make us pizzas."

The crying, broken, and abused *Darling* inside my mind was

begging to be left alone, pleading for solitude so she could wallow in self-pity and despair. So I pressed the mute button on her and nodded to Lucas.

"Absolutely. Pizza sounds amazing."

His hand found mine as we left my bedroom, his fingers linking us together as we started down the stairs. And somehow, with every step, I felt like I shed a fraction more darkness. Lucas was a part of me, tightly woven into my heart. I wouldn't be whole until I could be totally at ease with all three of my soulmates. That, I knew for sure.

Zed was in the kitchen, his hair still wet from the shower as he rolled out pizza dough on the stone countertop. The smile he gave me when we entered the room was the kind of smile that could light up the darkest of moods, and I returned it.

"Grab us drinks, Gumdrop," Zed suggested. "I'll have these ready in no time." The wink he shot me was way too damn sexy, and I bit my lip to stop myself from jumping him. That damaged version of me was on mute, not deleted. She wasn't ready.

So I helped Lucas pour us all drinks and headed out to the courtyard with him. It was warm enough not to need the firepit for heat, but we lit it anyway. The ambience a live fire brought was unbeatable.

A few minutes later, while the pizzas were cooking, Zed came out to join us and pulled a rolled joint from his pocket. He showed it to me, tipping his head in question, not asking if I wanted some, but asking if it was okay in general.

I nodded. I had no issues with weed, and to be fair, it would probably offer a hell of a lot of relief for my shoulder. So when Zed lit it, then held it out, I took it without hesitation.

He watched me with heated eyes as I closed my lips around the joint and inhaled deeply.

"Shit," he muttered, swiping a hand over his face. "I need to… uh…check the pizzas."

Lucas snickered and shifted to sit closer beside me while Zed rearranged his dick on the way back inside the house. Passing the joint, I gave Lucas a knowing grin and reached for my drink.

"I know I've already said this," Lucas commented, sinking back into the outdoor couch and draping his arm along the back of it behind me, "but it's so damn good to have you home."

I smiled over at him and leaned my head back on his arm. "Home. You know I've never really felt like I had an actual home before? Even the apartment I shared with Seph…it was just an apartment, never really my home."

Exhaling smoke up into the sky, he handed the joint back. I held it a moment, sipping my drink instead. Zed and I had enough years of mixing weed with alcohol that we were never at risk of a cross fade, but Lucas? I nudged his drink away with my toe, just in case.

"That makes me really sad for you, Hayden," he said after a while. "But also kind of happy…that you feel like you have a home now. Here. With us."

I smiled and leaned in to him more, tucking into his body as we sat and smoked in silence until Zed came back out with two trays of pizza balanced on his hands.

"That smells incredible," I moaned, my mouth already watering as I sat forward. Zed grinned, then fished his phone out of his pocket.

"Cass has been blowing up my phone," he told me, holding the phone out for me to take. "Feel like calling him back?"

I wrinkled my nose but took the phone from him. Sure enough, fifteen missed calls from Grumpy Fuck.

"Give me a slice of that, and I'll consider it," I replied, dropping the phone into my lap and holding my hand out for food.

"Call him back, and I'll give you food," he countered, mischief all over his face. I was high enough to play his game, though, so I grumbled but picked the phone back up to hit Redial.

"Zed, you dick," Cass snarled when the call connected, "why weren't you answering? I was fucking worried!"

"Because I'm mad at you," I drawled in response, even though I was having a hard time remembering why I was so mad at him in the first place. But hey, at least my shoulder wasn't hurting as much anymore.

"Red," Cass rumbled with a sound of relief. "You're high, aren't you?"

"Mmm." I narrowed my eyes at Zed. "Pizza."

Cass chuckled in my ear. "You're high on pizza? That's a new one."

I tried to correct myself, but Zed had just dangled a slice in front of my face and now my cheeks were full of cheesy goodness.

"All right, well, I'm on my way back to Shadow Grove," Cass continued when all he got out of me was muffled noises. "We can discuss you being mad when I'm back."

"Okay," I agreed, after swallowing my mouthful. "Come home to me, Grumpy Cat. I miss you." I really did. Cass was the missing link in our little quartet, and I felt his absence like a physical thing.

"I miss you too, Angel," he replied, his tone low and rough. "I'll be home soon."

There was an odd note in his voice as he said that, but maybe I was imagining things. Shrugging, I handed Zed his phone back and helped myself to another piece of pizza. The weed had hit me harder than usual, but I knew it wouldn't take long to fade. It never did.

Zed exchanged a few words with Cass before ending the call, then got comfy on my other side. His leg pressed against mine, and my body was against Lucas. Zed met my eyes as he lit a fresh joint.

"We okay?" he asked, nudging my knee with his.

I hummed a happy sound. He was asking if I was okay with the physical contact, but I was perfectly content.

For a while, we just hung out. We talked total shit about

nothing important and finished all the pizza. Then Lucas started snoring softly as his head lolled back against the couch, and I had to clap a hand over my mouth to hold in the laugh.

"Didn't he do this last time, too?" Zed whispered, pulling me out from where I'd been tucked into Lucas's side. He shifted me to lean my back against his chest as he reclined into the corner of the lounge.

"Mmm, yep," I replied, grinning at Lucas's sleeping form. "It's kind of impressive that he can fall asleep anywhere."

Zed's fingertips brushed down my bare arm, and he pressed a kiss to my hair, seemingly oblivious to how his light touches were making my breath speed up.

"I love when you wear this T-shirt," he told me, his fingers toying with the hem of it. Whether deliberate or not, his knuckles brushed across my belly, and I squirmed.

To distract myself, I glanced down to see what T-shirt I was wearing. Then grinned. Without even noticing, I'd selected his vintage, signed Blink-182 T-shirt that I'd stolen years ago and pretended I didn't have. It was well worn now, so thin in parts I was surprised it hadn't torn. I loved the hell out of it.

Zed's knuckles brushed my stomach again, and this time it was more deliberate. My breath caught, and I curved my neck as he pressed a kiss behind my ear.

"Zed…" I sighed his name, sinking back into his embrace further. Then all of a sudden, a dark thought reared its ugly head, making my whole body lock up.

"Dare, baby, what just went through your head?" he asked in a soft voice. His hands moved back to my waist—above my T-shirt—and he leaned away to give me some space.

I swallowed the sour taste in my mouth, then blurted it out before I could second-guess myself. "He made me come." Those words were like poison, and my chest constricted with dread. "He would trick me while I was out of my mind. He pretended to be you…" Bile rolled in my stomach, my whole body tensed as I prepared for Zed's rejection. His disgust.

It never happened, though. His arms just tightened around me in an instinctively protective gesture.

"I'll fucking murder him," he swore, his voice threaded with pure violence. "I'll gut him slowly with a blunt knife and make him choke on his own entrails. I'll—"

"No," I cut him off, "you won't. He's mine to punish." There wasn't a single note of weakness or uncertainty in that statement, just cold determination.

Zed, of all people, knew how serious I was about that too. Chase *would* get what was coming to him, and it'd be at *my* hand. When he eventually met his maker, there would be no question who had sent him there. Painfully.

CHAPTER 21

To my surprise—and Zed's, probably—I found myself crawling into his bed half an hour after I'd tried to go to sleep. I vaguely remembered mumbling about nightmares, then crashing out in his loose embrace.

Of course, then when I woke up some hours later, I had a moment of intense confusion and panic as I tried to remember where the hell I was.

"Fuck," I cursed on an exhale as Zed rubbed my back, soothing me. It'd only been a second, but he was right there with calming words and reassurances. "Fuck, I'm sorry. I forgot where I was."

I was trembling lightly and went willingly as Zed closed me back into his warm embrace. Somehow, sleeping with him had conditioned my skin to be used to his touch even more than before we fell asleep. I could almost pretend we were back to normal.

We stayed snuggled together as my trembles subsided, then Zed slipped back into sleep, his breathing slow and steady on my neck. I wanted to join him, but now that I was awake, I couldn't ignore the grumble in my stomach.

As carefully as I could, so as not to wake him, I slithered out of his bed and padded from the room. I needed a snack, or I wasn't getting back to sleep.

The lights were on in the kitchen, which seemed odd for the middle of the night. It wasn't until I walked in and spotted the big, tattooed gangster sitting at the kitchen table that I even remembered speaking to Cass about him coming home.

His head snapped up from the papers he was reading when I paused in the doorway, and his lips parted in surprise. When I said nothing, he pushed up out of his chair and took two steps toward me before I launched myself at him.

Fuck the noise, I missed my Grumpy Cat.

His strong arms caught me, wrapping around my back as I slammed into his body. I gave a hiss as I wrapped my arms around his neck—I'd taken my sling off—but pushed through the pain to hug him tight.

"Red," he growled into my hair. "I thought I was fucking dreaming."

"I was hungry," I mumbled back, relaxing my hold on him, and he slowly lowered me down to the floor. "So, I'm going to eat. Then *you* are going to explain just when the fuck you planted a GPS tracker on me and why in the hell you thought that would be a good idea."

Cass had the good sense to look guilty as hell, his gaze dipping away from my face as he rubbed a hand over his head. "I'll fix you something. Cheese and crackers work?"

And by that, apparently, he meant a whole-ass cheese board with four different cheese varieties, a plum paste, and a variety of cracker options. It only took him five minutes to prepare, too.

"Cassiel Saint," I murmured when he served it up in front of me with a sharp little knife to cut the hard cheeses, "have you been holding out on us? I thought Zed was the only chef in the house."

He just answered me with a sly grin. "So, you and Zed sorted things out?"

I hummed a sound of confirmation, taking a bite of my first cracker loaded with plum paste and a slice of vintage cheddar. "Did he explain it all to you?" I asked when I'd swallowed.

Cass shook his head. "I wasn't interested in hearing it. You were the only one he needed to explain himself to, and I trusted you to make the right call."

Well, that squeezed me right in the heart. Goddamn, Cass made it very hard to stay mad about the GPS tracker.

He watched me with dark eyes as I ate my cheese and crackers, then leaned forward on the counter with his elbows resting on the edge. "I'm not going to apologize for the tracker," he rumbled, like he *wanted* to start a fight.

I narrowed my eyes and licked some brie from my finger before replying. With my middle finger. Aimed directly at him.

"When did you do it?" I asked instead of taking the argument bait.

His brow quirked briefly, and he dragged his thumb over his lower lip, thinking about his answer—probably wondering how much worse his answer might make the situation.

"In my apartment," he admitted after a moment's silence, "after I made you come six times back to back and you passed out cold. You already had bruises and scrapes all over that gorgeous skin, so one extra mark went totally unnoticed."

A deep shudder ran though me at the dark possessiveness in his tone. In his eyes. He wasn't sorry at *all*. And I was weirdly more turned on than furious about it.

"Why?" I demanded, hardening myself against my natural reaction to everything Cassiel Saint. Fuck, this man could get under my skin something wicked.

He heaved a long exhale, tipping his head to the side as he stared back at me. "Because when you were lying there in my bed, naked and so fucking serene…I knew that you were my whole reason for existing. My *whole* damn reason. Then I started thinking

179

about all your enemies, all the threats to your empire, and the bastards who would constantly be challenging the *woman* in criminal power. I sat there for hours, letting the worst scenarios play out in my mind, and I just..." He let his voice trail off with a frustrated headshake. "I had to do something to keep you safe. Even if you didn't know about it."

I swallowed hard. "That's how you found me at the lookout that night?"

He nodded. "I don't check it constantly. You're not my fucking pet. It's *only* for emergencies. Like if you were abducted by your psychotic, obsessed, serial killer ex."

Well, when he put it in context like that, it made it really hard to stay mad about the whole situation.

I drew a deep breath, thinking it over, and Cass came around to where I sat. His fingers stroked a patch of skin at the back of my neck, showing me where the chip was planted. No wonder I hadn't noticed it after how rough our bedroom antics had been that night.

"Do you want it removed?" he asked in a low rumble.

Did I? That chip, no matter how sneaky inserting it had been, had saved my ass. Big time. As much as I liked to think I'd escaped Chase all on my own, I was also sane enough to know that if Zed hadn't showed up when he had...if Cass hadn't picked me up in that helicopter...I'd have never made it out.

"I need to think on it, Cass," I murmured. "You never should have done it without my knowledge, and you damn well know it."

His lips curled in a half smile. "You'd never have agreed, and *you* damn well know it. I won't apologize for doing it, because it means I still have you here to yell at me. But I *am* sorry for hiding it from you. Now, more than ever, I know how important truth and trust are for us." He flicked his eyes toward the ceiling and the second level, where Zed and Lucas slept. "For *all* of us."

I pulled the edge of my lip between my teeth, considering his question. Did I want the tracker removed? No. Not really. It kind of made me feel safe knowing Cass could find me anywhere. Or almost anywhere. Bad luck that Chase had created a Faraday cage within his house to block the signal.

"If you're not too angry, I had an idea that you might be into." Cass gave me a darkly mischievous look and excitement sparked within me.

"Oh yeah?" I replied, pushing the almost empty cheese board aside. "I'm listening."

His lips tugged in a grin. "Go change into something black and easy to move in."

With a hint like that, who was I to argue? Without question, I hurried back up to my room and changed out of my sleeping clothes. When I was dressed in activewear leggings and a long-sleeved black top, I tugged on a pair of Converse sneakers that looked more like they belonged to Seph than to me.

"Ready," I announced when I returned to the kitchen. Cass was already head to toe in black, standard Saint attire, so he'd just been waiting for me.

He motioned for me to spin around, then tugged his fingers through my hair, weaving it into a messy braid and securing it with my hair tie.

"Perfect," he murmured before pressing a soft kiss to my temple. "Let's go before one of these other assholes wakes up and wants to tag along."

He tucked my hand in his, and we quietly made our way to the garage. Cass pushed his bike out into the driveway, then indicated for me to get on before he fired it up. He didn't grab helmets for either of us, so instinct told me we weren't going far.

Sure enough, he stopped the bike at the bottom of the driveway, inside the main gate to Zed's property, and helped me off.

He grabbed a bag from behind a bush where he must have left it earlier, then shot me a smirk as he held the gate open for me to slip out.

"I'm all kinds of curious right now, Saint," I admitted as he slung the bag over his shoulder and led the way across the street. When he stopped beside Chase's fence and tossed the bag over, I stiffened with uncertainty.

He reached out a hand to me, the invitation clear. "Do you trust me, Red?"

Anxiety rippled through me, but despite myself, I placed my hand in his. "Yes. You don't fucking deserve it, but yes. Implicitly."

A full smile lit his face and he reeled me in with strong fingers around my hand. "Well then, let's do this quick. I promise, Red, this will be therapeutic."

I let him boost me over the fence, then he dropped down beside me with a quiet grunt.

"There's no one here," he assured me. "I thoroughly cased it before coming home. Wanted to make sure that one-eyed fuck wasn't lurking over here with his binoculars or something. Doesn't look like anyone has been here in weeks."

That made me feel a tiny bit less anxious, but still I gripped his fingers tight as we made our way up to the house.

Sure enough, the whole place was dark and silent. I expected Cass to pick a lock or something, but he reached into the garden and pried out a brick.

"Go on," he coaxed, holding the brick out for me to take. "It'll make you feel great."

With a short laugh of disbelief, I took the brick and hefted it in my hand. "If there's an alarm, we're going to have to run like hell," I reminded him.

"There's not. Just throw the brick, Red."

That was all the encouragement I needed. I hoisted the brick to my shoulder and let it sail through the window of the back door. Glass shattered, the sound of it jarring in the silent night air, but no alarms sounded.

"Told you." Cass chuckled, reaching through the broken window to unlock the door. "Mind your feet on the glass."

He steadied me with his hand as I stepped over the broken glass and followed him further into the house. Chills of anxious energy rippled through me with every step we took, but Cass was right. Breaking that window had shaken something loose inside me and lightened the heavy darkness in my mind a little.

"What the *fuck*," I muttered when we came out into the living room. Or what was supposed to be the living room. There was no furniture, but every available surface—walls, floor, windows, even the ceiling—was covered in text. Jagged, often illegible handwriting. Random words and sentence fragments, but over and over… *Darling.* On one wall, from floor to ceiling, the Darling logo that Zed had designed was painted. On closer inspection, though, I got a chilling feeling that it wasn't paint.

"This was supposed to make me feel better?" I muttered to Cass, my expression incredulous. "I'm going to have nightmares from this for weeks."

He gave the room a disgusted look, then tugged his bag open. "This? Hell no. This is creepy as fuck. *This* is what will make you feel better." He fished something out of the bag and held it out to me in his palm.

I peered closer at what he was offering me, then jerked my gaze back up to meet his eyes. "Is that—"

"Yup." His toothy grin flashed in the moonlight streaming from the windows. "Got a whole stack of them just begging to be used." He jiggled the bag to demonstrate, and I barked a sharp laugh.

"Goddamn," I muttered. "You really do know the way to a girl's heart, Saint."

He took a step closer, curling my fingers around the explosive device, then kissed my knuckles. "I'd burn the whole fucking world down for you, Angel."

Ugh. Be still my heart.

"All yours," he told me, handing over the bag as he released my hand. "You know how to set them?"

I scoffed, shooting him a dirty look. "Do I know how to fucking set them," I muttered, outraged. "How dare you!"

Humming a happy tune, I wandered through Chase's mostly empty mansion, placing and activating explosive devices as I went. I didn't want to go *overkill* and waste them. I knew firsthand how expensive the bastards were. But I sure as fuck wanted to ensure the whole house was little more than rubble when we were done.

Other than the living room, the only other room with any signs of habitation was the bedroom. Inside there was just a mattress on the floor and about seventeen thousand photos of *me* decorating every surface.

It was creepy enough, feeling so many of my own eyes staring back at me, that I barely took two steps into the room and just tossed an activated explosive device onto the mattress.

When I returned back downstairs, I found Cass waiting near the door we'd entered through.

"All done?" he asked, his hands tucked lazily in his pockets. Fuck, he was gorgeous.

I nodded, then sniffed the air. "Is that gas?"

His smirk was pure evil. "It seemed fitting."

I gave a low laugh as we left the house, a slight edge of hysteria shining through. The excitement and satisfaction of what we were doing pumped through me like the sweetest drug, and I couldn't wipe the smile from my face.

We hurried back down to the property boundary, and Cass boosted me over the fence once more with his strong hands firm on my waist. After he climbed over, he handed me the remote detonator.

I bit my lip, wrapping my fingers around the device as I peered up at him.

"What's wrong?" he asked when I didn't press the button.

I shook my head. "Nothing. Just…" Butterflies were going crazy inside me, and for the first time since my arrest, I felt totally alive. "Kiss me."

Cass didn't hesitate, gripping the back of my neck and crushing his mouth to mine in a rough, demanding kiss that flooded me with desire. His teeth scraped my lower lip, tugging playfully, and I groaned. Then pressed the detonator button.

Sixteen remote explosive devices all triggered simultaneously, igniting the gas we'd left filling the house. The collective sound was deafening, and for a moment we stood there, gaping at the fireball that had just shot up into the night sky. Then our lips were crashing back together in a desperate kiss.

Cass tugged me into the shadows beside Zed's front gate, his hands sweeping down my sides as I curved my body closer against him.

"Remember how you said you trust me?" he rumbled in a breathless whisper just a millimeter from my lips. Words failed me, but I nodded.

"Good," he murmured, turning me around to put my back to his chest. His face dipped to the bend of my neck, kissing me with lingering caresses. "Stop me at any time."

A short flash of confusion rippled through me, then his hands shifted around to the button of my jeans to flick it open. I stiffened up as he dragged my zipper down, my breath locked inside my chest, but I didn't stop him. There was no doubt in my mind I wanted him to continue. And I trusted him. Cass read my body better than anyone.

The flames licked the horizon in front of us, and I let my breath release as I acknowledged why Cass had turned me around. He wanted me to see the result of our handiwork. He wanted me to watch Chase's house burn down, all those pictures of me turning to ash inside the destroyed structure.

His teeth teased at the skin of my neck, and I groaned, relaxing into his hold once more. He whispered reassurances to me, and his hand slipped down the front of my jeans.

"Red," he groaned as he stroked me through my panties, "you're such a goddess. Blowing shit up gets you hot, huh?"

I gave a slightly nervous laugh, riding the razor edge of arousal and trauma while Cass blanketed me with his huge frame. "Violence and destruction," I murmured back, jerking slightly as his fingers slipped beneath the fabric of my panties and stroked me deeper. "It's part of our love language, isn't it?"

He responded with a throaty chuckle as he circled my clit with his thumb, making me squirm in his arms. "You're right about that, Angel." He continued teasing me, working me up.

I was so tightly wound. Between my fear and anxiety, worry that we might be caught, and almost overwhelming arousal, I was a goddamn mess.

Cass knew exactly how to handle me, though. His lips brushed my ear, his low voice coaxing and reassuring as his fingers brought me right to the edge.

"Trust me, Angel," he encouraged as I tensed up, fighting the release. "Trust me to keep you safe."

Fuck. With a pained whimper, I locked my eyes on the roaring flames of Chase's burning house and let go.

The orgasm flooded through me, making my muscles lock up and jerk, my head toss back against Cass's chest, and my hips writhe. Instantly, I knew I was okay. I was better than okay. Because the kind of climax Cass drew out of me didn't have a single thing in common with the drug-induced, forced orgasms Chase had stolen. They were as different as giraffes and rocks, and the realization filled me with such intense relief that I started laughing.

Pulling his hand from my jeans, Cass spun me around again so he could study my face. When I just gave him a loopy grin, he kissed me softly and muttered how much he loved me.

CHAPTER 22

I slept the rest of the night curled up in Cass's arms, and when I woke up, I wasn't instantly flooded with panic and confusion, just the intense feeling of security and warmth. The addictive, intoxicating knowledge that I was safe and loved.

Cass tightened his loose grip around my waist when I started to crawl out of bed, pulling me back into his embrace for a long and slow kiss.

"You doing okay?" he asked in a sleepy voice, his eyes barely open a millimeter.

I took a second to give myself a quick mental health check before I nodded and kissed him back. "I'm great," I corrected. "Last night was exactly what I needed. Thank you."

A lazy smile curled his lips. "Mmm, I need to restock my explosives. I'll never get enough of that look in your eyes when you watched that house detonate."

"That too," I murmured, brushing my lips over his and loving how his lids lifted higher in surprise.

"Oh, *that* part." He chuckled a deep, throaty sound. "I'm happy to revisit that right now, if you want."

I licked my lips, tempted. But I was also anxious to see Zed and

Lucas this morning. Since smashing though that barrier so perfectly with Cass, I was riding a jittery, happy high—the kind of mood that wanted to see what the fallout of our midnight mission had been.

"Coffee first," I suggested, sighing as he kissed my neck. I should have known intimacy would never be a long-term hurdle. Not when it came to my guys. Our bond was too damn strong.

Cass returned his lips to mine, kissing the breath right out of me before reluctantly pulling away. "Fine," he agreed, "coffee first."

I'd changed back into Zed's T-shirt when we'd returned to my room, so I didn't bother getting dressed before heading downstairs. Cass looped his arm around my waist before we entered the kitchen, and I couldn't help feeling like he was sending a not-so-subtle *fuck you* to Lucas and Zed.

Fucking men were never going to get past their competitive, jealous crap. I was sure of it.

"Good morning, firebugs," Zed greeted us, his narrow-eyed glare taking in the casual, intimate way Cass touched me. "I take it you two sorted out your issues?"

I aimed for innocence but couldn't wipe the smile from my face as I replied, "I don't know what you're talking about."

Zed huffed. "Smells like bullshit, Dare."

Lucas slid out of his chair at the table and came over to kiss my cheek, inhaling deeply as he did so. "Nah, smells like smoke. Like the ashy, delicious scent of Chase Lockhart's new house going up in a big old fireball at one in the morning."

Automatically, I frowned and lifted my braid to my nose to check if I did smell like smoke.

"Hah, caught." Lucas smirked.

I rolled my eyes but didn't try to deny it. Cass just tilted my chin up with a finger and kissed me softly before getting started making coffee.

Zed's gaze was heavy and hot, watching me intently. So I crossed the distance to where he stood gripping the counter and hugged him from behind, reassuring him that I was good and not just putting up a good front.

"Well, I had Lieutenant Jeffries on the phone first thing this morning," he told me as he shifted to hug me back, "spouting some crap about coincidences. Apparently, he thought it was suspicious Hades and I returned to Shadow Grove the same night as our neighbor's house blew up."

Cass just smirked. "Tell him to call back when he has proof. Guarantee there is none."

Zed gave a small grunt of approval. "You covered your tracks, then? Good."

"Like I'm some kind of fucking amateur," Cass grumbled, holding out a mug of coffee for me. I took it gratefully and made my way over to the table where Lucas was laying out various boxes of cereal and bowls.

I went straight for the sugary shit that Zed despised, filling my bowl up with colorful cereal hoops.

"Do you want me to arrange that meeting for today?" Lucas offered, taking the seat beside me and pouring his own bowl of the same sugary cereal. "Seeing as Cass is back?"

I glanced over at Cass, who was cracking eggs into a frying pan.

"Yeah, the sooner the better," I agreed. "Let's get that dealt with today, and then we can move on."

Lucas nodded, his mouth full of cereal, but he pulled his phone out and started tapping out a message while he ate. I relaxed into my seat, enjoying the moment of peace among the four of us. Zed was jokingly ribbing Cass, insulting his egg-cooking skills, and Lucas let his knee rest against mine under the table.

"You look calmer this morning," Lucas observed quietly when he put his phone back down and dropped his hand to my leg. "How's your arm?"

I wrinkled my nose. It hurt like a *bitch*, but I didn't want to spoil the moment by leaving to fetch my sling. "It's fine."

He gave my knee a squeeze, telling me he wasn't buying my shit. But he let it go, for now.

"Doc is coming by to see you in about half an hour," he told me between mouthfuls of food. "He might have a nonsurgical fix for your ACJ that could get you out of the sling sooner rather than later."

"That'd be preferable," I commented, finishing my bowl. "But, um, could I get a hand in the shower before he gets here?"

Lucas grinned. "Washing off the evidence of arson? Of course." He quickly finished his own breakfast and rinsed out our bowls while I took a few more gulps of coffee.

"Lucky prick," Zed grumbled as Lucas left the kitchen with me.

I bit back a grin, pretending I hadn't heard, but Lucas gave a low chuckle. "Next thing you know, Zed will have worked out a shower schedule." He glanced down at me, his eyes glittering with confidence. "But we all know I'm your favorite shower helper, right?"

In truth, I probably didn't even need a shower helper anymore. Or I wouldn't for much longer. But it was kind of nice, so I was going to hold on to it for a while.

All jokes aside, Lucas really was an exceptional helper. His touches only lingered slightly more than they had last week, and I found myself quietly hoping he'd push harder, like Cass had.

He knew it, though. As he was helping me dry off, he threaded his fingers into the back of my hair and tipped my head up with a firm grip. "Doc will be here any minute, Hayden. I refuse to rush things just to get a quick fix." He pushed me gently against the wall, his body pinning me and his lips hovering right above mine. "Make no mistake, though. I want you so bad it's physically paining me not to lock the door and ignore Doc when he comes by."

I groaned as his hard dick crushed against my towel and I didn't experience even a fraction of the panic I had a day ago. I had to give mental props to Cass's fingers for that breakthrough.

"I'm healing up so well I probably don't even need to see Doc," I murmured, slightly breathless.

Lucas's lips curled. "Nice try. We've got a lot to do today, and you need to take the Hades mantle back."

I pouted, but he wiped it away with kisses that made my heart race and my nipples harden. Damn those inconvenient life appointments getting in the way of my Lucas time.

He helped me get dressed, but I was still thinking about the press of his body against mine all throughout my medical checkup. It didn't help that he sat in on it all, listening intently to Doc's notes and inspecting how my wounds were healing.

By the time Doc left, I had clearance to remove all of my dressings and an appointment for that afternoon with a physical therapist in Rainybanks.

Lucas had picked up a new phone for me on our secure network from Dallas, and I barely paid attention to what the guys were saying as we climbed into one of Zed's cars as I swiped through my messages. It wasn't until he started the engine with a deep rumble that I glanced up.

"What happened to the Audi?" I asked, seeing as that was his usual go-to for a four-seater. We were in an Escalade, and last I checked, Zed didn't own one of those.

He cast me a quick look and shrugged. "It was time for a change."

"And this one is bulletproof," Lucas added with a grin from the back seat.

I arched a brow at Zed, but he just shrugged as he drove out of the garage. It was just the three of us for the day, with Cass left behind to avoid being spotted as risen from the dead just yet. He had been willing to risk it, but just the thought of some foolish gangster taking a shot at him for faking his own death made my blood pressure spike dramatically. So he'd gotten left behind.

"Vega confirmed for tonight," Lucas spoke up, his attention on his phone. "That's everyone."

"Maurice?" I replied, surprised.

Lucas shot me back a slightly feral grin. "He wasn't given the option to refuse."

Fucking hell. Vicious was *such* a hot look on Lucas.

"We have about an hour before we need to head over to your PT appointment," Zed told me, heading toward Shadow Grove's downtown. "Are you okay to stop in and see Nadia? She's been asking after you. A lot."

"I'd love to," I replied sincerely. "How did everything work out with the girls?"

"Other than the little girl who died, most were returned to their homes. One ran away, and two are still living with Nadia for the time being." Zed drummed his fingers on the steering wheel as he drove, his tanned forearms flexing with the movement below where he'd rolled up his sleeves. I didn't even try to hide the way I checked him out, and he glanced over at me when we paused at a traffic light some minutes later.

"Keep giving me that look, Dare, and we can forget going to Nadia's," he murmured teasingly. The light changed, and his focus shifted back to the road.

"I'm game," Lucas offered from the back seat. "If that was a genuine offer."

Zed glanced at him in the mirror. "It wasn't. Keep that anaconda caged, Gumdrop."

"Damn," I muttered, teasing. If I was totally honest with myself, I still didn't know if I could confidently fall back into bed with *anyone*, let alone multiple anyones. There was one easy way to find out, but in the back of Zed's car in the middle of the day probably wasn't the time or the place.

Zed just placed his hand on my knee while he drove, and I relaxed into the familiar touch. He drove us through Shadow Grove to Nadia's café, which Chase's paid goons had recently trashed. When we pulled up outside, it looked like her renovation was well underway.

"How much is this costing me?" I joked as we climbed out of the Escalade.

Lucas grimaced. "You don't want to know."

I gave a short laugh. Whatever it was, Nadia deserved it. She'd been so good to me, and now that I knew she was Cass's grandmother, she was an extension of my own little family. If she wanted to dip her coffee machine in twenty-four-carat gold, I'd let her.

"Hades!" The excited shriek made me tense up a moment after we stepped into the construction site of Nadia's Cakes. A small, red-haired demon came flying through the scaffolding and damn near knocked me off my stiletto heels.

"Diana!" Nadia hollered from the kitchen, "You get your scrawny butt back here and clean up this paint!"

"Oh, kid, you're in trouble," Zed muttered under his breath with a chuckle.

Diana pulled back from where she was hugging my waist and shot a wide grin up at Zed. "Told you she'd be back. No one gets the better of Hades."

Zed just rolled his eyes like he was resisting the urge to argue with a kid.

"Diana!" Nadia bellowed again, and the girl flinched.

"Yeah, okay, maybe a little trouble." Then she glared up at me with all the attitude of a six-foot-seven gangster. "Don't *leave*. I just have to clean up some paint."

She slouched back in the direction Nadia was yelling from, and I shot Zed a bewildered look. He just grinned back. "Don't ask me, I haven't seen the kid in weeks."

Lucas snickered. "Yeah, when we were searching for clues, Zed made some morbid comment about you possibly being dead where Diana could hear him. She looked like she was ready to fight him over it."

"She *was* ready to fight me about it. I had to explain that I was just being sarcastic, and she gave me a lecture about not being such

193

a Debbie Downer. Little brat." Then an affectionate grin crossed his face. "She reminds me of Seph at that age. All attitude, no manners."

"How old is she, anyway?" I asked. When I'd pulled her from the basement of Anarchy, I'd thought her to be only five or six, but now, having interacted with her, she seemed older.

Zed snorted. "We don't know."

"That's why I asked him to bring *you* here," Nadia announced, coming out of the kitchen with her hands propped on her hips and a moss-green stripe of paint down her cheek. "Stinking child won't give us *anything* useful to be able to find her family."

My eyes widened. "Uh...you asked me here to talk to a kid?"

Nadia folded her arms under her breasts. "Is that going to be a problem for you, sir?"

I glanced from her to Zed to Lucas and back. None of them offered me anything helpful, so I sighed and nodded. "Okay, sure. What do you need me to ask her?"

"Anything," Nadia replied, sounding exhausted. "Quite literally the only things we know about the little terror are her name and that she thinks the damn sun shines out of your vagina." Then she winced. "Uh, no disrespect intended, sir."

I bit back a laugh. "None taken."

Nadia nodded. "I'll sweeten the deal and plate you up some apple pie."

"With an offer like that, how can I refuse?" I muttered the comment somewhat sarcastically, but Nadia stopped me with a hand on my arm as I moved past her.

"I'm glad to see you back in one piece, Hades," she said quietly, patting my good arm. "I think the whole damn town gave a sigh of relief when you arrived home yesterday."

Swallowing the hard lump of emotion she'd brought up, I jerked a nod of acknowledgment, then continued on into the kitchen. Diana was on the floor with a rag and a bucket mopping up a spill of green paint and muttering curses that made my brows rise.

Glancing around, I didn't spot anyone else in the kitchen, so I figured we were probably okay to talk right there. But…how in the hell did I even start a conversation with this kid? I was *awful* with children. Just look at the mess I'd made of Seph, and she'd been thirteen when I took guardianship of her.

Clearing my throat, I tucked my fingers under the shoulder strap of my gun holster. Lucas had been dead against me wearing it, but I needed it. Being openly armed was as much a part of my costume as my red-soled shoes.

Diana sat back on her heels and threw her rag into the bucket with a scowl. Glaring up at me, her jaw took a distinctly stubborn set.

"I'm not going back to my parents, Hades. You can't make me."

I nodded thoughtfully, crossing my ankles as I leaned against a standing freezer. "Okay. How about if I kill them for you instead?"

CHAPTER 23

We left Nadia's an hour later with Lucas cradling a cake box in his arms. My stomach was pleasantly full of apple pie and ice cream, but Nadia had insisted we take a marble mud cake home, too.

I'd given Nadia the relevant information: Diana was eight years old—small for her age—and wouldn't be returning to her family. Beyond that, I'd kept the details confidential. I'd initially offered to kill her family just as a way to get her to open up to me, but as soon as Diana started telling me her story, I knew I would make good on that promise.

Poor kid deserved better, and I had every intention of making her father regret every hair he'd ever harmed on that tough little cookie's head.

Physical therapy sucked. Big time. Not just because it really showed me how bad my range of motion was in that shoulder but also because my therapist was a gorgeous man by the name of Misha. So Lucas and Zed felt the need to puff their chests out and piss all over me to mark their territory. Metaphorically.

The thin layer of silver lining to the painful process, though, was Misha's optimistic assessment that if I worked on it, I shouldn't need surgery at all. My ACJ had been nicked, but not cut or torn, and my healing so far had been just short of miraculous.

I didn't fully appreciate how badly the PT had exhausted me, though, until I fell asleep on the drive to Cloudcroft. Our evening meeting with all the gang leaders under my purview was being held at Timber, but the last thing I remembered was my eyelids drooping before we'd even hit the freeway.

Zed gently shook me awake sometime later, and I groaned my reluctance.

"I know, baby," he murmured, kissing my cheek. "Say the word, and I'll reschedule this meeting until tomorrow. We can just go home and sleep."

I yawned heavily, blinking myself awake and meeting Zed's eyes. I was in the back of his Escalade, having given Lucas the shotgun seat after my appointment, and had somehow managed to slip totally horizontal while I'd slept.

"I like the new car," I mumbled, rubbing the heel of my hand over my eye before remembering my makeup. Dammit. I couldn't go in there looking like a damn panda.

"Yeah?" Zed smiled, tucking my hair behind my ear with gentle fingers.

I nodded. "Mm-hmm. Spacious." I gave an exaggerated stretch, making the fresh scars on my ribs tug and itch. Maybe I *would* talk to Cass about covering that up for me, seeing as I definitely didn't want the start of Chase's fucking name on my skin forever.

Zed chuckled lightly, then helped me sit up. I'd fallen asleep with my sling on, and I cringed as I rolled my shoulders to loosen the stiffness.

"How bad do I look?" I asked, glancing around. We were in the underground parking lot for Timber, and Lucas was nowhere to be seen.

"You could never look bad," Zed replied with a sly grin.

I rolled my eyes. "Smooth, Zeddy Bear. Real smooth."

He laughed, then swiped his thumb under my eye a couple of times to clean up the makeup I'd just smudged. "Perfect," he murmured, combing his fingers through my hair to tidy it up. Lucas had helped me style it before we left the house, so it wasn't too out of control. "Lucas is inside keeping an eye on our guests. We wanted to let you sleep as long as possible. Besides, little Gumdrop seems to enjoy throwing some big-dick energy around."

I snickered. "If anyone can back *that* up…"

Zed huffed in a good-humored way, then helped me exchange the sling for a gun holster. The straps rubbed my wounded shoulder uncomfortably, but my tight, long-sleeved black top hid the scarring itself. All about appearances.

"You good?" he asked, grabbing my shoes from the floor where I'd kicked them off. He slid them onto my feet for me with a warm hand on my ankle, then offered me a hand to get out of the vehicle.

Drawing a deep breath, I smoothed my skirt down, tugging it into place before releasing my sigh. "Good," I confirmed. I rolled my neck and heard it crack. "Let's get this done."

I paused to wait as Zed fetched extra weapons from the trunk, slinging his favorite AR-15 over his shoulder. It was way more firepower than needed, but one never could be too cautious with a gathering of rivals. Besides, Zed had a reputation to uphold, just like I did.

We took the service elevator up to the storage area of Timber, then made our way out into the main club from there. My arrest and subsequent *disappearance* had put a hold on our plans for a grand opening, so the club was empty except for the small grouping of tattooed, tough-faced gangsters seated in a collection of velvet couches and armchairs in the middle of the main room.

One bartender and one waitress, borrowed from Anarchy, were serving drinks. Otherwise, the huge, converted church was vacant.

"Gentlemen," I said in a cold, hard voice as I approached my guests. "Good of you to come on short notice."

Ezekiel, the slimy bastard, gave me a long leer and adjusted his glasses. "The pleasure is all ours, Hades. After all the wild rumors floating around, I think some of us weren't sure you would be here in person."

Irritation bubbled in my bloodstream, but I controlled it with a cool, dangerous smile in his direction. "You should know not to listen to rumors, Ezekiel." My gaze shifted to Maurice, who looked like he'd been run over by a cement mixer. "You should *all* know better. I hope you learned your lesson, Maurice?"

His lip curled in a sneer, but his second gave him a not-so-subtle jab in the ribs. Maurice shot a death glare at the bruised man beside him, then glowered back at me. "Yes, sir," he gritted out, looking like the words physically pained him. "My mistake."

He was fucking lucky he was still breathing. But I didn't have the time or energy to deal with finding new leadership for the Vipers. The system we had right now worked. Maurice paid his dues and abided by my few rules, and I left his organization the fuck alone. Same for Vega's and Ezekiel's.

The whole reason I'd called this meeting was already adding more work to my pile than I really needed.

Letting my face remain hard and vaguely pissed off—my resting Hades face—I sat carefully in one of the vacant armchairs. Zed took up his post behind my right shoulder, and Lucas took the left without needing to be told. He really was a natural.

"I can imagine most of you just came to see if I was still alive, so I hope your curiosity has been assuaged. I don't have the patience for small talk tonight" as if I ever did in these meetings—"so I'll cut straight to business. Unless anyone has something they want to put on the table for discussion?"

Ezekiel, Maurice, and Roach remained silent, staring at me like I was some kind of venomous snake coiled to strike. In fairness, I did have a history of shooting people in these meetings.

Vega cleared his throat, though, sitting forward with his elbows braced on his knees. "Sir, if I may?" He paused for my permission, and I nodded. "Diego has been a great help these last few months, and I absolutely accept that oversight was a condition of my punishment for breaking the rules." I could hear the *but* coming, and I cast a curious look at Diego, who was standing behind Vega's chair.

He was one of mine, a Timberwolf, and loyal as they came. I'd assigned him as Vega's second after I'd shot the last one for fighting in my club a couple of months ago. His job was basically to babysit the Death Squad and ensure they were reporting correct balance sheets to pay their dues. It was insulting as hell for me to place him as Vega's second, but insult had to be better than death or maiming.

Diego met my gaze calmly and gave a barely perceptible nod. Whatever Vega was about to propose, he had Diego's support.

"If you might be so inclined," Vega continued, "I have someone that I'd really like to promote to the permanent second position."

I flicked my attention back to Vega, letting silence hang in the air for a few moments—just long enough to make him uncomfortable. Then I tilted my head to the side. "Send me the details. I'll take it under consideration."

If he simply waited out the oversight period, he wouldn't need my permission. So whoever it was, he must be worried they'd go elsewhere without a promotion, and that had me intrigued.

Vega bobbed a nod. "Can do. Thank you, sir."

Come to think of it, I wouldn't mind having Diego back. I needed all the help I could get these days.

Zed gave me a soft touch on my arm, silently letting me know that our additional attendees had arrived, so I swiftly moved on.

"Gentlemen, I called you here to keep you informed of some changes. Contrary to rumor, I am going *nowhere*. In fact, I'm expanding. You've all met Lucas already. Consider him my second Zed."

Ezekiel's brows raised, and his little squirrel eyes glittered with interest. He knew, like everyone else in the room, that comparing

Lucas to Zed was a high compliment on Lucas's marksmanship and lethality.

"As well as that, I'm swelling the Timberwolf inner circle ranks with some key, skilled individuals. The recent threats to my empire, which I don't doubt you're all aware of, have made me realize I've been too lenient." My words were threaded with cold fury. Maurice had pissed me off enough just sniffing around where he shouldn't be. *This* should squash any remaining thoughts of dissention.

The front door of Timber closed loudly, the sound echoing through the room, and I let a predatory smile curve my lips. Carefully, I savored each of their reactions as footsteps fell on the parquetry floor behind me. Mostly, I watched Roach.

"Gentlemen, I believe some of you will already know my two newly appointed Timberwolf enforcers." I could all but taste the chill of apprehension running through the other gang leaders when my men stepped into the light. "Rex Darenburg, returned from retirement. And Cassiel Saint, returned from the dead."

CHAPTER 24

When the dust had settled from my little necromancy trick, I asked Roach to stay behind as the others all left my meeting. He hadn't said a single word since laying eyes on his former gang leader and looked a little bit like his brain might have exploded inside his skull. That…or he was plotting Cass's assassination to protect the Reapers' honor. And that wasn't an option I was prepared to risk.

Our waitress, Bethany, brought over a round of drinks while we waited for the others to clear out, and Lucas leaned in close as he reached for his glass.

"Are you okay?" he whispered so softly I barely even heard him.

I met his eyes and gave him a small nod. I was hurting and tired as hell, but I was happy. This was my safe place, throwing my massive dick energy at tough-guy gangsters. Dropping little bombs and watching to see if today was the day someone felt like challenging my seat of power. It was exhilarating, making me feel all fluttery like I had when Cass and I planted explosives all over Chase's house.

Roach cleared his throat, giving me a small frown. "Hades, sir," he said cautiously. "Would you mind terribly if I spoke to Cass privately?"

I shifted my gaze to Roach's second, a midtwenties guy who

went by Skunk. Whoever gave these dudes their gang names needed a solid whack upside the head because some of them were straight up bad.

Skunk was eyeing Cass with suspicion and animosity, but it was nothing my Grumpy Cat couldn't handle. So I nodded and pushed to my feet.

Stopping in front of Cass, I reached up and pulled his face down to mine with a hand on the back of his neck. It was an aggressive gesture, and he let me do it. The power dynamic was clear in that *I* was kissing *him*, not the other way around. I'd likely make up for it later, anyway.

"Don't get any blood on the velvet," I told him, loud enough to be heard.

"Yes, sir," Cass growled back, his expression stoic but his fingers gentle where they rested on my hip.

Leaving him to speak with his former subordinates, I made my way over to the bar with Zed, Lucas, and Rex joining me.

Our bartender, Katie, was in the middle of rearranging the back bar, but Bethany bounced over with a smile to offer us more drinks. Rex ordered a beer while Zed and I ordered scotch.

"You're driving home," Zed informed Lucas after ordering him a soda.

Rex grunted a laugh, inhaling half his beer in one gulp. "And you're not legal to drink," he added, then burped. "Actually, I'd best be heading home. Can't trust those fucking kids of mine not to trash the house if I'm not all up their asses."

I arched a brow at him, and he shot me a grin.

"Don't worry, Boss. They're assholes, but they know how important their task is. They won't fuck it up." He jerked his head in the direction of Cass, who seemed to have Skunk in a choke hold on the floor. "He's a barrel of laughs, isn't he? Chatty." Guffawing, he finished his beer and put the empty bottle on the bar top.

Rex swaggered out of the club, and I stifled a sigh in his wake.

203

His reputation had more than preceded him, though. The look on Ezekiel's face had been pure panic, and it made me think the slippery squirrel was up to something he shouldn't be. I'd ask Rex to pay him a little visit another day.

A grunt of pain came from Skunk, which told me Cass was handling things just fine. I arched a brow in question at Zed, but he just grinned back at me. Yep, Cass was just fine in his new role.

Minutes later, a very pained-looking Skunk stumbled his way past us mumbling some respectful goodbyes as he limped out of Timber. Roach and Cass were not far behind but looked completely at ease as they shook hands.

Roach gave me, Zed, and Lucas a nod and tight smile, then followed his second out of my club.

"Everything okay?" I asked Cass now that we were alone.

He shrugged. "Yeah, fine. Roach is a smart kid. He knows what's what."

Lucas gave a short laugh. "Vague but typical Grumpy Cat."

Zed and I exchanged a smile, finishing our drinks. I had no desire to hang around any longer, my whole body aching with the need for rest. I was getting stronger every day, but it was still a process. I just thanked the fates that Chase hadn't shown his face back in town.

It was only a matter of time, though. He was still out there somewhere, plotting and scheming.

At least I knew where he *wouldn't* be. The burnt-out husk of his house this morning had reassured me of that.

The four of us started toward the service elevator, but Bethany called out after us, making me pause.

"Um, sorry, Hades, sir," she stuttered, shooting panicked glances at the three imposing men at my back. "Do you have just a minute? I know you're a busy person, so…" Her voice trailed off awkwardly.

I nodded, though. "Of course." I gave Zed a hand signal, telling him to wait there for me as I led Bethany back into the bar and away from the guys.

She drew a deep breath once we were alone, like she was giving herself a quick mental pep talk.

"Whatever it is, Bethany, I'm sure I can help. I protect my employees, so if someone is harassing you…" I don't know why I assumed that was what she was going to tell me. Maybe I was just jaded from years of running strip clubs and brothels. Ninety-nine percent of the time, when one of my female employees needed to speak with upper management, it meant someone was abusing their power.

Her eyes widened, then she gave a small laugh. "Oh, no. Not…that's not it. Um, okay, so I really hope this isn't out of line. Or, it definitely is, but not *too* far out of line…" Her eyes flicked up to the ceiling again, and she gave a small shake of her head. "Fuck it," she muttered with a sigh. "I heard you might be interested in recruiting more women into the Timberwolves, sir. I want to be considered."

My brows flicked up. "I see."

She nodded, firmer now. "Yes, sir. I think I can be useful." She hesitated, then indicated the slightly decorative and exceptionally sharp knives belted at the high waist of my skirt. "May I?"

Curious, I slid one of the slim blades free and held it out to her hilt first.

She flipped it once in her hand, testing the balance, then threw it with unexpected confidence right at Katie. The tip of the blade buried in the wooden pillar behind the bartender, pinning the small piece of docket paper she'd been using to alphabetize the bottles.

"Not fucking funny, Beth!" Katie shouted over her shoulder, yanking the knife free to retrieve her note.

Bethany just turned back to me with a wide grin on her face.

"Not bad." I bit back a smile.

She beamed, though. "I've been practicing."

I placed my hands on my hips. "And where did you hear this information, Bethany?"

Her smile slipped, and her eyes widened. "Oh. Um. One of the girls over at Club 22 was talking about it when I worked a shift there a couple of weeks ago. I don't know her name, I'm sorry."

"It's fine," I assured her, softening my voice and expression a fraction. Then I nodded to where she'd thrown my knife. "Keep practicing. I'll think it over."

She gushed her thanks, and I returned to the storage area where the guys were still waiting for me. If I were to guess, it was probably Sabine that she'd heard talking, and I wasn't even mad about it. Sabine had made an assumption based on the way I'd called in help for the girls rescued out of Anarchy's cellar, but it was a correct assumption.

Now, seeing Bethany's eagerness to join the Timberwolves, I had an idea.

"What was that all about?" Zed asked as we rode the elevator down to the parking level.

I grinned and told them what Bethany had done. Despite how cool my response to her request had been, I was impressed. And I didn't impress easily.

Zed tossed Lucas his keys when we got to the Escalade, then climbed into the back seat with me before Cass could get there.

"Oh, very mature," Cass muttered about Zed pushing him out of the way. He took the shotgun seat instead and turned to eye me over his shoulder. "Did that all play out the way you were hoping?"

I yawned, ruffling my fingers through my hair as Lucas started the car and drove out of the parking level. "Better, actually. And that makes me paranoid as fuck. Like Chase was watching the whole thing and telling Maurice what to do. Or Ezekiel. It was just too…civilized. Wasn't it?" I frowned at Cass. "Skunk looked like he wasn't thrilled to see you alive, at least."

Cass grunted. "Little shit. Roach can handle him, though."

Another long yawn tugged my jaw. "So long as they know not to try anything," I muttered. Zed saw how tired I was and coaxed me to lie down with my head in his lap. I tucked my knees up and relaxed into his warmth.

"What would you do?" Cass rumbled as I closed my eyes. "If they tried something."

Zed gently unclipped my gun holster for me, peeling it away without moving me out of his lap.

"I'd gut them," I mumbled in response to Cass. "Nobody touches what's mine and lives. I'd gut them, then mount their heads on pikes to warn everyone else away."

The sound of their soft chuckles lulled me to sleep, and I dreamed happy dreams that I was Vlad the Impaler, wreaking havoc on anyone who threatened my loves.

CHAPTER 25

"You're back!" Hannah's excited squeal made me stiffen as I stepped out of the elevators at Copper Wolf Enterprises the next day. I should have come to see her sooner, but it felt like there weren't enough hours in a day for me to do all the things and see all the people I needed to see.

She jumped out from behind her desk but stopped short of hugging me. Thank fuck. I was comfortable with the guys touching me now, and the hug from Diana hadn't sent me spiraling into darkness. But I wasn't willing to push my luck. Nightmares still haunted my sleep, and I woke up at least twice a night sweating and screaming.

"It's *so* good to see you, sir," Hannah enthused, tugging on her tightly braided hair. "Gosh, we have so much to discuss." She was already walking backward toward my office as she talked, then opened the door for me.

Macy, my accountant, shot me a small smile. "Good to see you back, Boss," she murmured. "We were all missing you."

"Thanks, Macy," I replied, then stepped into my office with Hannah tight on my heels. Zed had come into work with me, but I'd left him at the lobby coffee shop waiting for our order.

"Okay, sit," I told Hannah, pointing to the chair opposite my desk. "Take a breath, we're not in a rush." I clenched my teeth to hold back a wince as I peeled my jacket off and hung it over the back of my chair. "Zed's bringing up coffee in a minute. Until he gets back, why don't you tell me how *you're* doing, Hannah. Lucas said you were the one who found Gen."

Hannah's smile fell from her face, and her eyes pinched. "Um, yeah. I hadn't heard from her in about two days and neither had Demi. I checked her phone GPS on the company network, and it said she was at home, so..."

I nodded my understanding. "You went to check on her and found she was dead."

"Yeah," Hannah confirmed. "The police said it was a random act of violence or some bullshit." She rubbed the bridge of her nose, frowning. "But, on the upside, Maxine woke up from her coma."

I accepted her shift of subject. She was clearly troubled by seeing Gen's body, and I wouldn't push her on the topic. I already knew who was responsible, anyway. "Yes, I heard. That was surprising. The last time I saw her I thought her family was preparing to turn off life support."

"They did! They turned it off, and Maxine just...didn't die. She's such a badass." Hannah was smiling again, which made me feel like less of an asshole for even asking about finding Gen in the first place. My social skills needed *work*.

Zed let himself into my office, shooting me a warm look before handing Hannah a coffee from his tray. He came around the desk and placed mine down in front of me before kissing me softly, like we were totally alone.

Hannah cleared her throat. "Um, should I come back later?"

"Yes," Zed replied with a wicked grin.

I rolled my eyes and gave him a playful shove. "No. I'm sorry, Hannah. I don't know where Zed's professionalism is today."

She didn't look offended, though—rather the opposite as she

looked between the two of us with hearts in her eyes. Fucking hell, she was gazing at us like a kid whose divorced parents got back together.

Zed wasn't bothered. He just perched his butt on the edge of my desk and sipped his coffee with a satisfied look on his face.

"Okay," Hannah drawled, grinning. "Well, I made a list of all the things. Let's see…" She pulled out her phone and started running through all the notes she'd made, literally every single thing that had happened since my arrest that I might need to know about.

Lots of what Hannah told me I'd already heard from Zed or Demi, like the fact that Alexi had been found badly beaten in a hospital, marked as a John Doe until he woke up. Or the fact that my arrest had been leaked to all the major newspapers in the area, outing me as the leader of the Timberwolves.

"Sir, there's a gentleman here who claims to have an appointment with you." Macy's voice crackled through the intercom that we *never* used. Her tone was dry and sarcastic. "Says he's an FBI agent." There was a pause and then, "He's a mean-looking bastard with an eye patch."

A chill ran down my spine, and I straightened in my seat as Zed slid off my desk and pulled an AK-40 from the hidden panel behind my desk. Hannah gave a small gasp, her eyes wide as she eyed the gun, then turned to me.

"Do you want me to send him away?" She blinked at me with total sincerity. "I can tell him you've already gone for the day. The charges against you were all dropped, they have no right—"

"It's fine, Hannah," I murmured, even though every muscle in my body was telling me to fucking *run*. "Just let him in, then take the rest of the afternoon off. Macy, too."

That only alarmed her further, but I wouldn't risk her getting caught up in whatever bullshit Chase was playing at today.

210

"Go, Hannah," Zed pushed. "Now."

She tightened her lips but tucked her phone back in her pocket and stood up with a straight spine. "Understood, sir. Thank you for your time today."

Hannah opened my office door and gave a small gasp when she realized Chase was *right* there on the other side as if he'd been listening through the door like a fucking juvenile.

"Excuse me," she mumbled, brushing past him when he made no attempt to move out of her way. True to my request, she didn't even stop at her desk before heading to Macy and passing along my message to go home.

Chase peered over his shoulder at her, then stepped into my office with a wide grin on his face. "She's pretty, isn't she? Jumpy, too. Bet she has a lovely scream." He took another leering look in Hannah's direction, then closed the door behind himself. "Complexion is a bit dark for my liking, though. Freshly spilled blood doesn't contrast quite as nicely as it does on all that creamy porcelain of yours, Darling."

Bile roiled in my gut, and I could feel my palms sweating where I clasped my hands loosely on the desk in front of me. "I don't believe you had an appointment, Chase. Unless this is official *FBI* business"—my sarcasm was thick—"politely fuck right off. Feel free to jump straight out the window and do us all a favor."

Instead of doing as I asked—damn shame, too—Chase just sauntered over to the chair Hannah had vacated and sat his ass down like he owned the thing.

"That won't be necessary, old friend." Nodding to the assault rifle, Chase winked at Zed. "I sure hope that's licensed. I left my colleagues out in the foyer, but they really are sticklers for rules." He shifted his attention back to me. "You're looking good, Darling. How's that shoulder?"

"I don't know what you're talking about," I replied, using every damn shred of strength I had to keep my voice even, my expression calm. Beneath the desk, my knee was bouncing, but I managed to keep it subtle so Chase wouldn't see. "We're very busy. Do you have official business, Agent Lockhart?"

He grinned again. Fuck, I hated that smile.

"Always in such a rush," he purred. "I heard a whisper that your dead lover isn't so dead anymore. Maybe we could chat about that? Hmm? You made that look *very* real. I think I'm a little impressed."

I said nothing. Gave him nothing but silence and a level stare.

He made an irritated sound in his throat. "Very well, then." He reached inside his jacket, and Zed's grip on his gun shifted. But Chase just pulled out a thick linen envelope sealed with red wax.

"If you're inviting us to your Freddy Krueger–themed birthday party, unfortunately, we won't be able to make it," I drawled in the most casual tone I could muster while internally screaming. "I'm washing my hair that day."

Placing the envelope down on my desk, Chase gave a low laugh. The front of it was hand-addressed with looping script, made out to *Hayden Darling Timber*.

"The mayor of Cloudcroft is hosting a gala next weekend," he explained, his beady eye locked on me. "Given all the nasty press lately with your unfortunate arrest and dreadful abduction, she thought it would be really good for optics if you attended."

I blinked at him a moment. Was he fucking serious? Of course he was. He was straight-up fucking *insane*.

"What's in it for me?" I ignored the invitation and leaned back in my chair. Casual. Calm. Unaffected. Like nothing he'd done to me had *ever* happened.

Compartmentalization was my strongest asset, and I wasn't afraid to use it.

Shrugging, Chase stood. "Nothing at all, Darling."

He paused for a moment, standing in front of my desk and *looming* over me. I loathed to look up at him, but I also refused to be cowed into looking down at my desk.

"You *really* look good," he murmured again. "Like you got all your spark back. Bet you could run fast now, hmm?"

Oh fuck. I was about to crack. Just as the tremble in my leg started to creep up my spine, Zed closed his hand over my good shoulder. He grounded me, and I drew on his strength like a breath of fresh air in a stale room.

Chase stared at that connection, and I saw the briefest flicker of anger in his single eye—enough that I wanted to fan the flame. So I reached up and stroked my hand over Zed's, toying with his knuckles, and smiled as he linked our fingers together.

"If that's everything, *Agent*, I have a very busy afternoon planned." I loaded my voice with innuendo as Zed gave a soft, sexual kind of chuckle.

The corners of Chase's mouth tightened ever so slightly, but then that slick grin was back. "Cute." He made his way toward the door, then paused as he held it open. "Oh, you wouldn't happen to know what happened to my house, would you?"

I pretended to think about it, then shook my head. "Sorry, no. Nothing is sparking in my mind, anyway. I absolutely will tell you if anything ignites an idea, though. It's a shame you weren't home. I heard it was quite the explosion."

He huffed another forced laugh and sauntered back out of my office without closing the door. The second he was out of sight, Zed put his gun down and marched over to slam the door, then flicked the lock too.

For a moment, he planted his hands on the door, his shoulders bunched and his head hung low like he was desperately trying to get a handle on his anger. Then he pushed off again and scrubbed a hand over his face as he turned back to face me.

"This is probably the stupidest question that will ever leave my mouth," he said in a low, rough voice, "but are you okay?"

With Chase gone, my control had snapped. I shook violently all over, and my head swam like I might pass out.

"You're right," I replied, sounding *weak*. "That was a stupid question."

I was far from okay, and that "innocent" visit from Chase had shown me just how damaged I still was—no doubt exactly what he'd intended. But even knowing that, I couldn't stop myself as I broke down in Zed's arms.

CHAPTER 26

After Chase's friendly little visit to my office and my subsequent melt-down on the floor, wrapped in Zed's arms, it was no real surprise that sleep totally eluded me that night. I distracted myself by hitting the gym and working on my fitness. Even if my arm needed physical therapy, there was no reason the rest of me couldn't get back into shape, especially now that most of my injuries were healing well. My ribs still hurt, but as there was nothing to be done about that, I just...ignored them.

Mind over matter. It worked...to a point.

When the sun started cresting the horizon, I sent a message to Seph and asked if she wanted to grab breakfast with me. Even with all the stress and paranoia of Chase lurking around town, I couldn't keep shoving my sister aside.

She replied straightaway, which wasn't like her at all. She seemed excited to do breakfast, even suggesting we invite Demi. I thought that was a great idea, not just because Demi might offer a buffer if things turned sour between Seph and me, but because I also wanted to ask Demi a few things.

Heading upstairs, I made a mental deal with myself to regain some of the emotional ground I'd lost the day before. I was going to tackle the shower alone again.

Both Zed and Lucas had attached bathrooms in their bedrooms, but Cass and I used the main bathroom at the end of the hall. So rather than waking anyone up, I headed straight for that one and stripped out of my sweaty work-out clothes.

This time I didn't try to give myself a pep talk in the mirror, and I carefully avoided looking at the fresh scars decorating my ribs, wrist, thigh, and shoulder. Instead, I kept my mind working on my plan for those six people Chase had been speaking with when I escaped. He'd thrown me off with his little visit yesterday; it was about damn time I chalked up another win against him.

Blowing up his house had been fun, no question, but it wasn't enough. It hadn't hurt him or his plans, not really. I needed to start cutting him down at the knees.

Letting my mind wander, I worked on autopilot to turn on the shower and get it up to temperature before stepping in.

Vaguely, I recognized the way my muscles tensed and my skin prickled, but I was determined. Today was the day I regained another piece of myself.

Inch by inch, I backed myself under the water. Then the bathroom door opened, and Cass lumbered inside with a long yawn, tugging his T-shirt off.

"Cass, I'm fine," I snarled. "I can do this myself."

He paused with his hands on the waistband of his boxers. "Okay." Then he pushed them down and stepped closer with his big old tattooed dick swinging. "Can I shower with you, though? I'm late to go help Nadia with some heavy-lifting shit."

My lips parted, and I needed a couple of tries before I could make my voice work. "Oh. Yeah, sure."

I shifted slightly to the side, letting him into the cubicle that was suddenly way too freaking small. Why did this bathroom seem to have the smallest shower of the whole damn house?

"Thanks," he replied, flashing me a toothy grin as he dipped his face under the spray and saturated himself.

I bit my lip as the water cascaded off him and onto me, but I was too busy drooling to panic. "Grumpy Cat…what do you think you're doing?" I murmured as he spread soap all over his ripped, ink-covered chest.

He arched a brow at me, perfectly innocent. "Showering. What are you doing?"

I narrowed my eyes. "Showering too."

With a twitch of a smile, he dragged his eyes down my body. "Doesn't look like it. You need soap and water to shower, Red."

Gritting my teeth, I glared up at him, pointedly trying not to look at his dick. I'd seen it enough that I could picture it perfectly in my mind, though.

"You're taking up all the water," I pointed out with a shrug. "It's not my fault you're a shower hog."

Cass chuckled briefly, then stepped out of the stream of water and leaned his shoulders against the tile wall, leaving the soap suds clinging to his muscles like he was posing for a naked calendar. "All yours, beautiful."

The challenge was crystal clear, but I was stubborn enough to rise to the bait. Keeping my eyes locked on him, I moved further under the water. Further than I'd managed alone since…

Fuck. I was backsliding into dark memories, and that was *not* going to help.

Cass swiped a hand over his head, sending droplets of water flying as he eyed me hungrily. Okay. *That*, actually, was helping. I soaped up my hands and started spreading it over myself while Cass watched, unblinking.

"Shit, Red," he muttered as I cupped my own breasts, covering them in suds, "you sure know how to make a shower more interesting."

In case there was any question about just how interesting he found my showering, the rapid rise of his cock answered it. I shot him a heated look, playing into it by gently toying with my hard nipples.

When I slid my hand lower, soaping my belly and then heading south, Cass gave a small growl of frustration and reached out to snatch my hand away.

"You're killing me," he whispered, stepping away from the wall and into the water with me. Without asking permission, he placed my hand on his waist, then cupped my head with his fingers in my now soaking-wet hair.

He tilted my head back and claimed my lips in a hard, hungry kiss that made my knees weak and my pulse race. His hard dick pressed against my stomach, and a ripple of darkness shuddered through me. It was gone in a flash, though, when his lips moved to my ear.

"I've got you, Angel," he rumbled, his low, gravelly voice filling me with a heady sense of safety and security. "I'll never hurt you." He pulled away just far enough to shoot me a devilish wink. "Unless you want me to...later."

I huffed a laugh, then gasped as his fingers found my heated core.

"Cass," I breathed, but had no fucking clue if it was a protest or a plea. Either way, he brought his mouth back to mine, kissing me deeply as his thumb found my clit and made me writhe.

With firm, confident strokes, he worked me over as he kissed the breath straight from my lungs, until I was trembling and moaning in his grip. The warm shower continued beating down on us both, the water mixing with our kisses and heating my already flushed body to the point of scorching.

Right as I could feel my orgasm hanging on the horizon, I let go of the last bit of control I'd been clinging to. Acting purely on instinct, my fingers skated down Cass's hard abs and wrapped around his throbbing cock.

He grunted in surprise, then plunged his fingers deeper as my hand stroked him slowly. A moment later, I was moaning and shaking as I came. My grip on his dick tightened as my toes curled and my knees went weak, and as my orgasm started to fade, Cass jerked and huffed his own release.

I tensed up a moment, memories flashing across my mind in a lightning-fast montage of terror, but the shower water instantly washed away the evidence of his climax, and he kissed me again.

"You want me to wash your hair for you?" he asked, sounding husky and a little breathless. The water was pouring all over me, and I just gave him a loopy, relieved smile.

"Mm-hmm," I agreed, reaching for the shampoo, then handing it to him. "That was sneaky, Saint."

He flashed me a wicked grin and spun me around so that I was out of the water while he washed my hair. "No, that was positive reinforcement, Angel, replacing traumatic memories with stronger, fresher experiences of pleasure. And trust. And *love*." He kissed my shoulder. "It was Lucas's idea."

Of course it had been. Lucas knew Cass was infinitely more comfortable pushing me past my self-imposed limits, but that was exactly what I'd said I wanted. So they were working together to help me. I loved that more than I could ever express.

"Remind me to thank him," I murmured, letting my eyes close as Cass washed my hair. This time, though, it was a loving, borderline-sexual act. He wasn't helping me as an injured, fragile, damaged creature. He was worshiping the woman he loved.

I was late for my breakfast date with Seph. She'd asked me to pick her up from Rex's place because she wanted to show me something that she'd been working on, but after I'd asked Cass for some more *positive reinforcement* in the shower, I was breathless and rushed when I arrived.

"Good morning, Boss," Rex crowed as he opened the door for me. He lived in an apartment above his garage with his sons and now with Seph. "Lovely day, eh?"

I arched a brow at him. My hair was a bit wild—I'd run out of time to do anything but blast it with some heat—and I knew my lips were red and puffy from kissing that rough, bearded bastard in my shower.

"Superb," I replied with a flat, fuck-off tone. "Is Seph ready? I'm late."

Rex swiped a hand over his face like he was trying to hide a laugh. "Uh, yep, she was just having a small disagreement with Ford upstairs, but I'll give her a yell."

He led the way through the garage, past a beautiful Corvette in a soft lilac, and over to the door at the back, which was marked with Private—No Access.

The second he opened the door, I heard what he'd meant when he said Seph was having a "small disagreement" with his oldest son. Her unmistakable shriek echoed down the stairs, and on instinct I stiffened as a cold chill ran through me.

Before I could overreact, though, her shriek turned into scathing insults and curses, and I exhaled the tension out again. She was fine.

Rex clearly knew what they were arguing about because his shoulders shook slightly with laughter. Then he cupped his hand around his mouth and bellowed for her to come down.

"Come in anyway," he said to me, indicating I join him at the top of the first short flight of stairs. It opened up into a kitchen and eating area where a sleepy-looking teenage boy was eating cereal and watching anime.

Rex cleared his throat loudly, and the boy glanced up at us with half-asleep curiosity. As natural as breathing, his eyes ran over me with a spark of interest and a flirtatious smile curved his lips.

"Whatever bullshit is about to leave your lips, boy, I'd think fucking twice," Rex snarled. The kid gave Rex an arrogant sneer, then shifted his eyes back to me. This time, though, his brows rose with recognition. Seph and I looked *a lot* alike.

"I apologize for the fucking moron, Boss," Rex muttered to me, lumbering over to the kitchen. "Can I get you a cup of coffee?"

I shook my head. "No. I'm taking my sister for breakfast." Satisfaction rippled through me at how the boy paled when I said *my sister*. I flicked him a predatory glance. "I don't think we've met."

Rex grunted. "Sorry, Boss. This degenerate is Micah. Not technically one of mine, but he acts like he is." He gave me a long-suffering look. "I figure he's better off putting his hands to work here than getting in scuffles with Reapers or Wolves."

The boy flashed me a cocky smile, but this time it was more cautious and a whole lot less leering. "You're Hades, huh?"

Rex clipped him around the back of his head, and I bit my cheek to hold back a smile. "Apparently," I replied in a cool murmur.

"Ow, what?" Micah scowled up at Rex. "I wasn't being rude!"

Clattering footsteps coming down the stairs saved the kid from earning another wallop from Rex, and Seph burst into the room with bright-red, tearstained cheeks and venom in her eyes.

Instead of spouting off about whatever had upset her, though, she just grabbed me in a tight hug. "You're here! I thought you might have changed your mind or something."

I hugged her back awkwardly, cocking a brow at Rex over her head. He just shrugged and turned back to making his coffee.

"I just got caught up with Cass," I told my sister, desperately praying my cheeks weren't turning pink.

She gave me a sly grin anyway and waggled her brows. "Oh yeah?" Then she looked over to Rex. "Am I cool to go?"

Rex waved a hand at her in permission, and I had to clamp my lips together to stop myself from gaping. Seph never asked my permission to go anywhere. How was Rex more of a parent to her in a month than I'd been in five years?

"Head out and wait for me by the car," I told Seph. "I need to discuss something with Rex."

She nodded, taking the keys I offered her, and disappeared out the door. Rex gave Micah a nudge on his shoulder, and the kid scrambled to follow after Seph. I got the distinct impression that was less to give us privacy than to keep eyes on Seph. Good. That was the level of protectiveness I expected.

"She's a good kid," my uncle rumbled, "just got a few bad habits to iron out. That's what all that hollering was about upstairs, I think. My boys are sticklers for the rules around here, but she's getting there."

I gave a small shake of my head. The change in Seph was shocking, for sure, but that wasn't what I needed to discuss. "I've got a job for you," I told him, folding my arms carefully across my front. "Ezekiel."

Rex grunted. "Squirrely fuck? Assassinations are his game, yeah?"

I nodded. "That's right. He fancies himself in the same league as the Guild." Rex barked a laugh, and I couldn't help the smile creasing my own face. "He seemed particularly nervous the other night. I'd like you to pay him a friendly visit and see what's what."

His smile was all teeth. "How friendly are we talking?"

"Use your own discretion, Rex. Just don't cause any unnecessary problems for me to clean up later. I've got enough of those on my plate right now."

He inclined his head. "Understood, sir."

"Good," I murmured. "I'll drop Seph back around lunchtime."

Rex yawned, scratching his belly. "I'll make sure one of the boys is here all day, just in case. Can't be too careful."

I couldn't have agreed more. Rex and I seemed to have more in common than I'd previously realized. Maybe I wouldn't regret pulling him out of retirement after all.

CHAPTER 27

Seph was tight-lipped and flushed as she shifted uncomfortably in her seat for the fourth time since we'd left Rex's. Finally, curiosity got the better of me.

"All right, spill," I demanded as we turned into the parking lot beside the café where we'd arranged to meet Demi. "You look like you've been ridden hard and put up wet." I meant it as a joke, but then a wave of paranoia hit me. "Seph, you haven't—"

"What?" she shrieked, clapping her hands over her face. "No! Oh my *god*, Dare. As if! Ew. Gross. I wouldn't have sex with Ford if he was the last man on *earth*. I'd rather fuck a pineapple than *him*. Besides, he's my cousin. I can't believe that even crossed your mind!"

I was having a hard time holding my laughter back as we parked and got out of the car. I'd borrowed one of Zed's again, a silver Porsche 911. Technically, Rex's sons weren't our cousins at all. Rex was only related to us through his marriage to Demi, and they'd long since divorced. His kids were from his bit on the side.

I wouldn't fill Seph in on that, though. Better she think they were related by blood because the way her face was flaming told me she was trying to convince herself as much as me.

"Okay, if you say so," I said with a chuckle. "So why are you all squirmy and angry?"

She glared absolute *death* at me as she pushed through the main door to the restaurant. "I'm *not*."

The hostess took us over to the table where Demi was already waiting with a mimosa in hand, and Seph very gingerly lowered herself to her seat like she'd recently taken a hard smack across the ass.

I rubbed my forehead, debating whether to push the subject with her. Ultimately, I let it go. She was horrified at my suggestion there was something more with Ford, so I was guessing whatever their altercation was, it wasn't sexual. I *hoped* it wasn't sexual. It'd be such a shame to have to kill Rex's oldest son.

"Persephone, sweetheart," Demi greeted my sister with a bemused smile. "You look lovely. I hope Rex is being fair with you under his roof?"

Seph gave a tight nod. "Yep. We're cool."

Demi narrowed her eyes. "Hmm, well, you let me know if he's not. I'll pop by and have a little chat."

This made Seph crack a wide grin. "You're the best, Aunt Demi."

A waitress came over with mimosas for Seph and me, and Demi gave me a small shrug. "Figured you'd want one."

"You figured correctly," I agreed, taking a sip of my drink. "Only *one*," I warned Seph as she raised her own to her lips.

Demi smirked and changed the subject, asking Seph about what Rex had her doing around the garage. Apparently now that she'd graduated from high school and had very little in the way of career goals, Rex had started teaching her how to work on cars.

"I don't know why I thought he just had you doing paperwork and making coffee," I commented after Seph finished gushing over how she could now change a tire on her own without needing the boys to lift it into place for her.

My little sister cocked a brow at me in a gesture so familiar I might as well have been looking in a mirror. "That's awfully sexist of you, Dare. You of all people know women are capable of anything they set their minds to."

My jaw dropped, and Demi coughed to hide a laugh.

"Oh my god, brat," I exclaimed. "I didn't mean that's all you *could* do. I just didn't think Rex was an equal-opportunity kind of guy."

Grinning, Demi excused herself to use the restroom, and Seph turned to me with a thoughtful expression on her pretty face.

"Actually, there's something I've been wanting to talk to you about." She looked down, fiddling with her napkin. "Or, okay, it's a two-part thing. Firstly..." She drew a deep breath, her shoulder rising as she summoned up a bit of internal courage. "Firstly, I owe you an apology."

That...was unexpected.

"Uh, no, we're good," I murmured, deeply uncomfortable.

Seph shook her head, determined. "No, I really do. I never knew why you were so overprotective, why you threatened any guy who looked at me, or like...any of it. I didn't *know*...but I kinda knew, you know? Like...I wasn't totally oblivious. I knew there had to be a reason for it all, and I was really mad that you never talked to me or explained or...whatever. So I kept pushing you like I wanted you to snap and tell me, but you never did. And then I just..." She gave a sigh that sagged her whole body. "I let it fester, and I started resenting you. So I was a total bitch. I made things harder than they needed to be, and I convinced myself that you deserved it all. That *you* were somehow the villain in my story."

She gave a small, self-deprecating laugh and drained the last of her mimosa.

"I think it's safe to say I now know better. But I'm *sorry*. Like, I can't actually tell you how sorry I am, Dare. I saw how you were with Chase. I saw how depressed you were and how close you were to just…ending it. And I think now about how many times I threw Chase in your face during arguments. Or Dad." Her voice broke over that, and tears welled in her eyes.

I was at a total loss for words.

Seph didn't let the tears fall, though, dashing them away with a swipe of her thumb. "I was a total bitch, Dare. There's no making up for that. I'm glad Zed told me." She chewed the edge of her lip, the silence between us stretching as I still failed to find the right words to respond.

"He told me," she continued softly. "He said that the only reason you're still here, still fighting, was for me. So, I guess I'm kind of glad that Daddy tried to sell me to some creepy kiddy-fiddler. Because it gave you something to fight for."

Well. Shit. She wasn't wrong about that. I'd been in a *bad* place back then, a thousand times lower than after this recent abduction. If I hadn't overheard that conversation about Seph, would I have ever fought back? Would I have found the strength to simply fight for *me*?

I didn't know. I'd never know.

"I should apologize to you too," I replied, my voice rough with emotion. "I sheltered you so hard it ended up biting us all in the ass. Maybe if I'd prepared you better, trained you to protect yourself and raised you aware of the world we live in…maybe *Pablo* never would have gotten his paws on you." I sneered his name, and Seph chuckled.

"It was Paulo," she corrected me. "But it all worked out." Her eyes sparkled, and her whole mood lifted. "Dare, you should have *seen* Cass when he busted in there to save me. He was like something out of a movie."

I grinned. "I can imagine." Cass was pretty impressive; I wouldn't argue with that fact.

Seph bit the edge of her lip, then wrinkled her nose. "Could I maybe ask some questions? About…everything that happened back then?"

It made sense she wanted to know more about five years ago when I'd snapped and painted the streets of our hometown in blood. Or maybe about the *why* of it all.

Clearing my throat, I answered her as honestly as I could. "Yes, but could it wait a while? Things that happened... It's all a bit fresh for me right now, Seph. I'm doing my best to get through, to act *normal*, but I just don't think I can stomach those memories right now. Is that okay?"

Her eyes widened, and she nodded quickly. "Yes, of course. Fuck, I'm sorry, I should have thought. Shit, Dare, that was super selfish of me. You just seem so..."

I gave a short laugh. "Yeah. I know." I seemed so *fine* despite having recently suffered through some of my worst nightmares. And then some. But that was the thing about appearances—you never really knew what was going on beneath the surface.

Demi returned to us then, and Seph smoothly shifted the conversation back to more superficial topics, like lusting over a pair of shoes she'd seen while shopping last week. Eventually, though, the conversation came around to my business and the delayed opening of Timber.

"Actually, I've been meaning to ask you," I said to my aunt, "how *did* you manage to wipe the FBI records? That was a step up, even for your secret team of hackers."

Demi gave me a secretive smile while indicating to the waitress for two more mimosas and a water for Seph. "Ah, yes," she agreed. "Hence the delay in getting it all sorted out." She paused, grimacing. "I asked for help."

It took me a second to grasp what she meant, then I blew out a long breath and rubbed the bridge of my nose. "The Guild."

She nodded. "They were the only ones I could think of that had the capability. I heard a rumor years ago that one of their former mercenaries has risen quite high in the FBI ranks and built them little back doors into all the systems as payment for his resignation from the Guild. I figured it was worth asking, and then the next day, it was done."

I cringed. "What did it cost?"

Demi gave a shrug. "Nothing."

My eyes narrowed instantly. "The Guild doesn't do favors. It had to cost something."

She shook her head. "The merc I spoke to said it was a freebie."

Suspicion filled me up, and I groaned. "They're so fucking slippery, it's like making a deal with the devil." Then something occurred to me. "Who was it? That you spoke to."

"Same merc that was here a couple of years ago when Madison Kate had that stalker business going on. Leon."

I raked my fingers through my hair, trying to work out what vested interest Leon had in Shadow Grove or in *me*. Why would he do anything for free? And was that with the Guild's blessing, or had he gone rogue? Ugh, more trouble I didn't need.

"All right," I murmured. "I'll keep my ear to the ground. I'm sure he'll come for payment sooner or later."

Demi nodded. "Well, whatever it is, I'll pay it."

I seriously doubted the Guild wanted money. Not this time.

We finished our breakfast with Demi telling us about a new property she and Stacey had purchased in Italy. It was a renovation project in the gorgeous seaside town of Monterosso al Mare, and Stacey had stayed behind to work with their architect on plans. Also, I suspected, Demi wanted to keep her as far from Shadow Grove as possible right now.

After we said goodbye to her, Seph and I climbed back into the borrowed Porsche. As I started the engine, she turned to me with a thoughtful look.

"What's up, brat?" I asked her playfully.

She grinned. "Uh, I was thinking... You've got a lot going on right now—not just with Chase and stuff, but with all the bars and clubs and Copper Wolf. The guys talk about you like you're some

228

kind of eight-armed goddess with how much you're juggling at the same time."

The guys, hmm? Hopefully, that affection in her voice was of the familial variety.

"Yeah," I agreed, "I need a vacation."

Seph snorted. "No shit. But is there anything I can do to help you?"

It was on the tip of my tongue to say no, that I had it all handled. But a quick glance over at her showed me how sincere her offer was. She was extending an olive branch, trying to take the first steps in healing our relationship.

"Actually, yes," I replied, thinking of the perfect task for her. "I don't know if you know about this, but a little over a month ago, Zed and I rescued a group of girls who'd been either kidnapped or sold into slavery by their parents." Seph gasped, pressing a hand to her mouth. "It worked out okay. Most of them have already been returned to their families, but two of them can't go home and are staying with Nadia."

Seph blinked at me with huge eyes, pure concern and compassion practically pouring out of her. She really was *nothing* like me, except in appearance.

"What do you want me to do?"

I turned my eyes back to the road, swallowing my own failings for a moment. "If you have the time, I think Nadia would really appreciate some help. She's trying to get her new café renovated and opened, and she's, you know, not *young* anymore. Zoya only speaks Russian, from what I understand, and seems to be very quiet and well-behaved. But Diana is testing Nadia's patience a bit. Maybe you could stop by and give her a break now and then? Spend some time with the girls?"

Seph nodded without hesitation. "Absolutely. I can do that, for sure. Nadia seems super lovely, too."

I laughed. "She makes epic cakes and pies too, so there's that incentive. Just be aware that the girls have been through a lot. Like, a *lot*."

My sister beamed. "Don't worry about it, Dare. I've got this handled."

I didn't argue, but quietly I wondered if those would be famous last words when it came to Seph and Diana.

CHAPTER 28

My breakfast date with Demi and Seph had run late enough that I took myself straight to my PT appointment without going home first. It wasn't the *safest* thing I could have done, but I was Hades. I sure as shit didn't need a bodyguard shadowing my every move. Even hurt, I could take care of myself just fine.

Misha, my gorgeous trainer, made plenty of jokes about my guardians letting me out of their sight, but I knew it was in good humor. Misha was *not* interested in me, no matter how threatened Zed and Lucas had acted the last time I was there.

When I arrived home, half-dead on my feet, I found the house full of mouthwatering smells. The kitchen was vacant, though, so I wandered through the house until I found Zed and Lucas sparring in the gym.

They were both stripped to their shorts, sweating and jeering insults at each other while trading blows, and the whole thing was...*unbelievably* sexy.

"Get your guard up, Lucas," I barked after Zed's right hook clipped his cheek.

Lucas did as he was told, but Zed hesitated a moment to look over at me, giving Lucas an opening.

Smack. Right in the gut.

"Oof," Zed wheezed, doubling over. "Little shit."

Grinning, Lucas bounced out of reach and tore his gloves off as he approached me. "Hey, you." He swept me up in a sweaty embrace, kissing me long and hard, still breathless from his fight with Zed.

"You're in trouble, Dare," Zed called out to me, tugging his own gloves off and swiping a towel across his face. "How was PT?"

I smiled back at him, as innocent as an angel. "It was good, thanks. Why am I in trouble?"

Zed glared, and Lucas chuckled, shaking his head.

"Oh, relax," I told them. "I was armed, and Misha was a perfect gentleman. A better question is what's that incredible smell in the kitchen? I haven't eaten since breakfast with Seph and Demi."

I was no fool; I knew how proud Zed was of his culinary skills. It was the easiest way to deflect when he was in a mood: compliment his cooking.

"Zed's making lemongrass chicken with saffron rice," Lucas informed me as he released his hold on my waist.

Zed checked his watch and nodded to himself. "It should be ready in ten minutes. I'm going to take a quick shower, then plate up. Can you call Grumpy Dickhead and see if he's home soon?" Zed scooped an arm around my waist as he passed, pressing a soft kiss against my lips. "I missed you today. Will you sleep with me tonight?"

I grinned back at him. "Actually, I have a better idea. I'll explain over dinner."

His brows rose in curiosity, but he kissed me again and left the gym quickly to shower.

Lucas looped a towel over his neck and gave me a long look. "What's the idea, babe?"

I shook my head. "I said *over dinner*, Gumdrop. I actually have something *else* to discuss with you while we're alone."

His brows hitched, and he sauntered back over to me. The tattoo on his chest had healed beautifully, and I couldn't stop myself from reaching out to trace the lines of his scar hidden beneath the ink. His skin pebbled under my touch, and his eyelids drooped to half-mast. Bedroom eyes if I'd ever seen them.

"Cass mentioned that his positive reinforcement was your idea," I murmured, holding back a wince as I wound both my arms around his neck and pulled him closer. "So I wanted to thank you."

I peered up into his eyes, and he brushed his knuckles over my cheek softly.

"This morning I figured it'd worked," he confessed with a small grin, "when I woke up to the intoxicating sound of you moaning in the shower beside my bedroom."

A small laugh escaped me, and I leaned up to kiss him. "Well, next time...come and join us."

Lucas's brows rose, but instead of questioning me, he banded his arms around my waist and crashed his lips into mine. His kiss was hot and hard, demanding and full of pent-up longing. His arms tightened, lifting me up off the ground, and he walked us until my back pressed against the wall.

"Next time, huh?" he repeated in a husky whisper as his lips found my neck. "What are you doing right now?"

My response was to roll my hips against his rock-hard length crushing against my core. It no longer filled me with dread and sticky, black flashbacks. Nothing about Lucas could ever terrify me like that. Not a single shred of my body was scared of him hurting me.

"Lucas," I sighed, squirming in his grip until my feet hit the ground. "Let me show you just how much I appreciate your idea."

His eyes sparked with interest. Then as I switched our positions, turning him to lean against the wall, understanding seemed to dawn.

"Hayden..." He groaned as I sank to my knees and kissed his tight abs. "Are you sure you're okay with this? Because I could—"

My response was to tug his shorts down and palm his erection tightly. His words cut off with a hiss, and his fingers threaded into my hair ever so gently.

I knew he would happily swap places and go down on me instead, but *this* was what I wanted. I ran my tongue around his fleshy tip, tasting the salt of sweat and dick. Sure, post-workout blow jobs weren't the most floral-scented things, but Lucas wasn't a dirty human. He'd probably showered right before sparring with Zed, and really, when licking someone's genitals, could we be squeamish about sweat?

"Oh *fuck*," he groaned as I closed my lips around his crown, sucking him lightly as my hand explored his length. *This* I was okay with. This was something Chase had never tainted, probably out of his own sense of self-preservation.

I tightened my grip, stroking my hand down Lucas's huge dick as my jaw stretched to take him deeper. Goddamn, he was packing a *lot*. My cheeks hollowed as I sucked him, swallowing past my gag reflex, and I let out a small moan.

Lucas's fingers tightened in my hair, holding my head firmer as I bobbed up and down his cock. Groans and muttered encouragement fell from his lips, spurring me on and making me work harder. My pussy was hot with arousal, and my thighs clenched tight as I sucked Lucas closer to climax.

Unable to help myself, I squirmed, desperate to feel my own release as well. Lucas, sharp as ever, saw the motion and gave a low groan.

"Touch yourself, babe," he encouraged. "Make yourself come too."

I sure as shit didn't need to be told twice. Switching hands on his shaft, I flicked open the button of my pants and slipped my hand inside. My fingers found my swollen clit with ease, and I rubbed it eagerly.

Lucas gripped my hair tighter, bucking his hips to fill my

throat as he locked eyes with me. "I fucking love you so hard, Hayden," he groaned as I sucked him deeper and almost choked on his massive girth.

My fingers flicked my clit as Lucas's hips jerked and his breathing spiked.

"Shit, babe," he gasped, "I'm gonna come."

I gripped him tighter, sucked him harder. When his cock pulsed and thickened against my tongue, I rubbed my clit in just the right way to spark my own orgasm. I gasped sharply at the waves of pleasure tightening my cunt, almost drowning as Lucas came in my throat.

He released my head and slid free of my mouth with full-body shudders and his chest heaving, then gazed down at me with total adoration.

"Babe," he panted, tugging me up to my feet and seizing the hand that had been inside my pants. Slowly and deliberately, holding my gaze the whole time, he brought my hand to his mouth and sucked my fingers clean. A heady shiver of arousal coursed through me from head to toe, and I almost came again right then and there. "You blow my damn mind."

I moaned just a little as my pussy still throbbed with aftershocks. "You're pretty incredible yourself, Lucas."

He flashed me that panty-melting grin of his and kissed me long and hard. We'd barely put our clothes to rights when Zed yelled out that dinner was ready, and we both started laughing with an edge of post-orgasm delirium.

The look Zed gave us when we appeared in the kitchen said he knew full well what we'd been up to. Probably those damn security cameras again. Or just a good guess from how flushed and grinning we both were.

"Gumdrop, Jesus. Go and change. I don't want your sweaty ass tainting the food." Zed rolled his eyes and snapped a tea towel at Lucas's backside.

Lucas smirked, kissed me, then flipped Zed off as he jogged out of the kitchen to change.

Zed gave me a long look, and I smiled innocently.

"Uh-huh," he muttered, sarcastic as hell. "Name one time that angelic face has ever worked for you, Dare. One time."

Admitting defeat, I rolled my eyes and headed over to where he was plating our dinner. "Zed, this smells *divine*."

"Cute. I know your tricks, you know that?" He leaned in close and kissed my neck softly. "But I'll allow it."

"Honey, I'm home," a deadpan voice interrupted our intimate little moment. I glanced over to find Cass slouching his way into the kitchen with a sly smirk. "Smells tasty, Zeddy Bear."

In a deliberately antagonistic move, Cass booped Zed's nose, then swooped me up in his arms and carried me around the counter.

"Dick," Zed muttered, glaring as Cass placed me gently down on the edge of the counter and cupped my face with his tattooed hands.

Cass ignored him, though, kissing my lips softly. "How was your day, Red?"

"It was actually really good. Seph and I had a really nice breakfast with Demi, then PT was better than expected—"

"Her trainer is a flirt," Zed interjected with a growl.

Cass arched a brow at me, and I rolled my eyes. Then, just to punish Zed for being an alpha-male asshole, I cupped my hands around Cass's ear and whispered the reason why Misha was most definitely not a threat.

In response, he snickered at Zed's expense and kissed my neck.

"How's Nadia's looking?" I asked, noticing the moss-green paint smears on his arms. "Seph is going to put in some hours to help with Diana."

His brows shot up. "Fuck. Good luck to her. That kid is a damn firecracker. Repeats every goddamn bad word out of my mouth and isn't afraid to pass blame when Nadia hears her."

236

Lucas came jogging back into the kitchen looking fresh from the shower as Zed laid out plates on the table, and for a few minutes I just soaked in the domestic bliss of our unlikely foursome.

Then I cleared my throat and dropped the plan I had for the rest of the night.

"So, I want to go kill someone tonight," I announced.

All conversation stopped.

"Just...someone?" Zed was the first to recover. "Like, anyone? Or someone specific?"

I glared at him. "Funny. Yes, someone specific. Now is probably a good time to tell you I have a little revenge plot I'd like to work out before our *main* plan for Chase falls into place. When I was escaping his house, I listened in on a conference call. There were six people named on the call. I want them all dead, one by one, and I want him to know it's me doing it."

The three of them blinked at me, not speaking. So I elaborated.

"Starting tonight with a certain Brad Walshman, CEO of Chasing Trucking."

For another moment, they all just stared. Then Zed gave a wicked, deadly grin. "All right, let's do it."

CHAPTER 29

There was no way I would be in fit condition to go killing anyone without *some* sleep, so after we finished dinner I took my sleepy butt upstairs and crashed out in Zed's bed for a nap. He was given stern instructions to wake me at midnight, though.

I'd found Brad Walshman's home address and wanted to strike when he was least prepared. In the dead of the night.

Zed gently woke me up right on time, and the two of us quietly dressed and headed down to his Ferrari waiting in front of the house.

"How'd you win that argument?" I asked as we drove into the night. When I'd gone to bed, the three of them had been heatedly debating who would come with me to kill Brad. I'd put my foot down and said it wasn't a group activity. Either they agreed on *one* of them coming along for the ride, or I'd go alone.

Zed smirked. "Easy. I'm your *second*. It's just a simple matter of hierarchy, no one can dispute that."

I wrinkled my nose. "Really? That easy?"

He huffed a chuckle. "Nah, we had to do about sixteen rounds of rock, paper, scissors. Handled it like men, beautiful."

I wasn't sure if he was joking or not. It wouldn't be the first time they'd settled something with stupid rock, paper, scissors. Not that it mattered; so long as they weren't bickering, I'd take it.

"So," he said, changing the subject, "tell me more about this Brad Walshman." They'd asked shockingly few questions when I'd announced I wanted to kill a man they knew nothing about. I loved that.

I propped my head up on my hand, my elbow on the door, and yawned. I'd almost punched Zed when he woke me up, before remembering I'd asked him to do it.

"Brad Walshman, business major from UC Berkeley. Dabbled in multiple start-ups, evaded several embezzlement charges, ripped off a lot of unsuspecting people, now the CEO of Chasing Trucking." I gave a low grunt of disgust. "Can't believe I didn't spot that one sooner. Chase and Darling. Chasing."

Zed glowered at the road like it personally offended him. "Remind me again how much we're gonna make that sick fuck hurt?"

I grinned, focusing on our eventual plan for Chase rather than on the depraved things he'd done to me. "Anyway, from what I heard, Chasing Trucking was how those little girls were transported across the country and stashed in the Anarchy cellar. And if they've done it once, I'm willing to bet they've done it before. We're going to cut the head off the transport sector of Chase's human trafficking."

Zed flashed me a feral grin. "Literally?"

I smiled back. "Absolutely."

It was a decent hour and a half drive to get to Brad Walshman's home, so Zed turned the stereo on and told me to keep sleeping if I was still tired. I told him I was fine, but the next thing I knew, we were pulling into a park on the side of a fancy, tree-lined suburban street.

Every house was a miniature mansion with an immaculate lawn and zero security. Brad Walshman was a fucking idiot.

Silently, Zed and I strapped on our weapons—one could never be over-armed when on an assassination mission—then closed up the car and made our way over to the dark house, circling around the back and checking for cameras.

There weren't any, but just in case, Zed shot the motion-activated floodlight before it could flick on. With the silencer on his gun, it was barely more than the sound of a chipmunk sneezing, then glass breaking.

We paused for another moment, but no lights turned on inside the house, so we continued to the back door. I probably would have just broken the door to get in, but Zed had infinitely more finesse. He knelt and carefully picked the lock, letting the door swing open soundlessly. Why didn't people have dead bolts in their safe little havens?

"Show-off," I mumbled, following him inside. The alarm panel on the wall was flashing, the warning signal that it was about to scream, but I used my knife to flick open the panel and plugged our little override chip straight into it. It was basic as hell and only worked on cheap, domestic alarm units, but like I said...Brad Walshman was a fucking idiot.

The very thin file of information on Brad that Dallas had emailed me earlier in the day told me he lived alone. Wife and kids had left him years ago, and he'd made no attempt to maintain contact with them. He didn't even have any pets.

It made our task all that much easier as we confidently moved through his silent house, heading upstairs to the master suite.

Zed and I stepped into Brad's bedroom and found him spread out across the massive bed, flat on his back like a naked, snoring starfish. We locked eyes, grinning, and I pulled a roll of duct tape from the deep pocket of my coat.

When it came to the logistics of what we needed to do, I was glad Zed had come along. I didn't want to just put a bullet through a sleeping man's head. There was no satisfaction in that.

So I was more than happy to use Zed's muscle power to make things just a touch more dramatic—to give douchebag, child-sex-trafficker *Brad* the end he deserved and to make sure Chase got a front-row seat.

Working swiftly in unison, we wound the duct tape around Brad's ankles and wrists, binding him before he even woke up. When he did wake, jerking and thrashing in terror, we slapped a thick piece of tape across his mouth. No sense in waking the neighbors.

"Hello, Brad." I smiled down at him. Zed had jerked him off the bed and shoved him to his knees on the floor. "I hear you've built yourself quite the little business in trucking recently."

His eyes widened, pleading, but it was *far* too late for excuses. The second he'd dirtied his hands with those little girls, he'd signed his own death certificate.

"Let's get a witness, shall we?" I suggested, letting a cold, cruel smile touch my lips. Spinning around, I headed out of the bedroom, knowing Zed would drag Brad along with him as he followed. The office was downstairs, and I took a sick sense of satisfaction listening to the thump, thump of his body bumping down each step and the pained moans from behind his taped mouth.

In Brad's home office, I opened his laptop and pressed Brad's thumb to the fingerprint sensor to unlock it. Stupid system, really.

The screen unlocked immediately, and it took me no time at all to find Chase's contact—saved under his real name, no less—stored in previous calls. Before I connected the call, I pulled a little slip of paper out of my pocket and followed the instructions Dallas had typed out. The code would prevent the call from being recorded and ensure all traces would be erased when the call disconnected.

Zed pushed Brad into the chair as I clicked the button to call Chase, and we both ignored Brad's panicked mumbles and headshakes.

It took several attempts before Chase finally answered the call.

"This better be a fucking emergency," he snarled, the camera jostling as he grunted. In the background, the distinctive sound of bodies slapping together turned my stomach, and I swallowed bile when I realized he'd answered the call midfuck. "Oh. I see..." Chase's tone swiftly shifted as he focused on the video screen, which only showed Brad's terrified, duct-taped face and Zed's gloved hand around his neck.

"Is that you, Darling?" Chase purred, his breathing ragged as he continued fucking whatever poor woman had the misfortune of being beneath him. "This is an unexpected treat. What do you want, my sweet? A little revenge?" He leered at the camera, then turned his phone around to show me the woman beneath him. She was totally unconscious, if not dead. Her bright red hair spilled across the pillow, partially obscuring her bruised and swollen face.

"Remind you of better times, huh?" He started laughing like a maniac, his grunts and breathing coming harsher.

Waves of revulsion ran through me so hard my whole body shook, but it was *just* that. I wasn't terrified; I wasn't spiraling. I was just sick to my stomach.

Not interested in staying for the money shot, I decided to speed things up. Pulling a long dagger from the sheath on my thigh, I grabbed Brad's head by his greasy hair, jerking it back as Zed released him. Both Zed and I were in shadows, the light from the laptop only showing Brad, but Chase knew it was us. Just like I wanted him to.

Steeling myself, I brought the sharp edge to Brad's throat and sliced deeply. Blood sprayed all over the laptop, drenching the screen and camera, effectively cutting us off. My blade slid free on the opposite side of his neck, leaving his head barely clinging on. Without a word, Zed took the knife from me and finished the job, severing Brad's spinal cord and dumping his head on the desk.

The rich, hot, meaty smell of blood filled the air, turning my stomach, but I made sure to press the button on Brad's laptop to end the video call. It was the only way to be sure Dallas's code would wipe it properly.

For a moment, Zed and I just stared at each other across the decapitated corpse of Brad Walshman. We were both covered in blood, our black gloves and clothing sticky and glistening in the near darkness, yet I had the sudden urge to pounce on Zed and kiss the stuffing out of him.

"Come on," he murmured. "Let's get out of here and call the cleanup crew."

He took my hand and linked our gloved fingers as we left Brad Walshman's house and made our way back to the Ferrari. Before getting in, we stripped down to our underwear right there on the side of the street and tossed our bloody clothes into a waterproof bag in the trunk.

When I slid into my seat in just my bra and panties, I was grinning like a maniac.

"You're something fucking else, Dare." Chuckling, Zed buckled his seat belt and turned on the car. "That was crazy satisfying."

"You're telling me," I agreed, squirming slightly in my seat. Was I seriously turned on right now? My mind kept replaying the cold, vicious look on Zed's face as he'd hacked through Brad's spinal cord, and, yep, my cunt was hot and throbbing.

To distract myself, I pulled out my phone and called our cleanup crew. My instructions were clear: Wipe away any trace of Zed or me but leave the body and head. Chase could clean that mess up himself, and he would have to in order to protect his sick little trafficking line. I needed to tick off the other five names quickly, or he'd just replace Brad and continue on as normal.

"I think I'm too wired to go straight home," I confessed after ending my call to Robynne. "Can we go somewhere?"

Zed cast a long look at me from the corner of his eye, his lips curling in a smile. "I'd hoped you might say that. I have the perfect thing."

243

I quirked a brow. "Does it require clothes?" I indicated our state of undress. We really should have brought a spare change of clothes, but it'd been a while since we'd done something like this. We were rusty.

Zed grinned wider. "Nope, it does not. If you're okay hanging out in your underwear a while longer?"

My core flushed with heat again. "Fine by me," I murmured, turning my face to look out my window. It was either that or climb into Zed's lap while he drove. And that, albeit hot, sounded like an accident waiting to happen.

CHAPTER 30

Zed drove us back toward Shadow Grove, then took the mountain road up to the lookout we'd come to once before. It was still about an hour before dawn, and the stars were breathtaking as they twinkled over the sleeping city.

From the depths of his trunk—past our weapons and bloody clothes—Zed pulled out a stack of blankets and a picnic basket, then set us up in an area on the grass. When he was done, he patted the spot beside him, and I couldn't wipe the smile from my face as I sat down.

"You planned this in advance?" I asked with an edge of disbelief.

He gave a shrug. "Figured it was a possibility. It's been ages since we've done this, hasn't it?"

From the picnic basket he pulled out a box of homemade scones and some little jars containing vanilla whipped cream and raspberry jam. And a bottle of champagne. The *best* kind of breakfast.

"You're spoiling me, Zayden De Rosa," I murmured, watching him as he prepared the scones with toppings.

He handed me a plate, then popped the cork on the champagne. "You deserve to be spoiled, Dare." He draped a blanket over my shoulders as I took a huge bite of scone loaded with jam and cream.

I was incapable of response, my mouth full, so I just got comfy on the blanket and stared up at the sky. It was a magical time of day when the stars were still so damn bright but the sky no longer the deep ink of night.

We finished the scones in no time, then lay back on the blanket drinking champagne straight from the bottle as the sun started peeking over the horizon.

"I guess we should get back," Zed murmured reluctantly when we ran out of wine. "As much as I'd love to take advantage of the situation"—his fingers trailed down my bare skin, making me shiver—"I think that might be a bit of an asshole move on my part."

I bit my lip, *wanting* to disagree. But he knew, like I did, that I wasn't ready to sleep with him again. Not after the scars Chase had carved across my mind while masquerading as Zed.

So I swallowed hard, sat up, and tugged the blanket tighter around my shoulders. "I'm working on it," I said quietly.

He huffed a short laugh. "I know. I never thought I'd find myself *thanking* another man for making my girl come, but...there it is. I know you asked Lucas and Cass to push you, but I want you to know I won't. I'll wait, as long as it takes, until you're ready."

Reaching out, I cupped his cheek in my hand and pressed a soft kiss to his mouth. "I love you, Zed," I whispered against his lips. "You're my best friend. My fucking soulmate. No one can take that away from us, okay? We will get through this." I kissed him again, deeper, parting my lips and gasping as he kissed me back with barely restrained need.

At the point our kisses might have led further, Zed eased away with a grimace. "We should go," he muttered.

I nodded, hating myself a little, but helped pack up our picnic.

We got back to Zed's house just as Cass was leaving, and he gave us both a long look.

"Calm down," Zed muttered, grabbing the bag of blood-soaked clothes from his car. "I just didn't want blood all through the Ferrari."

Cass snorted. "Convenient. I'll have to use that excuse next time." He shot me a wink, and I pictured the two of us riding his motorbike in just underwear. It was a hot image, no lie.

I leaned in to his body when he looped his arms around my waist, kissing my hair as he rumbled a *good morning.*

"Where are you going so early?" I asked, tipping my head back to look up at him. In my bare feet, he was a long way up.

"Nadia's," he told me, tucking a stray lock of my hair behind my ear. "She's getting the furniture delivered this morning and wants me to move it around six hundred times before she's happy with the placement."

Using my ponytail, he tugged my head back further, then kissed me thoroughly enough that my whole body flushed with heat.

"Mmm," he rumbled, "you taste like champagne."

Zed muttered something about doing laundry and exited the garage, leaving Cass and me alone. I watched him go, troubled but at a loss for how to fix it. How to fix *myself.* But before I could voice those worries to Cass, he scooped me up with a strong grip and pinned me to the side of the Ferrari.

His mouth crashed back down on mine, kissing me even harder now that we were alone. My legs wound around his waist on instinct, and the hard bulge of his jeans ground against me in the most delicious way.

"How did you do it?" he asked in a husky whisper, his lips at my ear. "Did you shoot him between the eyes?"

Oh fuck. My hips jerked, rolling against him as a gasp slipped from my lips.

"No," I replied, breathless as he rocked against me, deliberately playing against my already sharp arousal. "No, I slit his throat while Chase watched on video call."

Cass gave a low groan, his teeth teasing at my throat as his fingers gripped my ass tighter. "Fuck, that's hot." He rocked his hips

247

again, the zipper of his fly rubbing right against my clit and making me moan. "I wish I could have seen you do it."

Shit, Cass knew exactly how to turn on the psychopath living under my skin. Another roll of his hips, another sucking kiss at my throat, and I exploded. I came hard with gasping moans, shaking against the side of Zed's car as Cass held me up.

He released me a moment later, letting my trembling legs drop back to the cold concrete floor as he kissed me stupid.

"Have a good day today, Angel," he rumbled, then let me go with a longing look as he sauntered over to his motorbike.

I didn't try to pretend I wasn't watching as he rearranged his dick before climbing on, and the look he gave me before tugging on his helmet was *pure* sex. Fuck, Cass was hot.

Making my way back into the house with weak legs, I decided to take a quick shower before changing into my sleep shirt. I needed a nap, and I needed to do it in Zed's bed...*with* Zed. But I didn't need to go rubbing his face in the smell of my recent orgasm.

After a quick wash, I slid into Zed's clean sheets a moment after he'd finished making the bed, and he arched a brow at me in question.

"What?" I muttered, glaring back at him. "Shut the blinds and come sleep. It was a long night."

He hesitated only a second, then did as I'd told him. He wrapped me in his arms, tucking my face into his chest, and I could feel the tension draining out of him. I made myself a promise right then and there to try harder with him. To push through my damage just like I had with the shower.

Zed deserved that much from me. To at least *try*.

Our morning nap turned into a full-day doze in bed. We got up only to have a midafternoon dinner, then retire back to bed for a lazy evening of movies and popcorn. Lucas joined us when he got back from visiting his mom, tucking into Zed's bed on the other side of me, and gave us all kinds of fun movie trivia as we watched.

Cass stopped by briefly when he got home but screwed up his nose at the teen musical movie we were watching, claiming he'd rather wax his own balls than watch that shit with us.

Fair call.

A couple of days later, Lucas asked if I would go with him to visit his mom, and I eagerly accepted. I was dying to ask her about Brant Wilson and what she knew about his involvement with the Guild or the FBI or the Lockhart family. There were *so* many questions, and I had a feeling a lot of them would go to the grave unanswered.

"You know how Big Sal has been pretty much exclusively minding my mom?" Lucas asked as he drove us over in the Mustang. He had that ball cap on backward again, with the edges of his hair curling out from under the rim, and was generally looking delicious.

"Yeah," I agreed. "You reckon he has a soft spot for Sandra?"

Lucas smirked. "Oh, without question, yes. But that's beside the point. He pulled me aside a couple of days ago and expressed some concern about my mom's medication."

I frowned. "What kind of concern?"

Lucas shrugged. "That's what I wanted to know. He said he had a relative with MS who takes the same medication as my mom and the pills look totally different."

I pursed my lips, thinking. "That doesn't really mean anything, it could be a different brand or manufacturer." I was no pharmacist, so I had no idea if that was really the case.

Lucas nodded. "Yeah, I wasn't sure what to do with that, but given my mom's other unexplained symptoms—the memory loss and slips into dementia? I dunno. I asked her nurse, Claudette, what she thought, but she wasn't very helpful, just pointed out that if there was something wrong with the drugs, then we should speak to Mom's doctor."

"And her doctor?"

He gave me a long look. "On vacation in Bermuda."

"Of course he is." I ruffled my fingers through my hair. "What do you want to do?"

Lucas gave a sheepish smile. "I told Big Sal to pocket a couple of the pills for testing. At best, they're exactly what they're meant to be. But..."

I nodded. "But they might not be. Then the question is who is responsible? Her doctor, the pharmacist, her nurse?" It was a rhetorical question.

"Or..." Lucas murmured after a long pause, "the Guild?"

My brows rose. "Possible. Definitely possible."

Lucas pulled into his mom's driveway, and we headed inside the house, only to pause at the sound of raised voices. It sounded like Sandra yelling at someone, then the low rumble of a man replying, calmer.

"Mom?" Lucas called out, heading for her bedroom. He pushed open the ajar door and glared at Big Sal, who stood stoically over Sandra's wheelchair with his thick arms folded. "What's going on in here?"

I arched a brow at Big Sal, and he winced when he saw me behind Lucas.

"Boss," he rumbled, "didn't know you were coming by today."

"Mom, what's going on?" Lucas demanded, giving Big Sal a shove to move him out of the way, then he crouched in front of his mother. "What happened?"

"He took my pills!" she wailed. "He took them, and he flushed them down the toilet! I *need them!*" She was almost hysterical, tears streaming down her puffy face like they'd been arguing for a while.

250

Lucas looked over at me with a flash of panic in his face like he didn't know what the hell to do. I gave him a small smile and indicated for Big Sal to leave the room.

"Lucas, why don't you get Sandra back into bed, and I'll fetch her a glass of water. Then Sal can explain things to me out in the kitchen." I tried to keep my tone soft and nonthreatening, but Sandra's head snapped up toward me, her eyes narrowed.

Deciding that I didn't need to exacerbate a tense situation, I quickly ducked out of the room and pulled the door shut.

Big Sal just threw his hands up in frustration, stalked back to the kitchen, and started stomping around, muttering to himself as he boiled the water for tea. Apparently, Sandra enjoyed chamomile tea in the afternoons.

Stunned, I just watched him with my hands propped on my hips until he finally stopped slamming cupboards and heaved a long sigh.

"You done?" I asked in a cool tone.

He flinched like I'd slapped him and nodded. "Yes, sir."

I pursed my lips. "Good. Now, can you explain what we just walked in on? Where is Claudette?"

"She went to get groceries," he muttered. "Did Lucas fill you in on my suspicion about one of Sandra's drugs?"

I nodded. "I take it you got the results?"

"Just now," he confirmed. "It's *not* what it's supposed to be. According to the lab, those drugs react really badly with her other meds and could be what's causing the worsening MS symptoms. So I grabbed them and got rid of them, then she just...*lost* it. Wouldn't fucking listen to reason."

I frowned. "What is it, then?"

Big Sal gave a frustrated gesture. "Can't remember the fucking name, it was some long word with not enough vowels. But I know what it does. It damages the bit of the brain that stores memories and shit."

Somehow, that information didn't shock me in the least. Whatever Sandra's history was with Brant, with the Guild, with her brother…someone wanted her to forget it. Badly.

"Here's the insanity, though." Big Sal grunted. "She said she knew."

Now *that* was unexpected.

CHAPTER 31

It took a couple of days before Sandra became coherent enough to provide any answers. Initially she'd needed to be sedated, she was in such a state over Big Sal flushing her medication. But several days later, her nurse contacted Lucas to let him know she was doing better and seemed willing to talk.

I'd been on my way to Anarchy for a meeting with Zed and Alexi when he called, and I immediately changed direction to head over there. Alexi could wait, but who knew when Sandra might be lucid again.

Lucas was waiting out on the porch when I arrived and greeted me with a tight hug.

"How is she?" I asked, peering up into his tired eyes. He hadn't been sleeping much, worried about his mom and stressed with his course load for EMT training.

A soft smile touched his lips. "She's good, actually, the best I've seen her in… I don't even know. Since we got back to Shadow Grove, I guess."

My brows rose because if that wasn't suspicious as hell, I didn't know what was.

"I feel like an asshole asking this of you, Hayden," he said quietly, "but do you mind…*not* coming inside? She's doing so good, but when I told her you were on your way, she got all twitchy and shit. Suddenly it was all warnings about getting mixed up with the Timber family and…" He let this voice trail off, shaking his head. "A bunch of bullshit, essentially. But I think you must look enough like your mom that it makes her jumpy."

I'd suspected as much. "Totally fine," I assured him with a smile. "I'll wait for you, though. I already told Alexi I'd see him tomorrow, so I've got nowhere to be."

Lucas's shoulders sagged with relief, like he'd thought I might be offended. "Okay. Maybe after we leave here, I can show you something I set up while I was playing Hades that week."

I grinned, curious. "Deal."

He kissed me quickly, then headed back inside the house to speak with his mom without his scary gangster girlfriend looming. I knew he was right; Sandra had reacted oddly to me every time she'd seen me. It was more important that Lucas get the answers he needed.

So, for lack of any better ideas, I headed over to the twin wicker chairs on the far end of the porch and sat down to wait.

A moment later, though, I realized I was sitting directly outside the sitting room and the window was open, allowing me to hear everything said inside the room.

For a while Lucas just talked to his mom about safe subjects— his gymnastics, memories of his childhood moving around the country—and he told her proudly about his EMT training.

"That's so great, Luca," she murmured after he'd told her, in vague but excited terms, about how Doc had let him suture up a real person recently. I smiled, running my thumb over the fresh scar on my wrist.

Lucas's next question was so quiet I didn't make out the words, but Sandra's reply was clear.

"I can't, Luca," she exclaimed, sounding pained. "I can't talk about it. Ever. You don't understand—"

"Of course I don't," he exploded, "because you won't explain it! Jesus, Mom, whatever it is, trust me when I say I can handle it."

"It's not that, Luca. It's...if anyone finds out... I can't... They warned me what would happen, and I won't risk it." She sounded resolute, but if anyone could get her to open up, it was Lucas.

His voice dipped low and quiet as he replied, his tone soothing. For a long moment, there was silence.

"They said they'd take you away," Sandra finally confessed. "They said if I ever told someone what I knew, they'd take you from me."

"That's..." Lucas sounded frustrated, and I didn't blame him. "Mom, are you serious? I'm nineteen, not some little kid who can be taken away."

Sandra mumbled something back, and Lucas let out some quiet curses.

"Mom, that was fifteen years ago. Don't you think things have changed since then? I can take care of myself *just* fine, and I really shouldn't need to point out that my girl is quite literally the scariest thing in the Tri-State area. I'm *not* in danger. But you are if you don't stop mixing these medications. Are you deliberately trying to erase your memory?"

Silence.

Lucas exhaled a curse. "You are, aren't you? Mom...it *can't* be that bad."

"It is," she replied, sounding like she was crying. A stab of guilt hit me for eavesdropping on this private conversation. But it was far from the worst thing I'd ever done, and I'd apologize to Lucas as soon as he came outside.

"Luca, baby, you need to understand. They didn't give me a choice." Her voice broke with a sob. The next few things she said were muffled like she was speaking into his chest while he hugged her. There was no mistaking his shocked response, though.

255

"Wait," he exclaimed, cutting her off. "Like some kind of genetic experiment? Test-tube babies?"

"No!" she cried in return. "No, it wasn't... Luca, this isn't some kind of Star Trek crap. It was just *normal* implantation. I was a surrogate, of sorts. They paid me to carry the babies and then... not ask questions. It happens all the time for couples who can't conceive on their own."

"This isn't a loving same-sex couple, Mom. They're a *mercenary guild*. What the hell did you think they were doing with those babies? Oh my god, is that what I am? Is that why we were always running?"

"No! No, no, no, Luca, *no*. You're different. I loved your father. He didn't even know about the other babies. Only Jack knew." She was sobbing between words, but it was clear enough to understand. My mouth had fallen open in shock, and I ached to run in there and comfort Lucas.

"Uncle Jack," Lucas muttered, bitterness coating his words. "Uncle *Jack* was in the Guild, Mom. Did you know that?"

There was no gasp of shock from Sandra, just another shuddering sob. She must have confirmed it because Lucas cursed again.

His tone hardened like he just wanted answers so he could go. "What do you know about Brant Wilson, Mom?"

Sandra drew a deep, shuddering breath. "Brant was my savior. He was the only *normal* thing in my life, and we were so in love. You're my only child born from love, Luca."

He laughed coldly in response. "Why lie about who my dad was, then? Why tell me it was Nicholas, who was *dead*, when Brant was still out there?"

"Because..." she replied, weak.

"Because Brant was in the Guild," Lucas answered for her. "And you didn't want me tracking him down and getting snatched up by the mercenaries and their fucked-up child soldier program?"

Sandra gasped. "What? No. Brant didn't even know about the

256

Guild. He just…disappeared one day. I didn't want you thinking your daddy didn't love you, so I pretended he was dead."

Oh shit. She really didn't know.

"Mom," Lucas sighed. "I love you, Mom. But are you honestly that gullible? Brant was Guild, then he was FBI. He was *here* in Shadow Grove just six months ago."

Sandra's response was a mess of mumbled words between crying, and Lucas soothed her with empty platitudes. It made no difference now, but I'd put money on it that his uncle Jack had known.

Lucas must have decided he'd gotten enough answers for one day because he shifted the conversation back to her medication. As calmly as he could, he explained to her everything our lab had told us about the mixture of drugs she'd been taking. That they would eventually kill her.

When she protested about the Guild coming for her, Lucas promised that we would keep her safe and that Big Sal had offered to move in and become her permanent bodyguard. *That* was news to me, but I was more than okay with Lucas making those decisions. It was all part of him taking a more active role on Team Hades.

Claudette arrived back from her shopping trip about twenty minutes later, and Lucas said his goodbyes to his mom before stepping back outside to where I was waiting.

I looked up at him from my seat outside the window, and I saw the understanding on his face.

"You heard all of it?" he asked softly, nodding to the window.

I inclined my head, stood up, and wrapped my arms around his waist. "Most of it."

He hugged me back tightly, my face smooshed into his chest. "Let's get out of here," he muttered. "I've got something to show you, anyway."

We'd both driven to his mom's, but Lucas decided to leave the

Mustang there and ride with me in the Porsche, offering directions toward the Shadow Grove industrial area.

"We're heading back to 7th Circle?" I asked as the streets became familiar. The club had been in a converted warehouse on the edge of Shadow Grove where there were no residents to complain about the noise. It'd been perfect for the type of hedonistic club it was, and I was still stinging about its destruction.

"Sort of," he murmured, shooting me a sly smile. I could recognize his compartmentalizing for what it was. His mom's confessions had blown his mind, and he needed to totally focus on something else for a while.

He pointed to a turnoff two streets before we would have arrived at the vacant lot that used to be 7th Circle and directed me to stop at an empty building.

Grinning, he hopped out of the car and waited for me to join him before approaching the front door. It wasn't locked, and Lucas pushed it open confidently, holding it for me to enter.

"Where are we, Lucas?" I peered into the darkness, noting that it was another empty warehouse. This one was different from 7th Circle, though—a bit smaller and made with lots of natural wood. In a way, the raked ceiling reminded me of Timber.

"Well…" He closed the door behind us and found my hand. The dirty windows only let slivers of afternoon sunlight in. He tugged me farther into the room, then shrugged. "Maybe the new 7th Circle?"

My lips parted in shock. It had definite potential, but…

"I'm so confused, Lucas," I confessed. "Give me more information."

Chuckling, he tugged me across the vast space to a wooden bench built into the side. "So, I remembered how your insurance company wouldn't pay out for 7th Circle."

Ugh, because Chase fucking owned them. "I had that decision

258

overturned," I reminded him. "They still need to pay out, and I'll make them do it."

Lucas shrugged. "Yeah, but I started thinking on this before that. It'd be cheaper to start over in a new building than rebuild from rubble." He hesitated, losing a bit of excitement. "Or, shit, maybe I'm wrong. This is definitely not my area of expertise, but I got a call about *this* place while you were missing and mentioned it to Zed. He told me to use my damn brain and ask myself, *What would Dare do?* So..." He waved a hand at the wall above where we stood. On it, someone had spray painted the word *Malebolge*.

I barked a laugh in disbelief at how thoughtful the whole thing was. "Malebolge," I repeated in a soft murmur. "The eighth circle."

Lucas's arms looped around my waist, and he kissed the bend of my neck as I gazed up at the spray paint. "7th Circle was where we met, Hayden. I couldn't just let it die. If you hate it or you don't want—"

I cut him off by twisting my neck and claiming his lips with my own. I spun around in his arms, holding him tighter as I kissed all my overwhelming emotions into him. Then when we were both panting, I pressed my forehead to his and whispered with total sincerity, "It's perfect."

CHAPTER 32

My wild plans for an early bedtime were thwarted before we even pulled into the garage. My phone started ringing on the Porsche's Bluetooth, and I glanced down to see it was Zed calling.

"Hey, you," I answered warmly. "You're not home yet?" We'd just parked, and his Ferrari was nowhere to be seen. Neither was Cass's bike.

"Unfortunately not," he replied, sounding irritated. "I'm at Anarchy, but you might want to get over here."

I exchanged a worried look with Lucas. "What's happened?"

"It's nothing too urgent," Zed gritted out, "but you'll probably want to get here before the fights start for the night."

I checked the time. Lucas and I had spent a while in the warehouse tossing around ideas for how the venue could be laid out. His main excitement had been around the stage and an aerial pole that he wanted to get installed. It was essentially a pole suspended from the ceiling and *not* tethered at the bottom, so it swung free.

"An hour?" I asked, even though I knew perfectly well what time the Anarchy fights started. "We just got home. I'll get changed and be there in forty-five."

"Good," Zed replied. Then shouts broke out in the background, and he ended the call abruptly.

"Uh…maybe we should be quick," Lucas suggested, following me into the house.

I grimaced but agreed. Zed hadn't sounded worried, just annoyed, which probably meant someone planned on fighting that he didn't want in our octagon. And if he needed *me* to handle it…"Fuck's sake," I groaned. "Cass."

"Cass?" Lucas repeated.

Breathing out a string of curses, I tugged my shirt off with a small wince as my shoulder tweaked. A week of PT had done *wonders* for my range of motion, but it'd be months before I was back to normal.

"Yeah. Cass. Anyone else Zed would be able to handle. If he's asking me to come down, there's only one person who could be causing him strife."

Lucas nodded. "Cass, for sure. I'll get changed quickly."

I headed for my own closet and automatically reached for jeans, then changed my mind. If Cass was stirring up shit with Zed, I'd dress for distraction. So I went further into my clothes and pulled out a formfitting black dress that boosted my tits up like something out of *Playboy* and hugged my ass like a lover's hands.

It was a tricky one to do up, being so damn tight, and I had to yell out to Lucas for help. When he came into my room to answer my call, he pulled up short and gaped.

"Oh shit," he chuckled. "Cass is in so much trouble. Please tell me I get to help punish him." His eyes flared hot and his tongue swiped over his lower lip like he was already imagining how he could hike my skirt up and bury his face between my thighs.

I grinned, agreeing to nothing. "Zip me up." I spun around to give him my back.

He took his time with it, his fingers trailing over my bare back

261

and making me shiver with desire before he secured the top of the dress with the little clasp.

Dancing out of his reach, I sent him a warning look and grabbed a pair of high heels from my closet. They were black Louboutins, of course, but had a sexy buckle around the ankle and zipper detail on the back of the thick stiletto.

"You look pretty edible yourself, Lucas Wildeboer," I commented once my shoes were on. I stepped up closer and grabbed the lapels of his suit jacket, pulling him close to kiss me. "But we need to go."

He let out a frustrated sigh but touched a gentle hand to my back as we hurried down to the car. I passed him the keys to the Porsche, letting him drive so I could do my makeup on the way over to Anarchy. It wasn't the easiest way to apply liquid eyeliner, but I'd done it often enough that it was doable.

It took us about twenty minutes to get from Zed's house to Anarchy, so we pulled into the staff parking lot earlier than I'd told Zed to expect us. Alexi was waiting, though, leaning against the fire escape door that would lead directly into the big top—my fight arena.

"Hades, sir," he called out, straightening up when we climbed out of the Porsche. His eyes widened, and he raked them down my outfit before catching himself. "It's so good to see you. I was really worried, and Zed wouldn't even tell me if you were okay. I thought—"

"I'm fine, Alexi," I cut him off with a tight smile. I still didn't trust him. Not like I had before. "As you can see, whatever rumors you heard were grossly exaggerated."

The thick leather strap of my gun holster hid the puckered scar on my shoulder, and a wide bracelet covered the one at my wrist. To the unsuspecting observer, I was totally unharmed.

A big smile of relief spread across Alexi's face, and he opened the fire-exit door for us to enter. The noise of the crowd reached us almost instantly, dulled only by the corridor we were in.

"Where's Zed?" I asked Alexi as he fell into step beside me.

It didn't escape my notice that he basically acted like Lucas wasn't here, so I reached out to take Lucas's hand.

Alexi flicked a look down at my movement, and a lightning-fast frown tugged his brow before it smoothed out once more. "Last I saw him, he was in VIP breaking up a fight. He's probably in the locker room now, though."

My eyes narrowed. "There was a fight? Between *who?*" Because fuck me, if any gangs were involved, I would rain hellfire down. They knew my rules; my clubs were off-limits for their petty disputes. Nothing drove paying customers away faster than the threat of being caught in crossfire.

Alexi gave me a nervous look, rubbing the back of his neck. "Uh, probably better for Zed to explain it all. He said he had it handled."

That just worried me even more. It was definitely Cass if Alexi was too chickenshit to tell me himself. Ignoring my head of security, I tugged Lucas along faster as I headed for the locker rooms, my heels clicking loudly on the concrete floor.

We needed to cut through the side of the main arena, and the roaring of the excited crowd was almost deafening. Our usual pre-fight entertainment was in full swing with the gorgeous dancers shaking their shit like crazy, riding the excitement high.

I stopped myself just short of kicking down the locker-room door and gave it a hard shove instead. Cass and Zed were inside, as expected, and Lucas didn't need me to tell him before he closed the door in Alexi's face. Whatever was going on, it was a family matter. Alexi wasn't family.

Propping my hands on my hips, I glared hard at Cass—who was stripped to the waist and in the process of taping his hands.

"Start talking, Saint."

He didn't even flinch when he met my gaze, cool as a goddamn cucumber. Fuck, I loved his grumpy ass, but *sometimes* I could happily smother him with a pillow.

"Your main event fight for tonight got canceled," he informed me. "But don't worry, Red, I've got you covered."

Lucas made a sound that bordered on a laugh of disbelief, and I felt my eye twitch with rage.

"Cassiel..." I growled his name with warning, and Zed came over to me, his body blocking Cass from my death glare.

"It's a good fight," he explained. "Have you seen the crowd out there? That was with just forty-five minutes of social-media rumors."

I blinked at him in shock. "You're supporting this? What the fuck, Zed? Cass, you were supposed to be *dead* a week ago, and now you're doing a highly public appearance in the octagon? For one thing, I thought you were retired—"

"Rude," Cass muttered, cutting me off. "I'm not a fucking senior citizen, Red. I think I proved that when I fought Johnny Rock."

I pushed Zed aside, storming over to where the big tattooed *asshole* was still calmly taping his hands like he didn't have a care in the world. "Cass. You were shot in the shoulder. Don't even try and tell me it doesn't still bother you. I know it does."

He finally stopped with the tape to grab my waist and pull me closer. "Red, are you angry or worried? It's hard to tell."

"Fuck you," I snarled back, sorely tempted to punch him in the face for mocking me.

He flashed me a smirk, his hands moving down to cup my ass through the skintight dress. "Well, this fight wasn't my idea. If you want to get mad at anyone, take it next door." He jerked his head in the direction of the second locker room.

My eyes narrowed further. "Who?" I demanded. "Who challenged you, Cass?"

The locker-room door burst open right then, the sound echoing through the room and jerking my furious attention toward the intruder.

"Hey, Cass, you ready in here? The crowd is going *nuts*, might be good to—" The blond bastard looked up from his phone and froze when he locked eyes with me. "Oh shit."

"'Oh shit' is fucking right, Kody," I snapped. I would have marched over there and kicked him right in the face if Cass hadn't tightened his grip on my ass and pulled me in closer so his legs bracketed me. Trapping me.

"Uh…" Kodiak Jones, CEO of KJ-Fit gyms, paled and jerked a thumb over his shoulder. "I'm just…gonna…go."

My lip curled in a snarl, but Kody was slick as hell, ducking right back out of the locker room before I could wriggle free of Cass's hold. No wonder there was such a frenzied crowd out there. Archer D'Ath versus his mentor? Fight fans would be foaming at the mouth to place bets.

"Those *motherfuckers!*" I raged. "How *fucking dare they*? No, fuck this. You're not fighting, Cass. You can't because I'm going to kill all fucking three of them."

Lucas did nothing to dissuade me, just watched with a vaguely concerned expression as he leaned against the lockers. Zed and Cass were in full damage-control mode, though.

"Dare, you can't kill them," Zed attempted to reason. "They're as close to friends as we have, and right now we're sorely lacking in those."

"Besides, they only came back to town because of me," Cass rumbled, grabbing my hand and reeling me back in. "They found out through the grapevine that I was alive again."

"And they were…somewhat put out," Zed finished, wincing as he said it.

My phone beeped, and Lucas pulled it from his pocket, since my dress was lacking in phone space.

"Seph," he told me, holding it out.

I grabbed it and checked the message. She was letting me know that Archer and Co. were back in town and super pissed that they didn't know Cass was alive.

"Bit late now, Seph," I muttered, tossing the phone back to Lucas before refocusing on Cass. "Why didn't you call me? If Archer started a fight in my venue—"

Cass cut me off, an edge of anger in his voice. "Last I checked, I was capable of handling my own disputes."

I ground my teeth in fury. "They broke *my* rules."

He tipped his chin back, meeting my gaze steadily. "And I'm dealing with that as a key member of the Timberwolves management. Or was that job title all bullshit?"

My lips parted, but words failed me. I wasn't used to sharing my power, and this was most definitely not how I would have handled things. But it wasn't a bullshit appointment, and I hated that he might think it was.

"No," I muttered, "it wasn't." I ground my teeth hard, trying to swallow down my anger. "Fine. If this is how you want to deal with it, then so be it. But if you threw any punches outside of the octagon, you'll also need to be punished."

A dark look flashed through his eyes, and the corners of his lips tugged in a smile. "I look forward to it."

His hands were back at my ass again, pulling me in closer, and I let him. Cupping his face with my hands, I tilted his head back and hovered my lips above his like I was about to kiss him.

"You'd better hand that little shit his ass on a platter, Saint," I told him in a hard whisper, "or your punishment won't be anywhere near as enjoyable as you think it'll be."

Cass gave a low groan, his fingers flexing on my ass. "I love it when you threaten me, Angel."

Rolling my eyes, I shoved him away and stormed out of the locker room. Vaguely I sensed Lucas following, but the second I got through the door, I locked eyes with a head-shaved prick leaning against the wall of the corridor next to the other locker room. His pretty girlfriend was beside him, chatting animatedly with Dallas's wife, but all three of them fell silent when I stalked closer.

"I want to see all three of you in my office the second this fight is over," I snapped to Max Steele—Archer's third musketeer—and the cold threat in my voice was as clear as a bell. "Conscious or not."

Dallas's wife, Bree, gave a feral grin, and as I continued down the corridor, I heard her snicker. "Oh, you're in so much trouble, Steele." She chuckled. "*So* much trouble."

She was right about that. I didn't give a shit what scores got settled in the octagon between Cass and Archer; they'd disobeyed me. That couldn't be ignored.

CHAPTER 33

Lucas and I headed up to the Anarchy big-top VIP room, which was really a small balcony area with awesome views of the octagon and a private bar. No way in hell was I fighting crowds to get a drink at the main bar, and I *needed* a drink. It was all I could do not to storm back down to the locker rooms and tear some shreds out of Archer myself.

But, like Zed had pointed out, this was great for business.

"You don't want to sit down there?" Lucas asked, indicating the front-row seats we'd occupied last time Cass had fought. It was an area reserved for his "team," but I was way too angry to play the part tonight.

"Nope," I replied, jerking my head to our private bartender. He gave me a nod back and set about mixing drinks for Lucas and me.

"Fair enough," Lucas murmured, pulling my phone from his pocket again. "Seph asked if she's allowed to come to the fight. She heard about it from MK."

I rolled my eyes and moved toward the balcony railing to peer down at the crowd below us. Sure enough, near the octagon I spotted a familiar copper-haired head.

"She's already fucking here," I muttered with a sigh. "But at least she asked…sort of." I was tempted to reply and say no, just to see if she would leave. But that was petty, and I was making an effort to do better with my sister.

I checked the time, noting we had about five minutes until the scheduled start of the fight. "Tell her to come up here," I told Lucas, still watching her as she hugged Madison Kate tightly and exchanged cheek kisses with Bree. Technically, I had no issue with her being friends with MK, who was actually a good influence. But right now I was pissed as hell at MK's husband, so by extension…

I saw Seph get the message and jerk her head up toward where I stood. From the way I'd designed the area, she wouldn't actually be able to see me. Clever lighting provided privacy for when celebrities or other private people attended a fight.

She spoke to MK a moment longer, then excused herself to head in my direction. I was relieved to see a teenage boy trail along beside her, his dark brows tight as his eyes darted around the room. Rex was training his kids well, that was for sure.

The security guard on the door let her in without question—they all knew my sister by now—and she gave me a tentative smile as she approached.

"I tried to tell you as soon as I knew," she said before I could launch into a lecture.

I just gave a small smile and shook my head. "It's fine, brat. I was already here." I nodded to her babysitter. "Ford, right?"

He dipped his head, folding his arms over his chest. "Yes, sir," he confirmed. From what I knew of Rex's boys, he must be almost twenty. It'd been a whole scandal when Rex's secret family was uncovered, but he'd done right by them and provided for their mother, even while he was incarcerated.

"You're keeping my sister safe, Ford?" I questioned him with an arched brow. The bartender delivered our drinks, and Seph took mine before I could pick it up. Brat.

Ford jerked a nod, his jaw tight. "Yes, sir," he repeated. "We agreed that we'd leave right after the fight and *not* drink." He gave Seph a sharp look at that, but my sister raised her middle finger at him and drained my entire cocktail in one go.

I needed to bite my cheek to keep from laughing, and Lucas swiped a hand over his face as he met my eyes with amusement. Oh yeah, Ford had his work cut out for him.

"Well…have fun with that." It was all I could say without totally losing my stern Hades face.

Seph grinned at Lucas and gave a pointed look at his drink on the table.

"Oh my god." Lucas chuckled under his breath. Then he nodded to her, and she snatched it up with a smirk of victory.

"Do you mind if I watch the fight from down there?" she asked me, cradling Lucas's cocktail and pointedly ignoring the way Ford glared daggers into the side of her face. "I haven't seen MK since Italy, and she's a bit upset with me about the whole Cass-not-dead thing."

I was quietly really proud she *hadn't* told her friend that Cass was still alive. I'd assumed she would, so it showed a good deal of maturity that she'd recognized the need for secrecy.

"Go for it," I told her. "But clear out as soon as Cass wins, understood? I have some business to handle with your friends."

Seph grinned. "Oh, after Cass wins, huh? What makes you so confident? Arch is, like, the best for a reason."

Lucas and I both laughed in response to that. Seph had missed Cass's fight against Johnny Rock.

"You'll see," Lucas replied, draping his arm behind me and letting his fingers brush my arm.

"Ew, you guys are totally about to get all PDA, I can just tell." Seph wrinkled her nose, and I leaned into Lucas a bit more. "Dare, can you come by Rex's tomorrow sometime? I wanna show you something."

I nodded. "Absolutely."

My sister beamed, then gulped down Lucas's cocktail quickly. She coughed a couple of times when she was done, then wobbled a bit when she stood up.

"Love you, Dare," she told me, then headed back toward the door.

Ford hesitated a second, and I speared him with a glare.

"Get her some water," I told him. "And don't let her out of your fucking sight, or I'll hold you personally accountable."

The kid—who, admittedly, was older than Lucas—winced and hurried after Seph. I was well aware she wouldn't make his life easy, but she also wasn't actively resisting the protection. She understood now that it was necessary.

Our bartender delivered fresh drinks to Lucas and me, murmuring that he had some food on its way up too, which was a relief because I was *starved*.

The Anarchy fight announcer entered the octagon, strutting around with his microphone in hand and wearing a sharp suit. He was totally the kind of guy who had Bruce Buffer posters all over his bedroom, I was sure. He did a good job, though.

The crowd went nuts as he started his spiel, rousing them even higher while Lucas pulled me closer to him.

I arched a brow, but he just shot me a wicked grin. "No one else is here," he pointed out, dipping his lips to my shoulder.

He had a point. Instead of pushing him away to maintain my *professionalism* if my staff saw me, I slid my hand into the back of his hair and pressed my lips to his.

He moaned lightly as he kissed me back, his tongue tracing the seam of my lips until I parted them. Lucas gave the most incredible kisses, like he was *worshiping* me.

"I knew I made the right choice coming up here," Zed interrupted with a teasing grin and flopped down on the couch beside me.

I pulled away from Lucas's kisses and glared. "Shouldn't you be down there coaching your fighter?"

Zed snorted. "As if Grumpy Cat would take advice from me during a fight against D'Ath. Nope, this is exactly where I'm meant to be."

The crowd roared below, their feet thumping the floor as music pounded through the speakers and Archer strode out into the octagon. He wasn't a showboater; he didn't do dumb, show-off flips or kicks, just gave a casual wave and headed to the side of the cage where Kody was giving him some last-minute advice.

When our announcer dramatically introduced Cass, the crowd was just as loud as they had been for Archer. There was no clear favorite for our patrons, which was always good for entertainment value.

"Huh, that was nice of Seph," Zed commented, leaning forward to peer down.

I shifted to see what he was talking about and spotted Seph with her babysitter in the section reserved for Cass's team. He knew I wouldn't sit down there, not tonight when I was *furious* with him, but it was adorable that Seph was there to cheer him on.

Cass strode into the cage looking like Death himself come down from the heavens…or up from hell. He didn't wave to the crowd, instead looking straight up at the VIP balcony lounge. Slowly and deliberately, he touched his fingers to his lips. Like he was blowing me a fucking kiss or something.

Nah, not Cass. He must have had an itch.

With a sigh, I sank back into Lucas's embrace. The fight started out fairly slow, with the two of them circling each other over and over. Cass had maybe an inch on Archer, but D'Ath was a fraction broader in the chest. With both of them covered in ink and bearded, at a distance it looked like they were fighting mirror images of themselves—especially once they actually started trading blows. It wasn't hard to see who'd given Archer his foundations in MMA.

"You think Cass is still sharp enough to win this?" Zed asked with a teasing grin, sipping his drink. "He's a bit rusty."

As if Cass heard him, a vicious uppercut sent Archer reeling against the cage, and the whole crowd hissed with pain.

I snickered. "Yeah, I reckon he's got it."

"I dunno," Lucas murmured, shifting to sit further forward. He was enraptured with the fight, so much more than Zed or me. "It might be a close one. Archer is a *weapon*. He's only had, like, two defeats in his whole career or something."

"How many has Cass had?" I asked, feeling like a bit of an ass-hole for not already knowing.

Lucas shot me a smirk. "One."

"Yeah, but he's also been retired for ten years," Zed pointed out.

"He hasn't exactly been sitting around eating junk food and getting fat," Lucas countered. "Meanwhile, doesn't Archer look like maybe he's gotten a bit soft now that he's all loved up and married?"

I laughed at that because, *no*, he did not. Still, I had total faith Cass would hand Archer his ass eventually; his ego wouldn't let his former student beat him in a public forum. Or private, for that matter.

Still, I winced as Archer's foot connected with Cass's ribs. That one had to hurt.

"My guess? They're going to keep playing with each other to drag out each round," I pondered aloud. "The last round will be the only one that counts."

Sure enough, they traded blows evenly for the bulk of the fight. They weren't pulling punches and blood was definitely flying, but neither pressed any advantages. They wanted it to go the distance. Hell, I was fairly certain they were just thoroughly enjoying themselves down there. Fucking alpha-male asshole behavior.

By the time the fifth round began, I had a nice, light haze of alcohol warming my body, and I was paying more attention. Lucas, Zed, and I had been keeping our own score, appointing two wins

273

to each of the fighters so far. As predicted, round five would be the decider.

They started out cautiously again, but then Cass must have said something incendiary because Archer flew at him in a frenzied rage. Sloppy. Meanwhile, Kody and Steele were at the cage, hopping up and down and shrieking at Archer. We were too far away and the crowd was too loud to make out their words. But it wasn't hard to assume it was some variety of "calm the fuck down, you idiot."

Sure enough, when the fighters spun around, a grim smirk danced across Cass's lips, and within thirty seconds he had Archer down on the mat all locked up in a rear naked choke. Blood smeared across both fighters as Archer thrashed around trying to free himself, but Cass just tightened his lock under Archer's chin.

The crowd was going *ballistic* and Archer's camp screamed at him, but the stubborn fool refused to tap out. Of course. Even when his face turned dark red from restricted blood flow, he still fought back, slamming his elbow ineffectively into Cass's ribs while the older fighter just waited him out.

A few moments later, Archer passed the fuck out, and the spectators lost their damn minds.

Cass pushed the unconscious weight of his opponent off him, then tilted his chin as he looked up at our balcony again. This time, there was no mistaking his smirk—or the deliberately blown kiss. Sarcastic fuck.

CHAPTER 34

Cass didn't hang around for all the pomp and ceremony of being declared the winner. He just slapped Archer awake, then gave him a hand back to his feet. They left the octagon together, and Cass accepted a manly bro-hug backslap thing from Kody and Steele. There was a lot of respect there, and against my better judgment, it softened my ire toward Archer and Co.

Seph bounced up to Cass as he made his way toward the locker rooms and wrapped him in a tight hug, not seeming to give a damn that he was sweaty and bloody. I watched him stiffen and glance up at me, but it wasn't Seph being a flirt. She just genuinely cared for him as *family*.

"You've got to be fucking kidding me," Zed exclaimed, rising to his feet with his eyes locked on someone in the crowd below. "What the fuck does she want?"

"Who?" I asked, searching for who he was scowling at. When I spotted her, there was no doubt in my mind. "Is that—"

"My mother," Zed snarled. "Wait here. I'll deal with her."

He started to leave, but I launched to my feet and grabbed his hand before he could make it more than two steps away. "Sit your ass back down, Zayden De Rosa. We will deal with her together."

His eyes blazed with defiance for a moment, but that was quickly replaced by relief. He didn't have to deal with her alone, and now that I knew everything she'd done, I had a few words I'd like to offer her myself. What kind of woman, what kind of *human*, could walk away from her own son that easily? Then to emotionally manipulate him into doing her dirty work? Veronica De Rosa—or whatever the fuck her real name was—deserved a bullet in the head. Or at the very least a broken nose.

It really depended on whether she was in my venue officially or not. I crossed my fingers for *not*.

"Sit down," I repeated to Zed. "I'll have her brought up." Not waiting for him to agree, I made my way over to our security guard at the door and gave him terse instructions.

While we waited, I checked my phone and found a message from Seph assuring me that she and Ford were safely on their way home. Good. One less worry on my mind, just in case the night got violent.

"Any idea what she's here for?" Lucas asked, giving Zed a curious look. We'd filled him and Cass in on the rough details of Zed's involvement with the FBI a few days ago.

Zed scowled, his hands balled into fists at his sides. "I can hazard a guess. My mother doesn't take kindly to being told *no*." Swiping a hand over his face, he gave a frustrated sigh. "I'm actually surprised it's taken her this long. Count on her having some kind of blackmail up her sleeve."

I scoffed. "I have no intention of letting her get that far. Do you?"

Zed met my eyes, a slow smile curving his lips. "You're such a badass, Dare. I'm with you, however you want to handle her shit. She's not my mother, she's just another easily corrupted law-enforcement agent."

Goddamn, that made my heart ache. He had idolized his mother when we were kids. She'd been the epitome of motherly kindness. I couldn't even imagine how badly it'd hurt when he'd realized it was all an act.

Decided, I gave him a short nod, then strode across the bar to intercept Veronica as she arrived. Her arm was firmly gripped by my security guard and her face flushed. She definitely hadn't wanted to be manhandled up here like that.

"What is the meaning of this?" she demanded, shaking him off as I indicated he could release her. "I'm an FBI agent here on official business, and this is assault."

I snorted. "Bullshit. My security guard acted fully within his rights in delivering a disruptive patron to management. As for *official business*, Veronica—"

"Rebecca," she corrected me with a twist of disgust in her face. "Special Agent Rebecca Laurence."

I sneered. "How unremarkable. I bet your mission undercover as Veronica De Rosa was the pinnacle of your career, huh? Now you're forever scrabbling to prove you're not all washed up."

I felt Zed and Lucas behind me. Zed's hand came to rest on the small of my back as he leaned in to kiss my hair. I didn't need to look up at him to know he was glaring at his mother with an expression that could *kill*.

"Zayden," she snapped. "I'd hoped to speak with you privately."

"I'd hoped you might have died in your sleep," he drawled back. "I guess we're both disappointed."

Oh, ouch. The cold hatred in his tone made me shiver a little.

Agent Laurence's eyes narrowed, and her lips took a cruel twist like she was preparing to launch her ammunition. But I sure as fuck wasn't interested in hearing it, and Zed had dealt with enough of her shit to last him a lifetime.

Stepping forward, I gave her a saccharine smile. "I think we're overdue for a little chat, don't you?"

Her lip curled. "Certainly not."

My smile chilled. "I wasn't asking." Quick as a whip, I grabbed a handful of her hair, yanking her head back to an uncomfortable angle. She immediately reached for her piece at her waistband, but the clicks of multiple guns aimed in her direction made her freeze.

"Oh, I'd think twice about that, *Rebecca*." Zed's warning was glacial, and his mother's eyes widened. She carefully moved her hand away from her gun, though, and I used my grip on her hair to march her back toward the exit.

"Whatever leverage you think you have," I murmured softly in her ear as we walked, "forget it. The only reason you'll walk out of here breathing will be as a courtesy to the life you brought into this world. You created one of the most amazing men on this planet, and for that I'll let you live today. But mark my words, *Agent Laurence*, I see you sniffing around Zed again, I'll ensure no one finds your remains. Not even your sick little friend Chase Lockhart. Clear?"

In response, she gave a low chuckle, like *I* was the idiot here.

Before she could get too smug with herself, I reached inside her shirt and ripped the recording device right out of her bra. I dropped it to the floor and stomped on it firmly, feeling the satisfying crunch of breaking electronics.

"You really don't understand who you're messing with, do you?" I commented, giving her a curious look.

Then, before she could retort, I spun her around and slammed her face into the wall beside the stairs. Blood sprayed and she shrieked in pain, but I just gave her a shove into my waiting security guard's grip.

"Oh dear, Agent Laurence. You really should watch where you're walking." I shot her a smirk. "I'd hate for you to trip and fall down these stairs on your way out."

My security smirked back at me, receiving the message loud and clear: Make sure Rebecca Laurence hit every bump on the way down.

"You can't do this," she spat back. "I'm *FBI*, you can't just—"

278

"I can," I cut her off, "and I will do worse if you don't heed my warning. I survived Chase Lockhart. I can *promise* you, Rebecca, I will crush you like a bug under my heel if you cross me again. Stay the fuck away from Zed. Move states. I never want to see your face in my territory again."

I nodded to my security guard and turned my back on the woman who'd created a man I loved with my whole heart.

Zed gave me a soft look as I returned to him and Lucas. "I could have handled her myself, you know."

"I know," I agreed. "But you shouldn't have to. And I owed her for that setup."

Lucas grinned. "Besides," he added, "Hayden's hot as hell when she gets violent."

Zed rolled his eyes but reached out to cup my face with his hand. "Thank you," he whispered, pulling me closer and kissing me softly.

I leaned into his kiss, crazy keyed up and turned on by the adrenaline pumping through my veins. I wanted nothing more than to drag my boys home and work off some steam.

But... "I suppose I need to go deal with those idiots in my office," I muttered against Zed's lips.

"Probably," he agreed, releasing me. He swiped a tired hand over his face and started for the exit.

Lucas snagged my hand before I could follow, though. He tugged me back into his arms, then kissed me until my knees went weak and I needed to hold on to him to stay upright.

He was in *no* hurry to let me go, until Zed stomped back over and punched him on the arm.

"Don't be a shit, Gumdrop," Zed snarled. "Dare has business to do, and it doesn't involve your dick down her throat."

Lucas quirked a brow. "But could it?"

I licked my lips and gave a shaking laugh. What was I meant to be doing again?

"Cass is waiting downstairs," Zed reminded me, and I ruffled my fingers through my hair to try to shake off the heady arousal.

"Right," I muttered. "Cass downstairs. Disobedient idiots in my office." I peeled myself out of Lucas's grip and headed for the stairs with wobbly steps. Quietly, under my breath, I added, "Game face back on, Hades."

It was harder than it should have been to shake off the goofy softness that Lucas and Zed had just brought out in me. I quietly loved how they bickered like that. It was no longer done with any real heat or resentment; it was just...friendly bickering.

Cass was indeed waiting near the bottom of the stairs, leaning against the wall with water still clinging to his hair and a fresh bruise swelling his cheek.

"Congratulations," I murmured, inspecting his face. He had small splits in his eyebrow and lip, but someone had already cleaned those up for him. I'd just spent the whole trip down the stairs pulling my Hades face into place; I couldn't drop it now, no matter how badly I wanted to launch into his arms and show him how proud I was of that win.

He studied me back, his eyes sharp and understanding. In response, he just dipped his head, then followed as I headed down the corridor to the admin office.

It was a tight squeeze inside already with Archer, Kody, and Steele taking up most of the space opposite my chair. Add Lucas, Zed, and Cass... Yeah, I probably should have told them to come up to the VIP lounge instead.

Whatever, I'd keep it brief.

"Good fight, D'Ath," I told the sulking, bruised-up man slouched in one of the guest chairs. His response was a narrow-eyed glare, like he wasn't sure if I was mocking him or not. Suspicious fuck. No wonder Cass won the fight. Archer clearly still had anger management issues, and Cass had exploited that.

"Hades, sir," Kody started to say, ever the fucking peacemaker, "we understand—"

"Save it," I snapped, folding my hands together on the desk. "I think Cass took care of things well enough on my behalf. In fact, you saved me the trouble of calling you next week."

My desire for their blood had well and truly faded. Now, I just wanted to move on with my bigger-picture plans.

"Steele, I'd like your help on a job tomorrow night." I arched a brow at the sharpshooter of their group. The name I intended to tick off my list was known to employ a heavy security team, and I wasn't interested in peaceful talks.

Kody drew a breath, and I knew the slick fuck was about to try to negotiate a payment for Steele's work.

"Believe me," I gritted out before he could try to extort a favor, "this is in your best interests." I shifted my attention to Archer. We were friends...sort of. We'd done three seasons of his grandfather's camp together.

"Who's the target?" he grumbled, still pressing an ice pack to his cheek.

I gave him a brittle smile in return. "A mutual friend. It would seem the Rainybanks dockmaster has reneged on our arrangement. He's working for Chase and bringing live cargo through the port."

The silence that followed my announcement was deafening. Then Archer threw his ice pack at the wall in frustration, his eyes flashing with fury.

"I'm coming too," he snarled.

I shook my head. "Sorry, this one is mine. Chase owes me multiple debts, and I'm claiming them in the flesh of his associates... for now. When I'm done, I'd like you to pay a visit to the new dockmaster and ensure he—or she—is in complete understanding of the agreement. Clear?"

Archer's teeth ground together so hard I could hear it. But he let out a frustrated breath and nodded. "Clear, sir. Steele will have your back."

I gave the three of them a tight smile. "Excellent. This will be fun."

CHAPTER 35

Muted gunshots rang out through the night air as I strode through the endless maze of shipping containers, my head held high and my shoulders squared. Cass was at my back, but bodies were dropping from their hiding places before we even reached them. The combination of Zed, Lucas, and Steele hiding out in elevated positions with sniper rifles was unbeatable. We were untouchable.

I didn't even try to hide the cruel smile on my lips when I raised my boot and kicked the door to the dockmaster's office open.

The paunchy dockmaster, Wayne, was cowering against the far wall, a gun in his hand and his phone to his ear. When I advanced into the room, unconcerned by his trembling gun, he held the phone out to me.

"He wants to talk to you," he told me, fear-sweat slick on his brow.

I strode closer, then shot his gun hand. Wayne howled, dropping the gun and phone both, but I scooped the phone up a moment later. Cass and I ignored his screams, and Cass pressed a gun to Wayne's forehead while I brought the phone to my ear.

"Are you there, Darling?" Chase asked in a low, breathless voice. "You are, aren't you? I hope you know what a turn-on this is. I've got my dick in my hand right now, thinking about how sexy you must look shooting that idiot." He groaned, and bile rose in my throat.

I didn't reply, just raised my gun and shot Wayne in the knee. Blood splattered across the wall, and he crumpled to the floor, writhing in agony. Chase's heavy breathing prickled my skin, so I tossed the phone onto the desk so I wouldn't need to hear him.

He could hear us, though. He could hear Wayne as the man begged for his life, sniveling excuses for why he'd reneged on our deal. He could hear as I gave the traitor zero mercy, shooting him six more times in nonlethal ways before finally delivering a shot between the eyes.

The sudden silence as the gunshots faded from the air was startling, and I locked eyes with Cass for a long moment, my own breathing rough. Not in the same way as my perverted nemesis on the phone—I wasn't getting off on the violence. I was just riding the adrenaline high.

Wetting my lips, I placed my hot gun down on the desk and picked up the phone once more. As expected, Chase was still there. Still listening.

"Another one bites the dust, Chasey baby," I announced, the cold violence in my voice shocking even me. "Better sleep with one eye open." Then I let myself release an unhinged laugh at my own joke before ending the call.

Swallowing back the bubbles of laughter, I dropped the phone to the floor, and Cass demolished it under his boot.

"We need to call Robynne," I murmured, peering down at the bloody mess on the floor. Wayne. Fucking *Wayne*. This one had been personal because that motherfucker had been taking more-than-generous payouts from me for years.

Cass nodded, placing his own gun down on the desk, and grasped my waist to pull me close. "It's done, Red." With one hand he tugged on my hair, tipping my head back. "Come back to me now."

I knew what he meant; I was deep within my cold, hard Hades shell. It was the only way I could kill with such callous disregard for human life. Necessary or not, it was hard to resurface again.

"I'm fine," I lied.

He tugged my hair harder, holding my gaze. "Bullshit."

I glared back. "I'll *be* fine. Call Robynne for cleanup."

He kept his fingers tangled in my hair, holding me tight as he pulled his phone out with his other hand. The call to Robynne took all of thirty seconds, and then he glanced at the time.

"She's twenty minutes away," he informed me. "Best we wait so no one else stumbles over our crime scene."

I laughed, then hissed as he tugged my hair again. "Oh yeah? What do you want to do to kill the time?" As if I didn't already have a fair idea.

The corners of his lips lifted, and he stroked a hand over my throat and down my front. "I want to bring my Angel back," he murmured, his fingers flicking the button of my jeans open.

I was still cold enough, hard enough, that I barely even offered Wayne's lifeless corpse a second glance before arching into Cass's touch. His fingers dipped into my panties, and his mouth crashed down on mine, hard and demanding. Cass wanted to snap me back to myself, and he wasn't taking no for an answer. Nor was he waiting until we got home.

His movements were rough as he pushed his hand further into my pants, his long fingers stroking my throbbing pussy. Then he released me with a growl of frustration.

"Not like this," he muttered, almost to himself as he gazed down at me with hungry eyes.

I shrugged lightly. "Fair enough." He'd always been unpredictable when I was like this, but also always distant and uninterested.

Cass gave a husky laugh, shaking his head. Then he tugged my jeans down further, taking my panties with them.

"Like *this*," he corrected, shoving me to sit on the edge of Wayne's messy desk as he sank to his knees in front of me.

My brows hiked in surprise, and I did nothing to stop him as he tugged my boots off and removed my jeans entirely. Then his huge hands gripped my ass, pulling me tighter toward him as his mouth found my cunt.

"Oh, *shit*," I breathed as his tongue penetrated me. My hand went to his head, encouraging him as he draped my leg over his shoulder. Ripples of desire ran through me from head to toe, shaking me to the core as he tongue-fucked me not six feet from a man we'd just killed.

I squirmed against his mouth, but his grip on my ass held me tight against him—so tight that for a moment I worried he might suffocate on my pussy—but then he popped up for air with his face slick and a sly grin on his face.

"Fuck, I missed eating this cunt," he confessed, bringing one hand around to toy with me. Holding my gaze, he pushed two fingers into my throbbing center, his tongue darting out to flick my clit. I convulsed, already on the edge of an orgasm.

"That's it, Angel," he purred as I bucked my hips, silently begging for more. "Fuck yeah, that's beautiful. Come on my face."

I groaned, wrapping my legs around his head as his mouth attacked my clit. His fingers filled me, fucking me hard as he sucked and bit my clit like it was his favorite food. The orgasm that hit me was hard enough to make me cry out as I shook and clawed at Cass's shoulders, but he was unrelenting. When my climax started to subside, he worked harder. His mouth was bonded to my clit, and he slipped one of his soaking fingers down to my ass, teasing me with a light press.

"Fuck," I gasped. "Cass—"

Whatever else I was going to say got cannibalized by my moans as he pushed inside. My feet arched with another intense orgasm, and I writhed all over the desk, collapsing backward as Cass finger

286

fucked my ass *and* my pussy while his mouth worked over my clit. I turned to a puddle of goo and screamed my release as I locked eyes with Wayne's corpse.

Fuck. We were messed up.

I wouldn't change us for the damn world.

"Look at me," Cass demanded, his fingers still buried inside me. Weak from my climax, I pushed back up onto my elbows and peered down at him. His face was slick and his eyes feverish, and I'd never been more in love with him. He wasn't turned off by my compartmentalization; he simply recognized it for what it was. A mask. And Cass never wanted to see anything but the real me.

"Much better," he murmured. He placed another teasing kiss on my cunt as he withdrew his hand, and I gasped. Those nerves were officially overstimulated, and he damn well knew it.

Licking my lips to wet them, I sat up and locked eyes with Zed, who was standing in the doorway of Wayne's shitty office.

"I came down to check what was taking so long," he commented, arching a brow. "Stayed for the show."

I couldn't fight the grin splitting my face. I didn't feel weird in the least about Zed having watched that. In fact, it was getting me hot and wet all over again.

"How long until Robynne arrives?" I asked Cass, my eyes still locked on Zed's.

Cass checked the time and shot me a wicked look. "Ten minutes."

I tilted my chin at Zed. "Close the door."

It was about damn time I worked through my physical roadblocks with him, and ten minutes seemed like a good start.

He did as I told him, then leaned his shoulders against the closed door, watching me cautiously as I pushed myself off the desk. My legs wobbled a bit as I quickly pulled my jeans back on—so I wouldn't be caught with my pants down if Robynne was early—then crossed the room to stand in front of Zed.

His lids drooped, and he eyed me with extreme suspicion. "Dare...what are you doing?"

I shot him a smirk and sank to my knees. "You heard Cass, we've got ten minutes."

Zed's brows hitched as I unbuckled his belt.

"Nine," Cass rumbled, and I moved a bit quicker.

Zed breathed sharply as I pulled his rock-hard length from his pants and stroked it. "Dare, this seems—"

"Like a fucking great idea," Cass said, cutting him off. "Quit complaining, and let her suck your dick, Zeddy Bear."

Grinning in amusement, I did just that. Zed wasn't exactly complaining, especially once I'd taken him into my mouth, sucking his sensitive tip with determination. His hands moved to my hair, his fingers tangling in the strands like he wanted to grip tighter but was at war with himself.

I showed him that we were okay by taking him deeper, swallowing his cock, and stroking his balls with my hand.

"Six minutes," Cass rumbled, sounding close. I cracked my eyes open, finding him with his own dick in hand, stroking it hard while he watched me suck off Zed. I reached out to him, batting his hand away to replace it with mine.

Smoothly, *quickly*, I pumped my fist up and down Cass's cock in time with how I bobbed up and down Zed's dick. Then I swapped over, taking Cass into my mouth as my hand tightened around Zed.

"Fuck," Cass hissed. "Four minutes, Angel, wrap it up."

I moaned around his tattooed dick, then sucked him just as hard as he'd done on my clit only minutes ago. Grunting, Cass wrapped my hair around his fist, then held me tight as he took over the pace. His cock slammed into my mouth, hitting harder and deeper while my hand furiously worked Zed over.

Cass came a minute later, holding me tight as his load pumped into my throat, and I swallowed in gulps. Then he released me, and I immediately gravitated back to Zed, my mouth sliding up and down his thick cock for another minute before he filled my mouth with his release.

When our cleanup crew knocked on the door, the guys both had their dicks tucked away and I was in the process of putting my boots back on. Robynne, the tiny, elderly battle-ax of a woman who owned the cleaning company, eyed me with suspicion. She said nothing, though, just swept her stern gaze over the body and blood splatter all over the room. It was a miracle I'd somehow avoided getting my bare ass right in a patch of blood on the desk, but I'd take the win.

"Same as last time?" she asked.

I nodded. "Yes, please. I'll have another for you on Saturday night in Cloudcroft."

One wiry brow twitched, and I saw the curiosity in her beady eyes. "The mayor's gala?"

I shot her a feral grin. "The very same. Always a pleasure, Robynne."

She just grunted and turned back to Wayne's corpse, dismissing us from her attention. Cass and Zed followed me outside, and I had to bite my cheek to keep from smiling like a loved-up fool. The only thing that could have made that little session better was Lucas, but he was likely keeping Steele busy.

"She creeps me the fuck out," Zed muttered, tucking his arm around my waist and kissing my hair.

Cass gave a low chuckle. "'Cause she could make you disappear and no one would ever find your body? Yeah. Same."

He had a point.

CHAPTER 36

I hadn't forgotten to stop by and see Seph the day after the fight at Anarchy. She'd wanted to show me the car she'd been working on with Rex—the lilac Corvette. It belonged to one of Rex's customers, but I couldn't help noticing the way my sister gazed at it with such pride.

A couple of days after my trip to the docks, I got the call I'd been waiting on from Rex.

"Two updates for you, Boss," he grunted down the phone. "The squirrelly killer, Ezekiel. He's clean, just a nervous little turd because he killed one of my cousins back in the day."

I sighed quickly in relief. "Well, that's one less worry on my mind. What's your other news?"

"The Corvette. He's willing to sell, but he wants double what it's worth." Rex sounded less than pleased to be delivering that information, but I just laughed hollowly.

"Of course he does," I muttered. "Take it. I'll send Lucas over with the money on Monday. But, Rex? Don't tell Seph yet. She needs to learn how to drive a shitload better before she gets that car. Understood?" She'd already crashed enough cars I'd bought for her.

Rex barked a loud laugh. "Understood. I'll get Linc to give her some lessons."

I ended the call and drummed my fingers on the countertop.

"What's up?" Lucas asked, leaning on his elbows opposite me. He'd been washing the dishes from breakfast, while both Cass and Zed had already disappeared into the gym together.

I frowned. "Chase," I muttered. "He's too quiet. I'm starting to regret blowing his house up because now I'm more paranoid than ever."

Lucas hummed thoughtfully, like he was in agreement. "You think he's planning something?"

"Oh, I *know* he is. My guess is that he'll go after one of the clubs again. Or possibly even Copper Wolf. There's no way he's just accepting defeat." I nibbled the edge of my thumbnail, and Lucas reached over to tug it out of my mouth.

"Whatever he tries," he assured me, holding onto my hand, "we will be ready. He's not catching us off guard again."

The steady confidence in his eyes warmed me inside. Lucas had slipped into his role on my team effortlessly, like he'd been born for this lifestyle. Part of me twinged with guilt over that, but the rest of me was just overwhelmingly glad to have him at my side.

"What do you have on for today?" I asked, changing the subject. Unless one of us suddenly developed psychic powers, we weren't going to predict Chase's next move. We could only continue on with our own plans and hope the scales continued to tip in our favor.

Lucas straightened up, stretching. "Uh, I need to hit the gym as well. Gotta stay in shape if I want a headline spot when Timber opens." He shot me a wink, and I grinned. He really did love stripping, something I was more than happy to take advantage of in private.

Luckily, I felt secure as fuck with our relationship, or I might stab every woman watching him dance when he was next onstage.

"I'll come too," I offered, sliding out of my seat. "I could use some exercise myself." And the view in the gym with all three of them working out was like something out of a dirty dream.

Lucas grinned, intercepting me before I left the kitchen to get changed. "Babe, as much as I love you drooling all over the gym floor...don't you have a meeting with your bar management team for Timber?"

Shit. He was right.

I groaned and gave him a sad face. "Remind me why I have businesses to run again?"

Lucas beamed back at me. "Because you're running a goddamn empire, Hayden, and slaying it, too. You would never be happy playing bored housewife, and you know it."

He was right, but I still rolled my eyes and grumbled all the way up to my bedroom to get changed out of my sleep shirt.

Zed came clattering up the stairs while I styled my hair into careful waves, shouting out that he'd be ready to come with me in ten minutes. Fucking men had it so damn easy. Guaranteed, he'd be ready in less than ten minutes and look like he'd just walked straight out of an ad campaign.

Sure enough, just as I was applying my scarlet lipstick, Zed slouched against the doorframe looking all effortlessly gorgeous in his navy pants, leather belt, and crisp white button-down.

"You ready?" he asked, rolling his shirtsleeves up to reveal his tanned forearms. Goddamn, did he know how hot that was? Rolled-up shirtsleeves with strongly muscled forearms are to women what great cleavage is to men. Or they were to me.

"Mm-hmm," I replied, smudging my lips together, then blotting them with a tissue. It'd taken a *long* time to find a red lipstick that wouldn't smudge, but this one was unbeatable. So long as I let it set for a few minutes, I could kiss Zed stupid and not smear it all over his face.

He cast his appreciative gaze down my body as I turned to face him, and a suggestive smile ticked his lips up.

"Do we really need to go to this meeting today?" he asked, tipping his head to the side. "Or can I just take you out for a lunch date?"

"Tempting," I replied, grinning as I slipped my arms around his waist and pressed a featherlight kiss to his lips. "Can we do both?"

He kissed me back just as softly. "Hell yeah, we can. Let's get this done quick." Wrapping his hand around mine, he led the way down to the cars and opened the passenger door to the Ferrari for me. Such a gentleman.

Zed's phone rang when we were halfway to Timber, and Katie, the name of Timber's bar manager, flashed over the screen. Zed frowned and answered the call on speaker.

"Hey, Zed," she replied to his greeting. "Look, I don't want to waste Hades's time today, but it might be best to reschedule this staff meeting."

Zed and I exchanged a look.

"Why?"

Katie sighed with frustration. "Because only six staff turned up for it. The others can't be reached for whatever reason. I dunno what's going on, but it's kind of a pointless meeting with only six here, right?"

Zed gave me a questioning look, and I shrugged. "We're already on our way, so we may as well come chat with those who did bother to turn up." I pursed my lips. "You haven't heard from the missing staff at all?"

"Nothing, sir," Katie replied. "I'm so sorry. I know staffing is my responsibility. I can't even imagine what went wrong. Even if they think it's a different day, surely they'd answer their phones."

I blew out a long breath. Somehow, I was afraid I knew what'd happened.

"Don't worry about it, Katie," Zed told her. "We'll sort it out. See you in twenty minutes." He ended the call and cast a long look at me. "They could be ill."

I scoffed. "How coincidental. No, this is Chase. I knew he'd been too fucking quiet. He was planning something."

Zed sighed. "And he's predictable, so hitting your businesses is

293

his logical move seeing as he can't strike at you directly again and you're hitting *his* business."

I rubbed my forehead. "My guess? Those missing staff won't be found. We'll have to push off the opening of Timber *again*."

"Fuck that." Zed scowled. "We've already pushed back because of his meddling. No, we can make it work. We just need to borrow staff from the other venues until Katie can train up a new crew."

His raw determination brought a smile to my face. "I guess we still have a few weeks to make it work."

Zed reached out, clasping my knee like he always did when we drove together. "That's more like it. No more letting that bastard win, not even on the small things."

I let out another long breath, letting some tension ebb. Zed was right. I couldn't let Chase have any win, no matter how minor. We'd open Timber as planned in three weeks, even if it meant shutting one of the other clubs to make it work.

Zed gave my knee a reassuring squeeze. "We've got this, baby. Everything is on track. You're hitting him back now, and he's scrabbling. This is what we predicted."

I nodded, swallowing hard. We had predicted backlash, yes. We'd even predicted collateral damage, and I'd made the decision that the loss of a few was worth saving the many. But now, with twenty of my new staff potentially dead in retaliation for my actions? That call was sitting on my mind like a black cloud.

We drove the rest of the way to Timber in relative silence and headed inside to find the six staff who'd been spared Chase's games. I was relieved to see Bethany among those six, along with a dancer who Bethany had told me was also interested in joining the Timberwolves.

Zed sat down with them all and ran through our hastily thrown-together plan to keep on track with our opening date in three weeks, and I sat back to observe each of the remaining staff. Were any of them working for Chase? He could have his spies anywhere.

Now that I knew he had access to the entire Lockhart fortune, his pockets were even deeper than mine. And mine were *deep*.

No one triggered my instincts, but that meant nothing. When Zed was done, I pulled Bethany aside and gave her the invitation to the mayor's gala that'd been secured for her. She beamed with nervous excitement, and I tried really hard not to grin back.

"Call my assistant, Hannah," I told her. "Tell her you need a dress, and she'll sort you out."

Bethany's eyes widened even further, but I dismissed her before things could get too sappy. With the staff gone, Zed and I took a look around the club to make sure everything was exactly how we wanted it to look and noted any areas that our builders needed to come back and fix.

As we were locking up some time later, my phone rang with Rodney's name on the screen.

"Boss," he grunted when I connected the call. "You got time to swing past 22 today?"

I frowned, exchanging a look with Zed. "I'm leaving Timber now. I'll be right there. What's going on?"

Rodney heaved a long sigh. "You're not gonna like it, Boss."

"Spit it out," I snarled.

"Club's fucked," he grunted. "Totally flooded."

"What?" I exclaimed. "How? When?"

Rodney sighed again. "Looks like the fire sprinklers activated sometime after we closed up last night and just…never shut off. Basement is almost full, and every stick of furniture is soaked through. It's a fucking mess, Boss."

"How the fuck does that happen?" I demanded. "Those sprinklers are linked to the fire alarms. Why was no one notified? Why did they not shut off in the allotted time?"

"Beats me, Boss," Rodney replied, as helpful as a lump of dog shit on the sidewalk.

I ended the call, too angry to continue talking to him about it without seeing it first for myself. I slammed Zed's car door so hard that he gave me a reproachful glance, until I explained.

He let out a string of curses and gave me a knowing look. "Chase."

CHAPTER 37

Rodney hadn't been exaggerating. Club 22 was totally ruined. It would take *months* to repair the water damage. All the drywall would need to be ripped off and the insulation replaced to avoid mold, and the furniture was totally destroyed. Velvet couches and heavy quantities of water did not mix.

Zed and I spent most of our afternoon there picking through the mess and talking to our *new* insurance company. Of course, now we were within a no-claim period, and they basically told us too bad, so sad.

When my phone rang again as the sun started to set, I groaned. My anxiety had been on high alert all damn day, and I just *knew* this call was going to carry more bad news.

"It'll be fine," Zed assured me as I stared down at my phone, not answering it. "Whatever it is, we knew this was coming. Lucas and Cass are safe. So is Seph."

And that was really all I could ask for. Everyone else...fair game. I couldn't save the whole world, after all.

"Alexi," I sighed, bringing the phone to my ear. "What's happened?"

The sound of sirens in the background sent a ripple of worry through me, and I held my breath as I waited for him to deliver Chase's next strike.

"Hannah," Alexi replied, sounding grim.

Oh fuck.

My chest tightened up, and my stomach turned to acid. "She's dead?"

Alexi grunted. "She's fine."

The relief that rushed through me was enough to weaken my knees, and I crashed down in a sopping armchair. "So, what happened?" I asked again.

"Someone came after her," Alexi elaborated. "She was shopping on Magnolia Street with the pretty waitress from Timber"—*Bethany*—"and after the other girl went home, Hannah was walking back to her car when she got jumped."

I swallowed hard. "How'd she get away?"

There was a scuffle of noise, and in the background I heard Hannah snapping at Alexi to give her the phone. Hearing her voice brought a smile of reassurance to my face.

"Boss?" she asked. "Fucking hell, I told that dickhead not to bother you. I'm fine. Alexi is just insisting I go to the hospital to get stitched up. But he *wasn't* supposed to call you about this. We've got it handled."

I smiled at hearing her with more steel in her voice than her usual submissive tone. "I'm glad you're okay, Hannah. Can you pass the phone back? I need to give Alexi some orders."

"Yes, sir," she agreed. "But also, I'm having Alexi drop your dress over tonight, and Bethany is all sorted out. I assume Zed has sixty thousand suits to choose from, but does Lucas or Cass need one?"

I laughed and ruffled my fingers through my hair. "We can sort something out tomorrow, Hannah. Go let the paramedics take care of you."

She huffed a sigh. "All right. Well, I'll call when I'm done at the hospital and get their measurements."

"Hannah," I said sternly.

"Yes, sir?" She was hesitant, like she thought she'd pissed me off.

"I'm glad you're okay," I told her softly. "Keep watching your back."

I could *hear* the smile in her voice as she promised she would, then handed the phone back to Alexi.

"Tell me what happened," I barked at him, all traces of softness gone.

He blew out a breath and paused for a moment like maybe he was getting out of Hannah's earshot. "Dude attacked her in the parking lot near her car. Hannah fought him off *somehow* and bolted back into the street. He chased her, but she ducked into the jeweler's here on Magnolia." He grunted a sound that was pure respect for what she'd done. "Then she smashed a display case to trigger the security gate. Kept her safe inside while she called me for help."

My brows rose. "That was smart."

"Damn smart," Alexi agreed. "Her elbow and arm are a bit sliced up from smashing the glass and she's got a few bruises and shit, but otherwise..."

I clicked my tongue, thoroughly impressed. "Otherwise, still breathing. Nice work, Hannah."

"Yep, I thought so too," Alexi agreed. "I'm gonna grab a copy of the security footage around here and see if we can get an ID, but my guess is that he was a paid thug."

"Go with Hannah to the hospital," I ordered him. "Stay with her until you can get one of your other guys on her for protection detail." Suddenly I found I needed to add Hannah to my list of nonnegotiables.

Alexi murmured his understanding, and I ended the call looking up at Zed with wide eyes.

"I got parts of that," he told me, folding his arms. "Someone attacked Hannah?"

I nodded. "She got away, though. I told Alexi to stay with her, so let's head over and review the CCTV footage ourselves. It'll be one of Chase's lackeys, no doubt, but goddamn, it'll make me feel better to cut down his goon squad by one more."

Zed flashed me a feral smile and held out a hand to pull me back to my feet. "Do you want to swing by home first?" he offered. "For some dry pants?"

I wrinkled my nose, inspecting my soaking-wet skirt. Sitting on a saturated armchair really hadn't been the best idea I'd had all day. It was a black skirt, though, so maybe I could get away with it.

"Is it noticeable?"

Zed tilted his head, squinting at my butt, then gave me a confused look. "What was the question?"

I laughed and headed out of our destroyed club. At the front door, Rodney was nailing up a sign informing our patrons that we were closed for the foreseeable future, and it made my skin prickle with frustration.

Still, it wasn't Rodney's fault. It was pretty damn clear that the sprinkler system had been tampered with, and there was no doubt in our minds who'd done that.

"Wait." Frowning, Zed stopped me before I could get into his car.

It took me a second to understand what his problem was, then I threw up my hands in exasperation. "Seriously?"

"What?" he protested. "You know that—"

"Oh my fucking god," I muttered under my breath, glancing around to check no one was watching before I shimmied out of my wet skirt. "Happy?" I snapped, sliding into the passenger seat in just my slightly damp panties instead, my skirt on my lap and *not* touching the leather.

Zed flashed me a wide smile. "Ecstatic." He closed my door and circled around to the driver's side to get in. The heated look he gave my bare legs said he was already considering a detour on the way to Magnolia Street.

"Don't even fucking think about it," I growled, my eyes narrowed in warning. "Last time I let you finger fuck me in this car, I ended up getting arrested with no panties on."

Zed winced and turned his attention back to driving as he pulled out of the parking lot. "I'm so freaking sorry for that, Dare," he murmured. "That must have seemed like the worst kind of unforgivable move. Trust me, if I'd known they were waiting to arrest you…" He shook his head, the anger and frustration clear in his face. "Shit, if I'd known, I would have had you on a plane to the Bahamas before they even realized we were coming."

I scoffed. "As if I'd ever run."

He gave me a sad smile. "Yeah, I know. Sometimes I wish we could, though. Just take a vacation and never come back. Do nothing but lie on the sand and drink cocktails…and fuck. We wouldn't even bother with clothes, there would be so much sex. It'd be amazing, don't you think?"

"Yeah, for you. I'd be lurking under umbrellas and bathing in sunscreen constantly to avoid turning into a lobster. Beach sun and my skin? Not friends, Zeddy Bear. Not all of us can tan as beautifully as you." Then I winced. "Sunscreen would probably sting if it got into places it shouldn't too."

Zed barked a loud laugh. "Thanks for ruining that fantasy for me. I'll start working on a new one. Maybe a cabin in the snow? Roaring fireplace? No clothes, of course, but also no sunscreen."

I smiled broadly. "Much better. That's one I can get on board with."

Zed slowed down as we drove through West Shadow Grove on our way to Magnolia Street—the trendy shopping area in downtown—and frowned through the windshield.

"Nadia's crew are working late," he murmured, nodding to the lights coming from Nadia's Cakes. The front windows were still all taped up because it was a construction site inside, but warm light spilled from around the edges of the paper.

"That's one of Rex's cars." I pointed across the street. "Seph must be here."

Zed arched a brow. "Want to stop by?"

I only pondered it for a split second before nodding. "Yeah, we've got time. Those tapes aren't going anywhere, and Hannah should be safe with Alexi."

"Should be," Zed murmured, pulling into a parking space behind the car that I recognized from Rex's garage. "We need to work out whether he's one of us or not. If not..."

I shook my head. "I'll rip his entrails out and stuff them down his throat until he chokes. He wouldn't be so stupid. Surely."

"I fucking hope not," Zed agreed. "Let's deal with him tomorrow so we can cross it off the list."

"Done," I agreed, wiggling back into my wet skirt before getting out of the car. Not that I gave two shits about anyone seeing my ass, but *Hades* had a reputation to uphold. One that didn't involve public nudity.

We crossed the road and tried the main door to Nadia's Cakes. It was locked, though, so I knocked and waited. Nadia was a smart woman; of course she kept the door locked if they were there in the evening. It didn't matter which gangs ran Shadow Grove, there was always going to be crime. There would always be random, opportunistic fucks willing to do immoral things...and now more than ever, Nadia had a target on her back for being associated with me.

There was a long pause, long enough that I quirked a brow at Zed in question and his hand shifted to his gun. Then came the subtle slide of someone moving the peephole cover.

"Oh shit," a male voice said. "It's Hades and Zed."

Nadia's voice was unmistakable as she barked back, "Which one of you shits called the boss?"

"Um...can we come in?" I asked, raising my voice to be heard through the door. "This is starting to get a bit suspicious." Understatement.

302

"Well?" Nadia snapped. "Don't just stand there with your dick in your hand, boy, let her in! You don't keep the boss waiting, learn that now."

The door bolts clunked as they were hastily unlocked, and then the door opened to reveal another of Rex's sons, whose name I couldn't remember for the life of me. The resemblance to his older brother, Ford, was uncanny, though.

"Hades," he said with a gulp, his eyes wide. "Hi. Hello. Zed. Sir. *Sirs.* Um, we haven't met yet, not officially. But I've heard... you know. A lot."

"Oh my god, Shelby, *shut the fuck up*," Seph bellowed from further inside the cafe.

Shelby. Now I remembered. Stupid Rex had named his three boys after cars: Ford, Lincoln, and Shelby. The man was obsessed.

She appeared in the doorway, shoving the boy out of the way, and gave me a wide, slightly feverish smile. "Hey, Dare, you probably wanna see the body, huh?"

I blinked at my little sister a couple of times. "Excuse me?"

"Did you say *body*?" Zed added, his hand still on his gun.

Seph's brows shot up high. "Oh. You're not here about the dead guy? Wow. This is awkward now."

Pushing past my sister and Shelby both, I marched into the main cafe and skirted around the pallet of plastic-wrapped furniture blocking the rest of the room from the doorway. Sure enough, there in the middle of the gorgeous, decoratively tiled floor, a man lay spread-eagled in a pool of blood.

"Boss," Nadia greeted me, "I take it you're here about this?" She waved a bloody frying pan at the dead man.

Diana was perched on the counter and sent me a sly smile. "He had it coming, Hades. We swear."

CHAPTER 38

Just like Hannah, someone had tried to kill Nadia. What he clearly hadn't been prepared for, though, was how handy Nadia was with a skillet or how quick-thinking Diana had been in running to get Seph and Shelby, who'd been about to drive away.

Shelby had officially earned his way into the Timberwolves by killing Nadia's attacker with one shot as Nadia had defended herself with her cast-iron skillet.

After we'd gotten the full story, I'd told Shelby to get in touch with Cass for a Timberwolf tattoo. He'd proven his worth in blood. The kid had been ecstatic, but Seph looked less than pleased.

Cass and Lucas were called to help Nadia clean up, while Zed and I continued over to Magnolia to collect the security footage of Hannah's attack. I was cold in my wet skirt, and we were both wrecked enough that we just collected all the tapes and took them home with us.

That was why Cass and Lucas found the two of us later that night curled up on the couch together, fresh from the shower, eating popcorn and watching Hannah hand her attacker his *ass*.

"Holy shit," Lucas murmured, standing behind the sofa to

watch it when we rewound the tape. "Hannah's a secret badass. Where did she learn that?"

Cass huffed in irritation. "She used to date that little prick Johnny Rock. Sounds like he liked to test out his punches on her, so she must have learned a thing or two to eventually fight back."

That made me feel sick…and at the same time so fucking glad she'd learned to fight because it'd saved her life today.

"The caliber of Chase's paid goons has definitely dropped," Lucas observed as he came around the couch to sit beside me, then snaked the bowl of popcorn out of my lap. Zed flicked the TV over to an action movie instead, since we'd seen enough of Hannah kicking ass.

"He was probably using a lot of Wayne's muscle," Cass suggested, dropping into a recliner and stretching his arms over his head in a way that made me stare straight at the V-line of muscles disappearing into his pants. Goddamn.

Zed gave a short laugh. "Probably. Two birds with one stone the other night."

"Did you see some of those shots Steele took?" Lucas asked Zed, his voice full of awe. "I didn't even *see* half of those targets until they dropped."

Zed rolled his eyes. "Less than I hit."

So damn competitive. I smiled and relaxed back into the couch as they chatted about sniper shots and trajectory and tossed out hypotheticals about whether being good at real-life guns automatically meant you'd be good at *Call of Duty*.

Cass wasn't really participating, so when he extended a hand to me, calling me over, I peeled myself up and went to him.

Holding my gaze, he pulled me into his lap on the recliner and cupped my face with his huge hand. "Rough day, huh?"

I offered a tired smile in return. "Could have been worse. A lot worse. I'd happily sacrifice my bars if the trade-off is keeping Hannah and Nadia alive."

His thumb stroked across my cheek, and his dark eyes studied mine. Then without a word, he pulled my face closer and kissed me with staggering intensity. When he released me sometime later, our breathing was equally rough and my lips buzzed with warmth.

"What was that for?" I asked in a husky whisper, leaning into the way his arm had wrapped around my waist, strong and possessive.

Cass gave a low chuckle. "Don't act like I need an excuse to kiss you, Red."

"Quit it, both of you," Zed snapped, shooting us a glare. "We're trying to watch a movie here."

Lucas snickered. "Zed's crabby because now he has to watch a Jason Statham flick while he's hard."

Zed walloped Lucas with a pillow while Cass shifted me to sit in his lap with my ass pressed against his own hardness. Well shit, now I really wasn't interested in watching a movie.

"Stop squirming, Red," Cass rumbled in my ear, his teeth nipping my lobe. His hand splayed across my stomach, holding me tighter against him as my breath caught and my core tightened.

Lucas tossed the pillow back at Zed and shot me a knowing smirk. "Keep squirming, Hayden. Torture his ass."

Zed snapped a sharp glare over at me. "Don't you, *Dare*."

I found that way too damn funny and started laughing, shifting on Cass's lap without even really meaning to do it. Or hell, maybe I did. Maybe my subconscious was sick of waiting for my mind to heal and just wanted some dick. Some long, hard, tattooed dick that was only a couple of layers of clothing away from—

"Shit's sake, Red," Cass growled, bucking his hips and sliding his hand lower on my belly. "You were warned." His fingers dipped under the waistband of my sweatpants, delving straight into my panties without a moment's hesitation and making me squeak.

Lucas and Zed both snapped their heads toward us, their eyes sharp as I let out a gasp and arched my spine, pushing myself onto Cass's hand harder.

"Seriously?" Zed asked, sounding pained.

Cass hummed a happy sound in his throat as his fingers slid into me with ease. "Shut up and enjoy the show, Zeddy Bear," he growled back.

Biting my lip against a laugh, I tugged my sweats and panties down, then kicked them off completely so there was nothing to block Zed or Lucas from seeing exactly what Cass was doing to me.

Fuck the damn movie, I was getting back on the horse. Maybe all three horses, if the night treated me right.

"Spread your legs wider, Angel," Cass purred in my ear, his spare hand hooking under my knee to drape it over the armrest. I obeyed his command, lifting my other leg up in a mirror image, and writhed my hips as his fingers stroked inside me. "That's it. Beautiful."

Lucas gave a low laugh, his head dropping back against the couch. His heavy-lidded eyes were on me, though. On my pussy and Cass's fingers working in and out, slick with my arousal. His hand shifted to his pants, grasping his erection through the fabric like he was trying to control it.

Soft moans slipped from my lips, and Cass sucked the flesh of my neck, driving me wild as he slid a third finger into my pussy.

Zed's gaze was like pure fire, totally unblinking as he watched. The lights were turned low, the flickering from the TV offering more illumination than anything, but I knew he could see everything.

I watched him right back, taking in the subtle way he shifted in his seat when I moaned. Or the way he ran his tongue over his lower lip, leaving it glistening. The naked, raw emotion in his eyes rocked me, though. There was nothing to fear there. No possible way I could ever confuse this Zed, the *real* Zed, with that bastardized, drug-induced version Chase had conjured up. No way.

"Are you gonna come for us, Angel?" Cass rumbled. "Do you want me to make you fall to pieces here in my lap?"

I wanted so much more, but my mouth wasn't listening to reason. "Yes," I panted, moaning and writhing, the pulsing of my impending climax growing more intense with every thrust of his fingers. "Yes, please, make me come, Saint."

He murmured his approval, then found my clit with his other hand. He stroked the pad of his index finger over that hypersensitive spot firmly and confidently, and I spasmed in his arms. My cunt was soaking; I could feel the dampness on my thighs as he pumped his fingers into me.

"Holy shit," I gasped, dropping my head back against his shoulder as he played with my clit. "Cass..." His name turned into a low moan as my orgasm started sparking.

His motions grew rougher, meeting the demand of my bucking hips, and continued even as I cried out and convulsed with my release. My toes curled, my pelvis pushing forward and begging for more as I came in long, shuddering waves and my breath came in rough gasps.

"Zeddy Bear," Cass rumbled before I fully came down from my climax. "Get over here. You know you want to taste this."

Just the suggestion of that had me shaking with hot anticipation, and I cracked my heavy lids to lock eyes with Zed, offering silent encouragement. He still hesitated a moment, until Lucas scoffed.

"If you don't, bro, I will. Hurry the fuck up."

Zed scowled at Lucas, who just grinned back at him. Then a second later, Zed was on his knees in front of me. In front of my spread-out and soaking-wet cunt.

"Dare, is this—"

"Yes!" I snapped, arching my hips. "Quit fucking asking for permission. If I didn't want it, I would've kicked you all in the balls and left."

Cass and Lucas both laughed at that, but Zed just did as Cass had told him. He leaned forward, bringing his mouth to my throbbing pussy to lick the slick cum from my flesh.

"Fuck," I hissed, my belly tightening once more. Oh yeah, I could go again, no question. I glanced over at Lucas, but he was slouched back on the sofa with his dick out and in his hand, stroking it lazily while he watched. A wide smile sat on his lips as he did so, too.

Cass shifted his hands to hook under my thighs once more, holding me open while Zed pushed his tongue inside my cunt. I groaned, tucking my face into Cass's neck and biting him, but I wasn't protesting. It'd been *too freaking long* since I'd had Zed's face between my legs.

"You gonna come again, Angel?" Cass murmured, his fingers gripping my thighs tight enough to bruise. "You make the sweetest sounds when you do. Gets my dick so fucking hard I could burst."

Zed shifted his mouth to my already swollen clit and slid his fingers into my pussy, making me buck. Cass gave a low chuckle, the fucking dick, and muttered something about how it would take no time at all.

He wasn't wrong, though. I wet my lips, looking over at Lucas and the weapon in his pumping fist. Oh yeah, I was definitely ready to get back on *all* the horses in my stable.

Zed's tongue teased me, dancing around my clit and only lightly brushing across it when I rocked harder on his face. His fingers worked faster, though, pumping into me in an echo of how Cass had just fucked me up.

Breathing hard, Cass released one of my thighs and brought his hand up to my face. "Suck," he ordered me, pushing two fingers into my mouth.

I didn't question him, sucking those fingers and tasting my own arousal in the process. Zed went harder, sucking my clit as I ran my tongue all over Cass's fingers. He grunted in approval as he withdrew them from my mouth and hooked them back under my leg once more—but not to hold my thighs open anymore. He took those fingers, slick with my saliva, and went straight to my asshole.

A scream of pleasure ripped from my throat as he pushed one finger inside, then quickly added the other. He was rough, but I fucking loved rough. Between him and Zed, they fucked both my holes with their hands, and Zed's mouth worked over my clit until I was a thrashing, trembling mess.

My orgasm hit hard enough to make me see stars, and I just barely peeled my eyes open long enough to see Lucas spill his load all over his own abs. Fuck *me*, that was hot.

"Don't fall asleep yet, Angel," Cass teased when I went boneless across his lap. "We've only just started."

Grinning, Zed sat up on his knees and licked his lips. Christ, that move in itself almost had me coming again. Especially when his hands shifted to his belt.

The shrill tone of a phone ringing cut through our little impromptu orgy, and all four of us paused a moment like we were all trying to remember whose phone that was.

"Shit," Lucas cursed. "Mine." He fumbled to tug his T-shirt off the rest of the way and swiped up his own cum with it before pulling his phone from his jeans.

He frowned at the display, and a cold chill ran through me. I hadn't forgotten the day we'd just had, all the coordinated strikes Chase had taken against us, and how he'd failed on two of them.

Cass and Zed sensed my panic. Zed got to his feet and Cass let me close my legs as I leaned forward to hear Lucas as he answered the call.

It only took a moment for his face to blanch, and I just knew. Hannah and Nadia had survived, but Chase's third strike had hit home.

"Who?" I barked, stuffing my legs back into my pants with angry movements.

"Maria," Lucas croaked, still with his phone to his ear. He paused another moment while he listened, then let out a long, shuddering breath before ending the call. He immediately dropped his face to his hands, taking a moment before he looked back up at me. "Car bomb. Doc caught some shrapnel and is being taken to emergency surgery now, but Maria was behind the wheel. She's dead."

Those words echoed through my head, stunning me. Maria was dead; Doc was in surgery. Chase was responsible, without a doubt. I was tearing apart his network, cutting down his allies, so he was returning the favor.

"Fuck," I whispered, swiping a hand through my hair and feeling utterly helpless. There was nothing I could do for Maria now; she was already dead. But I could damn well hit him back.

Good thing the gala was less than twenty-four hours away.

CHAPTER 39

Hannah, bless her tenacious heart, had tuxedos for both Lucas and Cass delivered first thing the next morning, while I was still yawning into my coffee. As she'd promised, Alexi had dropped over my dress and shoes the night before, so we were all sorted for the mayor of Cloudcroft's charity gala.

It was being held at the Cloudcroft Museum of Modern Art—because all charity galas need wealth dripping from every wall—and the guest list was impressive, to say the least.

I was only interested in *one* guest in particular, though—a certain gentleman by the name of Conrad Holmes, deputy mayor of Cloudcroft and third on my hit list.

"So, are you going to tell us what the plan is for tonight?" Lucas asked, munching on his bowl of cereal opposite me at the table.

I smiled back at him. "Nope."

Zed gave a soft laugh, already privy to my plans. "Gumdrop, you're only coming as arm candy, didn't you realize?"

Lucas flipped Zed his middle finger but tilted his head to me in question. I rolled my eyes and whacked Zed's stomach as he leaned close to refill my coffee.

"Zed's being an asshole," I murmured. "You're so much better than arm candy, Lucas."

"Although gumdrops *are* candy," Cass mused, still looking half-asleep as he scuffed his feet into the kitchen. He yawned hard, then blinked at the three of us. "What are we talking about?"

Lucas glowered. "I asked about Hayden's plan for tonight."

Cass grunted, scrubbing a hand over his head. "Oh yeah. It's a good one."

Lucas's jaw dropped, his spoon hanging loose in his hand. "What the hell? Cass knows the plan?"

I had to bite my cheek not to laugh, instead shooting a pointed glare in Grumpy Cat's direction. "No, he doesn't. He's messing with you, Lucas. Don't pay any attention."

Lucas looked like he wasn't sure who to believe, so I came around to his side of the table and slid into his lap with my arms around his neck.

"Hey, they're just being shitheads. I promise tonight's plan is the easiest one yet. I just don't want to ruin the surprise by telling you the details."

Dark circles sat under Lucas's eyes as he gazed up at me. He'd barely slept, having spent most of the night waiting for an update on Doc's surgery. He'd been doing a lot of his practical EMT training with Doc and Maria, so this attack was hitting him hard.

"I trust you." He heaved a sigh. "Sorry, I'm just tired. Crabby."

"Horny," Cass teased, and Lucas threw his cereal spoon at his face.

Cass and Zed both snickered like fucking children, but I cupped Lucas's face between my palms to kiss him.

"I get it," I whispered. "Give me ten minutes to wake up, and we can go visit Doc, okay?" He'd come out of surgery around three in the morning and been moved to the recovery ward. So far, it seemed like he might survive.

Lucas grasped my waist, kissing me back for a long moment.

313

Then he gave a small sigh. "No, you already have a full day. I'll head over there on my way to see my mom. Besides, you still need to check in with Hannah."

He was right, but I also wanted to be there for him. And Doc, who'd been working with the Timberwolves since before my reign. He must be devastated to lose Maria.

"I'll go with Gumdrop," Zed offered. "I'd like to check in on Doc myself."

I nodded, feeling slightly better to know Zed would represent us both. Glancing up at Cass, I raised a brow. "What are your plans today?"

He shrugged. "Gotta ink up your new recruit, then not much. Why, do you need something?"

"Yeah," I replied, my arms still looped around Lucas's neck. "I booked us a room at the Blanco for after the gala. Could I get you to head over early and secure it?"

Cass gave me a curious look. "You booked us a room, huh?"

I shrugged. "If tonight goes as well as I hope, we might be in the mood to celebrate. I figured it'd be nice not to have to drive all the way back here."

"No arguments here," Cass replied. "I'll sort it out."

He knew that I didn't simply mean to check us in and get access cards. With Chase lurking in every goddamn shadow, we couldn't take risks. Cass would ensure the room was clean of traps, bombs, gas canisters, listening devices, cameras...*anything* that might undermine our safety.

Smacking another quick kiss on Lucas's lips, I climbed out of his lap and went to get ready for the day. Unlike my guys, I had far less *important* appointments to get to after I'd been to see Hannah.

My assistant was quick to remind me of that fact when I knocked on her door, too. First, she reminded me that I was letting my humanity show—whoops—but then informed me I was late for the appointments she'd scheduled into my calendar and wouldn't even let me through her front door.

First, I needed a manicure. I used to keep my nails so perfect all the time, but between my captivity, my escape, and all the worrying I'd done…they needed some love.

Then, before heading to hair and makeup, I had my physical therapy appointment with Misha, who both praised my progress and scolded my lack of sling use. By the time I was done with him, I was sweaty and aching and sorely tempted to skip the damn beauticians.

But…the gala needed to go flawlessly, so I needed to play my part.

Several hours later, I was plucked, primped, polished, and *perfect* as I ascended the steps of the Cloudcroft Museum with my hand tucked through Zed's arm.

"In case I didn't mention it already," Zed murmured as we waited to enter the impressive old building, "you look sensational."

I flashed him a smile because he *had* already mentioned it. Despite the long sleeves on my formfitting black evening gown, I felt naked. Not because of the open back displaying the tattoo down my spine or because of the split skirt ending so high I needed to coordinate my panties. Nope, I felt naked as fuck because the mayor's gala didn't allow weapons.

"This still feels risky," Cass rumbled from behind us.

I quirked a flirtatious brow at him over my shoulder. "You saying you can't kill a man with your bare hands, big guy? I bet Lucas could."

Lucas beamed. "I totally could."

Zed pulled me closer as we advanced to the entryway and metal detectors. The mayor must've been paranoid about certain names on her guest list because the metal detector hadn't been on the original schedule for the evening. But so long as Chase was being held to the same standard, I wasn't concerned.

Okay, that was a lie. I was concerned enough that I'd slipped a fiberglass knife into a strap on my thigh and was pretty confident the guys had all done something similar. But my plan for the deputy mayor didn't require me to be armed.

We handed over our invitation at the door and passed through the metal detectors without a problem, then made our way into the main gallery where the party was being held.

For a while, Zed and I played our roles of influential investors and businesspeople. We smiled and exchanged polite small talk with political figures and various other company heads from the area, while I always kept the hapless deputy mayor in the corner of my eye.

"He's very well protected," Lucas observed as we danced together some hours after arriving at the event. We'd already eaten dinner and managed to elude Chase for most of the night. He was constantly watching but hadn't made any attempt to approach. Yet. He would, though. He couldn't help himself.

"He is indeed," I agreed, switching my attention back to the deputy mayor. "Even more so than the mayor herself. Which says he's feeling paranoid."

Lucas grinned. "I guess word gets around when someone starts killing off the men you've been colluding with."

I smiled back at him as we left the dance floor. There was a glimmer of vicious bloodlust in his eyes that turned me right the fuck on. I could hardly wait to get back to our hotel room later.

The Blanco was an iconic six-star hotel right across the road from the museum, and I'd booked us the honeymoon suite with a whole lot of fucking in mind.

Lucas stiffened a minute later, tension rippling through him in a palpable wave, and my breath caught.

"Go away, Chase," I said in a cool voice without turning to look at him standing behind me. "I'm busy."

Just as I would have walked away, Chase snatched my arm just above the elbow, jerking me back in to his body with a sharp movement.

"Now, now," he chided when I coiled my muscles to strike back at him. "Don't go causing a scene, Darling. We wouldn't want these nice people to think there was any ill will between Daria Wolff and Wenton Dibbs, would we? Or are we Hayden Timber and Chase Lockhart tonight? I tell you, it gets so hard to keep up some days."

Lucas's eyes were locked on mine, silently asking for a cue on what I wanted him to do. As badly as I wanted to tell him to stab Chase in the other eye, I couldn't risk messing up my plans for the deputy mayor. So I gave him a small headshake and a reassuring smile.

"Lucas, can I trouble you for another glass of champagne? I seem to suddenly have an awful taste in my mouth." I twisted my lip in a sneer as I looked up at Chase from the corner of my eye.

Lucas frowned, his jaw tight with tension. Before leaving, though, he leaned in close and kissed me tenderly. "Of course I can. I love you, Hayden."

I grinned, knowing he was messing with Chase's head. "I love you too, Lucas. So much." Taunting our enemy or not, it was the truth.

Chase's grip on my elbow tightened to painful, and I could almost hear his teeth grinding as Lucas sauntered away into the crowd. He firmly turned me around to face him, his other hand moving to my bare back like we were dancing.

"You're up to something, Darling," he muttered, full of suspicion. "I can smell the scheming on you. It stinks."

A hollow laugh bubbled from me, and I caught Cass's eye across the room. His face was a picture of rage, but I held his gaze steady until he got the message that I didn't need saving.

"Don't be silly, Chase," I replied, my skin crawling under his touch and my stomach like a lead weight. My heart was beating so hard it hurt my still healing ribs, but I refused to show my fear. He'd had enough of that for ten lifetimes; I wouldn't give even an inch more. "You invited me, after all."

"You've been a busy little demon lately, Darling," he observed, ignoring my reply. "Painting the streets red. Now that I think of it, Chasing Trucking was a little obvious, but tell me…how'd you find out about Wayne?"

I almost reacted to that. Almost. *This motherfucker doesn't know I have a list.*

I had assumed he knew I'd stood there and listened to his call. I was operating on the expectation that he *knew* I was coming after his whole dirty crew. But he didn't. He thought I'd found Brad and Wayne by…luck? Research?

My smile broke through, and Chase saw it. His grip tightened, and he dropped his face to bring his lips right beside my ear.

"*What*," he hissed, "is so fucking *funny*, Darling?"

His ignorance was amusing enough that I didn't even feel the need to vomit on his shoes for him being within my personal space. Instead of replying, I just let the laughter roll out. Dumb, arrogant fuck. He'd work it out…soon.

I cast my eyes around the room, searching for my mark once more, but found someone else familiar.

"Chase," I snickered, "you really thought I would come for your head in such a public forum? You had to bring your own security guards to a *charity gala*? Wow, you really are afraid of me."

He visibly bristled at my insult, his eye narrowing. "Don't give yourself so much credit, Darling. I don't need to bring security here. You're no threat to me. We both know it's only a matter of time before you're back in my house chained to a bed, *screaming* my name. But next time, I'll be sure not to leave a single person alive to rescue you."

I spotted Zed making a beeline toward us with a curiously satisfied look on his face. I hadn't seen him in over an hour and had no idea what mischief he'd been getting up to.

"Ah, Special Agent Dibbs, isn't it?" Zed called out loudly as he approached Chase and me, drawing the attention of several people nearby. "It was so good of you to keep my *darling* fiancée company while I was in the restroom."

Chase stiffened harder than a board, and I had to bite my lip not to laugh in his face again. Zed tugged me out of his slimy grip and spun me around, using my body as a shield while he deftly slipped a ring onto my finger.

"What did you just say?" Chase hissed as Zed looped his arm around my waist. Casual as fuck.

"Hmm?" he replied, acting innocent. "Oh, I said thank you for keeping Daria company. Not that she needs it. She's so independent, this *fiancée* of mine."

We still had the attention of several other guests, including the mayor of Cloudcroft herself.

"Oh, Zed, I didn't know you two were engaged," the mayor gushed, all smiles. "Congratulations." A waiter passing with a tray of champagne paused, and I grabbed one.

Zed laughed easily while Chase's face turned an ugly shade of red. It was glorious.

"It's a recent thing," Zed replied to the mayor, and I almost choked on the sip of champagne I'd just taken. *Recent* was putting it mildly.

Smiling, I focused on the mayor as if Chase no longer existed. "Sometimes true love comes along and makes you realize how shallow and meaningless all your past relationships were," I commented as though I was just musing on the nature of love. "Like any previous engagements were just *trash*."

Chase jerked as if to stomp away but collided with a waiter, sending a whole tray of champagne flutes crashing to the floor and soaking him in wine.

"Oh no!" the mayor gasped. "Agent Dibbs, what a mess."

"I'm *fine*," Chase snarled when the waiter tried to offer him a cloth. "I'll just...go dry off in the restroom." He shot me an acidic glare, and I gave a pointless flourish with my hand just to draw his attention to the ring Zed'd slipped onto my finger.

"Hurry back though, Agent Dibbs," I suggested. "The best part of the evening is about to begin."

"Yes, you're right," the mayor agreed, nodding to her silent husband at her side. "The auction is due to start shortly."

I smiled. I wasn't talking about the auction, and Chase damn well knew it.

He stalked away like there was something snapping at his heels, but it wasn't long until he returned in a fresh shirt with an even darker glower on his eye-patched face.

Lucky for me, though, he'd returned *just* in time to see my night come to fruition.

Not far from where I stood chatting with the Cloudcroft fire chief and a humanitarian lawyer named Elise, there was a clatter of noise and several shocked gasps. Then a woman screamed.

"Call an ambulance!" she howled, crouching on the floor over a convulsing, tuxedo-suited man. People closed around them quickly, everyone eager to see what the drama was, but I hung back. I didn't need to look to know it was the silly, hapless deputy mayor dying on the marble floor.

I also knew that there was no possible way for an ambulance to save him. Not from *that* toxin.

Across the room, Chase met my gaze, and I smiled.

I smiled and raised my glass to him as the lights refracted off the black diamonds of my ring.

"Cheers, asshole," I murmured under my breath. "Three down, three to go. And then you."

The gala dissolved quickly from that point as paramedics rushed in to try to help an already dead man and finely dressed guests flowed out of the museum. My guys and I left with them, and I headed straight for the stunning young blond woman waiting on the steps. She was dressed in a striking red Valentino gown and oozed money, just like every single one of the other guests at the party.

But this one? She was special.

"How'd I do?" the woman asked, breathless with excitement.

I gave her a proud smile. "Flawless. Welcome to the Timberwolves, Bethany."

CHAPTER 40

The four of us were in high spirits when we arrived at our penthouse suite at the Blanco, and Lucas headed straight for the champagne on ice that had been left out for us.

"I see why you wanted that to be a surprise," he told me over his shoulder as he opened the bottle. "I *never* saw that coming. Very impressive."

I grinned, smug as shit that the plan had been executed so perfectly. Chase had been so laser-focused on me, so sure I was the one who was up to something, that it'd never even crossed his mind that I was the decoy. Zed's trick with the engagement announcement had been the perfect finisher. It'd drawn a lot of focus, not just from Chase and the mayor, but from other guests too. So much so that it was all too easy for the gorgeous blond flirting with Deputy Mayor Conrad Holmes to poison his drink.

"Bethany impressed me," I commented, exchanging a knowing look with Zed. "I'm excited for this new era of Timberwolves."

Zed's arms slipped around my waist, pulling me close as he dipped low to kiss me. "You impress me, Dare. Every damn day."

"The ring was a nice touch," Cass rumbled, tugging his bow tie undone and snagging my attention. Cassiel Saint was sex in leather most days, but in a tuxedo? Holy mother of orgasms. *That* was something special.

Zed caught my hand in his and brought it to his mouth. "I thought so," he murmured, kissing the ring still on my finger. It definitely hadn't been a part of the plan I'd discussed with him, but now that I took a better look at it...

"Fucking hell, Zed," I whispered. "It's gorgeous."

Cass reached between us to grab my hand and took a closer look at the ring. It was rose gold and set with one large, blood-red diamond in the center and two inky-black diamonds to either side. Dozens of smaller black and red diamonds decorated the setting, which looked almost like a little bloodied crown around my finger.

I knew they were diamonds, not any other stone, because I knew *Zed*. He didn't half-ass anything, and red diamonds were his favorite stone.

Mine too.

"That doesn't look like costume jewelry, Zeddy Bear," Cass muttered, shooting Zed an accusing look. "What'd it cost? A mil? Two?"

"At least," I murmured. The average red diamond ran some-where in the realm of a million dollars per carat. At a guess, I'd say that central stone was at least two carats—and *flawless*. Most red diamonds in existence were barely a half carat at best.

I started taking it off—to give it back so he could return it to wherever he'd borrowed it from—but he swatted my hand away.

"You take that ring off, Dare, and we've got problems." His tone was low and dead serious, and his eyes held mine with an intense warning.

My brows hitched. "I'm not marrying you, Zed."

Instead of hurt, his face flashed with something far more dangerous. Determination.

Fuck's sake. The last thing on my agenda for the night was a blow-up argument about the pointless nature of a marriage certificate or how it was totally impractical given we were now a polyamorous heterosexual foursome. At least...I thought that's what we were defined as. Maybe just *reverse harem*.

Biting my cheek against my own instinct to argue, I forced a shrug. "Fine. It's safer on my finger than in your pocket, anyway. We can return it to its rightful owner tomorrow."

Zed flashed a grin of victory. "Deal."

He released me then, heading farther into the room and tugging his bow tie free from his shirt.

Cass gave me a side-eye. "That seemed too easy."

"Agreed," I replied under my breath.

Lucas handed me a glass of champagne. "I'm with Hayden on this, Zeddy Bear. You can't go proposing to a girl without a proposal. That's cheating."

Zed shrugged but didn't reply as he wandered through to the bedroom, checking out the suite. He'd unbuttoned the top few buttons of his shirt and shed his jacket, but otherwise seemed totally at ease in the designer tux.

Cass, on the other hand, downed his champagne in one gulp, then put the glass down to strip out of his shirt.

"No," I protested with a pout. "Keep it on. I never see you all dressed up, Grumpy Cat."

He huffed a laugh, shrugged out of the starched white shirt, and flexed his muscles. "Not a chance, Red. Suits should only be worn at funerals or—"

"Weddings?" Lucas teased, refilling his glass for him.

I rolled my eyes. Apparently, they were all in a *mood* tonight. And Cass in nothing but a pair of tuxedo pants was also a pretty spectacular look, so who was I to complain.

"One of you want to help me out of this dress?" I asked, heading toward the bedroom. It held a massive bed all scattered with rose petals—it was the honeymoon suite after all—and more champagne on ice beside the bed.

"Hold that thought, Red," Cass growled, swatting my hands away from the dress clasp at the back of my neck. "Are we gonna talk about this?"

I spun around to face him and bit my lip when I locked my eyes on the fresh Timberwolf tattoo on the side of his neck. It marked him so clearly as mine; I loved it more than any of his other ink—even the Darling logo on the top of his ass cheek.

"Nothing to talk about," Zed replied, slouching against the doorframe to the bathroom, his hands tucked in his pockets. "Like Dare said, tomorrow the ring will be returned to its owner, and we won't discuss it again."

Cass shot him a glare, and Lucas backed him up.

"Okay, but how about that casual way you just tried to snare Hayden into marrying you without even an attempt at a romantic proposal? That's severely uncool, bro." Lucas folded his arms, his tuxedo still perfect.

I sighed heavily. "Guys, come on. Zed was just playing, *right?*" I shot him a sharp look, silently warning him not to escalate the situation.

He just smirked and shrugged. Fucking hell.

"Okay, now you're all pissing me off," I snapped. "I thought we were going to come back here and…you know…work on some physical therapy." I tilted my chin up to meet Cass's eyes. "Don't you wanna provide more positive reinforcement, Grumpy Cat? Because I really want to finish what we started last night in the movie room."

His jaw clenched, his dark eyes flashing with desire. "More than anything on this planet," he muttered back. "But this is the first time I've ever even heard the prospect of marriage raised in your presence, and it feels important."

I could see the determination in his face, and a quick glance at Lucas said I would get no help from that camp, which wasn't surprising, despite his age. Lucas, of all three of them, had always been the surest. The most unwavering and determined.

With a groan, I flopped down onto the bed and felt the rose petals scatter. "Zed, I'm going to kill you." Lifting my hand in front of my face, I peered at the ring again. I doubt I could have imagined a more perfect engagement ring if I'd put my mind to it. But that wasn't the point.

Blowing out a breath, I sat back up and eyed all three of them. They were just fucking *watching* me, waiting for me to say something. Not fair at all, when they were the ones who'd started this whole pointless conversation.

I ground my teeth together, knowing full well that what I had to say on the matter would totally ruin the night. But I was also unwilling to lie to them, so...fuck it. Rip that Band-Aid off.

"I'm not marrying anyone," I told them. "Ever."

Yeah, that statement landed about as well as I could have expected. Lucas frowned like I'd slapped him with a piece of rancid ham, Cass simmered with defiant anger, and Zed? Zed just smirked like I was deluding myself and it was already a done deal.

"Red—" Cass started, his eyes flickering with fury like a pissed-off wet cat.

"Maybe you could explain that to us," Lucas interjected before Cass and I could start yelling at each other.

I flicked my gaze over to him, softening when I saw the genuine concern on his face. "Do I have to?" I asked, feeling somewhat childish. Screw them for putting me in a corner, though. I'd been caught off guard.

Lucas's brow tightened. "No. I won't make you do anything you don't want to do."

Cass glowered at him. "I will."

Lucas rolled his eyes. "No, you won't, and you damn well know it."

"Dare is clearly not in the mood to explain why she doesn't believe in marriage in the traditional sense," Zed mediated, even though it was his fucking fault we were having this conversation.

"Suffice it to say the three of us disagree with her position, but we don't all *need* to agree tonight."

I wasn't stupid; I could read between the lines. We didn't all need to agree *tonight* meant he fully intended to get my agreement another day. Stubborn fuck.

He *was* giving me an easy out, though, so I gritted my teeth and went with it, giving a nod.

Sweeping a hand through his hair, Lucas sighed but gave me a small smile of reassurance as he went back into the living room to grab the champagne.

Cass had folded his arms over his chest, though, and looked like he was ready to hash it all out right then and there.

"What?" I snapped, glaring up at him.

His eyes narrowed. "So you never want to get married. What about kids?"

Oh, for the love of fuck. Is he serious?

"What about them?" I replied, just as stubborn as he was. "They're usually small humans with sticky hands."

Cass glowered harder. Zed said nothing, his gaze locked on me and offering no assistance. Prick.

"Do. You. Want. Kids?" Cass bit out, one word at a time, just in case I misunderstood the question again.

I laughed sharply. "Hell no. Do you?" His brows hitched, and I shook my head. "Forget I asked. I don't want to have this conversation."

Officially pissed off, I pushed up off the bed and tried to brush past him, but he grabbed me before I could leave the room.

"Red," Cass snapped. "Don't you think—"

"No!" I shouted back, whirling around to give him the full force of my anger. "No, Cass, *you're* the one not thinking. Where the hell is all this coming from? Marriage? Kids? Who the hell do you think we *are*? We just had the deputy mayor poisoned in front of hundreds of witnesses to seek revenge on my psychotic, abusive, obsessed ex. I'm the head of one of the biggest, bloodiest gangs on the West Coast. You think I want to leave my offspring orphaned when Mommy gets killed by some up-and-coming gangster one day? You wanna create pawns for our enemies to kidnap, torture, ransom, or leverage against us? You want one of *our* children to be the target of some punk gangster kids trying to prove themselves to dear old daddy by killing them in their sleep?" I shot a sharp look at Zed when I said that.

He knew. He and Chase had tried to kill me when I was just ten years old. *That* was the kind of life the children of gang leaders led. Dangerous. Deadly.

That was no fucking life for a kid. I wouldn't ever wish my childhood on someone else.

Cass seemed speechless, as well he should. He wasn't thinking with his brain. Not his rational one, anyway.

"Wake the fuck up, Saint," I told him in a cold voice. "I'm not that woman. I'm Hades, and that's never going to change. Either take me as I am...or not at all."

Panic flooded through me the moment I offered that ultimatum, and I immediately knew I didn't want to hear his answer. So I jerked my arm free of his grip and stalked away, snatching the bottle of champagne from Lucas as I brushed past.

For lack of any better ideas, I took myself to the bathroom off the living room and locked myself inside, then sat down on the heated tile floor and trembled with silent tears. I'd finally imploded our perfect harmony.

CHAPTER 41

They didn't leave me there for long—I knew they wouldn't—just long enough to show they respected my need for a moment alone, but nowhere near long enough that I ever felt *alone*.

When a soft knock sounded on the door, I fully expected to find Lucas there with a warm hug and soothing words. So I was caught off guard when the big stubborn bastard let himself into the bathroom and sank down to the floor with me.

He didn't speak. He just sat down beside me, his warm, tattooed arm pressed to mine as he gently took the champagne bottle from my hand and took a sip.

I sniffed hard, swallowing back the water that had been stupidly leaking from my eyes. When had I become so fucking *emotional?*

For a while, we just sat there in silence, sharing the bottle between us. Then eventually, when I had a better grip on my shit, I snatched a washcloth from the vanity and wiped the mess of mascara and eyeliner from my cheeks.

The blackness of my makeup stood out harshly against the whiteness of the cloth, and I tossed it aside with a huff of annoyance. Stupid waterproof mascara never was waterproof.

Before I could say anything, Cass put the nearly empty

champagne bottle down on the tiled floor and cupped a hand around the back of my neck. His nose booped mine gently as he turned my face toward his, then his lips were on mine in a kiss that warmed me all the way from the inside out.

He kissed me with all the messy, soft emotions that we both struggled so hard to express. All the love and devotion that, for us, came out as frustration and stubborn defiance. Cass kissed me until my cheeks were wet with tears once more, then he kissed the tears away and dragged me into his lap to hold me tight.

"I'm sorry," he whispered against my neck. "I'm an asshole."

I huffed a watery laugh. "No joke."

His chest rumbled. "I never want you to be anyone but you, Red. I wouldn't change you for the fucking world." His lips moved on my neck, kissing me between words and making my breath catch. "I saw Zed's ring on your finger and...lost my damn mind for a minute." He kissed my neck harder, his teeth scraping my skin as I sighed.

"Why?" The question came out a little more than an exhale as he sucked a mark on my throat.

He kissed the mark, then shifted back to meet my eyes. "Because a small part of me still thinks you're going to choose. Eventually, you'll only keep one of us...and it'll be Zed. Because it's always been Zed."

I frowned. There was no way I could tell him his fear was unfounded, because it *had* always been Zed. He was my soulmate. But the human heart was capable of so much more than just one great love. And they *could* all sit equal in importance. I knew my own heart. I knew that the love I felt for Zed, for Lucas, and for Cass were entirely different things, yet each just as important and just as deeply woven into the fiber of my being.

But Cass didn't know that. Nor did Lucas or Zed. For them, I was their one and only.

Holding his gaze, I stroked my thumb over his lower lip.

"Cassiel Saint," I whispered, full of sincerity and promise, "I swear to you I'm not choosing. Not now, not ever. You're a part of me now, all three of you. We're in this to the end, the four of us. We don't need a legal document to confirm what we already feel in our hearts."

He blew out a breath, relief passing over his face. "I know," he murmured. "I *know*...but I just reacted without logic or reason."

I got it. I did. So I clasped his face between my hands and held his gaze firmly. "Saint. I love you. Even if I believed in the construct of marriage—which I don't—I still couldn't marry all three of you. So, can we just cohabitate? Is that enough for you?" I held my breath, waiting on his response.

"Shit, Red," he whispered back, his gaze soft, "of course it is. *You* are enough in whatever way you'll let me have you."

Ah, damn. That set the butterflies free inside me.

"No more jealous bullshit?" I asked, my eyes narrowed suspiciously.

He huffed a laugh. "Now *that* I can't promise you. But I want to be clear, my issues with Zed and that fucking massive-dicked teenager out there, they're with *them*. Never you. You're my angel."

I grinned, all fucking warm and squishy inside. Why did I secretly love that they couldn't get past their jealousy with each other? It was such a turn-on.

"I guess that's good enough," I murmured, brushing my lips over his softly.

Cass tightened his grip on me, pulling me in closer to his body. "Did I totally ruin the mood?"

Biting my lip, I shook my head. "No...but I probably need to talk to Lucas now."

He quirked one brow. "Not Zed?"

I brought my hand back in front of my face, eyeing the *perfectly me* ring that fit as if it were custom-made. "No. That asshole won't hear sense tonight. I'll deal with him tomorrow when we get home. That way we can break shit and not pay the hotel damage waiver."

Cass smirked. "I'll make popcorn and take bets."

Chuckling, I climbed off him and inspected my face in the mirror. Another swipe with the washcloth was needed to wipe away the Gothic look of dripping mascara. Cass waited while I cleaned it up, his hands resting on my hips and his lips against my shoulder like he couldn't bear to be apart just yet.

I understood what he was feeling and leaned back into his warmth for a moment.

When I opened the bathroom door, I found Lucas and Zed slouched on the huge leather lounge with the massive flat-screen displaying breaking news. Footage of glittering guests flowing out of the Cloudcroft museum filled the screen as the solemn-faced reporter spoke of the tragic passing of the deputy mayor.

I pursed my lips as I listened to the praise she heaped on the dead man, and a fire burned inside me. Conrad Holmes hadn't been a *good man*. He'd been a sex trafficker, a drug distributor, and a pedophile. He shouldn't be remembered as any kind of *great man*.

"You need me to kick Cass in the balls, babe?" Lucas offered, jerking my attention away from the news story. He and Zed were both staring at me with caution, like they weren't *totally* sure what kind of mood I'd emerged in.

I gave a weak smile. "Tempting."

Cass, though, growled in warning and gripped my hips tight again. "Only one person in this room is touching my balls tonight, and it ain't you, Gumdrop."

Swatting Cass's hands, I made my way over to the lounge that Lucas and Zed were both occupying. Undecided on where to sit or what to say, I perched my butt on the coffee table so I could look at them both.

"We're good, Hayden," Lucas assured me before I could dredge up the right words to address all the *intense* subjects floating around

332

tonight. Marriage and kids. Fucking hell, Lucas was nineteen. I was quietly surprised he hadn't run away entirely.

I arched a brow. "Are we, though?" Because I'd seen the stricken look on his face when I'd said I would never get married.

His smile tightened somewhat. "We've got our whole lives ahead of us, babe. I'm in no hurry to tick boxes. Are you?"

In other words, let's agree to disagree for the time being. I had no doubt this would be a heated discussion with him one day, but that day didn't need to be today.

"No," I agreed softly, "I'm not."

I flicked my gaze to Zed, but he just met my eyes unapologetically. He knew he'd sparked that whole argument, then stood back and let Cass feed the flames. I wasn't shortsighted enough to think he was being a coward because Zed already knew my stance on both of those topics. He was giving me an opening to clearly voice my opinions and get it all out in the open, even though he disagreed.

"Tomorrow," I told him sternly, and he just grinned as he glanced down at my hand. I hadn't even noticed that I'd been spinning the ring around my finger in a subconscious fidget like how I sometimes bite my thumbnail.

"Can I take you up on that offer now?" Lucas asked, sitting forward and clasping his hands on my waist. He lifted me off the coffee table and put me down in his lap, my knees to either side of his hips.

I tilted my head in question. "What offer?"

He grinned, his gorgeous eyes sparkling with mischief. "You asked if one of us wanted to help you out of this dress. I'm feeling *so* helpful right now." His hands slid up my sides, brushing over my breasts and skating gently across my shoulders. His fingers dipped under my hair, seeking the clasp of my dress, but paused there, waiting for permission.

Wetting my lips, I tipped my face to look over at Cass, who still loomed near the bathroom door. He dipped his head in answer, assuring me we were good. Zed's response was to swat Lucas's hand out of the way and flick open the clasp holding my dress closed.

"Dick," Lucas muttered but then smiled as he peeled my dress off my arms for me. The dress was backless, allowing no bra beneath, and a moment later my dress was bunched around my waist as Lucas's hands palmed my breasts.

Zed cupped my cheek, turning my face to him, and kissed me long and hard. Then he tugged me to my feet and helped me shed my designer gown the rest of the way. Cass joined us then, eyeing my tiny black thong and the fiberglass dagger strapped to my thigh.

"I can help with that," he murmured, moving to the opposite side from Zed, and plucking the knife from my thigh strap. He slid it gently between my hip and thong, gave a sharp tug, and cut the thin fabric.

I rolled my eyes, even though I'd gasped in arousal at the caveman gesture. "That was so unnecessary."

He smirked back. "You love it." He tossed the blade down onto the table and unstrapped the thigh sheath rather than cutting it, which I appreciated. They were harder to replace than thongs.

It was only then, with Zed and Cass towering on either side of me and Lucas on the couch in front gazing adoringly up at me, that it hit me. This was the first time I'd been totally naked with the three of them since my arrest.

"Dare," Zed murmured, "are you okay?"

It was also the first time that I felt *completely* comfortable in my own skin and with my own sexuality. These three men loved me unconditionally. They would lay down their lives for me, as I would for them. I had *nothing* to fear, not here, not with them.

I'd never felt safer or more powerful.

CHAPTER 42

Somewhere between Cass cutting my thong off and Lucas losing all his clothes, we moved through to the bedroom and swept all the rose petals off the huge bed.

Champagne was buzzing through my head as Zed kissed me, his hands banding around my waist and pushing me onto the bed. Before I could wiggle up to the pillows, though, Lucas grabbed my legs and tugged me back to the end of the bed before sinking to his knees between my thighs.

I'd made my point during our movie make-out the night before, and they'd stopped treating me like I was breakable. I appreciated the hell out of them for it too. Normalcy was all I wanted.

Cass dragged a chair over from the corner of the room, positioning it near the end of the bed, then slouched down into it with his hand inside his pants. He caught my eye, arching a brow with silent command as Zed kissed and sucked at my breast.

I grinned and hiked my foot up to rest on the edge of the bed, giving him an unobstructed view as Lucas stroked his fingers into me.

Cass's lips tipped up in a smile as I moaned and arched my back, and I caught the way he mouthed *good girl* before Zed claimed my lips again.

Zed kissed me breathless, his fingers playing with my nipples, tweaking and rubbing them. When Lucas's tongue found my clit, I shuddered a long moan into Zed's kiss. Cass just reached out with his foot, nudging mine wider on the edge of the bed. Then he gave an appreciative murmur as Lucas sat back once more to show off how wet I was.

"You see something you like, Saint?" I teased, my voice a breathy gasp as Lucas slowly pumped his fingers in and out of me, torturously slow.

Cass flashed me a grin. "Fuck yeah, I do." As evidenced by the tight grip he held on his hard dick. He didn't get up and join in, though. Instead, he nudged Lucas with his toe and exchanged a pointed look with my Gumdrop.

Lucas grinned, then gave me one more long lick before getting to his feet.

"Wait, what?" I protested, and Zed propped himself up on one shoulder, looking confused.

"Zeddy Bear, you've always been into a bit of exhibitionism, haven't you?" Cass asked, giving me a fiery-hot look. The muscles in his arms were tight, and I could tell it was taking all his willpower to stay put and not pounce on me.

Zed danced his hand down my naked body and found my soaking core, which Lucas had just abandoned to…drag another chair in from the living room. Oh. *Oh.*

I'd mentioned to Cass several days ago that I was hitting roadblocks with Zed when it came to sex, thanks to the drugged mess of horrible memories crowding my brain. Clearly, he and Lucas had discussed it and decided it was important that *Zed* be the one to help me cross this line.

"You wanna sit there and watch?" Zed asked with a short laugh. "Be my fucking guest."

I grinned because I was all kinds of okay with this. I'd never been one for exhibitionism myself, but with Lucas and Cass watching and getting off on the show we were providing? God, yeah, I could see the appeal. So I helped Zed strip out of his tux and tossed it across the room.

Kissing me, he sank back into the mattress and lifted me to straddle him.

I met his eyes as I shifted my position, my throbbing pussy grinding against his hardness as I braced my hands on his chest.

"Thank you," I whispered because he'd put me in charge. He'd given me the control...for this first time anyway.

Zed's response was to clasp my hips, lifting me in just the right way to line us up, and he bit his lower lip as I sank down onto his dick an inch.

I looked over my shoulder, locking eyes with Cass and shooting him a hot smirk. "How's the view, Saint?"

His answering grin was pure sex, and he stroked his cock teasingly. "Incredible."

Lucas huffed a laugh, and I turned my head over my other shoulder to peer at him. He was stark naked—I was starting to think that was his most comfortable state of being—and his eyes were hot with desire and need.

"Are you gonna tease him all night, babe?" He nodded to how I was poised, with only the tip of Zed's dick inside me. "I mean, he deserves it for sparking that argument earlier, but I'm really hoping these old bastards will blow their loads and pass out soon so I can have you all to myself."

I laughed. Zed reached behind him to toss a pillow, but his throw went wide as I sank further down on his cock. A low moan vibrated his chest under my hands, and I focused on him once more. Just him. Zed. My best friend. He'd once told me that if I took a leap of faith, he would catch me.

"Zed," I gasped, pushing down further and taking him all the way inside. I moaned, feeling the familiar thickness of his cock and the heat of his arousal. Holy shit, I'd missed this.

His hands gripped my ass, his hips rising to push deeper, encouraging me to move.

I loved the way his fingers bit into my flesh with such desperation, and I couldn't wipe the grin from my face as I started to rise and fall. I rode him slowly, savoring the delicious slide of his erection as he gazed up at me feverishly.

"Fucking hell, Dare," he groaned, "you feel so good." He sucked in a breath between his teeth, bucking his hips up, begging me for more.

Heat flushed through me, my nipples hard and my pussy tightening, making it all too clear that I was torturing myself too. Yeah, I was fine. No dark shadows were clawing out to ruin sex for me. No monsters were jumping out from under the bed and tearing my face off.

It was just me and Zed.

"Shit, Hayden, I'm going to come in my hand if you keep up this slow show," Lucas groaned, sounding pained.

Cass gave a low chuckle. "Amateur."

Okay. So it was just me and Zed, with Lucas and Cass watching and playing with their dicks. Actually, that was even better.

Reminded of our audience, I leaned forward.

"Nice," Cass rumbled, his breathing heavy as I arched my back. Zed took the opportunity to grab my nipple between his teeth, toying with it gently as I increased my pace.

It wasn't enough, though. I needed more. I needed...

"Zed," I gasped, leaning in closer so that my breasts pressed to his chest. "Zed...fuck me hard."

He grunted in surprise, then shifted his grip on my ass. "Yes, Boss," he replied with a grin, then kissed me deeply. "Hold on, baby. I want you to come all over my dick."

I nodded my agreement, and he gripped my ass tighter, holding me still. Then he gave me what I'd asked for, fucking me hard and fast from below until I was crying out his name and turning to jelly on his chest. It was an orgasm so intense that my head filled with fuzz and my fingertips tingled as I gripped Zed's face, kissing him between gasping breaths.

"Feeling better, Boss?" Zed murmured, easing his grip on my ass cheeks but still rock hard inside my contracted cunt.

"Mmm," I hummed back, feeling like a damn goddess, all weightless and free.

Kissing my neck, Zed gave a low chuckle. "Good. Because we're just getting started."

A startled yelp escaped my throat as he flipped us, somehow landing me flat on my back with my head dangerously close to the end of the bed. Zed slammed back into my pussy, making me cry out, and I locked eyes with Cass from upside down.

"Hayden, babe," Lucas groaned. "Can I take your mouth?"

Cass smacked him on the arm before I could reply. "Upside down like that? You'll fucking choke her with that thing."

I moaned as Zed thrust hard, my legs banding around his waist to hold him closer, to take him deeper. "One of you," I panted, "put your dick in my mouth. Now."

"I've got you, Angel," Cass rumbled, shoving his pants down further as he stood from the armchair. He fisted his cock, stroking the length right in front of my face as I licked my lips. "Open that pretty mouth for me."

I did as I was told, even as Zed fucked my pussy harder and my body rocked with every thrust. Cass didn't seem concerned, though, gripping my hair to tilt my head back more and threading his dick between my lips.

He groaned when I ran my tongue around his crown, tasting the salty precum leaking from his slit.

"That's cool, guys," Lucas muttered. "I'll just hang out here with my hand. Again."

I almost laughed, but Cass pushing his cock further into my mouth refocused that energy, making me moan around his girth instead.

"Shit," he growled. I swallowed around his length, sucking him hard as my back arched with Zed's hard thrusts.

Losing myself in the intoxicating sensations, I clawed at Zed's strong arms, my nails biting deep as I held on for dear life and ran headfirst toward another intense orgasm. When Zed had said we were just getting started, he hadn't been joking.

Death by multiple orgasms was definitely not the worst way to go.

Cass had his fingers in my hair, tilting my head back further as he thrust into my throat with his balls smacking my nose. As undignified as the position was, he was grunting and cursing like a damn sailor, and I knew he was going to blow his load soon.

A hand slipped between Zed and me, seeking out my clit, even though my fingernails were still deep in Zed's biceps. Oh yeah... those weren't Zed's fingers. Only Lucas played my clit with such fluid strokes, like my vagina was a tiny, complicated instrument.

I exploded, moaning my release around Cass's cock as my back arched and my toes curled. His thrusts hit harder and deeper, his breathing rough as his shaft thickened and jerked against my tongue.

"Shit," he growled, "Red—" His warning came a bit late, but I was ready for him, swallowing around his cock as it pulsed streams of cum down my throat.

He pulled out, releasing my head in time for me to see Zed's brow tighten and biceps flex as he chased down his own climax with a primal roar.

Panting heavily, he kissed me—not bothered by the taste of Cass in my mouth—then collapsed beside me on the bed. Lucas had his elbows propped up on the mattress to my other side, a mischievous smirk on his face.

"Zed looked like he needed a hand," he confessed, holding that same hand out to me in an invitation. As exhausted and boneless as I already was, I still took it and let out a delirious giggle when he hauled me out of the bed.

Lucas manhandled me effortlessly into his lap, back in the chair he'd been sitting in to watch me ride Zed.

"Hey, babe." He grinned, kissing me teasingly as his hands smoothed down my sides, gentle over my ribs even though they were more of an annoyance than a pain these days.

"Hey, yourself," I murmured back, reaching down between us to wrap my hand around his huge dick. "Feeling left out?" I rose up on my knees, bringing him to my core, and let out a breathy groan as I started to sink down.

"Not anymore," he replied with a gasp. His eyes widened as I pushed down with more determination, taking him deeper and deeper and stretching my pussy in the best kind of way. "Shit, Hayden. I missed this."

His teeth gripped his lower lip as he tightened his hold on my waist, pulling me down until I could swear his dick was touching my diaphragm, it was so deep.

I braced my hands on his shoulders, rising and falling to feel that fullness all over again, and gasped anew. "Same," I agreed. "Holy hell, Lucas."

My legs were like jelly from two orgasms already, and my muscles screamed at me as I rose and fell a couple more times. Panting, I rested my forehead on his shoulder and took a break.

Lucas just laughed and kissed my neck as his hands slid down to grip my ass. "I've got you, babe." Just like Zed had done earlier, he started fucking me from underneath, sparing my legs and making me moan and thrash with every thrust up into my cunt.

He didn't fuck me fast, though, taking his time and savoring the way I trembled and whispered pleas in his ear. Cass had collapsed in his own chair, watching us with hungry eyes, but after a few minutes he got up and crossed the room to fetch something from the overnight bags he'd dropped off earlier in the day.

When he swaggered back over, his dick was on the rise again and his lips were curved in a sultry smile.

He didn't ask permission, just met my gaze and hitched a brow. I grinned back and leaned further into Lucas's chest. Lucas slowed, his thrusts becoming shallow and gentle as Cass's husky laugh shivered across my skin. He paused beside us, making sure I could see him squeeze out a generous amount of lube onto his fingers.

I gasped when his slick fingers pushed into my ass, rising enough to tease that pain-pleasure line, and my whole body flushed hot with intense arousal.

"Fucking hell," Lucas groaned. "The way your pussy just tightened on my dick, Hayden…" His hands flexed on my butt cheeks, holding them open for Cass to fuck my ass with his fingers.

Words totally escaped me as I trembled and moaned, anticipation building as Cass stretched out my back door, preparing me to take his cock. I was *more* than ready for it too.

"How you doing over there, Zeddy Bear?" Cass rumbled, shifting to the side to let me watch as he slicked lube down his cock. Oh man, he was driving me *insane*. Meanwhile, Lucas was teasing me with these shallow thrusts that were sending me into a spiral of *What the fuck is going on?*

Zed muttered some curses under his breath, but a moment later appeared on the other side of the chair with his dick half-hard again already.

"Amazing what this woman does for a guy's refractory period," he murmured with an edge of surprise, stroking himself to coax it back up harder.

Cass huffed a laugh. "See, it's not just teenagers who can go all night."

"Oh my *god*," Lucas exclaimed. "Can you two stop chitchatting and hurry the hell up?"

Cass chuckled as he withdrew his fingers from my ass and repositioned himself behind me. "Kids these days," he muttered as he guided the head of his cock into my lubed-up asshole, "so fucking impatient, am I right?"

"Saint," I snapped, "shut the hell up and fuck my ass!"

Lucas, his lips at my breast, gave a startled laugh underneath me. Zed's brows hiked in surprise. But Cass? Cass wrapped my hair around his hand and gave me exactly what I asked for, slamming in with one hard thrust.

I screamed, and he pulled out, doing it again.

"Like that, Angel?" he asked in a dark rumble as I shuddered and gasped.

I groaned, my ass burning but my whole body flushed with intense pleasure. "Finally," I replied, my voice husky with need. "Zed..."

"Yes, Boss," he murmured, stepping closer without needing to be told. I parted my lips and ran my tongue around the hot tip of his cock, watching it twitch.

Lucas was *done* waiting, though. He shifted his grip on me, then resumed his long, hard thrusts as I gasped and moaned. Grinning up at Zed, I opened my mouth wider, inviting him in. He stroked my cheek tenderly, then pushed his cock down my throat so hard I gagged before swallowing around him.

The three of them, for all their differences, knew just how to work in harmony, fucking me senseless from all directions until I was coming again and again and *again*. I lost count as Lucas's huge cock pumped my pussy, Cass slammed in and out of my lubed asshole, and Zed fucked my throat like he had something to prove.

In hindsight, Zed was really taking chances with fate, but I somehow avoided biting him as my orgasms increased in potency.

Cass came first, his dick buried deep in my ass as he grunted his release. But even done, he was still directing things. He plucked me up off Lucas's lap with a strong grip on my waist, tossed me back onto the bed, and shot me a wink as he flipped me over onto my hands and knees.

"Angel," Cass purred, crouching down beside my face as Zed climbed onto the bed behind me, his hands stroking my

343

fingerprint-bruised ass cheeks. "You know what Lucas told me recently?"

Lucas groaned, once again sitting in his chair with his hand stroking his dick.

"You're an asshole, Grumpy Cat," he muttered. "I was high as shit when I told you that."

Cass just smirked, and color me intrigued, I could guess. Lucas had confessed to me that he was a virgin when we met, but I had a feeling there was something more.

"Sweet little innocent Gumdrop," Cass teased, "told me something he *really* wanted to do but didn't want to ask you."

"You're *such* a dick, Cass," Lucas snarled, getting up from his chair and giving Cass a shove out of the way. Cass just seemed highly amused, though, and returned to his own chair, slouching into it with a challenge all over his face.

Meanwhile, Zed had his fingers back inside my pussy, teasing my swollen, throbbing flesh with yet another climax. Still, I rocked onto his hand anyway, hungry for more.

"Whatever it is, Lucas," I said in a throaty whisper as I looked up at him, "I'm game."

His brow raised with skepticism as his hand stroked my cheek and he gravitated closer. Unable to help myself, I leaned forward and licked his dick, which was bobbing so close to my face already.

"Yeah, Gumdrop," Zed teased, flicking my clit with his thumb and making me writhe, "she's game."

Lucas bit his lip as he met my eyes but didn't protest as I closed my mouth around his tip and sucked him like a lollipop. In fact, he let out a long exhale and shifted closer, giving me full range to suck his dick properly.

Cass slid off his seat to kneel on the floor and leaned his elbows on the mattress. Sweeping my hair away from my ear, he brought his lips close to whisper what Lucas was too shy to ask for.

I hummed around Lucas's cock, giving my approval. It wasn't

even weird, either. I'd been expecting some kinky shit, but Lucas's request was actually pretty normal. So I didn't even stop to tell him it was okay, just pushed forward to take him further into my mouth.

"See?" Cass slouched back into his chair, his hand fondling his dick again.

Zed stopped teasing my cunt with his fingers and lined up his cock once more, but not at my pussy. I sucked in a breath around Lucas's girth, feeling the stretch in my ass once more, and pushed back onto Zed's dick.

Lucas was way too big for me to take all in my mouth, and Zed's thrusts in my ass were too forceful to risk taking a hand off the bed, but Lucas helped out by fisting the base of his own cock while I sucked the rest.

My head bobbed up and down his shaft, encouraged by a firm hand on my hair, and Zed's breathing came in rough gasps as he pumped my ass.

"Spank her," Cass growled, and my pussy throbbed just hearing him say it.

Zed didn't need telling twice and cracked a hand on my already bruised butt cheek. I jerked, moaning with my mouth full, and Zed whispered a string of curses when the rest of me tensed up.

"That's it," Cass murmured. "Spank her again, make those cheeks glow, Zed."

I barely got a second to catch my breath as Zed's next three smacks came in quick succession. Then he plunged his fingers into my soaking cunt, and I exploded.

Lucas took over, gripping my hair and fucking my throat as I trembled and moaned through an earth-shattering climax. Zed fucked my ass hard as he chased down another release himself, coming with a breathy gasp deep inside me.

"Go on, Gumdrop," Cass encouraged as Lucas withdrew from between my throbbing lips. "Don't be shy now."

A quick glance told me he was fully erect, his gaze hot as he watched me panting and gasping on my hands and knees.

Flicking my gaze back up to Lucas, I smiled, then opened my mouth wide, my tongue extended. He gave a whispered curse, his own hand jerking his cock faster. A moment later, his hot cum splattered across my cheeks, lips, and tongue, narrowly missing my eyes—thank fuck—and dripped down my chin. My sweet gumdrop had been too shy to ask if he could come on my face.

Deliberately, I held his gaze as I retracted my tongue, swallowing his load, then licked my lips.

His expression was well worth it. He probably could have come again, just from how dirty I'd made that whole thing.

Exhausted, I rolled onto my back, collapsing into a boneless heap, but Cass smirked and stood up, still pumping his own dick.

"Angel..." he purred. "Do you mind?"

I grinned and watched with heavy-lidded eyes as he came all over my tits, painting them with his seed.

"Fucking hell," Lucas muttered, dropping back into his chair with his cheeks pink and his breathing labored. "What did you do, old man, pop a Viagra or something?"

Cass barked a loud laugh as he crossed over to the bathroom and grabbed a stack of washcloths.

"Don't be jealous, Gumdrop," he replied, smirking. "It's just experience over youth."

Zed grunted. "Hell yeah." From his nearly passed-out position, he raised his closed hand and fist-bumped Cass. Ugh, some days I prayed for them to go back to bickering instead of teaming up.

Then again...they did *so* well as a team. All three of them.

I'd be walking funny for days, no doubt about it.

CHAPTER 43

Just in case there was any potential that I wasn't going to be walking like John Wayne the next morning, the guys took turns waking me up all fucking night to fuck.

Okay, in fairness, I initiated at least fifty percent of those. But who in their right mind would say no to a lazy, half-asleep dirty spoon? Or…double spoon…as it might have been on several occasions when my first spoon wasn't subtle enough.

It was well past midday when I finally migrated to the shower, only to end up pinned to the wall by Lucas's relentless anaconda. He'd definitely felt the need to prove the benefits of youth, and I was amazed he had anything left in the tank.

"Hey, babe?" he murmured in my ear as he pounded me into the wet tiles. "Can I…"

I gave a low chuckle as my wet breasts slid against his hard chest. I knew exactly what he wanted. "Yes," I replied with a groan, "but give me a few days to recover from this weekend."

He grinned, then kissed me deeply as he picked up the pace. We both came together, the hot water beating down uselessly beside us as we continued kissing.

"Awesome," he whispered a few moments later, dragging me back under the water to rinse off.

When I eventually made it into clothes and out to the living room, where room service had just been delivered, I was ready for a nap.

The guys had set up our food at the circular dining table, and I gingerly lowered myself into my seat with a wince.

"You all right there, Dare?" Zed asked with a wicked glint in his eye.

I flipped him off and snatched up one of the coffee mugs. "Fuck you," I muttered before taking a gulp of the already cooling coffee.

Zed grinned. "Again? Damn. All right, I won't say no." He pushed his chair out from the table and patted his lap in teasing invitation.

I glowered. "Remind me why I tolerate your shit?"

"Because you *love* me." He pulled me out of my seat and perched me carefully on his lap, dropping the jokes. "And I love you, Hayden Darling Timber. Always have, always will."

"Blah blah, till death do we part," Lucas added, shooting me a grin. "Zed gets all sappy after blowing his load too many times. You'd better let him sit out the rest of the weekend."

Wrinkling my nose, I sipped my coffee and snuggled into Zed's warm embrace. "I'd better sit myself out too," I admitted. "But Zed and I don't mind watching if you and Cass wanna continue without us."

Zed shook with silent laughter, burying his face in my hair and grinning against my neck. Lucas looked confused for a moment, then tilted his head at Cass with a shrug.

"Fuck off, Gumdrop," Cass snarled, his breakfast burrito half-way to his mouth. "My asshole is off limits."

Lucas cracked up, ribbing Cass about being insecure while Zed hugged me tighter and kissed my neck softly.

"Don't act like you'd be into that," Zed murmured in my ear. "We all know you would need to be the filling in that sandwich."

Lucas must have heard him because he gave me a loved-up smile. "Sandwiches without meat are just bread, and that doesn't sound appetizing. Besides, you're my *favorite* kind of filling, babe."

Cass scoffed. "Says the kid who's never tried anything else."

"You offering, big man?" Lucas shot back, then frowned like his quick wit had spoken before his brain. He shook his head. "Actually, I take that back. I'm more than happy with what I've got, thanks."

"This conversation got strange fast," I commented, gulping my coffee. "And we need to get home. I'm anticipating some kind of fallout from last night's strike, and I still haven't come up with a solid plan for the next name on the list."

Cass sighed. "Back to reality already?"

I grinned, nodding. "Yup. We need to plot three more executions, and I promised Diana I'd kill her parents for her."

Lucas gave me a lopsided smile. "Some might find that an odd thing to promise an eight-year-old, but from you to her? Cutest fucking thing ever."

"They sound like they deserve it. She gave me her home address, I just need to make the trip to get it done. In the meantime, I don't think Nadia minds playing foster grandma to both her and Zoya."

Cass scrubbed a hand over his beard. "Nadia loves Zoya already. I think she sees her as the Russian daughter she never had."

It reminded me of when he told me how Nadia had been gifted the Fabergé egg by her one true love, a Russian thief. I needed to get that whole truth of what happened out of her one day, but while I had no doubt it would be an incredible one, I already knew how it ended. She never married the thief, her love. Her husband had died, her daughter had been murdered, and now her grandson was a gangster. Nadia's tale wouldn't be a romance. It'd be a bitter-sweet love story with no true happily-ever-after.

"Seph seems to be happy helping out, too," Lucas noted. "Which is kinda…you know…un-Seph-like?"

I snickered. "She's changed a lot in the last month. I didn't ever think I'd say this, but Rex has been a good influence on her. And I spent *years* keeping her away from him for fear that he was just like our father, a sleazy, immoral, opportunistic fuck."

Zed hummed in agreement, his hands linked around my waist and his face resting on my shoulder. "Rex has been a pleasant surprise, that's for sure—not to mention that kid of his who saved Nadia the other night."

"Shelby," Cass grunted. "Nadia probably had shit handled herself, but I'm glad he was there to back her up."

Lucas's phone beeped on the table, and he picked it up to check the message. His brows hitched, and he tapped out a quick response before looking over at me. "Speaking of retaliation for last night, someone shot up the KJ-Fit in south Shadow Grove this morning."

My mood instantly soured. "Was anyone hurt?"

Lucas shook his head. "Doesn't sound like it. Steele just said Kody was *pissed* and out for blood."

"Tell him to get in fucking line," I murmured. Zed was already pulling his phone from his pocket to check in with Archer, and I gave Lucas a curious look. "When did you and Steele become friends?"

His answering look was flat. "Maybe the other night while you were sucking these two off beside Wayne's bleeding, bullet-riddled body and I needed to stop him from checking in on you?"

I tilted my head, grinning. "Fair call."

"Asked Archer if anyone in his crew got hurt in the shooting," Zed told me with a huff of laughter. "He told me not to fucking insult him."

Cass chuckled. "Sounds like him."

Chase was a fucking idiot for thinking he could go after my allies like that, but then again, he was probably more interested in being a pest and fucking up our businesses than actually killing anyone. It left me feeling uneasy, though.

"We need to get home," I said again, but made no move to get out of Zed's lap. I was so comfy there. These moments sitting around with the three of them, eating, drinking, or smoking, they were my favorites. Okay, second favorites. But in moments like these I could see us all being together forever, even as far-fetched as that seemed.

I snagged a pancake from the table, and the sunlight through the windows flashed across my ring, reminding me I still wore it.

"Mmm, we need to sort this out," I commented, then took a mouthful of pancake and waved my finger in Zed's face.

He dropped his phone back to the table and returned his hands to my waist. "Sort what out?"

I shifted to scowl at him. "You know what. You agreed to give this back to its owner today, so…" I put the rest of the pancake in my mouth and wiggled the gorgeous ring from my finger. "Do it."

The command was a bit muffled around my full mouth, but he knew what I was saying.

With a sigh, he took the ring from me and held it up, twisting it in the light. "I saw this ring, Dare, and I knew it was made for you. There is probably no more perfect ring on this planet for a woman like you."

"You're right about that," Lucas agreed.

Cass said nothing. Just stared at me across the table.

"Zed," I murmured. "You agreed." And if he kept pushing, I'd probably cave and keep it because it was already paining me to have it off my finger.

Zed sighed again, nodding. "All right." Taking my hand in his, he slid the ring back onto my finger. "Done."

I frowned, confused. Then Cass started laughing his low, husky laugh.

"Sneaky fuck," he muttered. "You bought it in Red's name, didn't you?"

I whipped my head around to stare at Zed, who looked *way* too fucking smug for his own good. "Zayden De Rosa, you wanna tell me you *didn't* steal this?"

"Bought and paid for, Boss. Paperwork is all in your name too, so consider the rightful owner back in possession." He closed my fingers and kissed the ring. "So quit your bitching about it."

Snorting a laugh, I elbowed him in the ribs. Conflicting emotions flooded through me as I gazed down at my hand, though.

"It's not a proposal," Zed added softly, and I caught Cass muttering something under his breath about what finger the ring was on. "*But* we did fairly publicly announce our engagement in front of Chase last night. Might be worth maintaining the ruse until he's dealt with."

Lucas snickered. "Sure, Zed. The *ruse*. You're so full of shit."

Zed flipped him off but kept his gaze locked on mine, waiting for me to reply. He *was* right, though. Him calling me his fiancée in front of Chase had pushed more buttons than I'd achieved since the moment that sick fuck had walked back into our lives. I'd thought he might burst a blood vessel, he was so worked up. And we could keep playing that up. An impulsive, irrational Chase would be so much easier to trap than a clear-thinking one.

"My opinion of marriage hasn't changed, Zed," I told him sternly. "Especially now." I tipped my head toward the other two vital ingredients in our recipe.

Zed kissed my lips gently. "It's just a ring, Dare."

I sighed, knowing he'd already won this battle. He'd won it the second he chose the most perfect-for-me ring ever created. So I looped my arms around his neck and kissed him back, but deep down, all four of us knew he was lying.

It wasn't *just* a ring. It was so much more, and that was something we'd need to work through. Together.

CHAPTER 44

Lucas ended up chatting some more with Steele on the way home from our hotel stay and got the full lowdown. The gym had been closed for some renovation work, so only Kody, Steele, and Archer had been there when the shooting happened. Madison Kate had been hanging out with Seph, which was lucky.

No one had been shot, but the gym was messed up and Archer had a decent cut on his ass from when he'd slipped on broken glass. Of course, he'd never have told Zed that himself. Fucking tough guy.

Monday morning, Lucas came with me back into Cloudcroft to visit the bank. I needed to pay for Seph's car before the owner changed his mind and doubled the price again. It was already way over value, but…I couldn't put a price on the pride in my sister's eyes when she talked about that car she'd put so much work into.

Obviously, I couldn't make amends for five shitty years by buying her things. But her birthday was only a few months away, so…whatever.

"Why do we need to go into the bank to get cash out?" Lucas asked as we parked in the lot across from my primary bank. I had vaults in loads of banks, in loads of cities, and even in other countries. That was just smart in my line of business. But this one was the first I'd used and still the most accessible. I had it on good authority that I wasn't the only less-than-legal customer at this bank, but that worked for me. The employees didn't ask stupid fucking questions about fake IDs.

Grinning at Lucas, I slid my sunglasses on, and we got out of the Porsche. All four of us had stayed up way too late again the night before. So much for giving my cunt a break. Maybe it'd just get used to the constant traffic instead. I, for one, was willing to give that a try.

"Because," I replied, leaning in to him as his arm looped around my waist, "I'm not the kind of moron who keeps all her dirty money and valuables inside her house, you know, just in case it gets set on fire or the whole building gets blown up."

Lucas winced. "Yeah, good point. When you put it like that… smart move using banks."

"Don't worry, I covered my bases on bank robberies too. This isn't my only stash." I sighed quickly. "That was one of the very few good things I learned from my father. He used to lecture me on the importance of splitting up assets. His rule was to never store anything more than you're willing to lose in each location. If one was lost, would it ruin you? If so, don't leave so much in that place. It makes you vulnerable."

Lucas nodded, understanding. "What about investments? Shares and shit? Digital wealth."

I smiled. "That's all done with Copper Wolf money." I shot him a wink and reached into my purse for the key to my bank vault as we approached the main entrance.

I needed to fish around a bit to find the damn key, so I was distracted as someone held the door open from the other side for us to enter. My manners not totally lacking, I glanced up to give the tall, suited man a nod of thanks before continuing into the old-school bank.

My high heels clicked on the marble floor as I took all of four steps inside, then froze and whirled around.

"What?" Lucas asked, alarmed.

My gaze darted around, searching for the man who'd just held the door open. "That man," I said, not clearly articulating my wild thoughts. "Where'd he go?"

He'd held the door open, which meant he was probably leaving. I rushed back outside, searching the street. It'd barely been fifteen seconds, and he was a big guy. He couldn't have disappeared so quickly.

"Hayden, what's wrong?" Lucas asked, clearly concerned about my erratic behavior.

I shook my head, frustrated. "The guy who held the door open. Did you see where he went? He was huge, he can't have just fucking vanished." And yet the street outside the bank in both directions was totally vacant.

Lucas frowned. "I don't even remember what he looked like."

I threw my hands up with frustration. "He was like…Cass's size—six foot five, easy—and broad across the chest. Wearing a sharp suit and carrying a briefcase."

Describing him was somewhat pointless, though. He was well and truly in the wind. Who fucking *was* this guy? That was officially the fourth time I'd seen him, and every interaction seemed stranger than the last. He hadn't truly caught my attention until the gala, though. When I'd spotted him and joked about Chase needing security, Chase had been confused.

Which meant that mysterious dude who'd stood back and let me punch Chase in the face over dinner wasn't working for him. So…who *was* he working for? Why did our paths keep fucking crossing?

I pulled my phone out and dialed Dallas, tapping my foot on the pavement as I waited for him to answer. When he did, I could hear a toddler throwing a tantrum in the background.

"Bad time?" I asked, a bit rhetorically.

"For you, Hades? Never. What's up?" Dallas laughed nervously, then tried to ineffectively shush his screaming son.

I cringed. "Sorry, I'll make it quick. I'm at Guardian Bank in Cloudcroft and just saw someone I thought I recognized. But he disappeared before I could verify. Any chance you can pull some security footage and get me a freeze frame to confirm?"

Dallas huffed. "From the Guardian Bank? No chance. They're tighter than Fort Knox. You could ask me to break into the Pentagon, and it'd be easier than them."

I groaned. "Figured you'd say that."

"I'll pull cameras from all the surrounding stores, though. Maybe your guy will show on one of those as he's coming or going. Who am I looking for?"

"Good fucking question," I muttered. But still, I gave him my *vague* description of the guy. Somehow, despite his size, he was as nondescript as they came. Which only made me more suspicious because what better way to fade into the background?

Dallas assured me he'd do his best, and I ended the call. Lucas arched a brow at me in question, and I blew out a frustrated sigh. "I dunno," I told him. "That guy keeps showing up, and it's making me suspicious as hell. I thought he was working for Chase, but now I'm not convinced."

Lucas tilted his head. "Could he be from the Guild?"

I'd wondered about that. "Maybe," I murmured. "But I don't know. Now it's going to irritate the hell out of me until we can get an ID on him."

"Dallas will sort it out," Lucas told me with confidence. "He's an *actual* genius, I'm totally convinced."

I grinned at his positivity, then raked a hand through my hair. "Yeah. If anyone can, it's him." Still annoyed that I'd let the stranger slip through my grasp, I headed back inside the bank and tucked my sunglasses up on top of my head. "Ready for this?" I asked Lucas with a teasing smile.

He gave me a curious look in return but followed along silently as I presented my key to the concierge desk. It was old-fashioned as hell, but most criminals I knew had a bit of a dramatic flair. Ancient keys on ribbons to access hidden vaults was right up there on that list.

The concierge teller didn't speak a word as she led the way to a tiny, two-person elevator at the back of the bank. Then she turned her key in the access panel, and I turned mine, calling the elevator car.

"Lovely to see you again, Ms. Timber," she murmured softly as the elevator doors clunked open. Again, totally old-school, totally dramatic.

Lucas grinned at me when the doors closed behind us, and I gave him a suspicious look back.

"I feel like I'm in *The Sopranos* or something," he whispered as the elevator *clunk-clunked* its way down to the vaults. The Guardian was the biggest chain of privately owned banks in the world, and most of them had a sub-basement level of vaults like this specifically for assets and valuables that the owners didn't trust in traditional banks.

The door rattled open once more, and we stepped out into the cool, narrow corridor. I led the way past multiple locked doors, then stopped in front of my vault and inserted my key into the lock.

"Seven-zero-six-nine," Lucas read aloud from the ornate plate on the door.

Shrugging, I pushed the door open. "Seventy is the branch number for this location. Sixty-nine...because Zed's a fucking child and thought it was funny when he saw it was available."

Lucas chuckled as he followed me into the tiny room and closed the door behind him at my gesture. The vaults each had their own private area with a table and chair, should you need to stay a while and sort your crap out. On the far side of the room, another heavy vault door was protected by both key and code.

With practiced ease, I spun the dial to enter my access code, and the foot-thick door clicked open smoothly. I hauled it open further and chuckled to myself when Lucas whispered a curse behind me.

"*This* is an expendable amount?" he asked in a strangled voice.

I grabbed a few stacks of neatly organized cash and tossed them into my handbag as I calculated the amounts in my head. "Mm-hmm," I replied, making sure I had enough to cover Seph's car and pay Rex for all the work he'd done on it.

"Are those gold bars?" Lucas exclaimed, pointing further inside the walk-in vault where I had a reinforced shelf neatly stacked with a dozen gold bars.

I shot him a grin, closing the vault door again. "Yup. But those are just for fun. The rest of my gold is in coins."

Lucas quirked a brow. "You gonna make me ask you to explain that logic?"

My laugh echoed through the small space. "The bars are just…a novelty. You know how hard it would be to actually try and trade in one of those bastards? Nightmare. Coins, on the other hand, hold significant value in a compact, easily transported size. They also continue to rise in value, so coins that I bought four years ago at, say, four hundred dollars per ounce are now worth over two thousand. *And* they're a physical commodity, not an intangible idea of wealth like printed paper."

I spun the vault dial, locking it up once more, then turned back to Lucas to continue my explanation, seeing as he seemed genuinely curious.

"Gold sovereigns—coins—are usually a quarter ounce each. So one coin can be worth four hundred dollars or so. Hell of a lot easier, and less attention grabbing, to trade in than a ten-ounce bar." I tucked my bag over my arm, and Lucas opened the door for us to leave. "Not to mention if society ever collapsed and the internet disappeared, gold will still hold international value. Paper money? Not so much."

Lucas grinned as we made our way back to the elevators. "Okay, so for one thing, I'm scary impressed and kind of intimidated to see how fucking rich you actually are. Although that definitely explains your taste in shoes and Zed's in cars." I grinned. "But for another, I had no clue you were a closet doomsday prepper."

I rolled my eyes, still grinning as we stepped into the waiting elevator. "I'm not. But only a fool leaves all his eggs in one basket and hopes it won't be dropped."

The elevator door clunked closed, and Lucas pushed me up against the wall, kissing me senseless while the car shuddered to life.

"You're so fucking sexy when you're in Daria Wolff mode," he muttered when he released my lips. His hard cock ground against me, and I was sorely tempted to drag him back down to my vault.

I licked my lips, resisting the urge as the elevator shuddered to a stop and Lucas stepped back to rearrange his pants. "What's Daria Wolff mode?" I asked.

He grinned. "The sharp, savvy businesswoman. Hayden Timber might have seized control over the Timberwolves and gotten her hands dirty to maintain that seat of power, but Daria Wolff is the reason you're sitting on an *actual* gold mine. I somehow doubt your father, or the previous Timberwolf leaders, ever built an empire like you've done."

I said nothing in reply as the door clunked open once more and we stepped out into the main bank. We made our way out, nodding to the concierge as we passed, and Lucas linked his fingers with mine as we stepped out into the sunlight.

His assessment rang true, though. I compartmentalized like it was an Olympic event, to the point that I'd created separate personalities for every aspect of my life. Not quite so extreme that I'd developed a mental disorder along with it, but certainly more intense than simply changing hats.

I loved that Lucas saw that. He understood me and didn't cast judgment over why I was the way I was. More than anyone I'd ever met, Lucas loved me exactly as I was.

Before we got back into my car, I pinned him to the door and dragged his face down to mine. We kissed until we were both panting and hot with need; then I whispered my thanks to him. For simply being *him*.

CHAPTER 45

We didn't make it home until after noon, and then we needed to go our separate ways. I had another physical therapy appointment with Misha that I couldn't miss—my shoulder was not happy with some of the positions I'd put myself in over the weekend—and Lucas needed to visit with his mom.

Zed was at Copper Wolf running things there, and Cass was at his grandmother's again, helping her hang pictures. The fit-out crew definitely could have handled that, but I got the feeling Cass was enjoying spending time with Nadia.

Misha was less than impressed at how sore my shoulder was, and I earned a stern lecture about overusing the joint before it was fully healed. I also earned a lecture about adequate stretching before a marathon fuck session that had me in stitches. Misha knew what he was talking about, too. In college he'd paid his bills with porn.

On my way out of the PT clinic, my phone rang with an unknown number, and I gritted my teeth. The laughter and lightness from my session with Misha evaporated in an instant, and I brought the phone to my ear with a scowl.

"What?" I snapped, bracing myself to hear Chase's voice.

"Hades," *not*-Chase replied, shocking me to a physical halt beside my car.

My gaze darted around, checking my surroundings out of habit. "Leon," I said. "I take it you're calling in that debt for helping with my FBI mess recently."

He gave a low chuckle on the other end of the phone. "That *was* quite the mess," he murmured. "I'm glad to see you've recovered well."

Motherfucker was watching me. My gaze darted around the parking lot but found no one. He could be anywhere, though. With his skills, he could be in a different country and still be watching me.

"I have," I confirmed. There was no point denying I'd been hurt; the Guild knew everything. The only thing I was relatively confident about was that they weren't working with Chase. "What do you want, Leon? I can assume it's not money."

"Money," he repeated with a laugh. "What a waste of an opportunity that'd be."

Unease tightened my chest, and I unlocked my car. Getting inside and closing the door was a mere illusion of safety, though. If the Guild wanted something, they'd get it. One way or another.

"Well?" I prompted. "Whatever it is, I'm sure we can get it sorted. I don't leave debts unpaid."

"Good," Leon replied. "I want a conversation."

I waited for him to elaborate on that, but nothing but silence followed that announcement.

"Okay..." I rubbed the bridge of my nose, sensing the unspoken catch. "With *who*? I can assume it's not me since we're talking right now."

"Lucas," Leon replied. "I'd like a private conversation with Lucas, and we can consider your debt cleared."

I blew out a long breath. "No."

"No?" Leon repeated with a dangerous edge.

I gritted my teeth. "No, not private. I'll allow a conversation, but only if I'm there too."

There was a long pause on the phone, and I briefly wondered if Leon had ended the call. But then he gave a hum of consideration.

"Anyone would think you didn't trust me, Hades."

I snorted. "Anyone would be right. I'd be a fucking idiot to trust anyone from the Guild without a binding contract in place. So, no, I don't fucking trust you. I'll arrange a meeting for you with Lucas, but I'll be there, too, keeping *my* asset safe." I had to speak in terms Leon would understand. Telling him shit like how I loved Lucas and the thought of the Guild harming him made me want to burn entire cities to ash…would mean nothing. Telling him I was concerned with an asset being corrupted? He got that.

Another long pause.

"Done," he replied eventually. "I'll be in touch with a time and place shortly."

A huge wave of relief ran through me, and I sagged in my seat. "Understood," I murmured back.

"Oh, and Hades? This one is just between us," Leon added. "Unofficial, if you will. I'd rather you not mention my presence in Shadow Grove to anyone else. Are we clear?"

Well, *that* was interesting. "Crystal clear," I agreed. Then the sound of the call disconnecting beeped in my ear.

Feeling anxious, I texted Lucas to check in on him. I wouldn't put it past Leon to call me as a decoy or some shit. Everything about Lucas's links to the Guild—his uncle training him as a kid, his mom's IVF program—pointed at the Guild doing some dodgy shit with training child mercenaries. While part of me was sure Lucas was in no danger of being snatched away in the night now that he was an adult, the other part of me was terrified they'd take him by force.

I hardly breathed as I waited on his response.

My phone buzzed a moment later, though, and the relief was staggering.

Lucas: All good, babe. Just left Rex's and heading to my mom's now.

He'd dropped off the cash for Seph's car and hung around for a subtle check-in on her. They were still friends, sort of, and it was less intimidating for Rex's boys if Lucas checked in rather than me.

Lucas: Unless you had other plans?

He followed his message with a wink-face emoji, and I laughed out loud.

My idiot pussy throbbed at the suggestion, too, with total disregard for its own survival.

I bit my lip and resisted temptation as I wrote my reply.

Hades: Have fun with your mom. I'll meet you at Anarchy later?

I had meetings there with our promotions team about the next few months of fights. Without 7th Circle, and now with Club 22 out of operation, my main focuses were on Anarchy and getting Timber open, so I couldn't keep dropping the ball with work.

Lucas: Absolutely. I'm stopping by Nadia's to get cake for my mom now. I'll make sure Diana hasn't driven Cass insane.

I grinned as I tapped out my reply, telling him that ship had sailed days ago. Diana was *fascinated* by Cass. Between his tattoos, his size, and his gruff voice, she had never-ending questions. I'd watched them when I stopped by a few days earlier. Cass was painting some trim, and Diana held the paint bucket, chattering nonstop. Occasionally Cass would grunt a one-word response, but Diana didn't seem to need it. She carried the conversation all on her own as she gazed up at him with puppy eyes and asked if he'd ever cut someone's hand off.

Diana was a strange kid. Maybe that's why I liked her so much.

I had a couple of hours to kill before my meetings at Anarchy, so I drove home to Zed's house with plans for a quick nap. I'd been operating on caffeine all day, and it was starting to catch up with me.

No sooner had my head hit the pillow, though, than my phone rang again. Fucking phone was about to get thrown at a wall.

I cracked one eye to peer at it and saw that Zed was calling.

"What?" I grumbled, answering the call.

"You sound cranky," he replied.

I huffed. "I was about to nap. Is this important?"

"Aw, sorry, Boss. You didn't see that three o'clock appointment in your calendar? You're late." He was way too damn amused about this, and I squinted at my phone. Ten past three.

Frowning, I opened my calendar app, and sure enough, there was a 3:00 p.m. marked in my day. "What the—" I could have sworn my afternoon was empty. Clicking into it, I couldn't help a snort of laughter. "Very fucking funny, Zeddy Bear."

"What?" he asked, laughing. "It's in your schedule, so..."

I dropped my head back onto the pillow. "I'm not late for my *dick appointment*, you fucking child. I came early to that one. Several times, if I remember correctly." I yawned, emphasizing my point. "Leave me alone. I'm napping."

I ended the call on him but was completely unsurprised when I heard footsteps coming up the stairs a couple of minutes later. I'd heard the familiar beep of our garage remote while he was talking to me.

The bed dipped, and a cool breeze hit me as the blankets were lifted. A moment later, I was wearing my very own Zed-skin coat.

"Hey," he murmured into my neck, "can I nap with you?"

365

I grinned into my pillow. "Only if you promise to keep your dick in your pants." I totally didn't mean that.

"I *promise*," he replied with emphasis, and I was pretty sure he didn't mean it either.

We dozed together for a few minutes before I rolled over and snuggled into his chest, my hands slipping under his shirt to stroke his sides.

"Dare..." he mumbled with an edge of amusement. "We're napping. Keep your hands to yourself."

I tilted my head back, meeting his heavy-lidded eyes. "You don't mean that," I whispered.

His lips curled. "I really don't."

Our mouths crushed together like magnets, our tongues meeting and tangling in a synchronized dance for dominance that lit my whole tired body on fire and turned my brain to liquid.

"Dare," Zed groaned as I kissed his neck and my hands pushed his pants down. "Isn't that your phone ringing?"

"Hmm?" I really needed to break that fucking phone. Now that he mentioned it, though, that *was* my phone ringing incessantly under my pillow.

With a heavy sigh, I rolled away from the temptation that was Zed and fished my phone out. I frowned, seeing two missed calls in addition to the one coming through now. All from Lucas.

"Hey, Lucas," I answered. "What—"

"Hayden," he croaked, cutting me off. "I need you."

CHAPTER 46

Zed and I broke every road rule and speed limit imaginable on the drive to Sandra's house, but it made no difference. When we arrived, Lucas was sitting on the front steps, his eyes red and puffy as a body bag was loaded into the back of a coroner's van.

Even so, I leapt out of Zed's Ferrari before he'd fully stopped, my bare feet slapping the concrete path as I sprinted toward Lucas. He saw me coming and caught me in his arms as I threw myself at him, burying my face against his neck, my hug tight enough to suffocate.

"Lucas," I whispered against his skin as he held me close, his body trembling, "I'm so sorry. I should have come with you."

His chest heaved under me as he drew a shuddering breath. "It wouldn't have changed anything. Claudette thinks she took the pills hours ago, when she said she was going down for a nap. She was already cold when I found her."

How? How had her live-in nurse and her bodyguard not noticed she was dead?

"Claudette and Sal both thought she was sleeping," Lucas mumbled, answering my silent question. "She naps at the same time every day, so they had no reason to worry."

Zed sat down heavily on the step beside Lucas, squeezing his shoulder in a comforting gesture. "I'm sorry, Lucas."

Lucas tightened his grip on me like I was his tether to calmness. "Thanks," he murmured. "She did it to herself."

I bit my lip, frowning. Given how many attacks Chase had launched on us lately, I wouldn't put this past him. "Are you sure?"

Lucas nodded, burying his face in my hair. "I'm sure. She left a note, and no one else entered the house. Big Sal was here the whole time. She overdosed on her own pain meds and died in her sleep."

Fury swept through me at his words. *How could she? How could Sandra do this to Lucas?*

"What can we do?" Zed asked, saving the moment before I flew into a Sandra-hating rage.

It was a quick reminder of what was important: Lucas. Spitting curses about his selfish, cowardly mother wasn't going to help him, and she was gone and couldn't hear me.

Lucas drew another long, shuddering breath, releasing it heavily against my neck. "Honestly? I just want to go home. I don't want to be *here*. Nothing about this house feels comfortable or safe."

"Done," Zed replied, squeezing Lucas's shoulder again. "I'll order from Massimo's on the way home and cancel our meetings for tonight. Dare can drive your car."

Nodding my agreement to all of that, I climbed out of Lucas's lap and offered him a hand up. He just gave Zed a watery smile, though, nodding to the cherry-red Mustang in the driveway.

"My car, huh?"

Zed rolled his eyes but didn't deny it as he headed back down the driveway to the Ferrari.

Lucas wrapped his fingers around mine, letting me pull him up to his feet and lead him over to the car. He hesitated as I opened the door, his eyes going to the coroner pulling out from the curb and a teary-eyed Claudette wringing her hands near the road.

"I've got it, Lucas," I assured him. "Just give me two minutes, okay?" I gave him a gentle push to get in the passenger seat, seeing the signs of shock all over him. The sooner we got him home, the better.

He gave a numb sort of nod and didn't protest as I closed his door. Hating that I needed to leave him for even a minute, I hurried back across the front lawn to where Claudette was still staring after the van.

She snapped back to focus as I approached, though, sniffing away her tears and straightening her shoulders.

"Hades, sir," she croaked. "I'm so sorry about all of this. I had no idea—"

I shook my head, cutting her off. "I'm not blaming you, Claudette. I met Sandra. I fully believe she would have figured out a way even if you were watching her around the clock." Raking my fingers through my hair, I gave a frustrated sigh. "Selfish bitch that she was."

Claudette's brows shot right up, and I bit my tongue.

"Where's Big Sal?" I asked, changing the subject.

The nurse nodded to the house. "Inside. He's taking it hard. He and Sandra had grown close recently."

I'd figured as much. So had Lucas. Still, I didn't have the time or energy to comfort a man in my employment when a man I loved had just lost his mother.

"I take it you can handle all the paperwork, Claudette?"

She nodded swiftly.

"Good," I muttered. "Send a copy of everything to my office when it's done. Then ask Big Sal to have this place cleaned out and closed up. Lucas won't be coming back here."

Claudette bobbed her head. "Yes, sir. Understood."

Casting another long look at the house, I padded over to the Mustang, my feet sinking into the damp grass. When I'd gotten his call, I hadn't paused to get dressed, leaving the house in my men's sleep shirt and cutoff sweatpants. No bra, no shoes. Hell, even Zed had barely tugged on a pair of sweats over his boxers.

"Hey, you," I whispered once I was inside the car. Lucas was just staring blankly up at his mom's house. His uncle's house. "Want to talk about it?"

He shook his head, and I respected that. I knew all too well how it felt, not wanting to verbalize all those dark, painful thoughts.

So I kept my mouth shut and backed out of the driveway, heading toward home.

We'd been driving for maybe five minutes when he shifted in his seat, turning to look at me with sad eyes.

"Do you ever think about how many secrets just go to the grave? Like…how many mysteries we're forced to simply live with, no fucking answers, because the last person who knew never told anyone?" His voice was cold. Bitter. I totally understood.

I nodded. "All the damn time."

He said nothing back to that, just turned to look out his window again, lost in his melancholy thoughts for the rest of the drive home. It made me wonder, though, what secrets Sandra had still been holding onto, what pain she'd been so desperate to run from that she'd rather leave her only son than deal with it. As mad as I was at her for hurting Lucas, I could also kind of relate.

The lights were all on when we pulled back into the garage, and Zed's Ferrari was already in its usual spot, having beaten us back. Lucas and I got out, and he found my hand with his as we made our way into the house.

Zed was in the kitchen mixing a cocktail for me. For Lucas, he handed over a freshly rolled joint with a flash of a smile. "Stole it out of Cass's room," he confessed. "That grumpy bastard gets the best shit from the Reapers."

Lucas arched a weak smile in return, accepting the gift. "Thanks, bro," he muttered, then wandered out to our usual spot in the courtyard to light it up.

Zed gave me a long look as he slid my Sazerac over the counter to me. "Despite the pretty face, that kid is tough as nails. He'll be okay."

I nodded, giving a heavy sigh. "I feel useless. Nothing I have to say about Sandra right now is kind."

He gave a one-shouldered shrug, pouring himself a neat whiskey. "Because we have no experience with *good* parents. Lucas still loved his mom…and that's not something either of us, or Cass for that matter, can relate to. Our parents were all better off dead."

If that wasn't the truth… "What do you wanna do about Veronica, anyway? We can kill her if you want."

Yes, I was aware of the inappropriateness of suggesting matricide when Lucas was grieving his mother's suicide. But he was outside slouched into a lounge chair blowing weed smoke up into the night sky. And Zed's mother could still cause problems.

Zed drummed his fingers on the counter, seriously considering it. Then he shook his head. "Nah, not yet. She lacks the spine to take any real swipes at us, and now that her 'big win' on your arrest fell apart, she'll have a hard time getting anyone to take her seriously."

"All right," I agreed, sipping my Sazerac. "The offer is there if you change your mind."

Zed flashed me a grin, shaking his head. "You're adorable. Come on, let's take care of the sad Gumdrop. You can't kill anyone to make him feel better, you can only be there for him."

I knew that, but it didn't stop me from itching to go shed some blood in Lucas's name. Except there was no one to punish for Sandra's death. No one to take responsibility. And that sucked.

Lucas glanced up at me with hooded eyes as I approached, then draped his arm around my shoulders when I sat down beside him. Wordlessly, he handed me the joint, and I took a deep inhale before passing it back.

Zed joined us, and we sat in silence for a few minutes sharing the joint. Then his phone beeped to announce our pizzas had arrived from Massimo's, and he went to collect them from the front gate.

371

"Hey, babe?" Lucas murmured when we finished the joint.

"Mm?" I replied, slouching deeper into his embrace.

His arms tightened around me, pulling me into his lap and turning me to face him. "Distract me. Give me something else to think about. Right now all I can focus on is what a selfish bitch my mom turned out to be, and I hate thinking those things about her."

I bit my lip, nodding. "You wanna talk about the next name on my list? How we're gonna kill him? Or..." I quirked a brow and skated my fingers across the firm muscles of his abdomen, just above his jeans.

Lucas gave me a lazy, high sort of smile. "Death and sex. Your favorite pastimes, huh?"

I shrugged because he wasn't wrong.

He seemed to consider it for a moment. "Can I ask for both? Is that too greedy?"

"No such thing, Lucas," I told him sternly, my fingers working the button of his jeans open. I had a pleasant, relaxed buzz going, and if Lucas had asked me to take him to the moon, I probably would have been on the phone to Elon Musk. "Next on our list is harder to get to," I informed him as I dragged his zipper down.

"Yeah?" he murmured, slouching back into the cushions and tugging on the hem of my shirt, asking me to take it off.

I whipped it over my head, leaving me naked to the waist, seeing as I hadn't stopped to put a bra on earlier. Lucas hissed out a breath as his warm hands cupped my breasts, his thumbs rolling my peaked nipples.

"Uh-huh," I confirmed with a breathy moan. "He knows we're coming for him sooner or later. He's doubled his personal security since I came back to town."

"Well, this just got more interesting," Zed commented, dropping the pizza boxes down on the table and giving me a long look.

I grinned back at him. "Lucas needs distracting, Zeddy. Give

372

him a slice of pizza and tell him what we're thinking for the next name on the list."

Grinning, Zed dropped back into his seat and flipped open the top pizza box. He handed a hot, cheesy slice to Lucas as I wiggled off his lap and sank to my knees in front of the couch.

"Best distractions around," Zed muttered, watching with hungry eyes as I palmed Lucas's cock and ran my tongue around the tip. "Pizza, death, and sex."

Lucas gave a relaxed chuckle, then groaned as I closed my lips around his dick. "Fuck yeah. All right, tell me the plan, and make it bloody."

If I wasn't already head over heels for this man, that'd do it.

CHAPTER 47

Cass arrived home shortly after Lucas had passed out. The combination of weed, pizza, blow job, and tragedy had hit him hard, and his eyes had drooped closed less than a minute after he came.

Zed and I were happy to let him sleep while we talked in low voices, but Cass scowled at us both and picked Lucas up in a fireman's carry to take him up to bed.

He returned back down to us a few minutes later, a fresh blunt between his fingers and an accusing glare at Zed.

"What?" Zed asked before Cass could say anything. "It wasn't for me, it was for Gumdrop."

I nodded, keeping my face as serious as possible. "It absolutely was."

Cass rolled his eyes, then sat down and pulled me into his lap. "Sorry it took me so long to see your message," he rumbled to Zed. "Fucking kid had taken my phone to play games while I was sanding woodwork."

Zed must have filled him in after we'd left Lucas's mom's house. I'd been in too much of a panic when we'd gotten the call from Lucas.

"How is he?" Cass asked, jerking his head up in the direction of the bedrooms.

"Hell of a lot better now." Zed chuckled. "Amazing what a good blow job will do for a grieving man."

Cass arched a brow at me, and I just grinned. It was the least I could offer, considering how shitty I was at platitudes and emotional support.

"We also discussed our plans for the next three names," I added. "All three of them are a whole lot harder to get access to, and two of them will make a big splash when the media catches wind. They need to be *perfect*."

He gave a thoughtful hum around the joint resting gently between his lips. Lush, kissable lips. As much as I'd like to blame my high for how horny I was, it really had nothing to do with it—and everything to do with how addictive my men were.

"Keep looking at me like that, Red," Cass growled, "and I'll want an encore performance featuring my cock in your mouth."

I gave a throaty laugh. "Like that's supposed to be a threat. Sounds more like a promise..."

He gave a sultry smile in return, and his fingers dipped below the waistband of my shorts when he shifted me on his lap. "Well, hold that thought, beautiful. I have a lead that might help on one of the names."

My brows twitched in curiosity. "Yeah? You found an access route?" Because I knew who was next and I knew *how* I wanted to kill him, and that was what Zed had detailed for Lucas as I'd sucked his dick earlier. But we didn't *currently* know how to get to the man.

Cass took another drag, his dark gaze teasing. "Sure do," he murmured. Then he shifted his gaze across to Zed. "Do you remember that annoying shit whose little brother was harassing Madison Kate?"

Zed frowned for a moment, then nodded. "Yeah, I know the one. What about him?"

"He wants in with the Reapers. Since the Wraiths were eradicated, he's got no protection. And he rejected Chase's recruitment drive, for whatever reason, but now he's feeling *exposed*. Wants a new daddy."

I snickered, remembering when Lucas had called him Daddy Cass. Suddenly that was way funnier than it had been back then, and I laughed harder.

"Ignore her," Zed said with a wide grin. "She's high and horny. Guarantee she just heard 'daddy' and thought about you spanking her."

I squirmed, and Cass's arm around my waist tightened.

"Is that right?" Cass murmured, his fingers dipping lower under my waistband.

The smile wouldn't budge off my face. Goddamn weed high. "No," I lied. Rather unconvincingly, I might add.

"So, Officer What's-his-face can get us access to our mark?" Zed redirected the conversation back on track.

Cass was *such* a good multitasker. He returned his attention to Zed but slipped his fingers into my panties as he replied. "Yup, I think he can. All we need is one weak link, and the whole chain is broken, right?" He kissed my shoulder. "Angel, you're *soaking*."

I groaned, writhing against his fingers. "I'm well fucking aware of that, Captain Obvious."

He gave a husky laugh, biting my shoulder gently. "Go wake Gumdrop up. Let him take care of this." His fingers stroked my throbbing clit, and I moaned. "Remind him that just because his mom is gone doesn't mean he's alone. He's got family, still. He's got us."

"Fucking hell, Saint." I cupped his face with my hands and kissed him deeply. "You're just a big pussycat, huh?" I grinned, teasing, but also *painfully* in love. I kissed him again, then climbed out of his lap with a small wobble.

Zed smirked. "You need me to carry you, Boss?"

I extended my middle finger. "Bite me, De Rosa."

"Before, during, or after that spanking you want from Daddy Cass?" Zed was way too amused. "Because I'm cool with any of those options. How about you, Grumpy?"

Cass flashed a toothy grin and flexed his hand. "*Any* time, Angel."

Snappy comebacks eluded me because I was already picturing that scenario—with Lucas added into the mix—in my mind. Oh yeah, I was into that. I just hummed to myself and made my way upstairs to Lucas's room.

He cracked one eye open, giving me a slow smile as I stripped out of my clothes and slid under his blankets. "How'd we get up here?" he mumbled. "Did I fall asleep again?"

I chuckled. He did have a habit of falling asleep out in the courtyard. "Yeah, Cass tucked you in."

"Mmm." His warm hands found my naked body and pulled me close. "Suddenly I'm not so sleepy."

Grinning, I tugged at his clothes. "Good. Me neither."

We were both lying our asses off and passed out cold still tangled up in each other's sweaty, naked bodies less than twenty minutes later.

The deep sleep of sex and weed only lasted so long, though. Lucas woke up multiple times that night, cold sweat coating his skin and his pulse racing fast. Shitty nightmares plagued him, and there was nothing I could do to stop them. All I could offer was the comfort of my presence when he snapped out of each dream.

He finally seemed to rest easy just before morning, but I was too wired to sleep. So I just lay there with Lucas's cheek on my chest, his arms and legs wrapped around me like I was his favorite stuffed animal. I lay there, stroking his hair and plotting. It was my new happy place.

Zed quietly slipped into the room with a mug of coffee in hand around midmorning, meeting my eyes as I raised my finger to my lips. He gave a nod of understanding and waited silently as I extracted myself from the Lucas squid and threw a T-shirt over my head.

"Mine?" I whispered, taking the coffee from him before we were even out of the room.

He grinned and closed Lucas's bedroom door softly. "Of course. How is he doing?"

I wrinkled my nose, taking a long sip of the fresh coffee. "As you'd expect, I guess. Or better? I have no clue what the standard is on grief. I've never lost anyone I truly loved." My own mother had been the closest, and I was so young I barely remembered her.

Zed shot me a hard look, then pinned me to the wall and kissed me hard enough to spill my coffee. Not that I cared much. Locking lips with him woke me up better than any caffeinated drink.

"I fucking hope you never do, either," he told me in a rough voice when he released me. Then he grimaced at the coffee soaking into his carpet. "Head downstairs. Cass has news. I'd better clean this up before it sets in."

"Your fault," I teased, sipping what was left of my coffee.

Zed smirked. "Worth it."

Laughing, I left him there and made my way down to find Cass in the kitchen. He sat at the island finishing off his breakfast and looked up at me with a sleepy, rumpled smile when I hugged his waist.

"Red, you look tired. Lucas keep you up all night?" His eyes were sharper than with casual interest, and I heard the thread of jealousy, despite him having sent me to Lucas last night.

I tilted my face to kiss him, then swapped my empty coffee for his half-full one. "Not like that. He was having a rough sleep."

Cass grimaced sympathetically. "We've all been there," he muttered. "Zed tell you the news?"

I slid onto the stool beside him, shivering when the cold seat met my bare ass. "He didn't. Just told me to come find you. What have you got?"

"I've got our access route sorted," he told me with a sly smile. "Officer Dickhead came through. He's on protection detail tonight at the Sullivan Hotel downtown."

My lips parted in surprise. "Tonight?"

Cass nodded. "Apparently our mark has a standing Tuesday-night appointment with a competitor of yours."

More shock. "Swinging Dicks?" I guessed. Cass nodded again, and I laughed. "No way. Seriously? Shit…I wouldn't have picked him as the Swinging Dicks type. So, what are we thinking? Switch out the escort?"

He reached out to tuck some wild copper hair behind my ear. "Yep. Our officer looks the other way, and our fake prostitute walks straight into the hotel room unchecked."

The scenario ran through my mind over and over as I mentally tweaked the details to make it work. Then I shook my head. "It can't be you or Zed, you're too well known. Lucas, too. They've seen him with me too often now. We will need someone else… someone who can just leave the door unlocked for us and walk away without a second glance before the blood starts spilling." I tapped my chin thoughtfully.

Cass grunted. "Needs to pass as a Dicks escort, too. Other security will see him arrive and raise an alarm if he looks like a gangster instead."

I nodded, on the same train of thought. "I think I have some-one who could be perfect. Maybe. I'll have to ask nicely, though. He's not intimidated by my mean face."

Cass gave me a curious look. "All right, well, if he can be trusted to get us in, I think Lucas should be the one to do it."

My spine stiffened. Not that I was against the idea. Lucas had shot people before. Whether he'd killed them or not, I wasn't sure.

But this would be up close. Personal. *Messy*. Did I want to corrupt my sweet Gumdrop like that?

"Lucas should do what?" Lucas asked with a yawn, scuffing his feet as he entered the kitchen.

Cass arched a brow at me, asking for my approval. I sighed and gave a shallow nod. Ultimately, it wasn't my choice whether to corrupt Lucas or not. He was his own man and could make his own choices. I wouldn't force him to do it, but I also wouldn't stop him if he *wanted* to.

"What should Lucas do?" he repeated, leaning his elbows on the counter and peering into my coffee mug.

"Kill Lieutenant Jeffries," Cass answered with a wicked little smirk on his lips. "Tonight."

Lucas blinked a couple of times, still sleepy as hell. Then he nodded. "Done."

CHAPTER 48

"How do I look?" Misha asked me for the fifth time, checking his appearance in the rearview mirror. He'd been skeptical when I'd asked him for this rather large favor, but when I explained what Jeffries was party to, what crimes he'd been allowing to pass unchecked since transferring to SGPD, he was all in.

"You're hot as hell, Misha," I replied with a grin, even though I could feel Zed's glower from the back seat. "It'll be a breeze. Get in, block the door before it closes, distract him for *maybe* five minutes, then walk away when we arrive. I'll take it from there."

Misha gave me a long look. "If I get arrested for this—"

"I will personally bribe every single person in Shadow Grove to have you released," I assured him. "But you won't."

Zed's watch beeped, and he made an impatient noise. "Time."

Misha drew a deep breath, released it in a gust, then pushed his door open and got out.

"You sure he's good for this?" Zed murmured as we watched Misha cross the road to the hotel.

I shrugged. "No. But I think he's our best bet for a man pretty enough to be a gay prostitute, totally unaffiliated with any gangs, and willing to look the other way when Lieutenant Jeffries turns up dead on the morning news."

Zed just huffed a sound in response, leaning his tanned forearm on the edge of the passenger seat so our faces were only inches apart. "What does it say about us," he asked after a moment, "that we're about to assassinate another city official and all I can think about is dragging you into the back seat here and impaling you with my dick?"

I laughed quickly, then shot him a hot glance. "It says we're two peas in a pod, Zayden De Rosa. Fucking soulmates."

Officer Shane Randall exited the hotel lobby, lighting up a cigarette. Our cue. Without another word, Zed and I got out of the car, and he looped his arm around my waist. We made our way over to the hotel, giving each other hot and steamy looks that weren't even remotely staged, like a couple about to check into a room purely to fuck.

We bypassed the check-in desks—no one even glanced at us twice—and headed straight for the elevators. As planned, no one stopped us. Officer Randall was the man on duty to watch the lobby, and he was now officially on the Reaper payroll.

Zed and I played up our *newly engaged* vibe, our lips locking before the elevator doors even closed, discouraging an older couple from joining us in the car. Still, we didn't separate in any great hurry once the doors *did* close and we started climbing to Jeffries's floor.

"Do you think this is a good idea?" I whispered to him when we did finally peel ourselves free. "For Lucas, I mean."

Zed gave me a contemplative look. "I don't know. But I know it helped you. When you were at your darkest, the violence and killing seemed to act as therapy for your damaged soul. Maybe it'll be the same for him? He definitely gets off on the violence like you do."

I scoffed. "Oh yeah? Like I'm the only one. You and Cass are just as bad. Or do I need to remind you about our dockmaster?"

Zed grinned, no doubt remembering how I'd sucked both him and Cass off five feet from a dead man. "Good times," he murmured with a chuckle.

The doors slid open, and we stepped out onto the fifteenth floor where Jeffries had a room reserved under a false name. This recurring appointment with a Swinging Dicks prostitute was by far the weakest point in his security. He clearly didn't want anyone to know about it, so he stripped off the outer layer of his personal protection. Only two men guarded him for the duration of these appointments, and one of them was now in our pocket.

As for the other? He was at the end of the corridor, struggling and red-faced with his eyes rolling into his skull as Cass calmly choked him into unconsciousness. Or death. It was unclear what kind of mood Cass was in.

The fact that he had to wear a hotel employee uniform—complete with a silly little hat—probably meant the man was dead.

He met my eyes as he dropped the security guard to the floor, and I shot him a toothy grin. He had that lethal look in his eyes that made my nipples hard. Yeah, I was a touch more than *slightly* damaged. Whatever. I was who I was.

Silently, we made our way to room 1507, and Lucas slipped out of the room opposite, where he'd been camped out watching, to give us the information.

As instructed, there was a plastic swipe card jammed between the lock and the doorframe of Jeffries's room, and low male voices issued from inside. Neither sounded panicked in the least, and I caught Misha's husky laugh a moment later.

Biting back a grin, I pushed the door open and strode in with my guys behind me as if we were expected. In fairness, we were. Just not by Jeffries.

"Oh, Misha," I murmured, striding forward to where he stood, "I'm *very* impressed. Have you ever considered a life of crime? The Timberwolves could use a man of your skill."

Jeffries made panicked mumbles, but we just ignored him. Good thing Misha had just secured a gag ball in his mouth to keep him quiet. Thick, leather bondage cuffs secured the good lieutenant to a chair at the wrists *and* ankles, and he was stripped down to his boxers.

"The Timberwolves need a full-time physical therapist?" Misha asked with total innocence. "I had no idea. Hmm, thanks but no thanks. I like my nice boring life." He shot a grin at Zed and Lucas, who he'd met before. "Boys, lovely to see you again."

They eyed him suspiciously. Damn, Misha hadn't even unbuttoned his shirt, and he'd gotten Jeffries all trussed up like a Christmas ham. I was *super* impressed.

"Thank you, Misha," I said with a laugh. "I'll see you on Thursday."

"Mm-hmm," he agreed. "Make sure you do your exercises and, for the love of god, stretch before another of those athletic orgies, all right?"

Lucas's eyes widened and Zed glowered, but I just grinned and showed Misha the door.

Once it was closed securely behind him, I flipped the dead bolt and turned back to our bound victim, who was making muffled protests behind his gag ball.

"Lieutenant Jeffries," I said, crossing back to him as Lucas unzipped the duffel bag he'd brought from his room. One by one, he started laying out knives on the low coffee table. "You know, you *almost* had me fooled into thinking you were one of the good guys the first time we met. Almost. But you made a *big* mistake getting into bed with Chase Lockhart. Even bigger mistake when you became involved in his extracurricular activities. He must have given you some juicy incentive to have you kill Agent Hanson for him."

That was something Dallas had uncovered for me after I'd given him those six names while I was still at Foxglove Manor. Sending him the list had been one of the first major steps I'd taken toward healing my mind, and he'd been working on it nonstop since then.

We didn't have concrete proof that Jeffries had been the one to kill Hanson, but his proximity during the time of her death and the subsequent cover-up, with SGPD declaring her death a suicide, waved enough red flags to connect the dots.

Jeffries was making noises, likely defending himself or denying all accusations. But he didn't realize I'd seen him on Chase's conference call. I'd personally seen each of the six men working with Chase and heard them speak. Their fates were already sealed; I didn't need to hear confessions or denials.

"All yours, Lucas," I said softly, stepping out of the way.

He already wore gloves—we weren't amateurs—and his face remained impassive as he picked up the first knife from the table. Jeffries thrashed against his bonds, but Misha hadn't been messing around. He wasn't going *anywhere*, especially after Cass clamped his hands down on the back of the chair, stopping it from toppling over.

Lucas froze, though. He stood there, scowling down at Jeffries with a deadly sharp blade in hand...but he went no further. His jaw was tight and his shoulders were bunched with tension, but he made no move to start gutting the dirty cop.

"Lucas," I whispered, jerking his attention up to meet my eyes. I gave him a small shake of my head. "You don't *need* to do this. We can handle it. Fuck knows our hands are already stained so red they'll never wash clean."

His brow dipped, and I could see the indecision clearly in his eyes. He wanted this. He *wanted* to cleanse his aching soul with the blood of a bad man. But he just wasn't there yet, and *that* was perfectly understandable. He hadn't been raised with casual violence and death like the rest of us.

Zed understood that too. Without explanation, he pulled out his Glock, clicked a suppressor into the barrel, then swapped Lucas's knife for the gun. "Or just make it quick. Don't jump in the deep end before you can swim, Gumdrop."

Lucas shifted his gaze to Zed's, searching as though he thought he'd find judgment or pity. But I knew without even looking at Zed that he wouldn't find anything but calm understanding. We all had a first kill, a first victim that we'd looked into the eyes of and questioned all the choices that had brought us to that point. There was zero shame in hesitation, and not a single one of us would judge Lucas if he decided not to pull that trigger.

Bang.

That answered that.

"Shit, Gumdrop," Cass growled, "could have warned me to get out of the way." He swiped a hand over his blood-covered face.

"Lucky he's a good shot," Zed snickered, taking the gun back from Lucas and putting it away in his holster.

I ignored Cass and Zed, focusing my attention on Lucas as he blinked down at the lifeless body of Lieutenant Jeffries still strapped to the chair. "Hey, Lucas." I spoke softly, bringing my hand to his cheek to tilt his face to me. "You okay, babe?"

His brows hitched as he refocused on my face. Then he nodded. "Yeah. Yeah, I'm fine. I'm sorry I froze."

I shook my head. "Nothing to be sorry for. At all." I glanced over at Cass, who was drenched in blood and brain matter, having been positioned behind the chair. "Take Cass across the hall and make sure he gets all that blood scrubbed out of his beard, okay? Zed and I can finish up here."

Lucas frowned. "No, I can stay and help. I should have—"

"Come on, Gumdrop," Cass growled. "Let these two do their thing. I need to shower, and you need a drink."

The big, blood-soaked man started for the door without waiting for Lucas to agree. I bit back a smile and gave him a nudge to go with Cass. Lucas gave a small sigh, then exited the hotel room with Cass to get him cleaned up.

386

When the door clicked closed behind them, Zed arched a brow at me.

I glared back at him. "I never pressured him," I defended before he could even say anything. "He *wanted* to do it. I would have happily done it all myself and left all three of you at home."

Zed gave me a slightly irritated look. "He wants to impress you, Dare. He wants to be *one of us*, even if he's not ready."

"Don't you think I know that?" I shot back, angry. "But I promised I would treat him as an equal. I'd have given you or Cass the exact same freedom to make your own choices."

He blew out a breath and ran his hand over his hair. "I know. I just feel bad."

I threw my hands up. "And I don't?" I stalked away a couple of paces, looking out the window to the lights of Shadow Grove. "I think maybe we need to give Lucas some credit. We're not dragging some poor, innocent soul into the murky underworld. He's diving in headfirst with his eyes wide open."

Zed gave a long sigh before he picked up one of the knives from the table and tapped it against his palm. "Yeah, that's true. And he seems to be thriving, too."

I bit my lip. "I know what you're saying. I'll keep an eye on how this sits with him."

"As will Cass and I," Zed agreed. "But…I think you're right. He's a natural." He turned his attention to Jeffries. "What do you wanna do about this, now?"

I parked my hands on my hips, peering down at the dead man. It hadn't been the dramatic, bloody statement we had planned, but sometimes *dead* was statement enough. Besides, Chase didn't need to be party to every death; it'd be pretty damn obvious who was responsible.

Just in case, though, we'd leave him a message.

"Do his ribs," I told Zed. "Then let's leave it as it is." Bound in bondage cuffs in his boxers with a gag ball in his mouth? Yeah, that worked for me.

Zed jerked a nod. "Yes, Boss."

He made quick work with his knife, cutting the design directly into Jeffries' ribs in the exact same spot Chase had started to cut me before I escaped—except this one was complete. The *Chase* logo he'd tried to put on me.

When he was done, he wiped his bloody blade off on Jeffries' boxer shorts, and I checked my phone to see how far away Robynne and her cleanup team were. Once again, they'd erase every trace of evidence from the room, scrubbing it sterile, but leave the body.

"Robynne's on her way up now," I murmured. "Good timing."

Zed smiled, tossing all our knives that hadn't been used back into the duffel bag. "Like riding a bike, Boss."

Chuckling softly, I headed for the door, but Zed grabbed me by the waist as I passed him. He hauled me back against his body and kissed me long and hard. I sighed into his hold, melting with every brush of his lips and stroke of his tongue.

"We need to go," I whispered when I was damn near ready to climb him like a tree.

He kissed me again, lingering a moment longer, then released me with a sigh. "I know. It just…hit me again how fucking lucky I am to still have you, Dare."

Swallowing hard, I simply linked my fingers together with his, and we left our crime scene together.

Four down. Two to go. And then the main event.

Chase's demise was getting closer, and I was buzzing with excitement to see it all unfold.

CHAPTER 49

Ultimately, Zed and I were thinking way too hard about how killing Jeffries would affect Lucas. He was annoyed at himself that he'd frozen up at the thought of really making it messy and hearing Jeffries's screams of agony—albeit muffled. But Zed's gun had been the easier option. Lucas was comfortable shooting and had no regrets over wiping another rodent out of a position of power.

In fact, he'd been more than eager to prove how *okay* he was with it all by jumping me while Cass was still in the hotel shower in the room across from Jeffries. Zed had reluctantly sat back and serviced himself while Lucas fucked me hard and fast against the door, and all three of us had found our climax before Cass even got out of the shower.

Not that Cass was one to miss out on anything, though. He dragged me into the spacious back seat of the Escalade as we left the hotel. Somehow, he managed to fuck me doggy style while Zed drove and Lucas watched from the front seat. Safe? No, not even close. Hot as fuck? Oh *god,* yes.

Yeah. Sex and death. What better combination was there, really?

The next day I found myself sleeping right through my alarm

and waking up when Seph pounded on my bedroom door and yelled at me that I was supposed to pick her up an hour ago.

I raised my sleepy head, blinking some brain function to life, then grinned. The fact that she was pounding on the door and hadn't just burst in told me she was *learning*. Good fucking thing, too, because I was stark naked, curled up in Cass's heavy embrace, and crusted with an unseemly amount of dried jizz. I needed to shower *badly* before my little sister saw me, so thank fuck we were in Lucas's bed.

The shower was already running in the attached bathroom, so I yelled back to Seph that I'd meet her downstairs, then slid out from under Cass's arm and hurried into the bathroom.

"Good morning, gorgeous," Lucas murmured, swiping water from his face as I let myself into his shower. "Last night was fun."

I grinned, pushing him out of the water so I could start scrubbing my skin clean. "What part? Killing that revolting piece of shit Jeffries? Or all the sex afterward?"

He gave a low chuckle while handing me the soap, then watched with hooded eyes as I washed. "All of it," he replied after a long pause.

I took my sweet-ass time soaping up and washing out every damn crack and crevice on my body, enjoying the way he watched me with his huge dick standing hard and proud between us.

"I was supposed to take Seph out for lunch today," I told him as I rinsed under the water. "She's here to inform me that I'm over an hour late."

His grin arched wider. "Oh, well, if you're already *that* late"—he pinned me against the shower wall, his hands hitching my legs up around his waist and his dick sinking into my hot core—"then what's ten more minutes?"

"Fuck," I breathed in response, feeling him push deeper, and I groaned at how fucking good it felt. My arms looped around his neck, and his lips found my mouth as he started moving, pumping into me slowly and lazily while I shuddered in his grip.

A cool breeze touched my legs as the shower door opened again and a half-asleep Cass lumbered his way into the shower cubicle.

"Room in here for three?" he asked, a wicked gleam in his dark eyes.

Lucas grinned against my lips, shifting his grip on my ass and turning us around so his back was to the wall and mine was to Cass.

"There is now," Lucas replied, holding me tighter and planting his shoulders against the tiles as he pumped his hips. My knees were against the wall, my ankles crossed as I held on tight to Lucas, but when Cass ran a wet hand down my spine, I groaned and leaned back into him.

He kissed my neck, his beard tickling my skin and sending delicious shivers all through me. "I could get used to showers like this," he murmured against my throat, his hard cock against my ass. "Hold onto my neck, Red."

Doing as I was told, I raised my good arm to loop around Cass's neck behind me, gasping as he pushed fully inside with one forceful thrust. My nails dug into his flesh, probably drawing blood as I tensed up, quivering, then relaxed with a long moan.

"Saint..." I breathed, clinging to both of them as they started to move with shallow thrusts, their motions synced up beautifully. "Did you lube up your dick before getting in the shower?"

He huffed a laugh, his teeth scraping over my neck. "Damn right, I did. Always be prepared, Red."

I turned my head, seeking his lips, and moaned when he fucked my ass a little harder while we kissed. Then I turned back to kiss Lucas. It was heavenly, switching back and forth between them as they fucked me senseless and the shower continued to run.

When I came, Lucas swallowed my screams with his kisses, then his own movements became rough and deep, his hips jerking and his body tensing as he finished.

Cass wasn't quite done, though, giving a gruff order for Lucas to stay put as he fucked me harder. His fingers slipped down between Lucas and me and pinched my clit hard, which instantly forced another sharp, fast orgasm to ripple through me as he came.

Lucas gasped as my pussy clenched tight around him. Then he found my lips and kissed me breathless as Cass eased away to grab the soap.

By the time I made it downstairs, my cheeks were flushed and my lips puffy. Just in case my sister was under any illusions about what had taken me so damn long, Cass and Lucas followed closely behind me with *freshly fucked* grins painting their faces.

"Seriously?" Seph asked, deadpan, as she folded her arms and eyed me. "You kept me waiting while you had another round with *both* of them?"

I shrugged. "I regret nothing." I made my way into the kitchen and pinned Zed to the counter, kissing him thoroughly. Then I promised I'd call him later and headed out to the garage with Seph, who muttered under her breath behind me.

"I already ate, by the way," she told me when we climbed into the Porsche. "Zed was cooking waffles, and it seemed rude to let them go cold while you were upstairs getting your brains screwed out."

I chuckled, not even slightly embarrassed. "How'd you get over here?" Because I hadn't seen any of Rex's boys lurking around Zed's house.

"Rex dropped me off," she replied. "He was heading over to Demi's office for something or other. I'm pretty sure he's still a little bit in love with her, by the way."

I scoffed. "He's barking up the wrong tree there. Demi would *never* leave Stacey."

Seph grinned. "I know that. But it's kinda funny to watch him try. Whoa! What the fuck is *that*?"

Her sharp tone made me do a double take before I realized what she was gawking at in shock and disbelief.

"Oh. Nothing. Just…a gift." *Oh yeah, real believable, Hades. Nice work.*

"Bullshit!" Seph exclaimed. "That's a fucking engagement ring! Who the fuck asked you to marry them, Dare? Tell me!"

I rolled my eyes. "No one." Technically true. "It was just part of a plan. I'm not *actually* engaged."

Her smile was coy. "Sure, you're not." There was a long pause, then she nodded. "It was totally Zed. That has his style all over it. Anyway, what did you want to do today?"

I glanced at her, glad she was dropping the engagement ring topic—sort of—and pleased to see her so…content. She seemed like she'd grown up so much in just two months, it was crazy.

"I have a friend I want to visit," I told her, "if you're cool to come with? She just got out of hospital not long ago. I've been meaning to stop by, but…" I let my voice trail off with a shrug.

"But you've been too busy getting fucked six ways to Sunday?" Seph teased. "I'm so freaking glad I'm not living with you anymore. I bet you're even more of a sex addict than MK."

I laughed but didn't deny it. In fairness, this week I was just making up for lost time.

"Well, anyway," I moved on, ignoring her comment, "do you mind?"

Seph shrugged. "Fine by me. I'm just glad to be away from all the testosterone at the garage today. I swear, ever since you took Shelby into the Timberwolves before Ford and Linc, it's been nothing but fights and arguments between them. Rex has them all deep cleaning the garage with toothbrushes today, Micah and Nix, too."

I remembered meeting Micah the last time I'd picked Seph up, and Nix must be the other friend of the boys that Rex had unofficially adopted.

Tapping my fingernails on the steering wheel, I shrugged. "Shelby earned his place. I don't run a fucking charity. If the other boys want a Timberwolf tattoo so damn bad, they'd better prove it."

Seph wrinkled her nose. "I'll be sure *not* to pass that advice along, thanks."

393

There was an edge to her tone that suggested she was less than amused. Almost resentful? I gave her a long look from the corner of my eye, frowning. "What's that supposed to mean?" I asked.

She huffed a sigh and ruffled her fingers through her hair in a movement identical to my own frustrated gesture. "Nothing," she muttered. "Forget it. Who's this friend we're visiting again? I didn't think you *had* any friends besides Zed."

That was a fair assessment. "Maxine," I replied. "She's—she *was*—a dancer at Club 22."

Seph frowned thoughtfully, then nodded. "I remember, she was your Friday-night main attraction, right? Crazy awesome pole dancer?"

I nodded. "That's her. She's also the one who got beaten nearly to death with a stripper shoe and who Zed's bitch mother tried to frame me for attempted murder on."

Seph's mouth dropped open in shock. "Whoa. Wait. Zed's *mom*? I thought she was dead!"

I sighed. "We all did. I guess she is, in a way." I glanced at Seph, debating if she was really ready for all this info. But she wasn't that sweet, innocent, bratty thirteen-year-old anymore. I think in some ways I had never stopped seeing her like that, but she was almost nineteen now. She *was* grown up; I just hadn't acknowledged it.

"Turns out Zed's mom was undercover FBI the whole time she was with his dad. When her cover got blown, she shot Zed's dad and ran back to her old life." Just saying it out loud made me wish I'd killed Veronica when I'd seen her at Anarchy. Or whatever her fucking name was now.

"Whoa," Seph breathed. "That's…wow. And she just never contacted her *son*? What kind of—"

I cut her off with a bitter laugh. Fuck it, if I was going to treat my sister as an adult, to *trust* her, then she might as well know the rest. "Oh, she got in contact. Five and a half years ago, when Zed was in the hospital after the Timberwolf massacre, she manipulated him into becoming some kind of pseudo agent, undercover for the FBI."

Seph's jaw dropped, and she stared at me in horror. "What?" She shrieked after a moment. "Zed's *FBI*? No freaking way. Nuh-uh. No *way*."

I shrugged. "He's not *now*. I doubt he was *ever* officially on the books. They just made him think he was to force him into delivering intel and shit. I dunno, it was a whole fucking thing that we needed to work through together."

She made a sound of shock. "I feel like my head just exploded. How did you not fucking kill him when you found out?"

I grimaced. "Like I said, it was a whole…*thing*."

She sat with that information for several minutes of silence as I drove us toward Maxine's house. I didn't try to make excuses for Zed, nor did I elaborate on the intricacies of our relationship and forgiveness. I trusted that she could see we were in a good place now and understand that it was nothing more than a speed bump.

"Well…" she finally muttered, exhaling heavily, "I'm glad he's not dead."

My brows hitched. "You are?"

She nodded. "I know you guys only got together really recently, but in my head you've been a couple since forever. He's family, you know? I've *always* known how much he loved you. So…whatever he did with the FBI, I don't think he ever would have done it to hurt you."

I was speechless for a moment, my eyes hot with something dangerously close to tears.

"Thanks, Seph," I whispered eventually. I hadn't known how much her understanding meant to me, not really, until she gave it. But it'd struck something deep inside me, shifted that tiny remaining piece of resentment I was holding toward Zed over the whole FBI thing. I hadn't even known I was still hurting over it, but all I'd needed to do was talk to my sister.

She smiled at me, a bit smug. "I'm smarter than you give me credit for, Dare."

I hated to admit it, but she might be right about that.

"So, how is the pretty purple Corvette coming along?" I asked, changing the subject.

Seph rolled her eyes dramatically. "It's *lilac*, Dare. And she's a dream. I'm going to be so sad when she's finished and her owner picks her up."

I smiled to myself as she launched into an explanation of the work she and Rex were doing on the Corvette, totally impassioned with her topic and with no clue *she* was the new owner. I never would have guessed that my spoiled, bratty sister would find her calling in fixing cars. Never. But there was no denying the way she lit up while telling me about the inner workings of an engine.

"That's great, Seph," I murmured when she paused for a breath. "I'm glad you're happy."

She smiled brightly back at me. "I am." Then she tipped her head to the side, her gaze curious. "Aren't you?"

What a complicated question that was. I shook my head. "No. Not yet. But I will be soon."

Really fucking soon…I hope.

CHAPTER 50

To my intense relief, Maxine didn't slam the door in my face when we showed up on her doorstep. Quite the opposite, she almost knocked me over by hugging me and dropping her crutches. Once I got her steady once more, she ushered Seph and me inside and tried to make us coffee.

She'd refused to go home to her parents, citing that she was twenty-two and a grown-ass adult. Her bruises had all gone, and she looked shockingly alive considering that the last time I'd seen her she was one step from dead.

I tried to apologize to her—without me, she never would have been targeted—but she waved it off, joking that it was technically Zed's fault, seeing as it was *his* exes being killed. Instead, she just wanted to catch up. As *friends*. It was…weird. In a good way, I guess.

When we left her several hours later, Seph teased me that I was turning into a human. But she kind of had a point.

I drove her back to Rex's garage but came inside with her instead of dropping her at the curb. Call me paranoid, but I wasn't leaving my sister unprotected for even a moment while Chase was still free.

We found Rex's boys in their living room, fighting over game controllers, and my mood went ice-cold as I noticed their reaction to Seph joining their mix. She didn't notice, not one freaking bit, but their fighting paused as she entered the room and every single one of them kept her in their line of sight as she made her way to one of the couches and flopped down.

"Gimme that," she demanded of one of the boys, the one I'd threatened outside Club 22 when I first got back to town. Lincoln.

He handed over his game controller without the slightest hesitation, and I cleared my throat loudly. It wasn't often that my presence went unnoticed in a room, and I didn't like it. Not because my ego was so huge I couldn't handle being overlooked, but because they were *that* focused on my little sister. Crazy as it sounded, I didn't want Seph turning into me. I didn't want her falling for a gangster...or five.

"Oh, shit," Micah sputtered, choking on the corn chip he'd just stuffed in his mouth before he spotted me.

"Oh yeah," Seph drawled, "my sister wanted to make sure you guys were home before she left me here." She said it *so* casually, but the wicked glint in her eye said she knew exactly how badly I'd just spooked them.

A couple of the boys started talking over each other, tripping on their words, and I leveled a hard look at Shelby. I didn't say anything, just tipped my head to tell him to follow me back outside.

"Bye, Dare!" Seph yelled as I left the room. "*Loooooove you!*" She said it sarcastically enough that I didn't feel bad ignoring her as I headed back toward the door to outside. Shelby hustled to catch up with me and was on my heels as I pushed the door open.

"I'm sure I don't need to have this chat with you, Shelby," I murmured, my voice like quiet death, "but my sister is off-limits. To all five of you."

His eyes widened, and his Adam's apple bobbed as he swallowed hard.

"I have a job coming up that I could use you for. Your dad tells me a couple of you are pretty good drivers?" I changed the subject without even a hint of emotion, and I could see him reeling to catch up.

He nodded quickly, though. "Yes, ma—Uh, sir. Yes, sir. All of us, really, but Linc and Nix are the best."

I arched one brow, surprised at his honesty in not claiming to be the best himself. "I see. I'm still working out the finer details, but clear your nighttime schedule for the next few nights. Dallas will be in touch with more info later today." I pursed my lips, thinking. "Which of you is the worst driver?"

Shelby tilted his head to the side, considering the question. "On a racetrack or urban driving?"

"Urban," I replied.

He nodded. "Ford. He'd kill me if he ever heard me say it, and he excels on a drag track. But with city distractions? He'd lose."

I bit back a laugh because Ford struck me as the top dog in their crew. His ego wouldn't like this blow. "Good. Leave him out of it, then. He can stay on Seph detail."

Shelby barked a sharp laugh before clapping a hand over his mouth. "Sorry, sir. Um, yes. Of course. Whatever you want."

I stifled an eye roll. "I want you to stop picturing my little sister naked. Reckon you can fucking handle that, Shelby?" His face paled and he started to nod, but I held up a hand. "Don't even think about lying to me, kid. Just keep your dick in your pants and make sure your brothers get the same message. Or I'll cut them off."

With a pointed look at his pants, I turned and headed for my car. "Keep an eye on your phone, Shelby. This job has plenty of room to impress me."

I felt like a total asshole as I drove away. Seph clearly didn't want these boys involved in the Timberwolves…and I'd just created a golden opportunity for more of them to earn a place. It was like I couldn't fucking help myself. Two steps forward, one step back.

My phone rang when I was halfway home, and I answered it without checking the caller ID, expecting Dallas. So I slammed my foot on the brake a little harder than necessary when a different voice spoke my name.

"Leon," I sighed. "To what do I owe this displeasure?"

"You have a lot of animosity for someone on the Guild client list, Hades," he commented. "What could have caused that, I wonder? I'm sure you didn't keep digging into Guild files *after* I told you to stop."

I gave a low chuckle. We both knew I'd never had any intention of following that order. "I take it you want to arrange this *conversation* with Lucas?"

"I do," he replied. "I'll be back in Shadow Grove this evening. You own that big old amusement park with the clown-face entrance, don't you?"

"Anarchy," I told him. "You know I do."

"Good. Let's meet there at midnight. The drama of that place appeals to me."

He ended the call before I could accept or decline, and I gave a long sigh. Fucking Guild were creepy bastards on the best of days, no matter how *normal* they tried to appear. Now he wanted to meet at midnight in my old amusement park? I shuddered.

I hadn't told Lucas—or *anyone*—about my first discussion with Leon, either. It'd completely slipped my mind until now, and I already knew it'd get pushback from Cass and Zed. But I'd negotiated for me to be present with Lucas, not all four of us. And I wasn't going to push Leon any further.

Tapping my fingers on the steering wheel, I continued home. Maybe I'd take the easy way out…tell them in the middle of sex when they weren't paying attention. That certainly seemed like my best option to avoid arguments. Or better yet, maybe it would *cause* an argument that would then require angry argument sex. So many good options.

By the time I got home and headed inside, I still hadn't come up with anything better.

"Hey, you." Zed greeted me with a warm smile when I found him in the gym with Cass. They both wore fight gloves and no shirt, and I instantly forgot what I needed to tell them. "How was lunch with Seph?"

"Ummm..." Goddamn, they were sweaty, like they'd been sparring together for a while already. Shouldn't they both have work to do? Not that I was complaining... Maybe I could just curl up in the corner and watch them...

"Red," Cass barked, snapping me out of my daydream. "You're drooling."

I narrowed my eyes at him in a sarcastic glare, but shit, he wasn't far off the truth. Clearing my throat, I ruffled my fingers through my hair. Focus, Hades. Come on, you're not *that* dick drunk.

Okay. I was an addict.

But that didn't mean I needed to turn into an idiot about it. So I screwed my eyes shut in an effort to stop getting distracted—yes, it was that bad—and gathered my scattered thoughts.

"Where's Lucas?" I asked because this information directly impacted him.

Someone ripped their gloves off, the tearing Velcro crazy close to my ear. Then fingers grasped my chin and tilted my face up.

"Why are your eyes closed, Dare?" Zed asked in an amused voice, his warm breath feathering my lips.

Cass gave a low, husky chuckle from nearby. "Insatiable."

"Where's Lucas?" I asked again, keeping my brain on task even as I cracked one eye open. Zed was right there in front of me, his lips close enough to kiss if I leaned forward just a little...

Those gorgeous lips curved up. "Upstairs," he told me. "He was down here working on some new tricks with the pole but headed up about half an hour ago."

401

I sucked in a shaky breath, mentally cursing my hyperactive libido. "Cool. I'll go get him. I've got *news*."

Zed's brow arched in question, then he nodded. "All right, we'll get cleaned up. I need to get dinner started anyway." Before stepping away, though, he crashed his lips into mine for a lingering kiss that made my insides turn to horny jelly.

It took a crazy amount of effort to peel myself away and turn to leave the gym, but Cass was right there, waiting for me. His strong arm swept around my waist, lifting me up and pinning me to the wall as his mouth found mine. A gruff noise escaped his throat as he kissed me stupid, and his hard dick ground me into the wall through our clothes. *Fucking hell.*

"Yeah, and *I'm* the insatiable one," I muttered when he released me. I gave him a mocking headshake. "You're the worst offender here, Grumpy Cat. Go take a cold shower, you'll want to hear this."

His deep, sexy laugh followed me as I made my escape out of the gym, and I needed to scold myself for thinking with my cunt too damn often. The four of us were in a whole new honeymoon phase, and it was safe to say we were *all* insatiable. I kind of hoped that never wore off, even though I knew my life wouldn't just sit on hold while I stayed in bed around the clock chalking up record numbers of orgasms.

It was tempting to try, though.

I found Lucas curled up in the middle of his bed, staring up at the ceiling. The distress on his face instantly washed my head clear of sex, and I climbed onto the bed to curl around him.

"Hey," he said softly a moment later. "Sorry, I was just—"

"You're fine," I replied, cutting off his unnecessary apology. "You don't need to explain or apologize."

With a soul-deep sigh he rolled to wrap his arms around me, tucking me into his warmth. He was wearing just his boxers, and a wet towel was draped over the edge of the bed. "I got a message," he told me, his face buried in my neck, "asking about my mom's funeral arrangements."

Oh shit.

"Do you want me to handle it for you?" I offered softly. I couldn't imagine how hard that would be as a child who loved their mother. Funerals were such a *final* thing. My heart ached to think what Lucas must be feeling.

He didn't reply for the longest time, just held me close. "I think I need to do it," he finally said. "For my whole life, it was just the two of us. No one knew her like I did... It just... I don't know. I feel responsible."

I didn't know what to say to that. So I just shifted back until I could cup his face in my hands, our foreheads and noses together. "I'm here, if you need help. Or a distraction. Or support. Or... whatever."

His lips curved in a sad smile. "I know, and I love you for it more than you know. But I think I'll regret it later if I turn my back on her at this last step."

Goddamn, Lucas had a huge heart. His capacity for love and forgiveness, his emotional maturity...it blew my mind. I was insanely lucky to have him in my life.

At a loss for words, I just pulled him close and kissed him softly, hoping he knew how deeply he touched my soul, despite my inability to vocalize those feelings.

We stayed snuggled up together in silence for a long time, just existing within each other's arms and letting the soft rhythm of our breath, our heartbeats, soothe us both into relaxation.

Eventually, though, I remembered why I'd come looking for Lucas and peeled myself up with a groan. "I came up to get you," I admitted. "I've got news that concerns you...but we should all discuss it."

Lucas pushed up from the bed with a curious look on his face. "Why do I feel like this is bad news?"

Because it probably was. We didn't often get *good* news these days.

I shrugged and waited while he tugged on some jeans and a T-shirt, and then he reached out a hand to pull me to my feet. Before leaving his room, he kissed me gently, inhaling deeply.

"Thank you," he whispered.

"For what?" I asked, licking my lips to savor the feeling of his kiss.

He gave me a wise sort of look. "For loving me."

"You're late," a voice called from the shadows as Lucas and I got out of our car. Leon stepped into the light from the Anarchy clown face, but his deep hood kept his face shrouded in total darkness. Drama king.

I gave an unaffected shrug. "Traffic was terrible." At midnight on a Wednesday on the outskirts of Shadow Grove. "I think I prefer that nice, nerdy act you were putting on the first time you came to town, Leon. This one is far too *Dungeons and Dragons* for my liking."

"Oh, I was thinking more *Assassin's Creed*," Lucas commented, tipping his head thoughtfully. "But now that you mention it…"

"Shut the fuck up," Leon snapped. "We don't have all night."

Rolling my eyes, I started into the park with Lucas at my side. Leon paused a moment, no doubt bristling at the idea of *following*, but I wanted to go somewhere that I knew we wouldn't be overheard. There was no better area than the back of the park, where we'd stored all the old rides that were so rusted they were beyond repair.

I waved a hand to one of the teacups that had lost its door. "After you, Leon."

His hood had shifted enough that I caught his suspicious glance, but he still climbed in and took a seat before Lucas and I joined him.

For a moment, no one spoke. I wasn't about to go breaking the ice first, though. Leon called this little clandestine meeting; he could cough up whatever he wanted to say and fuck off.

Eventually, the Guild prick huffed in frustration and tipped his hood back properly.

"Lucas, we haven't officially met," he said by way of an opening.

Lucas cocked one brow, sending me a what-the-shit look. "We haven't met at all," he replied, "officially or not."

Leon just blinked. Impassive. Shit, his poker face could rival mine on the best of days. "Sure. Anyway, I'm sure Hades already told you who I am and who I work for."

Lucas dipped his head in acknowledgment, but below the little circular table his hand gripped mine tightly. "You're with the mercenary guild. I'm aware."

Leon just stared at Lucas for a long moment. Long enough to be awkward.

"Why don't you get to the point, Leon?" I suggested, running out of patience. "You're here to offer Lucas a job, am I right?"

The mercenary shifted his cool green eyes to me, still as blank as fuck. "No," he replied. "Like I said on the phone, this is unofficial. A personal matter."

Lucas's brow creased. "Personal?" Then he gave a rough laugh. "Don't tell me you're my brother. What is this, a family reunion just in time for Mom's funeral?"

Something flashed across Leon's expression, a lightning-fast crack in his mask, but with the darkness it was impossible to get a good read on him. Lucas had hit the nail on the head for what *I* suspected, though. After all of Sandra's involvement with the Guild, her IVF cycles, and her own confirmation that there had been other babies before Lucas…yeah, I'd pondered on Leon being Lucas's brother, too.

"No," Leon replied, cutting that train of thought cold. "I'm not related to you, Lucas."

"Oh." Lucas's shoulders slumped. For all his sarcasm, he'd quietly hoped that was the case, that he still had blood family out there somewhere, even if it was in the cold, sociopathic form of a Guild mercenary.

A small frown touched Leon's brow, and his gaze flicked to me briefly like he was irritated that I was there to witness whatever he'd come to say. "I'm not your brother, Lucas. But that is why I wanted to talk to you. I'm assuming you know something about your mother's involvement in the Remus project."

I squeezed Lucas's fingers, silently urging him to play along.

"Yeah," he said, getting the message. "She told me about the test-tube babies she handed over to the guild. Am I one of those?"

Leon shook his head. "No. You were the product of a different manipulation, an experiment in a different type of conditioning that fell apart when your mother ran. When she didn't report back within the set time frame, the project was dropped. The variables were too great for a conclusive outcome."

I couldn't help myself. "Dropped? Or just started again on some other innocent child?"

Leon blinked at me like that differentiation was irrelevant and shifted his attention back to Lucas. "You're not some genetic freak, if that's what you're thinking. This isn't *The X-Files*. There was just some heavy guidance when you were young to push certain skills—athleticism, marksmanship, shit like that. You're not going to suddenly grow wings."

Lucas gave a shaking laugh. "That's a relief. So, if you're not here to recruit me, why are you telling us all of this?"

Leon linked his hands together on the rusty bar. "Because you need to be aware of your surroundings. Your uncle didn't have a heart attack, he was killed by the Guild. Someone is cleaning up all evidence of Project Remus."

"Uncle Jack was involved in that?" Lucas sighed. "Of course he was. And now I'm in danger?"

Leon shrugged. "No. Like I said, you weren't a Remus baby."

Well, now I was confused. But I bit my lip to keep from speaking up; this was Lucas's situation to handle however he saw fit. I was merely protection.

"Okay..." Lucas said slowly, squinting at the mercenary. "So, I'll ask again. Why are you telling me?"

Leon stared down at his hands a long time before responding. When he did, it was in a carefully neutral, emotionless voice.

"I knew your sister. She asked a favor of me, and I'm finally upholding that agreement. As far as the Guild is concerned, Lucas Wildeboer, you don't exist. No trace of your birth remains in any system on earth. You're a ghost. I suggest you pick a new name and get some records drawn up to bolster that identity, but the bottom line is that you're no longer a target for the sins of your father... or uncle."

Leon shifted his gaze to me, giving me a long look, and I got the message. We were done.

I gave Lucas's hand a small tug, then climbed out of the teacup to let Leon out.

"That's it?" Lucas asked, frowning.

Leon just stared back at him. "What more do you want? A hug? Fuck off. I just gave you the greatest gift on this planet. Say thank you, and forget we ever met."

He stalked away into the night without another word, melting into the shadows like he was made of inky darkness himself and leaving Lucas and me standing there speechless.

"Thank you," Lucas muttered after a long silence. Then he turned to look at me with a bewildered expression on his face. "What the fuck just happened, Hayden?"

I shrugged. "The Guild are creepy bastards, but Leon's one of the worst I've ever met. Guarantee that if you ever see him again, he will be a totally different person. You'll actually question whether they're just identical twins, not the same person. I know I did."

Lucas stared out into the night, then gave a long sigh. "Did you hear what he said?" he asked me in a pained voice. "I have a sister."

My chest tightened, and I looped my arm around his waist. "Had," I corrected gently. "He spoke of her in past tense."

A shudder ran through him, and his shoulders drooped. "Oh. Yeah, you're right. That did feel like a debt-to-a-dead-woman kind of thing, huh?"

I nodded. I hated it, but that was *exactly* what it sounded like. Lucas's sister had been someone Leon cared for enough that he'd fulfilled her wishes after she was gone. He hadn't been joking when he said he'd given Lucas a gift. With his entire existence erased, Lucas was safer from the Guild than I could have ever hoped.

"Fuck," Lucas breathed as we slowly started toward the exit of Anarchy. "He erased my whole life? Everything documented is gone?"

"That's what he said, and Leon's one of the best hackers in the world. If he says you're a ghost, then it's *all* gone."

He groaned, running a hand over his face. "What does that mean for my EMT assessments? I'll have to start over again."

I cringed. "Yeah. Probably. I'll get Dallas working on your new identity tomorrow, though, and we'll work something out."

Lucas tugged me to a halt as we got to the car, the cherry-red Mustang, and turned me around, kissing me deeply. I rose up higher, kissing him back with an edge of desperation born of the anxiety I'd been holding ever since taking Leon's call. Before I knew it, Lucas had boosted me onto the hood of the car and my leg was hitched up around his hip.

"Babe," he whispered between kisses. "Are you okay with public sex?"

I chuckled softly, then let my actions speak for themselves as I unzipped his jeans.

CHAPTER 51

Dallas was more than happy to get out of the house a couple of days later and arrived at Zed's with a haggard look on his face. Apparently Maddox was going through a sleep regression, and he and Bree had spent the entire night playing jack-in-the-box to get him back to sleep.

I shuddered just hearing about it.

"New identity," he announced, tossing a thick envelope down on the table for Lucas. "Everything you could possibly want to be a real person, right down to school transcripts and a police report for graffiti."

Lucas picked up the envelope and pulled out his new driver's license. Then he smiled.

"Twenty-one-year-old Lucas Wilder." He gave me a long look. "Cute."

I grinned back. "It seemed like the obvious choice."

"There wasn't much I could do with your assessment records," Dallas continued, "because so much needs to be done in person. You'll have to redo the ones you've already passed."

Lucas sighed. "Not the worst thing ever. At least I'll be really good this time."

Zed came into the room tugging his top shirt button undone and flopped down onto the couch beside Lucas. "Hey, cool," he commented, peering at the license in Lucas's hand. "Now you can legally drink."

"Because I was so worried about being carded," Lucas responded, dripping sarcasm.

"As for the other matter I've been looking into for you," Dallas continued, focusing his attention back on me, "I have a lead."

Excitement zapped through me. "On which one?"

Dallas smiled. "Both."

I sat forward, my eyes wide. "Really?" He nodded. "Well, shit. You just became my favorite person."

Dallas laughed, placing a much thinner envelope down in front of me. "There's not *much*, especially on the rat. But it should, hopefully, be the window of opportunity you've been waiting for."

My brows rose. "Street race?" It was the *only* angle we had been able to work on the fifth name on the list. When I'd initially sent it to Dallas, he'd thought I must have remembered it incorrectly—there was *that* little information on this man. But on further reflection, I'd remembered seeing a flyer for a street race pinned to the noticeboard behind him while he chatted so casually with Chase and the other five slime buckets. It was from a past event, but we were hedging our bets that he might attend the next one.

"Sure is," Dallas confirmed. "This weekend in Rainybanks. I've registered your drivers already. They'll get a text message with the starting point an hour before it begins."

My grin couldn't have been wider. I had started to worry we wouldn't catch the rat, but this was perfect. Especially now that I had drivers who could activate the trap for me.

"Dallas. You're the best."

He flashed a smile back, then shot a nervous look at Zed and Lucas before clearing his throat. "Well, as for the last mark, there's a copy of his calendar in there, showing all his public appearances for the next two weeks. I spotted a few that could work, but I'll leave it up to you." Dallas checked the time on his watch and grimaced. "I should go. I told Bree I was going out to get us coffee."

Zed gave a sharp laugh. "You're a dead man. Coffee doesn't take this long."

Dallas cringed, then yawned and hurried out of the house to return to his overtired wife and cranky toddler. Poor guy.

When he was gone, I turned my bright grin to Lucas and Zed. Cass was still asleep.

"You guys wanna help me map out a rat trap?"

Lucas grinned back, and Zed gave me an amused shake of his head.

"You're adorable when you're plotting murder, Dare," Zed told me with a huff of laughter. "But you know I'm in. Let's take it to my office so we can print out a map to draw on."

"Good idea," I agreed, bouncing to my feet. "Lucas?"

He checked the time, then wrinkled his nose. "I want to, but I asked Sabine if I could join her choreo session at Anarchy this morning. I just kind of…need to stay busy. I thought maybe if I get back into shape, I can pick up some shifts when Timber opens too."

My gaze darted to Zed out of habit before returning to Lucas. "Totally understandable," I assured him. "I heard Sabine has been working the dancers twice as hard since she took over from Maxine."

Lucas arched a lopsided smile. "Good. But I'll be home by this afternoon, so don't have too much fun without me."

Zed laughed as he headed toward his office. "No promises, Gumdrop."

I lingered a moment longer, and Lucas swept me up in a tight embrace. His mom's funeral was just one day away, and I knew it'd been steadily darkening his mood.

"I'm okay," he murmured into my hair before I could say anything. "I'm just…sad. But it'll be okay. I just want to go and dance for a while today."

I nodded my understanding. "Have fun, then."

He cupped my face and kissed me hard. "Will you let me go onstage this weekend if Sabine approves?"

I groaned. "Can I think about it?"

He gave me a low chuckle, kissed me soundly, then shook his head. "I wasn't asking, babe. I'll tell Sabine to put me on the schedule." He kissed me again—dammit, my kryptonite—then smacked my ass as he left the room with a swagger.

Shit, who was I to tell him no? If that was what made him happy... I wasn't so insecure as to make my men keep their bodies covered in public for fear of other women ogling them. I was confident in the knowledge that Lucas might be stripping onstage for hundreds, but he was coming home to me.

"Dare!" Zed shouted, snapping me out of my daydream. "We plotting this murder or what?"

Grinning in excitement, I headed through to his office where his oversize printer was already spitting out a large-scale map of downtown Rainybanks and his desk was cleared off.

The loose plan we'd already devised should be implemented easily enough; we just hadn't known which city we'd be working with. I tapped my chin, thinking while the map printed. We'd need to grease the right pockets to keep the roads clear of cops, although the race organizers themselves would likely have taken care of a lot of that.

Then there were the other racers to deal with. And how to work out which car held our rat...

"You're overthinking it," Zed told me, and I realized I was thinking out loud. "We've already *got* the plan, we were just waiting for the race to be announced. It'll work."

I bit my lip. "It has to. We're so close to the end. I just want to map it out. Do you have a highlighter?" The oversized printer was *so* slow, and it looked like Zed had printed in high resolution or something.

Zed tugged his desk drawer open and held up a collection of bright colors. "That map is going to take a while to print, though." My thoughts exactly. He slammed the door shut and slouched back in his chair, giving me a predatory look.

With a knowing chuckle, I came around his desk to where he sat and perched my ass up on the top of it. "Oh really? What were you going to propose we do while waiting, huh?"

He sat forward, sliding his palms up the outsides of my thighs and pushing my skirt up as he went. "I think you know." His voice was a sultry murmur as his fingers hooked the elastic of my panties, and when I lifted my butt, he dragged them back down my legs.

"Did someone say we're plotting murder?" Cass rumbled from the doorway. "I love plotting. And murder. And whatever else is going on in here." His sharp gaze locked on the panties dangling from Zed's fingers. "Count me in."

Zed pushed my skirt up higher, bunching it around my waist. Then he pulled me to the edge of the desk, spreading my knees so that his chair was tucked in between my legs. "Wait your turn, Grumpy Shit. That's what you get for sleeping in." Without waiting for a response, he parted my pussy with his fingers, then dove straight in tongue first.

"Ah, shit," I gasped. Bracing my hands on the desktop, I met Cass's hot gaze as he prowled closer. Zed took that as the encouragement it was, tonguing me with determination as I moaned and rocked against his face.

Cass must have slept well because he didn't argue with Zed's direction. He just dragged over a chair and kicked back to watch, his feet up on the corner of the desk and his eyes fucking me through my clothes. I held his gaze for a few moments while Zed ate me out, then I tugged my shirt over my head and popped the clasp on my bra. Why not give something Cass to really eye-fuck while he so patiently waited his turn?

He slowly shook his head. "That's just teasing now, Red," he growled, rubbing his beard.

I laughed softly, panting as Zed slid his fingers inside my pussy. "No," I replied, cupping my breasts with my hands. "This would be teasing." I pinched and rolled my nipples as I moaned.

Cass's gaze darkened. "You're asking for trouble now, Angel."

Grinning, I rolled my nipples again. Zed scraped his teeth over my clit, and I let out a small cry of pleasure. "Oh yeah, Saint?" I taunted. "What are you going to do about it?"

Zed froze, peering up at me with a you're-so-fucked look on his face.

"What?" I asked, frowning down at him.

He swiped his tongue over his lips, tasting me, then groaned. "I think you just waved a red cape, Dare."

Seeming to agree, Cass pushed to his feet, looming over me with a darkly delicious expression on his face. "Zeddy Bear, sit back a moment, would you? Little Red just threw down the gauntlet."

Zed shot me a look that screamed *I told you so.* Then he smirked. "Yes, sir."

I gasped my outrage as he did what Cass told him, pushing his chair back from the desk to watch. "I can't believe you just *yes, sir*-ed him," I hissed. "Traitor."

Cass was already tugging me off the desk, then pushed my bunched skirt down to the floor and helped me step out of it. "Hands on the desk, Red," he growled.

I squeaked a protest, but it was all an act. I was all too happy to plant my palms on the desk and waggle my bare ass at Cass. Now that I'd started taunting him, I couldn't seem to stop.

He gave a low laugh and smoothed his palm down my spine. "Further," he ordered, and I obligingly pushed my hands to the back of the desk. My nipples brushed the smooth wooden top, and my breath caught.

"Now, what was the question again?" Cass murmured thoughtfully, his broad hand stroking my buttocks.

Zed coughed a laugh. "Pretty sure Dare asked what you were gonna do about her teasing you."

I bit my lip, grinning over my shoulder. "Is that what I said?"

Cass leveled me with a hard glare. "Sounds right to me."

Before I could find any better sense and talk my way out of it, his hand cracked across my bare ass. The smack was hard enough to make me yelp, and my pelvis hit the edge of the desk when I jerked forward. But it was so quickly followed by that delicious, stinging burn of red skin that made me moan when Cass massaged the flesh.

"Did I make my point?" he asked in a husky voice.

I arched my back, pushing back into his grip. "Was that it?"

This time, all I heard was Zed's laughter before Cass's palm met my ass cheek, and I trembled with anticipation. Still, I tossed another bratty comment over my shoulder at Cass, urging him on. Each time he smacked my ass, he immediately massaged the flesh. Pretty soon, my backside was glowing and stinging, and my cunt was so wet I could feel it on my thighs.

Cass's next smack hit so close to my pussy that I screamed and was rewarded with two very masculine chuckles in response.

"Zed," Cass grunted, "help our Angel out. She seems like she needs something to do with that mouth of hers."

I moaned, my fingers gripping the edge of the desk and my breasts against the top as Cass kicked my feet apart, spreading my legs.

Zed moved without protest, coming around the desk with his dick already in hand and a wide grin on his lips. Anticipation, arousal, and excitement curled through me, and I opened my mouth wide, my tongue out in invitation as he stepped closer.

Zed gathered my hair up in his hand and tilted my face up to hold my gaze as his dick slid into my mouth. My lips closed around him, and I sucked his tip, tasting the salty precum already leaking from his slit.

"Oh, shit yeah," he groaned as he pushed forward.

Cass smacked me again, but this time, instead of massaging the flesh, he plunged his fingers into my cunt, and I bucked against him, moaning around Zed's dick. My fingers gripped the desk tighter than ever, and Cass pumped his fingers in and out of me like a man on a mission, pushing me right up to the edge of climax while Zed fucked my mouth.

Then Cass stopped, taking his hand away entirely and making me whimper and writhe with wordless pleas for more. Zed held my hair tighter, shoving his cock deeper into my throat as I swallowed around him.

"Shit," Zed panted, his hips jerking as I sucked. "Saint, make her come."

Cass grunted in agreement, then slammed his dick into me right up to the hilt with one rough thrust.

I shattered. My screams muffled to nothing as Zed continued fucking my face, and Cass didn't pause. He just grunted and thrust deeper as my pussy tightened and pulsed with my orgasm. When I started to come down off it, he propped a foot up on the desk and fucked me harder.

My front ground against the edge of the desk, and I instantly came again, right on the heels of the first one. Zed's movements became rough and jerky, his dick pulsing against my lips, and a moment later, he pulled out of my throat so he could come on my tongue. The second he was done, he pulled away completely and opened my mouth with his fingers to watch as I rolled his seed over my tongue; then he whispered a curse as I swallowed it.

Cass finished a scarce second later with a couple of slamming thrusts that shoved me so hard into the desk I would have bruises on my hips for *weeks*.

In the heavy, exhausted silence that immediately followed, the printer chirped a happy tune to announce the finished project, and I started laughing.

CHAPTER 52

Sandra Wildeboer's funeral was an intimate thing. No churches or overabundance of flowers. No weeping friends giving lengthy speeches about all the *good times* they'd had. It was just six people along with a priest around her grave site. After all, she'd spent her whole adult life on the run, never forming friendships or connections strong enough that anyone would care to attend her farewell.

The priest kept it brief, per Lucas's request. Claudette and Big Sal each took a moment at Sandra's casket to toss in a rose and say goodbye, then left, and it was just the four of us.

After standing in silence for several moments, Cass shifted and squeezed Lucas's shoulder. "We'll give you some privacy," he rumbled, tipping his head to Zed to follow him back to the parking lot where we'd left the Escalade.

I glanced up at Lucas, wondering if he wanted me to leave as well. His fingers tightened around mine, though, holding me tight as he stared down on his mother's coffin. I took the hint and leaned in to his side in comfort.

"She was a coward," he murmured after the longest time. His voice was rough with emotion, but he hadn't shed a single tear, like he was numb to it all. "She took the *easy* way out, killing herself rather than facing the sins of her past. I had a sister, and she never told me. For all I know, I have other siblings out there too. Or *had*. It doesn't sound like their child-assassin program was a huge success."

I didn't try to defend Sandra. Lucas was just speaking his thoughts aloud, not seeking contradiction. I wiggled my hand free of his, then wrapped my arms around his waist, holding him tight.

"She was a fucking coward," Lucas whispered again, his voice cracking, "but she always loved me. Before she got sick, she did *everything* to support me and give me all the opportunities I could have hoped for. She was a good mom."

I nodded, then tipped my head back to look up at him. "She was a great mom, Lucas. She raised *you*."

Tears spilled from his eyes, and he hugged me back, crushing my face to his chest. His face was buried in my hair, and his body shook with grief. We stayed like that for a few minutes, then he drew a deep, shuddering breath before relaxing his hold on me.

"Let's go," he murmured, kissing my cheek softly. "Cass promised we could piss Zed off by smoking weed in his new car."

I snickered, loving how my guys showed their affection for one another. Zed would be *severely* unimpressed to replace that new car smell with musty marijuana smoke, but he'd also allow it because Lucas just buried his mom.

We walked slowly back toward the parking lot, my arm still locked around Lucas's waist and our steps in sync. Zed and Cass were already seated inside the Escalade, so we climbed into the spacious back seat. Lucas pulled me against his side.

Cass glanced over his shoulder, then without a word passed back a freshly rolled joint and lighter.

"I hate you," Zed muttered to Cass, who just shot him a wicked smirk back.

"Simmer down, Zeddy Bear," he rumbled. "Gumdrop deserves it."

Zed huffed, glancing at us in the mirror. "Getting high? Or hotboxing in my car?"

I met his gaze in the reflection, smiling softly. Cass was the one who answered, though. "Both."

Zed rolled his eyes but didn't disagree. "Home?" he asked.

"Lookout," I suggested instead. "A storm is about to roll in. It'll be nice to watch from up there."

"While high," Lucas agreed, taking a long drag on the joint.

No one disagreed with *that* part of the plan, and Zed sighed as he pulled out of our park to drive us up the mountain behind Shadow Grove. It wasn't a long drive from the cemetery, but by the time we arrived, we were all buzzing with a nice, light high.

Rain began pelting down on our windscreen as we parked, and for the better part of an hour we stayed there. Conversation stayed light and relaxed, and Lucas held me in a warm embrace the whole time. Eventually, when Zed murmured that we should head home, Lucas let out a soft snore.

The three of us all grinned, but I carefully fastened our seat belts without waking him up, and Zed drove us home.

"Want me to carry him upstairs?" Cass offered when we pulled back into our garage.

I shook my head, my eyes on Lucas and the way he was curled up against the door of the car. "Nah, leave him. I'll hang out here until he wakes up. Didn't you say you had something to do this afternoon?"

Cass grunted, checking the time with slightly bloodshot eyes. "Shit. Yeah, I do. Zed, you coming with?"

Zed grinned showing teeth, a feral sort of smile that suggested they were going to do something bad. Damn, now I wanted to join them too.

"You wanna come too, don't ya, Dare?" he teased me in the mirror.

I rolled my eyes. "Yes, and I don't even know where you're

going." I glanced at Lucas again and gave a small sigh. "Lucas needs me tonight, though, I think. You two have fun, just don't get caught. Or killed."

Cass smirked, jerking a nod as he climbed out of the musty vehicle. Zed gave me a small salute of acknowledgment and a grin. "Yes, sir. Don't wait up."

I shook my head, groaning internally. As if *that* wasn't worrying. The sound of Zed's Ferrari pulling out of the garage rumbled through our car. Then a moment later, it faded away and the garage door whirred as it closed. For a second, there was nothing but silence. Then Lucas's hand on my waist flexed, grabbing me tighter.

"Are they gone?" he mumbled with a sleep-thick voice.

I grinned. "Yup, both gone."

His eyes cracked open, and a smile of pure evil crossed his lips. "Finally. Come here." He lifted me by the waist, pulling me to straddle him as he unbuckled his seat belt.

"Lucas *Wilder*," I purred as his hands pushed my black dress up my legs, "were you *faking?*"

His response was to crash his lips against mine, his kiss tasting like smoke and grief as his grip on my hips begged for a distraction. It was something I was *more* than happy to provide.

"First you smoke weed in Zed's car, now you wanna fuck in the back seat?" I laughed. "Lucas, you're choosing violence today, and I'm here for it."

"Good," he breathed. His fingers hooked my panties, pulling them aside, and plunged deep inside my pussy.

I gasped, my back arching. He knew what he was doing, though. In seconds, I was moaning and riding his hand like a sex-starved vixen as an early orgasm started building. And he was only warming up.

The bouncers at Hot Spot recognized me and let Lucas and me in ahead of the *huge* line of waiting patrons. It wasn't one of my bars, nor was it owned by any of my associates. It was a *normal* nightclub, owned by clean operators. Bouncers just tended to know who the scary bastards were to avoid uncomfortable misunderstandings, which I was grateful for when it gave us easy entry into the club.

"You call that anonymous?" Lucas laughed in my ear as we made our way through the packed club, heading for the bar.

I shrugged, tugging him closer to my back as I led the way. "As good as it gets within driving distance, hot stuff. Tequila?"

"Absolutely, yes." His hands gripped my hips possessively as we waited our turn to be served—proving my point that I was decently anonymous here—then downed two shots of tequila each.

Lucas's eyes flared with heat as I sucked on the lime wedge, and he dragged his tongue over his lower lip with a groan. "Fucking hell," he murmured.

I smirked, then looped an arm around his neck and crushed my body to his as I kissed him. "I thought you wanted to dance," I teased when his hands groped my ass.

"I did," he groaned. "I do. But I was unprepared for how *scorching* you would look tonight."

When Lucas had said he wanted to go out dancing, I'd dressed with public sex in mind: tight minidress and no underwear whatsoever. I wasn't even wearing my guns—but had loaded Lucas with a spare in case of emergencies. I wasn't totally dense.

But, shit. Fucking in a nightclub supply room held special sentimentality to us.

"Come on, Wilder," I teased, using his new name like I used to when it was his stripper alias. "Show me those dance moves."

Linking my fingers through his, I led the way through the dense crowd until we were in the middle of the dance floor. Lucas didn't need to be cajoled into dancing with me; this was *his* element. The thumping music tugged at my hips, and I spun around to face him as he moved in time with the beat.

We danced together like we were fucking on the dance floor,

421

all sexy glances, roaming hands, and grinding hips, until I was so sweaty I was dripping. Or, hell, maybe that wasn't sweat.

"Wanna find a supply room?" Lucas whispered in my ear, his voice low and drenched with desire. As if the hardness he was pressing against my ass hadn't clued me in already.

I groaned, grinding back against him. "Fuck yes, I do."

That was all the permission he needed, and he snatched my hand, making a beeline for the back of the club where we'd both already scouted out the most likely location for a supply room, accessible bathroom, or even just a dark corner to fuck in.

"Score," Lucas announced, as he pushed open a dark, employees-only door. Inside was an accessible bathroom that was being *used* as a storeroom. So there was a lock on the door. A lock that I flicked the moment we closed the door behind us.

Lucas dropped straight to his knees and peeled my short dress up, making me shiver when the air hit my soaking pussy.

"Shit," I whispered, "let me check my messages real fast, make sure Zed and Cass haven't been arrested for public indecency or something."

Lucas huffed, but handed me my phone from his pocket. He was acting as my purse and holster tonight, which he was more than happy to do, considering the easy access it was giving him.

"Do you know what they're up to?" I asked curiously, obliging when he lifted one of my legs to drape over his shoulder.

He grinned, then licked a long line down my pussy to make me moan. "Yeah, I do," he admitted. "I'm the distraction. Can't you tell?"

Oh yeah, now that he mentioned it. "You're the best distraction in the whole fucking world, Lucas," I replied, then gasped and shuddered as his tongue pushed inside me, flicking and tasting.

Shit. I had messages and missed calls. Of course I did.

Not willing to pause Lucas's distraction techniques, I gripped his hair tight with one hand, holding him against me as my hips rocked, and I rode his face. With the other hand, I swiped through the notifications and found they were all from Alexi.

I frowned. What the hell did he want?

Deciding I didn't have the patience or concentration to read his messages, I just fired back one of my own.

Hades: Is this urgent? I'm busy.

His reply dinged almost instantly.

Alexi: Yes

That brought a frown to my face, but it was quickly erased as Lucas slid his fingers into me.

"Oh shit," I gasped, my legs shaking. "Dammit. Give me two seconds, Wilder."

With *extreme* effort, I pushed him back and dropped my leg to the ground so I could focus on replying to Alexi. I only typed out half a message before glancing down at Lucas, still on his knees, and tilting my head to the side.

"Pull that gorgeous dick out, Wilder. Show me how much you love being a distraction."

He laughed huskily but leaned back to do as instructed.

I hit Send on my message and watched with hungry eyes as he stroked his huge dick, the tip gleaming with precum already. Alexi's reply buzzed in my hand, and I glanced down at it.

"All right. We've got ten minutes," I told Lucas, holding out a hand to pull him to his feet. "Make me come at least twice."

Grinning, he lifted me by my thighs and crushed me against the door. "Yes, sir."

Oh yeah. Just like old times.

It was more like twenty minutes before Lucas and I tumbled back out of the supply room, giggling and sweaty. Alexi had texted multiple times to say he was here, but I'd told him to fucking *wait*.

I'd cleaned up as best I could with some napkins from the supply room, but still I groaned as Lucas and I threaded our way through the crowds toward the exit.

"What's that face for?" Lucas asked with a smile as we stepped out into the cool night air.

I wrinkled my nose. "I can still feel your cum dripping out of my pussy," I confessed, and his lips parted in shock.

"Holy fuck," he whispered on a laugh. "That just *instantly* got me hard."

Rolling my eyes, I tugged him farther down the street to where I'd told Alexi to wait. There was a diner around the corner where I wanted to get a snack before Lucas and I called a cab to get home, seeing as we were both way past too intoxicated to drive.

I spotted the heavyset, bulky figure stepping out of the alleyway beside the diner as though in slow motion. Something about him screamed *threat*, and my body flooded with adrenaline as he raised a gun.

Lucas wasn't the naive, clueless, teenage stripper anymore, though. He spotted the man—the threat—at the same time I did. He grabbed me, wrapping his body around mine, and tugged me to the side right as the gunshot cracked through the night, echoing and deafening me by how close it'd been.

A hard jolt shocked through Lucas, knocking us both to the ground, and sticky, wet blood sprayed the pavement.

Terror swept through me, and I reacted on autopilot. I reached around Lucas's heavy form to grab one of the guns from the holster in the small of his back and fired off three shots in the direction where our attacker had been located.

"Lucas!" I exclaimed, my free hand shaking him in a panic. There was blood. He'd been shot. "Lucas, talk to me!"

He groaned. Good sign. "I'm fine," he replied, flexing his shoulders to push up off me. "What the fuck—"

His confusion faded along with mine when we saw whose blood it was. Alexi must have been nearby too. He'd thrown himself at both Lucas and me, knocking us down and taking the hit himself.

"Check him," I ordered Lucas, pointing in the direction of our fallen attacker. I had no clue if I'd killed him or just hurt him, but at least one of my bullets had found its mark.

Lucas didn't argue as he pulled his own gun and stalked cautiously closer to the gunman while I knelt beside Alexi and touched a hand to his cheek. The amount of blood pooling beneath him didn't indicate a good outcome for my head of security, but he was still conscious. Just.

"Alexi, what the fuck were you thinking?" I hissed, emotion clawing at my chest.

"He was gonna shoot you, Boss," he mumbled back, blood bubbling from his lips as his eyes rolled back. "Knew I'd found him out," he continued, his voice weak. "I hope you killed him."

I glanced up at Lucas for confirmation, and he gave me a sharp nod, his posture relaxing somewhat but his gun still in hand.

"Yeah," I told Alexi, "he's dead."

More blood bubbled from his lips. "Me too, huh?"

I wrinkled my nose, but shit. That was the life we lived. "Yeah, Alexi," I breathed. "I think so."

He released a small sigh, his eyes closing. "Good way to go," he murmured after a painful silence. "Don't ever stop fighting, Boss. Make that bastard pay."

I gave a heavy sigh. My fingers found his bloody ones and held tight. "I will," I promised my friend—because despite my recent doubts, tonight proved that's what Alexi was. A damn loyal friend. "He'll get what's coming to him."

Alexi tried to say something more, but more blood bubbled from his lips and then...nothing. He was gone.

Swallowing back the unexpected tears burning at my eyes,

I peeled my fingers free of his lifeless hand and stood up. In the distance, the sound of police sirens wailed, no doubt called by the gunshots, and I knew Lucas and I needed to get the hell out of there. Fast.

"We need to go," I told Lucas in a cold, hard voice.

He nodded, stony-faced, but indicated to the dead man he stood over. "You need to see this first."

Dread filled my stomach, and I crossed over to where he stood, then looked down into the lifeless eyes of Rodney, my Club 22 manager.

CHAPTER 53

Maxine gasped in dismay on the phone as I filled her in on Rodney's death and what that meant for his involvement with Chase. The reason I was telling her—aside from the fact that she had been calling me every day just to chat—was because I suspected he'd been the one to attack her.

"Yeah," she agreed, "it could have been. He wore a mask, but now that you suggest him…yeah, the height and build fit. I think. It's a bit hazy, you know?"

"Totally understandable," I replied with a sigh. I had her on speakerphone while I did my hair and makeup after a particularly dirty shower with Zed. It was Friday night, and we were expecting a text with the starting point of the street race at any time. This was an appointment that required *full* Hades face.

Maxine hummed thoughtfully. "Kinda irrelevant now, though. I'm alive and he's dead, so, like, Rodney can suck my spirit dick."

I snickered at that imagery. "He would have been acting on Chase's instructions anyway." I paused, drawing a deep breath. She didn't know the whole Chase story, just enough to understand who was responsible for nearly killing her. "And I'll deal with him. Don't worry about that."

She gave a throaty laugh, and I could see why Zed had been attracted to her. Even after the violent attack that'd nearly killed her and left her relearning how to walk properly, Maxine oozed sex.

"I never doubted that for a second, H," she told me with a chuckle. "Hey, did I tell you that I finally got an appointment with the physical therapist you recommended?"

I smiled. Misha was crazy overbooked, but I'd sweet-talked him into accepting Maxine as a patient too. She needed the best for her recovery, and that was Misha.

"Really?" I feigned surprise. "Well, that's great."

She scoffed. "Yeah, nice try. His voicemail was literally 'Hades told me I don't have a choice, so be at my clinic tomorrow at twelve.' But thank you. What are friends for if not leveraging their scary-ass reputations to get shit?"

"I'm sure I have no clue what you're talking about." I laughed. "Must be a different Hades running around threatening people to get you shit. Did Cass sort out your security?" When I'd visited her place, I'd been quietly horrified at the lack of security on the building. She'd been targeted once; she could easily be targeted again.

Maxine made a sound of confirmation. "Sure did. I'm locked up tighter than a nun's cunt."

Cass, entering the bathroom as she said that, met my eyes in the mirror and gave me an amused look.

"You're a classy bitch, Max," I replied with a chuckle, leaning back into Cass as he clasped my hips and kissed my neck.

"Uh-huh, that's why you like me so much," she shot back—and wasn't that the truth. "Anyway, you just got a whole sexy, sultry sound in your voice, which *probably* means you have company. I'll leave you to it."

I grinned. We'd spent *a lot* of time talking, and though we'd been friends for a short time, she read my tonal shifts better than anyone I knew. "Not gonna deny it," I replied, tilting my head to the side as Cass kissed higher, his beard teasing my skin.

Maxine groaned. "I'm so jealous. Wanna leave speakerphone on so I can listen in? It's been so long since I got laid I'm considering shares in Satisfyer."

"Bye, Maxine," Cass growled, reaching out to end the call before snaking a hand up my skirt. "Fuck, Red."

Dabbing concealer under my eyes, I smirked at him in the mirror. "This skirt shows awful panty lines," I lied. "Better to just go without."

Cass hummed happily as he peeled my skirt all the way up, folding it over at my waist. We still had time; the text message hadn't arrived with the race location yet. As for the trap, everything was in place. So I had no qualms about bending further over the sink and pushing my ass back into his groping hands.

"Hands on the mirror, Angel," he rumbled, already unbuckling his belt to free his thick, tattooed cock.

I bit my lip and grinned, locking eyes with him in the glass. "Yes, *Daddy*," I teased.

His eyes narrowed. "Call me that again, Angel, and I'll fuck you right to the edge of climax, then leave you there. Then do it again and again and again, denying you release until you're *begging* me. Then I'll remind you why you shouldn't push my buttons."

I shivered because that kind of sounded like a good time. But not right now. We definitely didn't have time for that. So I mimed zipping my lips and planted my hands against the mirror as instructed.

Satisfied with my submission, Cass didn't mess around teasing me. He knew, like I did, that we would have to leave the second that text arrived, and neither of us wanted to be left hanging. So he fucked me hard and fast, both of us coming simultaneously within minutes.

He grabbed my chin, tilting my face back to kiss me roughly, then smacked my ass and told me to hurry up with getting ready.

Shithead.

I made a mental note to call him *Daddy* later when we had more time to play.

Fifteen minutes later, as I was making my way downstairs, Zed called out that it was time to go. We had the location of the starting point, but that in itself didn't matter to us. We weren't racing; that was what I had Rex's boys for. But it gave us a reasonable time frame for when our rat would come scurrying into our trap.

We took the Escalade again so that we all fit into one car—not to mention the amount of trunk space for weapons and ammo. Also, with every passing day, Zed grew more paranoid that Chase would flip his lid and try to kill me outright.

I disagreed; Chase would want me alive for a *long* time before I died. But I also didn't put it past him to try and take out my guys with a car bomb or by running them off the road. So I had no objections to taking the bulletproof SUV when we were out together. Besides, the back seat was all kinds of spacious for sex.

The mood in the car crackled with anticipation as we drove to Rainybanks, and I spent the majority of the drive texting with Dallas. This was a long shot, and we still weren't totally sure the rat would show up for this race. Shelby had a photo of our guy, though, and would send confirmation if he was among the racers at the start line.

"You reckon these kids are good enough for this job?" Zed asked as we pulled into the old shipping yard. Every visible surface was covered in graffiti, and rodents scurried around in the light cast by our headlights. We were miles from the nearest residential area. Miles away from anyone hearing gunshots or screams.

I nodded. "Rex vouches for them. He's determined to get all five of them blooded into the Timberwolves as fast as possible. Makes me think he's got other enemies he hasn't told me about."

Zed huffed. "Rex? Unquestionably. So long as they're useful, though, I don't have an issue with it."

"Agreed. This will be a good test for the three helping Shelby tonight. We can always do with new skills in the Wolves, and according to Rex, one of them is some kind of auto electrical genius." I couldn't remember which one. It was either Nix or Micah.

We parked at our planned spot and killed the lights, then sat in silence a moment before my phone buzzed with a message from Shelby.

"We got him," I confirmed with a wicked grin. "Stupid, arrogant rat. Should have stayed in hiding where we couldn't reach him."

Dallas sent me a link to the GPS tracking app he had linked to each boy's car. We could follow their progress from the start of the race through the streets of downtown Rainybanks as they herded our mark all the way to us, like sheepdogs in fast cars.

Cass and Lucas got out of the car to load their guns while Zed and I watched the little colored dots moving on the screen. We couldn't see the actual race, but the way those dots all worked together had me wishing we could.

"Not bad," Zed murmured. We didn't have a tracker on the mark's car, but we could guess where he was based on the way the four boys were splitting up and blocking any routes other than the one carrying him right to us.

I sent him a wild grin, and he reached over the center console. He grabbed my face, bringing it to his to kiss me hard and fast, the thrill of our mission infectious. Zed and I, we were cut from the same bulletproof cloth.

"After," I promised him in a rough, husky voice, my pussy already heating with anticipation.

"Deal," he agreed, kissing me again, then climbing out of the car to arm himself up with the others.

I waited where I was, keeping an eye on the moving dots as I buzzed with nervous energy. Or not *nervous* so much as...determined. After this, there would be just one very high-profile name

431

left. Things were about to get crazy; Chase wouldn't leave this one unpunished.

Headlights caught my attention as they flew around the corner in the distance, and I reached over to turn the Escalade lights on high. All five cars came to a screeching halt in front of us, the mark's modified Supra trapped in a net of my making with nowhere to go.

Smiling a cold, cruel smile, I climbed out of the car and stalked to the front of the Escalade where my guys waited, each heavily armed. The bright headlights of the SUV backlit us in a dramatic way that would have made the Guild proud.

My mark revved his engine, like he was threatening to run us over to get out. That was his only option, too, with four other cars hemming him in.

I nodded to Lucas and Cass, and they moved as previously instructed, Lucas to the passenger window, his gun trained on the driver, and Cass to the driver's side. Not bothering to try the door, Cass used the butt of his rifle to smash straight through the window. He reached in, grabbed the shrieking driver by his shirt, and hauled him through the broken window before throwing him down on the hard ground.

The man twisted, rolling to his feet and immediately tried to make a run for it. He only made it as far as the shimmering gold Nissan 350Z when he pulled up short. The driver of that car had stepped out and aimed a gun right at my mark's head as he sprinted closer.

"Back it up, speedy," the boy ordered in a hard-edged voice that almost made me grin. Yeah, Rex was right about these kids. They'd be valuable assets to the Timberwolves if they had the stomach for what was to come.

The terrified target threw his hands in the air, spinning around again like he might be able to plead his way out if he could locate whoever was in charge.

"Over here, Anthony," I called, stepping forward so I wasn't

432

totally shadowed from the backlight. "You surely must have been expecting me by now."

His eyes rounded to the size of saucers, and he swallowed heavily. The kid from the gold Nissan stepped around his door and gave Anthony Yang a prod in the back, getting him walking back over to where I waited with my guys.

"Y-you," the sweating man stammered, licking his lips. "Y-you can't k-kill me. I'm FBI."

I laugh coldly. "I wasn't aware that gave you immortality. Pretty sure dead's dead, no matter what your job title."

The slippery fuck shook his head. "No, y-you can't kill me. They'll know it was you, and then—"

"And then *what*, Anthony?" I hissed, taking a step closer. My little helper with a gun to Anthony's back kicked out his knees, sending him crashing down to the dirt at my feet.

The rat peered up at me, a sneer twisting his face. "And then you'll end up right back where you were six weeks ago," he spat out, "chained to that bed in Chase's basement, screaming at all your delusions and begging him to kill you while he—"

I couldn't stomach hearing it. I did something I knew would shut him up, short of killing him. I shot him in the shoulder.

Anthony Yang had just confirmed the suspicion I'd formed when I realized his role in Chase's business. He was an FBI techie. The man could erase key pieces of evidence from databases, alter test scores for paid-off recruits, and delete any reports of crimes that Chase was involved in. He also, apparently, had a video feed into Chase's cell of terror.

This man. This slimy, pathetic man screaming in the dirt as he clutched his bleeding shoulder, was the Lockhart version of Dallas, but better connected. He was why it'd been so hard to track Chase down. That was why his loss would hit Chase *hard*. Without Anthony Yang to wipe security footage and erase evidence, Chase would have to be *so damn careful* from here on out.

"You *bitch!*" Anthony shrieked. "Chase should have finished you off when he had you! He should have just drowned you properly instead of—"

Oops. There went Anthony's knee.

Without speaking, because fuck chatting with this dead man, I gave Zed a nod. He gave me a cruel smile back and came over to grab Anthony by the ankle. Amusement rippled through me when he grabbed the leg I'd just shot.

Without paying attention to our nasty little rat's squeals, Zed dragged him over to the point we'd chosen for this specific death. It was a wide metal grate in the ground, leading down into the stormwater drain below the shipping yard. Lucas helped, making quick work of securing Anthony to the grate, hand and foot.

"Don't worry, Anthony. Your former employers won't be coming out to avenge a good, upstanding FBI agent's death. My associate took the liberty of forwarding some *very* damning evidence against you about five minutes ago. They'll know exactly why you're dead. Because you're a dirty, corrupt *rat*. So, consider this karma." I flashed him a toothy grin and exchanged my gun for a long-bladed knife.

Tugging his shirt up, I closed my ears to his screams and slid my blade into his flabby belly. The steel was so sharp it was like cutting butter as I dragged it across his body from hip to hip, splitting him open.

His blood ran freely over the grate, dripping down into the drain while he screamed and screamed, then passed out from the pain or fear, or both.

"Holy shit," the kid from the gold Nissan murmured, staring down at Anthony's opened guts. "Is he dead?"

I laughed. So did Zed. We were sick fucks some days. "Nope, not dead. A wound like that could take hours to kill him."

"Pity he doesn't have hours," Zed murmured, his eyes meeting mine with bloodlust shining bright. As if perfectly on cue, high-pitched squeaks echoed out of the drain below Anthony.

"Rats?" one of the other boys exclaimed, coming closer. Micah. "Oh man. Brutal." His smile was just as feral as Zed's though, and I decided I liked this kid.

"I trust you four can hang around and make sure this rat doesn't wiggle free before it's all over?" I arched a brow at Shelby, who nodded back. "Good. Shelby, I've forwarded you a phone number for my cleanup crew. She'll sanitize the scene when it's done. Don't leave until she gets here, understood?"

"Understood, sir," he agreed.

Satisfied with my new helpers, I headed back to the SUV. Zed tossed the keys to Lucas, telling him to drive, then followed me into the back seat. He pounced on me the moment the doors closed, hot and hard, riding the bloodlust like an aphrodisiac, and I was just as bad.

Cass got into the passenger seat, and Lucas gunned the engine, peeling away from our latest crime scene. It wasn't long before Cass climbed over into the back with us, though, and Lucas almost crashed twice while we celebrated a successful night out.

Anthony Yang made five. One more, and my list was done. One more...and I could take down Chase Lockhart himself. Just that thought alone was enough to make me come.

CHAPTER 54

The sun shone bright over the lush green of Shadow Grove Botanical Gardens, not a single cloud in the sky as we wandered into the upscale charity event. Blown-up pictures of smiling children were propped up on stands all over the place, but there were no children in attendance. That was a relief. I'd have hated to scar any innocent kids by killing a man in front of them…even though it wouldn't have stopped me.

"Ms. Wolff," a woman called out, and I pasted a polite smile on my face to greet the mayor of Cloudcroft, Julia Smythe. "I'm glad you could make it. The foundation is beyond grateful for your generous donation."

The fundraising event we were attending was for a charity specifically aimed at giving foster children a better start in life, ensuring they weren't falling behind in school and providing funding for textbooks, clothes, whatever was lacking. The irony of the situation made me sick.

"It's the least I could do," I murmured with a tight smile.

The mayor looked around me with curiosity, her brows raised in question. "Is your handsome fiancé not here today?" She smiled warmly, glancing down at the ring still firmly in place on my finger.

I hadn't taken it off once since that argument with Zed, and secretly, I think we all knew it was never coming off. It was *mine*.

"Oh, he's around here somewhere," I replied with a low chuckle as Lucas approached through the crowd. He was dressed impeccably, blending in with the rich crowd with ease, but his devoted gaze was only for me. "Julia, I don't think I've ever formally introduced you to Mr. Wilder."

I indicated for Lucas to come closer, and he wrapped an arm around my waist possessively, kissing my cheek. "Hey, beautiful," he purred, everything about him dripping sex.

The mayor's eyes widened to the size of saucers, then she gave a slow smile and nod. "No, I don't believe we've met." She held out her hand to Lucas. "Mr. Wilder. A pleasure."

Lucas shook her hand, his arm still holding me in a clearly intimate embrace. "Mayor Smythe, I'm so sorry about the loss of your deputy the other week. What a tragic event."

The mayor's lips tightened, but she looked more irritated than upset. "Yes, such a tragedy," she murmured, "an unfortunate allergic reaction."

I almost laughed out loud at that, but clearly Mayor Smythe was happy to be rid of her deputy. She'd just lacked the balls to do it herself.

"Well, I certainly hope you have some solid replacement candidates lined up, Julia," I commented with a sharp edge in my voice.

The mayor heard it and smiled back. "Absolutely, I do."

I knew, like she did, that her staff would send me a list of the names she was considering for my approval or veto. Julia and I had a good arrangement, and she didn't want to rock that boat—especially not now, while I was making so many high-profile power moves against my enemy. She may not understand the game, but she *did* recognize the danger.

"I saw a buffet of sweets over there," Lucas said quietly, then kissed my hair. "I'm going to grab some before things...kick off."

He shot me a wink and nodded to the mayor before disappearing back into the crowd.

Julia's gaze followed him for a moment, like she couldn't help herself, then she flushed when she realized I was glaring. "Handsome man," she commented with an uncomfortable laugh. "Will today's event be as…dramatic as the last you attended?"

It was a diplomatic way to phrase it, and I grinned showing teeth. "Probably."

She blanched but gave a tight nod. "I see."

Cass appeared at my side then. For such a big, tattoo-covered man, he slipped through the crowd like a ghost. It was scary, in a good kind of way.

"We're all sorted," he told me, ignoring the mayor entirely. His hands gripped my hips, and Julia quirked a brow. Because I didn't give a flying fuck about people knowing I had three lovers, I covered one of Cass's hands with mine. Our fingers tangled together, and his thumb stroked over my ring as though it was from him as much as it was from Zed.

Fuck, I wouldn't put it past him to have demanded Zed let him pay for half, just so he could lay claim too.

"Lovely to see you again, Julia," I told the mayor, dismissing her. "I suggest staying back from the stage during our lieutenant governor's speech."

That was as good as my warnings ever got. But like I said, Julia and I had an arrangement. I'd hate to have to start from scratch again if she became collateral damage.

She melted away into the crowd once more, and Cass turned me in his arms to press a soft kiss to my lips.

"I didn't know we were all public with this," he rumbled, his hands holding me close to his body.

It was understandable why he'd think that; I was usually careful to avoid public displays of affection with *any* of the three of them, at least when it came to those casual, intimate touches that implied

438

a relationship deeper than sex. I'd spent so long cultivating my reputation as a strong, independent woman to be feared and respected *without* relying on men that I'd shied away from all affection. But I was past that now. I was too fucking in love to care.

I shrugged. "Since when did I give a fuck what people thought of me? I won't hold back simply for societal expectations. If I wanna kiss you here in front of all these stuck-up pricks, then I damn well will. If I wanna drag you behind that hedge over there and let you fuck my ass, I damn well will. No one stops me from doing what I want, and I want *you*, Saint."

To prove my point, I cupped the back of his head, pulling his face down to meet my kiss. It wasn't a chaste, polite sort of kiss, either. I melted into his strong body and parted my lips to meet his aggressive tongue.

"Fuck, Red," he growled when he released me, his forehead against mine. "Now all I can think about is fucking your ass behind that hedge, and I didn't bring any travel lube."

Chuckling softly, I snaked a hand between us to squeeze his hard dick through his pants. "Save it," I whispered. "We'll have something to celebrate soon."

He gave a frustrated groan, but didn't protest as we went in search of Lucas at the dessert table.

For a while we played the part of polite—if scary—party guests. But eventually, a woman took to the stage and tapped the microphone, making it squeal painfully in the speakers.

She launched into her spiel about the charity and all the good it does, while a slideshow behind her displayed pictures of all the smiling, happy children they'd supposedly helped. Across the garden party, I caught sight of an eye-patch-wearing bastard and smiled.

"He knows." Cass chuckled in my ear. "He knows, and he can't do anything about it."

I grinned wider. It was why I'd picked a different method of death for each of his associates. He had *no* clue how the attack would be coming, so he couldn't prepare for it. Would it be poison again? Or a subtle knife in the back later in the day? Maybe a ranged shot or even an explosion? The options were endless and impossible to safeguard against.

Based on the grim scowl on Chase's face, he'd already accepted that I'd win this one, and he wasn't even going to *try*.

He started crossing the party, his eye locked on me, and I forced my lingering fear back in its box where it damn well belonged. He wouldn't *ever* get the satisfaction of seeing me scared again, that was a goddamn promise.

The guests clapped as the woman from the charity finished her speech and announced their patron, the lieutenant governor of our state.

"Darling," Chase greeted me, ignoring the important man taking the stage behind him. "Somehow I knew you'd be here today."

I smiled wide, all teeth, and leaned back against Cass. "Of course I am," I replied as Cass slid his hand around my waist and splayed it across my midsection possessively. "I give generously to foundations like this. Foster children are so easily preyed on by bad men, they need all the help they can get, don't you think?"

Chase's lip curled in a sneer, then his eye flicked down to where I'd placed my hand over Cass's. My ring was on full display, and it was short-circuiting his pea-sized brain. His claim of ownership over me was the cornerstone of his obsession, so the idea that I could be engaged to—going to *marry*—someone else? Unacceptable.

"Hush, Pirate Chase, the lieutenant governor is about to begin telling us what a great man he is. You won't want to miss this." I laid a finger over my lips and winked, making his eye twitch with anger.

The silver-haired politician started his speech onstage, talking about how the matter of foster children was so *near* and *dear* to his heart. Meanwhile, the slideshow behind him faded from smiling kids to something far more sinister: security footage of a shipping container and a dozen crying girls being herded inside at gunpoint. And there he was, our *charitable* lieutenant governor, shaking hands with one of the armed men, his face tilted just the right way toward the camera to make his identity unmistakable.

The crowd was gasping and whispering, horrified at what they were seeing, but I just grinned at Chase. Neither of us was watching the stage when the suppressed sniper shot sounded and blood splattered the projector screen. The video clip froze on an image of the lieutenant governor receiving head from a woman chained to the wall like a dog, and I couldn't have timed it better if I'd tried.

"Oops," I murmured, "my mistake. It was *Zed* who didn't want to miss this one."

A vein pulsed in Chase's temple, and I could hear his teeth grinding painfully. He wasn't stupid, though. He knew I'd outplayed him again.

"There will be retaliation for this, Darling," he gritted out, furious. "Count on it. I'm coming for you, and when I succeed—which I will—you'll wish you'd never escaped my mountain home."

The entire party was in a panic, people running and hiding, women crying, and security running around like headless chickens. But the deed was done, and they'd never catch Zed; he was too damn good.

Chase stormed away, and I needed to bite my lip to hold back my glee as Lucas, Cass, and I made our way out of the garden party with all the other guests.

The Escalade pulled up with precise timing as we reached the main road, and the three of us piled inside. I grabbed Zed by the front of his shirt before he could pull back out into the traffic, dragging him close and kissing him long and hard.

"I fucking love you, Zayden," I murmured against his lips. "Take us home."

He licked his lips, shifting the car back into drive but keeping

441

his hot, hungry eyes on me. "Take your panties off, Dare. I'm not waiting that long."

I gave a low, throaty chuckle at that…because he damn well should have known I wasn't wearing any.

CHAPTER 55

It wasn't until late the next morning that I remembered to ask Zed and Cass about their secret mission from the other night. We were all piled into Zed's bed this time, and Lucas had awakened me with the push of his thick cock into my pussy from behind. I hadn't even fully woken up, grinding back onto him while still floating in a light sleep, until Zed had started sucking on my breasts, biting my nipples, and making me cry out.

When they were all done—each needing to take a turn making me come on their dick—we just lay there in a comfortable, naked, cum-soaked pile.

"So, when do I find out what mischief you two got up to while Lucas and I were getting shot at by Rodney?" I murmured, playing with Zed's fingers splayed over my hip.

Cass propped his head up on his hand and met my sleepy gaze. "I think Zeddy Bear was waiting for a special occasion."

Zed scoffed before brushing kisses against my bare shoulder. "I wasn't. But right after Alexi was killed didn't seem like a good time."

Lucas made a frustrated sound from the end of the bed, where he'd rolled so he could watch while Zed had screwed my brains out. "Just do it now," he groaned. "I hate keeping secrets."

I turned my head, giving Zed a pointed look, and he huffed a sigh.

"Fine," he muttered. "I guess early-morning group sex is as good an occasion as any."

He rolled out of his big bed and headed out of the room without bothering to grab clothes. Lucas immediately crawled up the bed and took the place at my back that had just been vacated, and I gave a laugh as he snuggled close.

Cass caught my chin between his fingers, pulling my face back to his, and kissed me hungrily as Lucas's hands found my breasts. The horny bastards were already keen to go again, apparently.

"Cut it out, you two," Zed snapped as he returned with a neatly wrapped gift box in his hands. He climbed back onto the bed to kneel at either side of my legs and presented the box to me. "This is from me."

Cass sat up and punched him on the arm, and Lucas kicked him on the leg.

"Fine," Zed grunted, "from *us*."

"Because we love you, Red," Cass rumbled before kissing me again.

As much as I enjoyed that, and the hardness of Lucas's dick grinding against my bare ass, I really wanted to know what was in the box—and why they needed a secret mission to get it for me.

So I pushed Cass away and sat up to take the box from Zed. I shredded the wrapping paper with my fingers and pried the box open to find...

"What?" I shrieked, stunned. "You... *How*?"

Zed grinned like the damn Cheshire cat as I ran my fingers over the familiar Desert Eagle inside the box. "A little birdie gave us a location where Chase was storing his prizes, and we made a little visit the other night while Lucas was taking a trip down memory lane with you."

"And we didn't *just* find this," Cass rumbled, smirking. "We also found a Guardian vault key."

My eyebrows shot up. Of course the Lockharts would have a Guardian vault. And if there was *anywhere* Chase might keep a fucking Fabergé egg, it was there.

"Have you checked it out yet?"

Cass shook his head. "Neither of us are clients, so we can't access the vaults with a key alone."

I smiled in understanding. You needed to be a known client to gain access without the red tape. And there was no way Cass could have pretended to be a Lockhart in order to use the key himself. But...I could. It would be easy enough for me to access the vault floor, then simply bypass my own door to find Chase's.

My fingers petted the Desert Eagle again, and I sank back into the pillows with a blissed-out moan. "You guys are spoiling me," I muttered. "A girl could get used to this."

Grinning, Zed tugged on my ankles, parting my legs around him. "You deserve to be spoiled, Boss. Now let us spoil you some more before we need to get up."

He slid back inside me with a breathless moan, and I clutched my Desert Eagle to my chest, hugging it like a psychopath as Zed fucked me between Lucas and Cass.

I couldn't have created a better scenario in my wildest dreams. It was goddamn perfect.

Getting access to the vault floor was a breeze, no one even glancing twice as I used my own key to open the elevator cage. Only Cass accompanied me, seeing as this was *his* mission, and I desperately hoped this would be the end of it for him. He'd been searching for this damn egg for so long; I badly wanted to help him find it.

"If it's not here," I said softly as the elevator clunked its way

445

down to the vaults, "we can keep searching. Even after Chase is gone. It's out there somewhere, so we'll find it sooner or later."

Shooting me a quick glance, he gave my fingers a squeeze. "It's here," he replied, firm.

I didn't disagree, just led the way out of the elevator when it stopped. We needed to be quick so we didn't catch the attention of anyone watching the security cameras. But the only way to find Chase's vault was to try the key in every door. Old school, I know, but we had no other options.

Cass blocked me from view as best he could, and I moved swiftly from door to door, trying the key in each lock until finally—on the seventh door—it clicked open.

"That's a relief," Cass murmured as I pushed it open and we moved inside. "I thought for sure it'd be way down at the end of the hall and security would drag us out before we got there."

Shaking my head, I made sure the door to the hall was closed fully before shooting him a grin. "We were due a small break, surely. Because *now* we still need to break into the safe itself." I nodded to the old-fashioned combination wheel, exactly the same as the one in my vault. "The keys only get us so far."

Cass scoffed a laugh. "Red, that's cute. You think this is the first vault I've cracked? Sit over there and watch, you might learn something."

Somehow, I'd thought he might say something like that. Cassiel Saint, man of mystery and many skills. Literally nothing could shock me about him anymore. He could turn invisible and walk straight through the vault wall, and I'd just nod and smile.

I leaned my shoulders against the door and watched as he went to work. A stethoscope-type thing was pressed between his ear and the door, and he took his time with each click of the combination, listening for the telltale sound of the tumblers falling into place. It wasn't the most high-tech system to start with, but a lot of the Guardian's security relied on the reputation of its clients. No one dared to rob these vaults because they feared the retribution of the vault's owner.

Me, though? I hoped Chase saw this. I was getting far too much glee from pushing all his buttons, but I knew my time was limited. I had to take my fun where I could get it.

After what felt like an hour, Cass stepped back with a broad grin and opened the safe door.

"Nice work, Saint," I whispered, coming closer to peer inside. The small room was crammed full of precious items: artwork by the greats, trays on trays of glittering stones, wads of neatly stacked cash...and there. Right in the middle of the vault on a specially made podium was a display case. An *empty* display case with an unmistakable egg-holder shape in the base of it.

Cass said nothing. He just stared at the empty display case for the longest time. Then his shoulders sagged with a heavy sigh.

"We're too late," he muttered. The resignation in his voice was enough to nearly break me.

I shook my head. "Bullshit. Chase must have worked out what you were looking for and moved it. We *will* find it, Cass. I promise you I won't give up." I planted my hands on his chest, giving him a stubborn glare.

He gave me a weak smile, then leaned down and kissed me. "I love you, Red, but I think this is my sign to give up on the egg hunt." With another heavy sigh, he slapped my ass and backed out of the vault empty-handed. "Come on, gorgeous. Let's go see Nadia and eat our body weight in cake."

I frowned, hating that our mission had been unsuccessful. But this was his call and the egg was very clearly no longer in the vault, so I just followed as he closed up the Lockhart vault and pocketed the key.

"Wanna come back here with a truck tomorrow and empty his whole vault?" I suggested as we got back into the elevator. "Just for fun? And then leave a big purple dildo in that display case or something?"

Cass huffed a laugh as the elevator carried us back up to the main bank. "Definitely," he agreed with a smirk.

Even so, the mood between us was somber the whole way back to Shadow Grove and Nadia's Cakes. Her grand reopening was just a day away, and she'd been hard at work for days to get everything ready and perfect. She was so busy that she didn't even see us come in or slide onto a pair of stools at the counter, where Diana spotted us.

"Hades!" she squealed, dropping the mop and bucket she'd been carrying and scurrying around the counter to hug my waist.

I patted her head awkwardly. "Hey, squirt," I replied. "You behaving yourself for Nadia?"

She snorted. "As if." Peeling away from me, she gave Cass a little nod. "Hey, Big Man."

"Hi, Little Shit," he replied, the affection in his voice thick.

"Have you guys killed my parents yet?" she asked point-blank. "I'm gonna be so pissed if they find me and drag me out of school next semester."

"Diana!" Nadia bellowed from the kitchen. "Why is there water on my floor?" She popped out, scowling at the dropped mop and bucket, then saw Cass and me sitting at her counter. "Ah, that explains that."

Diana had the good sense to cringe. "Sorry, Nadia," she muttered, hurrying back to clean up her mess as the old woman headed over to us.

"I think I might lose my sanity with that one before the new school year starts," she muttered, tossing an exasperated look over her shoulder at Diana. "That reminds me. I sent over the payment details for both girls to your office, Hades. Hannah said she'd sort it out."

I smiled. "Good." We'd managed to get both Diana and Zoya enrolled at Shadow Prep in the boarding school to give Nadia some room to breathe again. She was still happy to play the role of guardian to them both, but was too old to be a full-time parent of two preteen girls from a rough background.

"Oh, this is the kind of news to make an old woman smile," she exclaimed, snatching my hand up from the counter to peer at my ring. "About damn time, boy."

Cass huffed a disgruntled sound, and I grinned in spite of myself.

"It's beautiful," Nadia said warmly, inspecting my ring closely. "Very appropriate for the queen of the underworld." She shot me a wink, and I smiled wider.

"Oh my god!" Diana shrieked, coming back out of the kitchen and seeing my hand. "Are you guys getting *married*?"

"No," I said.

At the same time, Cass said, "Yes."

I elbowed Cass, but he just wrapped his arm around me and kissed my hair. "One day," he murmured just for my hearing.

I shivered but didn't argue. I had no doubt that one day they'd find a loophole and talk me into it. But that day wasn't today, so I just flicked him a warning glare and shook my head.

Diana propped her hands on her hips, frowning. She'd heard my denial much louder than Cass's confirmation.

"Well...are you marrying Zed, then?" she demanded. "Or Lucas? Because if you want my opinion—"

"She doesn't," Cass muttered.

"Then I pick Big Man. He's super grumpy and stuff but, like, he's totally in love with you."

Cass straightened up somewhat in his seat, like he hadn't been expecting that from sassy little Diana.

"Besides," she continued, "that means Lucas can wait for me to get older." She batted her lashes and grinned at me, teasing.

I rolled my eyes, fighting a laugh. Fucking kid had a death wish.

"You finished mopping that floor, Diana?" Nadia asked, redirecting the energy. "Still looks dirty from here."

The kid gave legitimately the most dramatic eye roll I'd ever seen and flounced back toward the kitchen. When she was gone, Nadia folded her arms and gave us both a long look.

"You two look like you've had a disappointing day."

Cass grimaced, running his hand over his head. "Yeah, you could say that." He looked down at me, his hand still resting on my hip. I said nothing because his egg hunt was his own personal mission to share or not as he saw fit.

"Whatever's eating at you, boy, you'd better just spit it out," his grandmother snapped, leveling him with a glare. "Especially if it concerns me."

She was sharp as a tack, this one. Nothing slid past her, no matter how *old* she claimed to be.

Cass blew out a long breath, and I leaned into him for support. "We just came from the Cloudcroft Guardian," he admitted, "where we broke into the Lockhart vault."

Nadia's brows rose, then a sly smile touched her lips. "Steal me anything pretty while you were in there?"

Cass laughed, but it was shaky. "I wish. I had hoped... I *know* that's where he was keeping your Fabergé egg. But when we got there today, it was already gone."

Nadia stared at the both of us for a long time, then burst out laughing. She shook her head at us like *we* were nuts and planted her hands on her hips. "Oh, you're funny, Cassiel, my boy," she chuckled. "I knew it was you."

Confusion rippled through me, and Cass gave a grunt. "What was?" he asked.

Nadia was still chuckling as she pulled out a couple of coffee mugs for us and grabbed the freshly brewed coffee pot to fill them up. "The egg," she said after a few moments, her smile wide and easy. "I knew it had to have been you who found it. You could have just given it to me, you silly goose."

Now I was *super* confused. Cass was too, if I was to guess based on his rigid posture and perplexed expression.

"No, it was already gone," he repeated. "We found the case, but it was empty. Chase must have moved it somewhere."

Nadia rolled her eyes. "Oh, I suppose you want me to believe Chase bloody one-eyed Lockhart left my priceless Fabergé egg on my dining table two nights ago? Hmm?" She shook her head at Cass. "Honestly, boy. Don't tell me you were high and forgot delivering it."

Shock held me speechless, and Cass seemed to be floundering for logic as well.

"What? No, I was... I didn't..." He wasn't lying, either. Two nights ago, we'd been dealing with the rat Anthony. There was no way he could have delivered an egg we hadn't even located.

Nadia just smiled and patted his tattoo-covered hand on the counter. "Thank you, my boy. It means the world to me." Tears gleamed in her eyes, and she sniffed them back. "Now, let me get you two some cakes. I've been sampling some new recipes."

She bustled away into the kitchen, leaving Cass and me peering at each other in shock. Chase hadn't moved the egg at all. It'd been stolen by someone else. Someone else...who'd then *returned* it to Nadia?

The pieces clicked together in my head, and I instantly knew who was responsible.

My mystery man.

CHAPTER 56

The shimmering gold Nissan came to an abrupt stop less than three feet from where I stood, its tires burning and brakes screeching. But that had nothing on the sound that exited my sister as she bounced out of the driver's seat and almost knocked me over with a hug.

"Dare, you're here! I didn't know you were here! Why are you here?"

I arched a brow at the boy climbing out of the passenger seat, the same one who'd stopped my rat from running a few nights ago. He just gave me a lopsided smile and shrugged.

"We figured it was better to surprise you, Sephy girl," Rex responded, clapping her on the shoulder. "Didn't want nerves getting in the way. Now, you could probably have taken that last corner a little wider. It'd give you more control on the—"

"No way, old man," the kid from the passenger seat scoffed, stomping over. "Don't go messing up my hard work with your antiquated bullshit."

Ah, Lincoln. The racer of the family. Made sense that he was the one teaching my sister to actually drive, finally.

Rex had called me down to the racetrack where Lincoln and the other boys had been taking Seph for driving lessons, but it looked to me like they were teaching her to street race, not parallel park. Rex wanted me to see how far she'd come in such a short time, and he'd been all puffed out like a proud peacock the whole time we'd watched her drive.

Lincoln and Rex were arguing over race strategy, but Seph turned to me with excitement in her eyes. "What did you think, Dare? Not bad, huh?"

I smiled back at her. "A vast improvement from the girl who drove herself into a ditch six months ago because it was raining, that's for sure."

Seph groaned. "You're never going to let me live that down."

Rex looked over at me, his brows raised in question. I pursed my lips, thinking, then gave him a small nod back.

"Persephone, kiddo, your sister got you something to celebrate your new ability to actually *drive* a car." Rex chuckled, clapping a hand on Seph's shoulder again. He stuck his fingers in his mouth and gave a shrill whistle, damn near deafening us.

On that cue, Shelby drove onto the racetrack in Seph's pretty purple Corvette and parked beside the Nissan.

Seph wrinkled her nose in confusion. "I don't get it," she admitted. "Why is Cora here?"

I frowned. "Cora?"

Lincoln answered with a smirk. "Cora the Corvette. We were high." Then he blanched and stumbled over his words. "O-on life. Obviously. High on life." Clearing his throat, he made a swift escape as far away from me as he could reasonably get while Shelby climbed out of the Corvette and tossed Seph the keys.

"Wait…" She turned to me with her mouth open in shock. "Did you—Dare! Did you buy me Cora?"

I shrugged. "You seemed attached. Happy early birthday or whatever."

The hug she wrapped me in was tight enough to suffocate, but I didn't push her away. I just patted her awkwardly on the back and

453

waited it out as she squealed thanks over and over, then babbled something about taking her Corvette for a spin around the track.

"Hold up, Seph," I said, grabbing her arm before she could skip back to her new car. "I want to talk to you about something, if you can spare a minute?"

She bobbled her head in agreement, and the two of us made our way over to the run-down bleachers at the side of the track, out of earshot from Rex and his boys.

"What's up, Sis?" Seph asked with a small laugh as we sat down. "You've got a whole serious vibe going on. Like, more than usual. Or different. Or something."

I was making her nervous, and that was far from my intention. Hooking my foot up underneath me, I shifted so I could face her more directly and pushed a smile onto my lips. "Sorry, I've just got a lot on my mind," I admitted. "But I did want to talk to you because I heard back from a contact of mine in Michigan this morning."

Seph gave me a small, rumpled frown of confusion. "Michigan? What's there?"

My smile warmed somewhat. "Uh, well, for one thing... Michigan Tech. It's one of the top-rated colleges in the country for automotive engineering."

Her brows shot up. "You...you want me to go to college? In *Michigan*?" There was a thread of hurt in her voice, and I knew why.

I shook my head, reaching out to take her hand. "I'm not *sending* you anywhere, brat. I'm offering you an opportunity, if you want it. My contact has given tentative acceptance for you to start next semester, and I would set you up with somewhere to live... Full disclosure, I'd also probably set you up with a security detail, at least for a while. But you don't *have* to go. If you'd rather stay here, then that's totally fine too. I just..." I blew out a breath and ruffled my hair. "I got the feeling maybe you'd be happier away from Shadow Grove and Cloudcroft. Away from...*me*."

454

Her lips parted, guilt flashing across her face. "Dare…" She groaned, throwing herself forward to hug me again. "No, not away from you. I love you. You're my big sister and the only person who has ever loved me enough to turn into a total psychopath just to keep me safe." She paused, pulling back with a grin. "Zed doesn't count. He did it for you."

I smiled weakly because I could hear the *but* coming. "But…" I whispered, hating how badly I'd fucked up our sisterly bond. "You'd probably rather go to Michigan."

Seph gave a halting nod, tears in her eyes. "I think I would," she admitted. "I don't… I don't want to leave you, Dare. But…fuck, I mean this in the least insulting way possible, but I don't want to turn into you." Her words were quiet, full of pain, guilt, and regret. "I don't want to live this life, with all the danger and bloodshed and killing… It's not me. And I hate that every time someone meets me, they see *you*. It's like I'm not even a real person within Shadow Grove, you know? I'm just Hades's little sister."

I swallowed the emotion clogging my throat and nodded. "I get it."

Seph chewed her lip, looking pained. "I'll still be your sister, Dare. But if I have an opportunity at a new life in Michigan…" She paused, turning the idea over in her head for only a moment before nodding. "I'd like to see what that's like."

It'd been my idea and I was the one who'd secured her a place at Michigan Tech, but part of me hadn't really believed she'd take it. Not that quickly. But I guess I was more right than I'd even known. Seph was miserable here, living constantly in my shadow. And I didn't blame her one bit for wanting to get out.

"I just have a couple of conditions," I told her with a quick smile, shoving aside my hurt and feelings of failure and rejection. "Number one is the *most* important. You can't leave Shadow Grove until Chase is dealt with. Okay? I can't risk him targeting you again, and the moment you leave town without protection, he *would* come after you."

She gave a firm nod. "Understood. That's reasonable. I'm guessing you plan on dealing with him soon, though?"

"Absolutely," I muttered. Then I drew another breath. "Before you go, I want Rex's boys to teach you how to defend yourself properly. You need to get approval from Cass that you've learned enough to protect yourself, okay?" I wasn't doing that to be a bitch, but it genuinely terrified me to think Seph would be hundreds of miles away with no protection detail eventually. She needed to know how to fight back, should anyone come after her.

She wet her lips and nodded again. "Can I ask something in return, in that case?"

I nodded quickly, overwhelmed by her lack of resistance on those stipulations.

"Will you and Zed teach me to shoot?" She gave me a hopeful look. "I wanna learn from the best, and that's you guys."

I grinned. "Don't let MK hear you say that or we'll end up with Steele and Zed in a pissing contest."

Seph barked a laugh. "Let them. You could beat them both blindfolded. You're the ultimate badass, big sister."

This time when she hugged me, I hugged her back.

"Hey, why don't we have a sleepover tonight?" Seph suggested, practically vibrating with excitement. "Maybe at a hotel so that the guys here don't actually piss themselves around you, and *your* guys don't suck up all your attention with their magic dicks. We can just hang out and order room service and Google stuff about Michigan? Maybe browse real estate?"

I smiled. Every word out of her filled me with warmth and reassurance, evaporating the feeling of rejection. My sister wasn't leaving me. She was simply leaving my territory. It didn't mean she loved me any less, and I loved her more for taking that courageous step.

"That sounds perfect," I whispered. "Go take your car for a spin around the track first. I have something I need to discuss with Rex."

She squealed with excitement as she bounced back to her feet. "Love you, Dare!" she shouted over her shoulder while running back toward the boys gathered near her car.

I watched as she slipped into the driver's seat, and dark-haired Micah claimed the passenger side while flipping off the other boys in victory. The sooner Seph left town, the better.

"That's one happy little girl," Rex boomed, heading over to where I still waited on the bleachers. "You're a good sister to her, Boss. Even if it doesn't always feel like it."

I gave a short, bitter laugh. "I need you to take a job for me, Rex," I told him, changing the subject. "I can't leave town right now and can't think of anyone better suited to this task." Especially after seeing how paternal he was with my sister. He was easily my man for this hit.

"Whatever you need, Boss," he agreed. He craned his neck back toward his other four boys and gave a hand gesture that had the tallest—Ford—come jogging over to us. "I'd like to take this one with me, if you approve."

I arched a brow. "This is a kill mission, Rex. I'm sending you to wipe out a little girl's family as retribution for selling her into slavery. You think that's the right time for bring-your-kid-to-work day?" I flicked a glance at Ford, whose brow was tight with irritation at my dismissal.

Rex knew me better than his boys. He just nodded, knowing I was testing how strongly he believed in this kid. "I absolutely do, Boss. Can't think of a better mission for him to get his feet wet."

I bit back a laugh but couldn't stop the cold smile curling my lips. "So be it. Bring me back evidence of death for the parents, and use your own judgment on the sister. If she was involved in *any* way, do not give mercy. This girl has been through hell and back while she was held captive, and they need to pay."

Ford stiffened with rage, but it wasn't directed at me. It was at that vague description of Diana's treatment.

"Leave it with us, Boss," Rex grunted. "We'll handle it, won't we, boy?"

Ford jerked a nod to his dad. "Yes, sir." Then to me, "Thank you for the opportunity, sir."

I gave him a grim smile. "Don't make me regret it."

CHAPTER 57

Seph and I ended up staying two nights at the hotel, and it was time we both needed. We found a whole list of possible apartments for her from online listings, and I arranged for my contact at the university to view them all for us. Seph also started working out all her classes and getting insanely excited over the prospect of college parties.

I bit my lip and didn't rain on her parade over those. But it would be some time before I could be convinced to relax her security *that* much.

When I got home, I was instantly greeted by the sound of enraged shouting and shattering glass.

Panicked, I raced through to Zed's office, where I found Zed dripping blood from his hand and broken mirror shards on the floor from where he'd clearly just punched one off the wall. He sucked in a ragged gasp when I burst into the room, his face a twisted mask of fury and...*pity*.

My eyes snapped to Lucas, who sat behind Zed's desk, staring in abject horror at the laptop screen as my own panicked, agonized voice filled the air, begging for death while the slick, wet slap of fucking bodies filled the background.

Snapping out of my shock, I stormed across the office and

smacked the laptop shut. Then I picked the whole thing up, tucked it under my arm, and headed for the door.

"Dare!" Zed shouted after me.

Ignoring him, I strode out of the office and took the stairs two at a time, *fleeing* to my bedroom. Once inside, I kicked the door shut, locked it, and slid down to the carpet as my heart thundered in my chest.

With shaking fingers, I peeled the laptop open again, and a low, pained moan escaped my throat as I saw the freeze-frame of the video on the screen. It was a scene I desperately didn't need to relive, so I slammed the fucking thing shut again and threw the computer across the room. Not because I was a moron who thought breaking the device would erase the video, but because I was no longer fully in control of my actions. That video was bringing back all the dark, slippery damage that I truly thought I'd overcome, and I needed to get it away from me.

A soft thud on the other side of the door made me jump in fright, and my arms curled around my knees tighter than ever.

"Dare," Zed's voice reached my ears, muffled by two inches of wooden door. "Baby, please, let us in. Please. *Please*, Dare, you don't have to deal with this shit alone anymore."

I said nothing back. I couldn't. My whole body was shaking, tears flowing like rivers down my face, and an uncontrollable whimpering sound came from my chest as I backslid into the dark memories. It was still *so* fresh.

Throwing the laptop had done nothing to curb the onslaught of mental images. They crashed down on me, one after another, until I was drowning underneath them all. I couldn't breathe. I was back under that water, the bag over my head and Chase slamming his body into mine—

"You're okay." A soothing voice cut through the deafening panic. "You're okay, Hayden. You *can* breathe. Take it slow. Deep inhale, long exhale. Come on, beautiful, you've got this."

Soft hands stroked my hair back from my face, long fingers combing through the strands in a comforting way, not a threatening one. My cheek was pressed to the carpet, and when I peeled my eyes open, I locked eyes with Lucas.

"There you are," he whispered, the relief palpable in his sigh. "Keep breathing with me, babe. Nice and slow, okay? Fill those lungs right up. Just focus on your breath."

He lay there on the floor of my bedroom for an indefinite amount of time, just breathing with me. His soft words of encouragement coached me down from sheer hysteria, slowing my jagged, gasping breaths to deep, calming ones.

When the violent trembles finally faded and my pulse no longer raced, I wet my lips and swallowed heavily.

"I'm okay," I whispered, my voice rough.

"I know," Lucas replied, stroking his gentle fingers over my wet cheek. "I just like lying here with you."

I cracked a weak smile at that, then groaned as I pushed myself up to sitting. I didn't remember collapsing to the floor or Lucas arriving. Frowning, I looked to the door we were in front of and found it still locked. Then I noticed the open window.

"Uh, I freaked out when you wouldn't open the door," Lucas admitted with a slight blush, seeing my sharp glance at the window. "I climbed around from my room and used the fingerprint lock to get in."

I blinked at him for a moment, then threw my arms around his neck, hugging him tight. "Thank you," I whispered against his neck. He hugged me back, pulling me into his lap and burying his face in my hair.

"Can we let Zed in?" he asked softly. "He's freaking out."

Shit. I winced. "Yeah. Sorry. That was—"

"A completely understandable and normal human reaction," Lucas finished for me, pulling back far enough to give me a firm look. "And not one that needs apologies."

In a smooth motion, he lifted me up in his arms as he stood. Then he flipped the lock and opened the door to reveal Zed sitting right there on the floor with blood staining the carpet where his cut hand had been resting.

"Dare," he exclaimed, climbing to his feet and reaching out for me. He hesitated before touching my skin, though, a worried frown etching across his face.

Lucas just gave a head motion into my room, then carried me over to the bed and got comfy with me still in his lap. Zed paused for a moment, seeming unsure, then climbed onto the bed with us. He leaned back on the headboard beside Lucas and rested his hand softly on my hair. His eyes locked with mine, but there was no pity, only love.

"I'm okay," I mumbled again, sounding weak and exhausted.

"Of course you are," Zed replied, soft and caring as he stroked my hair. "But sometimes it's okay for the cracks to show. We don't judge you for it, we just want to be there to share the pain. To help put you back together again."

Lucas nodded, his chin bumping the top of my head as I cuddled into his chest. "Exactly that," he murmured. "You're not alone, Hayden. We're here, no matter what. Nothing you could do—nothing we could ever *see*—will change that. Nothing. Not fucking ever. All Chase achieved here is to make us hold you tighter, to love you harder than ever before."

Zed huffed a laugh. "Too fucking right."

"This was payback for my list," I said, voicing my thoughts out loud. Focusing on my revenge was better than wallowing in shame over my panic attack. "Weak payback, if you ask me." My voice was hollow, and I didn't even believe what I was saying. Chase had struck me right where it would hurt the most. My sanity.

Zed offered me a lopsided smile. "So what are we gonna do in return?"

Chase had hit me in my sanity, my security with my guys...

He'd sent that tape to *Zed*, knowing it would hurt him the most to see what had been done to me because Zed knew it had all happened before. He'd targeted my biggest weakness. So we'd do the same to him.

Now that his most valuable contacts were all dead, there was just one thing that could push his buttons like he'd just done to me.

Sniffing hard, I peeled myself up from Lucas's chest and drew a deep, strengthening breath.

"Where's my phone?" I asked, looking around for somewhere I might have dropped it.

Zed pulled his own from his pocket and handed it to me. We had the same contacts saved anyway, so it was easy to use his instead. I didn't explain myself as I scrolled through his address book searching for...

"Aha," I murmured, finding the one I wanted and hitting Dial. The call connected after only a couple of rings.

"Zayden De Rosa," the woman answered, "to what do I owe the pleasure?"

"Nikki," I said back, "it's not Zed. Clearly. Do you have plans today?"

There was a stunned silence before she replied. "Nothing I can't reschedule for you, sir. What do you need?"

I grinned, meeting Zed's eyes as he smiled back at me with dawning understanding. "I need a photo shoot, today."

"Absolutely, sir, what am I shooting? New Copper Wolf advertising?" Nikki was our photographer for the ad campaigns on all the bars, as well as our vodka brand.

"Actually," I corrected her, "an engagement announcement. Zed and I are getting married."

I caught Nikki's startled gasp before she covered it with a cough. "Wow, sir, congratulations. Yeah, definitely. I can be there in two hours."

"Perfect," I replied, then ended the call to hand the phone back to Zed. "Call Hannah, tell her to get hair and makeup out here within half an hour, then call the *Shadow Grove Gazette*. They're to run a front-page spread on this. Tomorrow."

"Yes, sir," Zed replied, grinning wickedly.

Lucas looked less convinced, though. "You think that will bother him?" he asked. "Like, as hard as that video hit you?"

Zed and I exchanged a knowing look. "Oh yeah," I confirmed. "This is on par."

"I'll get it sorted," Zed assured me, sliding off the bed. He left the room with his phone already to his ear.

Lucas sent me a small frown. At first, I worried he was reading too much into this engagement announcement with Zed. But then he pressed a soft kiss to my knuckles. "What can I do to help?"

Smiling, I slid my hand around the back of his neck and sealed my lips to his in a gentle kiss. "You're already helping, Lucas. So fucking much. But...I need to shower and wash that sour smell of panic attack from my skin. Will you join me?"

"Shit, Hayden," he replied with a teasing grin as we climbed off the bed. "It's a hard ask, but I guess I could manage that."

I snorted, winking at him as I led the way to the shower. "Something will be hard, anyway."

By the time Lucas and I emerged from our shower, Zed had everything set up. The hair and makeup artists were waiting downstairs along with Hannah, who was unloading a huge armful of garment bags from her car.

"Boss!" she called out, beaming. "This is so exciting! I called in some favors and picked up some dresses in your size for the photo shoot. And Leonard Nelson from the *Gazette* should be here in about two hours to interview you for the article." She hurried up the front steps and glared at Zed. "You said you *had* suits. What the hell is that?"

Zed was still in his rumpled, bloodstained shirt from earlier with a loose bandage looped around his hand. "I was going to change," he grumbled, peering down at his clothes.

Lucas glared at the loose bandage. "I'd better sort that mess out for you first, tough guy." He pressed a kiss to my temple, then teased Zed the whole way back up the stairs, leaving me with Hannah.

"Boss, no disrespect," Hannah murmured, "but you need to stop drooling over your guys' asses and hurry the hell up. Uh, respectfully. Of course."

I shot her a smirk. "Of course." I tilted my head to the living room where hair and makeup had set up. "Come on, show me what dresses you chose for me."

Cass arrived home right as Nikki was setting up her cameras and checking lighting for different locations through the house, and his raised brow told me he was confused as hell. I just grinned and slid off my stool, rubbing my lips together to settle the ruby-red lipstick.

"Saint, you almost missed all the fun," I teased, rising up on my toes to brush a ghost of a kiss over his lips. My lipstick needed longer to set before making out properly.

He rumbled a vaguely irritated sound, his gaze sweeping down my black lace dress. It was dramatic, with a fishtail train and ribbon pulling the bodice so tight my breasts were almost falling out.

"Red..." he rumbled in warning.

I clicked my tongue and wove my fingers through his to tug him into the kitchen and away from all the people setting up for our interview and photo shoot.

"Chase took a swing at me," I told him quietly, not meeting his eyes but looking past him instead, "so I'm hitting back with a big, public, splashy engagement announcement. This changes nothing, though. I stand by what I said in the hotel that night."

Cass said nothing for the longest time—long enough that I got anxious and shifted my gaze to meet his eyes. Only then did his lips curl into a small smile.

"That's more like it," he muttered. "You look like a fucking dream right now, Red. Like the Queen of the Underworld come to life. What I could do to you if you let me drag you into that pantry right now..." His hand was on my face, his thumb teasing my jaw and his eyes hungry.

"Fuck," I muttered with a sigh. "You're bad news, Saint. Hold that thought until this journalist is gone, and I'll let you take this dress off me."

He shot back a devilish grin. "Deal. Where's the Gumdrop?"

I nodded upward. "Studying upstairs. He's rescheduled all his EMT assessments under his new name and wants to beat his previous scores."

Before I could slip out of his grip, Cass grabbed me tight and kissed me like he could fuck me right there in the kitchen. When he pulled away, my deep-red lipstick was smeared all over his mouth, but he couldn't have looked more pleased with himself if he'd tried.

Possessive shit. My makeup artist was going to be less than impressed.

CHAPTER 58

The interview and full-page spread hit the *Shadow Grove Gazette* the next day, as instructed. Just to be sure Chase would see it, I had a hundred copies of the paper couriered over to his apartment, which Dallas had located for me.

That night, the Copper Wolf Vodka Distillery blew up.

I watched the video footage from one of the parking-lot security cameras, feeling hollow inside. There was no point in rushing out there; the damage was done. And Chase would have done a thorough job of it, too. Like Cass and I had done to his house across the road. Not a single brick would be left undamaged.

"Shit," I whispered, sitting naked in Cass's bed and watching the flames lick the night sky on my phone.

"I'll get down there and deal with the fire crew," Zed told me, kissing my hair. He slipped out of bed and disappeared back to his room to shower and dress.

I bit my lip, thinking. "Lucas, can you go with him? I feel... uncomfortable having him go alone."

Lucas's brows shot up. He'd just pulled his sweatpants and T-shirt back on, having jumped up the moment I got the call about my distillery. "Really?"

I nodded. "I feel like Chase is plotting something bigger. I wouldn't put it past him to try to kill Zed if he catches him alone... I think I'd feel better if someone was watching his back. Is that okay?"

Lucas blinked a couple of times, his gaze shifting from me to Cass and then back again. He clearly wanted to ask why I wasn't sending Cass, but at the same time didn't want to say no. Truth was, I trusted Lucas and Cass equally to watch Zed's back...and Lucas was a slightly better shot than my grumpy cat. Not that I could say *that* out loud.

"Yeah, absolutely," Lucas responded, nodding. He raced out of the room, yelling at Zed that he was coming along and not to leave without him.

"That was nice of you," Cass murmured, kissing my bare shoulder, "making Gumdrop feel important like that."

I grinned, not contradicting him. Whatever made my big-ego men feel better.

Falling back against the pillows, I tapped out a message to Hannah to let her know Zed was on his way over to the distillery to handle things there. She replied to say she'd meet him there; then a few minutes later, my guys called out that they were leaving.

Left in silence once more, I rolled onto my side to face Cass. "Hey, you."

A slow smile curved his lips. "You're insatiable," he replied with a chuckle. "That four-way wasn't enough for you?"

I leaned in, grabbing his lips with mine. "It's never enough," I sighed, wrapping my body around his once more and feeling his hardness brush against my aching, well-used pussy. The three of them were *way* more willing to engage in group sex than I'd ever thought they would be. But I wasn't dumb enough to think it was because they enjoyed seeing other guys' dicks slamming into me; it was because they were all too competitive and jealous to *not* be involved.

Fuck it. I didn't care for the reasons, only the results. And when the results were multiple orgasms and the best sex of my life? No arguments here.

Cass had no sooner shimmied down the bed, his mouth finding my throbbing pussy, than my phone started ringing again.

"Ignore it," Cass growled, his fingers spreading my cunt open and dipping into the remains of his own release. Or Lucas's. "It'll be something Zed can handle."

I was inclined to agree. My hips rocked me into his face, and my hands pulled his head closer. But then my phone rang again. And kept ringing.

"*Fuuuucking hell*," I moaned, fishing around in the sheets to find the damn thing. Cass took that as an invitation to suck my clit, and I almost came before answering the call.

"What?" I snapped, breathless as Cass's fingers pushed into my slick core. I bit the inside of my cheek to stifle a moan but clamped a hand on his head to hold him tighter.

I only needed to hear the first few words from my Alexi replacement, Diego, to sit up with a curse.

Cass sighed but propped his head up on his hand to listen as I put the call on speakerphone.

"Just the club?" I asked, seeking clarity, seeing as I'd been distracted when I answered. "Or the big top too?"

"Everything," Diego replied, sounding grim. "The club, the big top, the training center, the supply rooms…every single structure within Anarchy is currently on fire, almost like it was a remote detonation or something because they *all* went off at once."

Cass's resigned gaze met mine.

I wet my lips, thinking. "Get it under control with the fire department, Diego. I can't get down there yet, someone just blew up Copper Wolf distillery too."

My new head of security let out a string of curses. "What do you want me to do, Boss? Where am I most useful?"

But the problem was that I had no idea. Chase was splitting our focus with multiple attacks. He was making us chase shadows. "Sort things out there, then get over to Timber as fast as possible. That'll be the next target."

"Understood, Boss," Diego agreed. "I'll send some guys ahead of me, too."

I blew out a breath. "Good. I'll meet you there." Ending the call, I looked up at Cass, who was shaking his head. "What?"

"You're not going to Timber," he told me with a hard edge to his voice.

My brows shot up in disbelief. "Excuse me?"

Growling in frustration, he rolled out of bed and grabbed his pants. "You *can't* go to Timber. That's exactly what he wants you to do. First the distillery, now Anarchy... He knows that *you* know he'll torch Timber next, so that's the perfect place to snatch you again."

I rubbed a hand over my face, both frustrated and exasperated. He was right, to a degree. "Since when was I that easy to simply *snatch*?" I snarled back, letting out a little of that frustration as anger.

Cass just gave me a long look, and my face heated. Fair point. Arguing that Chase'd set it up so well last time that there had been no chance of escape wouldn't support my case. It'd just strengthen Cass's.

"I can't just let him burn down my empire while I sit here and twiddle my thumbs, Cass," I protested, also fishing around for some clothes. It felt stupid having an argument while totally naked.

He snatched my bra before I could reach it, holding it away from me. "You're not," he barked. "You're being sensible and not playing directly into his hands. He can't come for you here, this place is *better* than Fort Knox now. While you were gone, Zed had every fucking window replaced with bulletproof glass, and the locks would even keep me out—if I didn't have the right thumbprint. Chase can't touch you *here*. But out there? Different story. So just…sit back and let your Timberwolves do the legwork this time."

I stared up at him for a long moment, then narrowed my eyes. "Fine," I gritted out. "Can I have my bra now?"

His glare darkened. "Are you going to stay in the house?"

My anger and irritation spiked hotter, but I nodded. "Your logic isn't totally unfounded," I reluctantly agreed.

He considered me for a moment longer before handing my bra back and watching me put it on. "He's losing his grip, Red. Exactly like we predicted. You just need to grit your teeth and let us keep you safe because ultimately *you* are his sole objective. If he catches you again…" He let his voice trail off, looking sick.

I heard him, though. Loud and fucking clear. If Chase caught me again, that'd be the end of it. They'd never see me again, and I… Well. I knew firsthand that there were plenty of things a whole lot worse than death. And Chase didn't want me dead.

"I know," I whispered with a whole lot less heat. "Call Rex and get him over to Timber, too."

"What do you want to do about Anarchy?" Cass asked, already tapping out a message on his phone.

Blowing out a heavy breath, I tugged my stretchy tank top over my head. "Let it burn," I finally decided. "It's too late to save it now."

A flicker of sympathy lit his eyes a moment before they shifted to his usual resting-Cass face. "All right. Let's double-check that the security system here is all operational. If Chase is trying to draw you out—which he is—then he'll be shit out of luck tonight."

Gritting my teeth with frustration, I pulled my jeans on and followed him out of the room to the security operation center in a closet downstairs. Everything was on, as it should be, but Cass still muttered some shit under his breath and tweaked the settings of something. Motion detectors, I think.

I pulled up a stool at the kitchen island while he worked,

anxiously checking my phone for a call from Zed or Lucas. Now that Cass had suggested it was a targeted attack to draw us out of the safety of Zed's fortress, I was stress-sweating that they would be attacked.

"The distillery is a two-hour drive away, Red," Cass rumbled without looking up from the display panel he was working on. "Even with the way Zed drives, they won't be there yet."

He was right. I *knew* he was right. But it didn't stop me from sending an anxious text message to Lucas to check that they were okay.

He replied almost instantly, and I let out a long sigh of relief. They were on the road, fighting over what music to listen to.

"They're fine," I murmured, feeling Cass watch me from the corner of his eye. I chewed my lip, checking the time. Diego wouldn't even be at Timber yet, so it was too soon for an update from him, too.

Cass finished what he was doing and came over to where I sat at the island, his hands caging me in and his chest against my back. "I know this doesn't come naturally to you, Angel, but you just need to *wait*. He's likely banking on your need to handle everything personally, so the *last* thing he will expect is for you to simply stay put."

He was right. I fucking hated waiting. My skin was almost crawling with the feeling of being a damsel in distress, of not getting out there and kicking ass myself. But running off to prove I had the biggest dick in the city would only fuck me, ultimately. There was no *need* for me to handle these attacks myself. The only thing that would be satisfied would be my own ego.

"I've got a bad feeling about this, Saint," I admitted, my fists clenched against the counter in anger and frustration. "Worse than just my businesses going up in flames."

Cass, his forehead resting on my shoulder, rumbled a wordless agreement. "I do too. That's why you have to stay put."

The breath that gusted out of me was pure irritation. "We need an activity so I don't go nuts," I told him. "And no, not fucking. We both need to keep our wits about us and our clothes on…just in case."

He chuckled roughly, then pressed a kiss to my neck. "Come on, let's check the weapons locker and load up some guns in the cars, just in case we need to leave for some reason."

I perked up at that suggestion and twisted around on my stool to face him with a grin. "Excellent idea."

His lips curled in a smile. "Then, maybe, if nothing else blows up, you can handle *my* weapon."

A startled laugh escaped my lips before I shook my head. "That was awful. Truly awful. Have you been hanging out with Kody behind my back?"

With a husky laugh, Cass lifted me off the stool and kissed my hair. "Come on, I'll keep you busy *with* clothes on. For now."

We made our way out to the garage where our weapons cage was located, and I scanned my thumbprint to unlock it. For the next hour and a half, we sorted through the enormous weapon collection Zed kept and ensured several cars were loaded up with guns and ammo. We also went through the house to check that all the hidden guns were loaded.

"Finally," I exclaimed when the message came through that Zed and Lucas were at the distillery. Diego and Rex had both checked in with me that they were at Timber, but so far it was all quiet.

Cass peered over my shoulder at the message. "Maybe we were being paranoid," he muttered.

I turned my face to meet his eyes with a squint. "You don't believe that."

He huffed. "No, I don't. He's still got something else up his sleeve."

Groaning, I rubbed a hand over my face. Because I agreed. This night wasn't over yet, but I was still overwhelmingly glad to hear

473

Lucas and Zed had made it to the distillery safely. No one had run them off the road or shot out their tires or, fuck, launched a missile at their car. Yet.

"Rex wants to know how long you want them to hang around Timber," Cass told me as we made our way back into the living room.

I frowned. "As long as it takes," I replied. "All night, if they need to. Actually, get Diego to leave a handful of Wolves to back Rex up, then ask him to start combing our security footage from Anarchy. Chase doesn't have his support network anymore, so he could well have slipped up and given us more evidence."

Cass nodded and fired off messages to carry out my orders without a word. I collapsed into the couch, yawning heavily. It was past midnight, and we'd been way too adventurous in our bedroom antics earlier in the evening. I was wrecked.

When Cass finished his messages, he sat down as well, pulling me closer until I was horizontal with my head in his lap and feet up on the cushions.

"Close your eyes for a moment, Red," he told me, fingers stroking through my hair. "I'll wake you up if anything changes, but right now it's safe to sleep."

I shook my head, even as my eyes drooped closed. "I'm too wired to sleep," I protested. But that was total bullshit. Sleep sucked me in faster than a black hole in space.

The sound of my phone ringing jerked me awake again what felt like only a minute later. Cass answered it before I'd fully sat up, and he smoothed his hand over my cheek as he listened to the call with a grim look on his face.

"That's smart thinking, Hannah," Cass replied in a voice edged with anger. "Block the door and window as best you can. We'll get someone there as quick as we can. Text us the address."

He ended the call and shifted his gaze to me. "Someone is in Hannah's apartment. She's locked herself in her bedroom, but…"

474

"It'll only be a matter of time," I agreed, frowning. "Why is she there? I thought she was at the distillery with Zed."

Cass quirked a brow. "Apparently Zed told her not to worry about heading out, that he and Lucas had it handled."

I groaned. Yeah, that sounded like him. But now Hannah was alone and being targeted while the majority of my trusted Wolves were in the next city over, protecting an empty building. "Fuck. We need to go."

Cass shook his head, stubborn. "Absolutely not. This is just another attempt to draw you out."

My phone rang again in his hand, and he handed it to me to answer.

"Boss?" Macy, my accountant, said in a shaky voice. "I don't know if you've already been told...but the Copper Wolf office is on fire."

I screamed internally. "The Copper Wolf office is on fire," I repeated, doing everything in my power to keep my voice calm. "Is anyone in there?" It was past midnight; it *should* be empty.

"Not that I know of, sir. I just heard the sirens and went to see what was going on. The fire crew won't tell me anything, not really, but the smoke is definitely coming from our level." Macy lived in an apartment only a short way down the street from our offices.

I ground my teeth. "Are you safe?" I asked.

"Y-yes, sir. Yes, I'm fine." She seemed confused by my question.

"Good," I replied. "Go home. Lock your doors. Plan a vacation or something."

She laughed hollowly. "Sure thing, Boss. You stay safe too."

I ended the call and dropped my phone to my lap. Scrubbing both hands over my face, I groaned. "We need to get to Hannah," I announced. "We're the closest to her, and she's already survived one attack. We can't just leave her to fend for herself."

Cass scowled, shaking his head. "No. No way."

I burst out of my seat in outrage. "Cassiel Saint, if you tell me *no* one more fucking time—"

"I'll go," he snapped, also rising out of his seat. "She only lives ten minutes away. I'll go, deal with her intruder, and then bring her back here."

I threw my hands up. "Cass—"

"Nonnegotiable!" he roared back at me. "Sit your fine ass down, and *stay put.*"

He gave me no opportunity to argue, just stomped his ass off to the garage while I stood there in a little bit of shock that he'd *ordered* me to do anything. Outside of the bedroom, that was. And yet I didn't go running after him, demanding to be included. Because that was moronic.

So, as much as it rankled, I did as I was told. I waited to hear his motorbike roar out of the garage, then reset the security system. I'd never felt more like a damsel in my entire life, locked up in my castle, helpless, while a fire-breathing dragon destroyed my empire.

CHAPTER 59

I lasted all of five minutes before blowing up Cass's phone to check on him. He grunted a response that he was pulling into Hannah's building—having halved the drive time—and hung up before I could ask dumb-shit questions that would only waste his time. As mad as it made me, I didn't disagree with his decision to cut me off.

So I sat there at the kitchen table, drumming my fingertips on the wood and going quietly insane. I wasn't so weak I'd snap and go off half-cocked, though. I *had* to trust that my guys could handle things without me. I had to trust in my Timberwolves to have my back.

Still, when Cass didn't call me back within ten minutes, I found myself anxiously texting him to ask for an update. The message immediately bounced back at me, undelivered.

I frowned, hitting the resend option. Once again, it bounced back.

A ripple of dread ran through me, and I hit the call button, only to be met with silence. My phone flashed that the call couldn't connect, then I noticed the tiny "no service" message where my reception bars should be.

"Fuck," I breathed. Our cell phones were unhackable, thanks to

Dallas, and totally secure. But if the mobile tower near Zed's house was damaged...then yeah, my service would go down.

I rose out of my seat, going to check a window. Maybe it was storming outside and that had interrupted cell service? Nope. Dead still.

Muttering curses, I checked that the security system was fully operational, then headed back to the weapons cage to grab myself a bigger gun. Not that I should need it, considering Zed's house was now fully designed to prevent any intruders breaking in...but it made me feel better to have it ready. Just in case.

Half an hour passed, and nothing happened.

Cass didn't return with Hannah, my phone still wouldn't connect for calls or texts, and no one attacked the house. What the fuck was going on? Was Chase trying to bore me to death? Or was the lack of reception just a coincidence?

Needing to stay busy, I headed upstairs and moved from room to room, checking that the windows were all closed and locked. I checked my own room last and stiffened when I saw a figure out on the lawn in the darkness.

"I fucking *knew it*," I hissed out loud.

He was too far away, too deep into the darkness for me to see his features, but I'd bet my whole damn fortune that it was Chase himself. He'd grown impatient with trying to lure me out and had come to handle things himself.

I pulled my phone from my pocket, checking it for the thousandth time, but sure enough...no service. I already knew before checking that the landline would have been severed too. Fucking Chase was cutting me off from help. It'd only be a matter of time before Cass came back, though. Whatever distraction Chase had organized to keep him gone this long wouldn't last forever. I simply needed to wait it out.

Not moving from the window, I watched Chase move closer to the house, his head tipped back as he looked up at me. The moonlight caught on his toothy grin, and he blew me a kiss before disappearing out of sight.

"What the fuck are you doing?" I murmured, leaving my room and heading for Zed's to get a better viewpoint. I couldn't see anything from his window, either, and I was loath to go downstairs where I'd be on the same level as Chase. He couldn't get in, but that wouldn't stop him from taunting me through the window.

I tried a couple more windows before I found him again, bent over and doing something to the wall of the house outside the living room. Frowning, I watched as he moved his way along the wall, unhurried.

Losing my patience, I raced downstairs to the security center to pull up the camera feed on that side of the house. The black and white night-vision flickered into focus, and I gasped sharply when I realized what he was doing. He couldn't get into the house; somehow, he knew that without needing to test the entry points. So he was going to make me come out.

A sharp knock on the window nearest where I stood made me jerk with fright, and I steeled my spine before crossing the room to where my one-eyed, smiling demon stood outside the glass.

He gave me a mocking wave, then waggled his now-empty can of gasoline at me. Taunting. It was probably only one of many, too, if he'd doused the entire perimeter of the house before I'd spotted him out there.

I had no words, my tongue locked up in my mouth as he held my gaze. He tossed the empty gasoline can over his shoulder, then pulled a silver lighter from his pocket. It was a gift I'd given him on his eighteenth birthday and was engraved with our names. Chase was even more obsessive than I'd given him credit for…though that explained the rather out-of-balance reaction to my engagement announcement.

"Come out, come out, sweet demon," he called through the window, "or I'll smoke you out."

I extended my middle finger, pressing it to the glass. "Kiss my ass, Captain Bluebeard."

He didn't react to my childish dig at his eye patch, just grinned wider and dropped the lighter. Flames exploded up between us with an audible *boom* as the gasoline ignited, and the red-orange glow lit up Chase's features. But I wasn't hanging around for a staring competition.

Turning my back on him, I squared my shoulders and walked calmly over to the control panel once more. There was an emergency button on there somewhere, and it should be hardwired rather than dependent on cell reception. I gritted my teeth and tried to ignore the flames dancing in every damn window of the ground floor, focusing instead on the security system.

The button was easy enough to find, but when I pressed it, nothing happened. Or...nothing that I could see. Had it sent a silent alarm to the security company? Fuck, I hoped so. Either way...I needed to use my damn head and not let Chase win out of sheer shock factor.

He'd set fire to the house, but only the exterior perimeter. The windows were bulletproof, so surely, they were also fire- and smokeproof. So...could I wait him out?

I turned back to check the window where he'd been standing, but he was gone. Shit. Now what? Where the fuck had he gone? I highly doubted he was just sitting back and waiting. No, he was up to something. This wasn't aggressive enough.

My mind whirred, ticking over everything I knew about the security of the house. Trouble was that a lot of the upgrades had been done while I was in Chase's clutches, and I hadn't bothered to get the full rundown from Zed. Seemed stupid in hindsight, but it hadn't occurred to me that Chase might actually lay siege to the fucking house.

I walked slowly, carefully, from room to room, my eyes scanning the windows for any sign of movement. He was alone, so far as I could tell. But hell, he could have a whole army out there in the darkness sneaking around.

As I passed through the living room again, my ears picked up a faint, mechanical whirring sound. Like...a drill. Or electric screwdriver.

Five seconds later, an alarm screamed through the house, and I raced back to the control panel to find where it was coming from. Red letters flashed on the screen, telling me what I already knew.

PERIMETER BREACH

No shit.

I tapped the screen and found the location highlighted on the little blueprint of the house. It wasn't a door or a window; those were all still secure. It was the air-conditioning vent.

What the fuck was he doing with the air-conditioning vent? It was too small for any human to fit inside. So what in the—

Boom.

The explosion rattled the whole fucking house, and I ducked for cover on instinct.

"Mother*fucker*," I hissed as the alarm system went mental on the screen. Surely *that* would alert our security company, at least.

I raced through the house in the direction of the explosion, only to be hit with a thick cloud of smoke. Whatever explosive he'd tossed into the air vent had made a mess and set fire to almost every visible surface. He must've guessed his perimeter fire wouldn't be enough, so he'd made sure the flames took hold inside the house.

"Shit, shit, shit," I muttered, backtracking from the fire billowing from the utility room beside the gym. There were several more points around the house where he could toss an explosive device inside, depending how small the incendiaries were. The last thing I needed was to be caught by shrapnel from an exploding door.

I grabbed my gun from where I'd left it in the kitchen and

raced upstairs. If I could get a good line of sight, I'd simply open a window and shoot him. Not fatally, of course. That'd be far too anticlimactic of an ending for this story. But enough to disable him until help arrived.

The only problem was he was keeping out of sight now. Sneaky, sneaky bastard. He somehow managed to blend with the shadows, darting between obstacles like he suspected I might shoot at him. I caught a flash of a gun in his hands now too, so I wouldn't be shocked if he was thinking the same. Or, knowing Chase, I'd bet that gun was loaded with tranquilizer darts.

Three more explosions went off downstairs as I frantically raced from window to window, trying to get a line of sight on him. He'd shot out all the security spotlights on the lawn, though, and it was like trying to target a fucking ghost.

Within a matter of minutes, the smoke rising from the ground floor had me coughing and lightheaded. Fucking hell. He was banking that my own sense of self-preservation would make me leave the house before I died of smoke inhalation, and he was probably right. I wasn't scared enough of Chase psychopath Lockhart to willingly burn to death. I'd get out, but I sure as shit wouldn't fall directly into his arms.

Racing over to Zed's room—because his overlooked the courtyard where Chase wouldn't be able to see me—I used my thumbprint to unlock the window and pushed it open as far as it would go. I leaned out, sweeping my gaze over all the visible areas to ensure no one was lying in wait, then ducked back into the room. I'd already strapped my shoulder holster on with my freshly returned Desert Eagle snugly tucked inside. But I ran back to my room to strap on some throwing knives and slide spare ammo into my pockets. Then, looping the strap of an M16 over my head, I climbed out of Zed's window and balanced my toes on the ledge as I straightened up.

For a second, I paused there, holding my breath and listening for any signs that I'd been seen. When nothing changed, I reached for a handhold above the window and started the painful task of climbing up to the roof. My shoulder screamed protests at me, but I gritted my teeth and pushed the pain aside. It wasn't anything compared to the pain I'd felt climbing trees naked in the forest while escaping Chase's den of horrors, so my pain receptors needed to shut the fuck up with their crying.

I took it slow, thinking carefully about each move, but eventually I hauled myself over the lip of the roof and collapsed there for a minute to catch my breath.

"Fuck me," I whispered to myself. "Unfit bitch."

Smoke billowed up out of the open window below me, and I groaned. Zed was going to be *furious* when he got back.

Digging my toes into the gutter, I started slithering up the sloping roof. I wasn't going to stand up and offer Chase a target to shoot at, but I sure as fuck wasn't going to wait for the house to burn down below me. I needed to take out the one person standing between me and safety—sooner rather than later.

I reached the crest of the roof and settled myself so that only the scope of my gun poked over the lip. I used that—with night vision, thank fuck—to search the area below. It took three sweeps before motion caught my eye.

Smiling to myself, I sank lower against the roof tiles. "Come out, come out, Chasey," I called loudly, taunting him with the same phrasing he'd used downstairs. "Come on, tough guy. Since when do you hide behind trees, huh?"

"Since I wasn't stupid enough to think you're not armed, Darling," he called back with an edge of amusement in his voice.

"Come out from behind that tree and I'll tell you if I am," I shot back. The flames were still licking the house below, and the billows of smoke coming out of Zed's open window didn't bode well for the amount of time I had left. "Come on, Chase. I *dare* you."

His slightly manic laughter carried back to me through the

night air, and a tiny movement twitched from behind his hiding place. I took the shot without hesitation, and based on the way he cursed, I'd bet I had hit him. Probably only a graze, but it still made me all warm and fuzzy inside.

"You're a better shot than I remember, Darling," he called out. "I don't know how I feel about that."

I scoffed a laugh, then raised my voice to tell him. "Scared, asshole. You should feel scared."

Another flicker of movement and I fired off another shot. It missed, but it still would remind Chase I wasn't so helpless this time. He'd caught me off guard once; I wouldn't make that mistake again.

"Wanna know how I improved my marksmanship?" I called, taunting him to try to get a better shot. "It was through months and months of intense *hands-on* training with Zed. He was so thorough, too. Unrelenting."

An enraged sound came from Chase, but he didn't shift from his hiding spot. Dammit. A moment later, sirens sounded in the distance, and the distinctive hum of a helicopter drew closer.

"Uh-oh, sounds like the cavalry is arriving, Chasey baby," I mocked. "Now what are you gonna do? You'll be caught red-handed trying to kill me…again."

He didn't respond. Instead, he threw something at the house, and a split second later it exploded. Foolishly, I flinched back, ducking below the roofline. When I popped back up, my sights on that same tree, I already knew he was gone. Like a one-eyed, evil magician. Fuck.

CHAPTER 60

Zed's house was toast. Burnt toast. He was going to shit bricks when he came back.

As it turned out, the alarm button I'd pressed on the security system *had* been a silent one, and they'd immediately sent out a pair of security guards to investigate. Two heavily armed men had been the first to arrive, rappelling down from a blacked-out helicopter, then sweeping the whole yard with their guns at the ready.

Only a few minutes later the fire trucks came barreling up the driveway and a ladder was thrown up against the side of the burning house to get me down.

A nondescript silver sedan pulled in behind the fire trucks, and Cass leapt out of the driver's seat almost before it had fully stopped. He snatched me off the ladder when I was still several rungs from the bottom and swept me up in a hug so tight I felt my ribs protest.

"Cass, let me down," I squeaked when he started walking with me still in his arms. "Saint, for fuck's sake, *put me down!*" I pushed steel into my voice, expecting him to immediately obey. It was what I was used to. But he didn't. The fucker just held me tighter until I threatened to kick him in the balls, and only then did he relax his iron grip around me.

"Look!" I snarled, pushing out of his embrace and spreading my arms wide. "Not a scratch on me. Takes a little more than some pyromaniac tricks to take me down."

"Fucking hell, Red," he exclaimed on a heavy exhale. His hand scrubbed over his beard, and I could see the barely constrained need to touch me all over his face. But he needed to get a grip. Despite how bad it must have looked when he drove up, I was unharmed and nothing but pissed off.

"I'm fine," I snapped. "Whose car is that? And what the fuck took you so long?"

He winced, and I stepped forward to place my hand on his cheek, softening my hard edges a little after seeing how my words struck him.

"I'm sorry," I whispered. "That came out wrong. I was worried about you. I thought you'd have been back half an hour ago."

He gave a shaky laugh. "You were worried about me?" His pained eyes flicked to the burning remains of Zed's house as the fire crew doused it in water from high-pressure hoses. "Angel...you could have died, or worse. Because I told you to stay put."

I rolled my eyes. "I hardly think either of us expected Chase to do *this*. Besides, I'm fine. And I think I clipped him with a bullet, too." I peered back to the mystery car he'd pulled up in. "Is that Hannah?"

"Yeah, she's fine. Little shit too." He gave a grumpy huff, and the back door of the car burst open as if on cue. Diana came tumbling out and launched herself at me in her overgrown-octopus impersonation.

I patted her head awkwardly, giving Cass a puzzled look, and he just rolled his eyes skyward.

"Dammit, Diana!" Hannah yelled, coming after the little girl. "I told you to wait!"

"It's fine," I assured Hannah before she could peel Diana away from me. Still patting the fiery little girl's hair, I sank down to her level. "Hey, kid. What the hell are you doing here?"

Diana quirked a sassy brow. "Nadia would say that's swearing, Hades."

I wrinkled my nose. "Bullshit. Now *that's* swearing. But don't evade the question. It's almost two in the morning. You should be tucked up safe in bed, not running around with known gangsters." I tipped my head up at Cass, and Diana smirked.

"I couldn't sleep," the little shit lied, "so I went for a walk."

Hannah snorted. "A walk with a bag packed, kid? Try again."

Diana rolled her eyes. "Whatever. You should be *thanking* me. If I hadn't seen that guy climbing the fence here, Hades might have *died*."

I wrinkled my nose in confusion, and Cass passed a hand over his mouth to hide a smile.

"I'll fill you in," he murmured. "You should call Zed, though, and tell him what's happened to his house."

"Can't," I replied. "Don't you think I would have called *you* if I could? Chase must have damaged the cell tower near here."

Cass groaned. "Yeah, that makes sense. We should go, then. Get set up at a hotel."

I glanced over at the fire trucks and found one of the crew waiting to get my attention. "I need to stay here and sort this out," I told Cass. "You go. Get Diana home, and sort out a hotel for us all."

He barked a laugh. "You must have hit your head, Angel. I'm not fucking leaving without you. Not again."

"Diana and I will go," Hannah offered before Cass and I could spiral into a full-blown argument. "We'll sort it all out. Come to the Shadow Majestic when you're done here."

Diana started to protest, but Hannah smoothly steered her back to the silver sedan, then hesitated at the driver's side, glancing at Cass in question.

"It'll be fine," he told her with a grunt. "Just don't turn the car off until you get there."

She nodded in understanding, then shot me a smile. "I'm glad you're okay, Boss."

They pulled out of the driveway once more, and I glared at Cass. "I need an explanation."

He shrugged. "Someone slashed the tires on my bike, so I hot-wired that thing."

Yeah, that made sense. "And Diana?"

"Ran away from Nadia's," he rumbled with a pissed-off look on his face. "Was coming here to stay with us, but saw Chase climbing the fence when her taxi pulled up. So she asked the driver to bring her back to town so she could call the cops. Pure coincidence that I spotted her outside the police station near Hannah's apartment."

I yawned heavily and lifted the strap of the M16 over my head, handing it to Cass. "Smart kid," I muttered. Then reconsidered. "Dumb fucking kid for running around Shadow Grove at two in the morning, but smart for going back to town for help. Do we know why she took off from Nadia's?"

Cass shook his head. "Nope. I imagine she'll tell you, though."

Giving him a faint nod, I made my way over to the waiting firefighter, who was holding his hat nervously.

"Hades," he greeted me, then gave Cass a nod as well. "I'm guessing you already know the cause of the fire?" I nodded. "Okay, good, makes our job easier. We've almost got the flames out but will need to come back and assess the damage tomorrow. This goes against our usual safety protocols, but since you're *you* and this is Mr. De Rosa's house, do you want us to pull the cars out?"

My brows hitched. "The cars survived?"

Cass drifted away behind me, moving across the grass to speak with the black-clad security guards who'd completed their sweep of the property.

"Yes, sir," the firefighter confirmed. "Looks like the concrete walls kept the flames from spreading into the garage at all. They might be a bit smoky, but otherwise are undamaged. If you can tell us where to find the keys, my crew can pull them all out, just in case the structure above collapses as it cools."

Talk about small mercies. That might *slightly* dampen Zed's ire over the house. I directed the fire chief to the hidden panel where all the keys for Zed's vehicles were kept, and they went to work carefully driving each of Zed's prized cars out of the ruined building. I directed them to park on the grass, figuring that would have to do until morning.

Eventually the fire crew told us there was nothing more for us to do, so Cass and I took one of Zed's Aston Martins and headed into town.

Hannah had organized for us the penthouse suite at the Shadow Majestic, and I was asleep almost before my head hit the pillow.

I slept so deeply that I didn't even wake up when Zed and Lucas arrived, despite it probably not being long after we'd checked in. Instead, I woke up late the next morning to find myself curled in Lucas's strong embrace while Zed and Cass talked in hushed whispers over the top of us.

"We're in a *suite*," I grumbled, without opening my eyes. "Go and talk in the next room. I'm *sleeping* here."

"Same," Lucas mumbled, kissing my neck as he snuggled closer.

Zed wasn't inclined to respect my beauty rest, though, snatching me out of Lucas's arms to drag me on top of him. His mouth crushed to mine, and he kissed me until I was groaning against him, then he released me with a kiss on my nose.

"Hey, you," he murmured, his voice husky and his eyes sparking with heat. "Are you okay?"

I frowned. "Of course I am. Are you? On a scale of one to *furious*, how are you feeling about losing your house last night?"

"Are you kidding me?" he asked with a sharp laugh. "Fuck the house. All the important things survived."

I nodded my understanding. "Yeah, that was lucky getting all the cars out unscathed."

Zed gave me a flat glare. "*You*, Dare. You were the only important thing that was in that house."

"So, I guess that answered my question about whether the engagement announcement would bother Chase," Lucas mumbled, still half-asleep.

Zed shot a grin at Lucas, then tipped my head back to kiss me again. "New plan," he murmured against my lips a moment later. "No more splitting up the team. Not ever."

I scoffed. "Like shit. I had that totally under control. Go debrief with Cass while ordering us room service. I want to sleep a little longer."

Zed kissed my hair, then wriggled out from under me, telling Cass to hurry up while Lucas drew me back into the warmth of his sleepy embrace. They left the bedroom door open halfway, so we could still hear the low hum of their voices out in the living room. I huffed a sigh.

"You want to sleep?" Lucas teased as I wriggled my ass against his hard morning dick. "Or sleepy fuck?"

Rolling my hips again, I gave a low chuckle. Someone had taken my jeans off while I slept, so I was just in panties. "What do you think?"

He groaned softly as he hooked his fingers under the elastic of my panties to tug them down. "You've got to be *super* quiet," he breathed against my ear, "or we'll have company. And I want you all to myself this morning."

A quiet gasp escaped me as his fingers danced over my clit, getting me warmed up. "Quiet," I agreed in a whisper. "Done."

My confidence was a touch ambitious, though, because I found myself biting the pillow to stifle my moans as he pushed into me from behind, his hand hitching my leg up to hook over his hip and give him better access.

"Shhh," he chuckled against my hair when I started grinding back against him, desperate for him to move. "Pretend we're asleep, babe. Just tell me before you come, okay?"

I swallowed back a moan and nodded instead, holding my

breath as he slowly, torturously rocked into me. My eyes fell shut, my teeth sinking into my lower lip as I tried to keep up the illusion of sleep, but goddamn, Lucas didn't make it easy. When he dropped his hand down to rub my clit, a full-body shudder rolled through me and my toes curled with the start of a climax.

"Lucas," I gasped, my hips pushing back on him with each thrust, "I'm so close."

"Shhhh," he whispered again. His other arm was under my pillow, and he raised it up to cover my mouth with his palm. "Come for me, babe, but stay quiet."

His thrusts increased in intensity, his fingers teasing my clit as he gagged me with his huge palm. I exploded, thrashing and writhing as I came, my moans muffled by his hand. Then he rolled me onto my stomach and pounded me harder, making me come a second time before he found his own release.

"Subtle," Zed drawled from the doorway. "Real fucking subtle."

Lucas gave a relaxed laugh, and I just moaned, still trembling and clenching around his dick with aftershocks.

"Shut up, Zeddy Bear," Lucas panted. "Hayden needed that."

"Uh-huh, *she* needed it, did she? Room service should be here in ten minutes." He came around to the side of the bed and offered me his hand. "I'll help you clean up, seeing as we're all being so selfless this morning."

I laughed at that but took his hand and let him pull me out from under Lucas. He didn't even bother letting me walk, just hauled me straight out of bed and tossed me over his shoulder to carry me to the shower.

My coffee and waffles were already getting cold by the time I wobbled out to the living room, wrapped up in just a hotel bathrobe.

Cass met me with a deep kiss and seated me in his lap, and I gulped half the coffee before starting on the food.

"I've got good news for you, Red," he murmured when the

rumbles of my stomach were at least partially satisfied. "Everything is lined up for Friday night. We're solid."

I arched a brow at him, swallowing a mouthful of waffle and coffee. "You're sure?"

He inclined his head. "As sure as we're ever going to be. It's all in place. Last night was the missing piece of the puzzle."

I stared at him for a long moment, letting that information sink in. I grinned and twisted on his lap to kiss him fully. Then that kiss turned into something a whole lot better, and I finished my breakfast while riding Cass's dick. Life just didn't get much better than that.

CHAPTER 61

It wasn't until Monday that the fire department gave their final assessment on all the damage across our properties. Anarchy was salvageable; the individual fires hadn't caught fast enough to burn everything down. My staff had used their brains, grabbing extinguishers to contain the worst of the blazes until help arrived.

The Copper Wolf office had come off the least damaged, the building's sprinkler system having kicked in fast enough to prevent any structural damage and stop the fires from spreading to other floors. We'd need to gut and freshly refit it, but all in all, not the worst.

The distillery and Zed's house, though, were another matter. Both were condemned by the fire department, and just a day after receiving the news, Zed had a demolition crew at his property to knock the whole thing down.

Better yet, he turned it into a publicity event and invited journalists to witness the wrecking ball smashing through the once rock-solid structure. With Hannah's help, it was spun into a front-page story, and I happily posed for happy-couple shots with Zed as we bullshitted about our grand plans for a rebuild.

By the time Friday rolled around, I was starting to worry Chase wouldn't follow his predictable pattern. The article about Zed and me building our *dream house* had gone live this morning, though, so I was banking on that to draw the little one-eyed scorpion out of hiding.

Hannah had my afternoon booked solid with beauty appointments, but for once I actually enjoyed the pampering because Seph joined me for all of it.

"So, what now?" she asked, flicking through the rack of designer dresses that been delivered to my suite courtesy of Hannah. "Will you rebuild everything? Or just focus on Timber for a while?"

I sipped my champagne and gave her a smile. "Since when did I admit defeat, brat? Hell no, I'll rebuild everything Chase has taken from me and then double it. This time next year, they may as well give me a key to the city."

She huffed a laugh, pulling out a champagne-colored minidress embroidered with thousands of glass beads. "I'm going to try this one," she announced. "Cool?"

I nodded. "Not really my color, so go for it."

"Good point." She grabbed a second hanger off the rack. "This one has your name all over it, anyway." Holding it out to me, she grinned. "Thank you for inviting me tonight, by the way."

I smiled back at her. "For the opening night of the club literally named after our family in our father's old gang headquarters? I wouldn't dream of excluding you. Go try that dress on, and I'll see if Hannah sent shoes to match."

My little sister skipped off to the bathroom, and I checked my phone for the seven thousandth time that day. Nothing had changed, though, so I entertained myself by whipping my shirt off and sending a picture of my tits to the new group chat I'd started with the boys.

All three of their bubbles popped up as typing at the same time, and I chuckled, tossing my phone aside to try on the dress Seph had chosen for me. She was right; it was like it'd been made just for me.

"Ta-da!" My sister popped back out of the bathroom in the champagne minidress looking like a damn supermodel, all long legs and pouty red lips. She looked like my polar opposite, even more so now that I wore a dramatic, sexy black evening gown with blood-red embroidery.

I grinned. "Which one of the boys is on Seph duty tonight?" I asked, pitying the poor boy.

She scoffed. "Like they'd fucking notice. But all of them are coming, if that's okay? Rex said it'd be good to have extra eyes in the crowd."

"Fine by me." I shot a message to Hannah requesting shoes for the two dresses we'd chosen, then refilled both of our glasses with champagne. "Did you tell them about Michigan?"

Seph shook her head. "Not yet. Rex knows, but he won't say anything. I just don't want to get too excited until it's actually real, you know?"

I nodded. "I know. Here." I handed her a glass of champagne. "I want you to know, brat, that I love you. Things haven't been easy. I was a *crappy* guardian, but maybe now we can just go back to being sisters?"

Seph stared at me for a long moment, then wrinkled her nose. "Did you just display *feelings*? Ew, what the hell? Are you feeling okay? Oh my god, don't tell me you're pregnant! Ah, I fucking knew it, you ate so much fucking pie at Nadia's the other day!"

"Jesus fucking Christ," I muttered, gulping my entire glass of champagne with one sip and leveling a hard glare at my sister. "You're an asshole, Nadia's pie is amazing, and *sometimes* a girl just wants pie without her hormones driving that need. Fuck me."

She screwed up her face, squinting. "Okay, but that's not a no. So, am I gonna be an aunty or—" Her teasing cut off with a yelp as I threw a pillow at her from the couch.

"No!" I shouted. "Most assuredly, unquestionably *not* pregnant!" Not for lack of sex, but thank *fuck* for contraceptives. I'd rather keep my sex life just as active as it currently was for as long as it could possibly last. Hopefully forever. I wanted to be gray and wrinkly with my tits swinging all over the place while those three men fucked all my holes at once. Hell yeah, that was my idea of a happily-ever-after.

Seph still snickered with laughter but let the matter drop as Hannah arrived with our shoes, and we finished getting ready for Timber's opening night.

Zed and Cass were waiting in the lobby for me when we got downstairs, and I spotted one of Rex's boys, Nix, lurking near the exit waiting for Seph. Those boys had impressed the hell out of me with their dedication to the job I'd assigned, and I was pleased to see a fresh Timberwolf tattoo on his forearm when he pushed his hair back from his face.

A limo took us over to Timber, but Zed and Cass had such a hard time keeping their hands off me on the way that Seph bolted the second we arrived. She yelled over her shoulder to us that she needed more alcohol to stomach all the PDA, then disappeared into the crowd with Nix trailing behind like a loyal bodyguard… or lovesick puppy. Unclear.

"Hades, sir," Bethany greeted me as we stepped into the lively, glittering club. Her smile was bright as she indicated for us to follow. "Right this way."

I knew where to go, but it was good practice for my hosts. So we didn't argue as Bethany led us through the partying crowd and over to our reserved table directly in front of the main stage of Timber. It was a semi-circle booth with a high back, offering the illusion that whoever was on stage was giving a private show just for whoever sat there.

The table was already laid out with an ice bucket and champagne, but Zed ordered us cocktails as well. Bethany assured us that food would be brought over too, so there was no need for us to leave the table unless we wanted.

Ordinarily, when I visited my own clubs, I stuck to VIP lounges, not wanting to be among the guests. But tonight was different. Tonight, I wanted the full experience. We were already hours late, the opening party having started much earlier in the evening, but I was only there for two things.

Seph floated past our table, announcing that she was going to hang out with Rex's boys rather than sit with us, which was more than fine by me. Now I didn't need to feel weird about my uncontrollable urge to make out with both Zed and Cass *constantly*.

A waiter delivered a huge array of sample plates to our table—what looked to be one of every item on the menu—and a few minutes later the house lights dipped. Excitement lit me up inside, and I sat up straighter while the music shifted to something more dramatic.

A hush fell over the crowd, and with an explosion of glitter, our first dancers took to the stage. It was Sabine and one of the other girls from Club 22, and they were perfection. The whole room watched entranced as they moved with the music, then made their way to secondary platforms, climbing the dance poles like they were made of air.

But I wasn't there to see them. I wasn't on the edge of my seat with anticipation for my employees. Nope, I was here for the main event.

My entire breath gusted from my lungs in a heavy sigh of relief when Lucas appeared on stage. I finally had to admit to myself how anxious I'd been to have him out of my sight all damn day, but there he was, all in one piece and dancing *just* for me.

His eyes locked with mine as he moved, and I wet my lips. Fucking hell…it was like sex onstage. Maybe I *wasn't* secure enough to have him take a regular shift.

"Sit back and watch the show, Boss," Zed murmured in my ear, his teeth nipping my lobe teasingly.

I gave him a knowing look, but obligingly relaxed back into the relative privacy of our high-backed booth. His hand was already on my thigh, but as Cass tugged our table closer, Zed slipped his fingers under the slit of my skirt, finding my heated skin.

"Zed..." I murmured in warning, but he just nodded to the stage where Lucas was unbuttoning his shirt. All around us the screams of excited women filled the air, but his attention was entirely on me.

Zed's hand moved higher, finding my bare pussy, and paused. "Dare, did you forget your panties?"

I grinned. "This dress didn't lend itself to panty lines."

Cass chuckled. "I've heard that one before." His hand gathered up my skirt on the other side, drawing it up high enough that he could join the party under the table. "Oh, Angel. You're drenched."

I sucked in a breath as his fingers sank into me, but I didn't stop him. Instead, I reached out for my drink and took a sip as Lucas eye-fucked me and Cass dragged my own wetness up to tease my clit. Zed wasn't going to be left out, though, his own fingers sliding up into my cunt.

"Oh fuck," I muttered with a laugh, realizing they actually intended to finger fuck me *together*. Why was that so damn hot?

"Just sit back and watch the show, Angel," Cass ordered with a smirk. "Lucas has been practicing this *just* for you."

No way in hell was I arguing with that. I lifted my hips, silently asking for more, and locked eyes with Lucas once more. Goddamn, he could move. Throughout his set Cass and Zed took turns fucking me with their fingers and teasing my clit, then toward the end, when Lucas was down to his briefs, they both had their fingers in me at the same time. It was pure heaven, and I came hard, gasping and writhing on their hands while Lucas oozed pure sex and covered his dick with a hat before whipping off his last garment.

Zed, ever the gentleman, cleaned me up with one of the linen napkins so I wouldn't have a wet patch on my silk dress for the rest of the night. Then Cass licked his fingers clean and almost made me come again. Fucking hell.

The lights came back up, signaling the end of the first show of the evening, and the volume of the crowd rose back to drunken-chatter level once more. As badly as I wanted to race backstage and jump on Lucas's dick, I checked the time instead.

An excited smile crossed my lips. "It's almost time," I murmured to my companions.

Cass grinned smugly. "I think he might be early," he murmured.

Sure enough, Bethany was heading our way with wide, excited eyes. "Boss, your guest has arrived," she told me with a grin. "He's being held at the door for you."

"Perfect, thank you, Bethany," I replied, standing and smoothing my dress back into place. Good thing it was black because even with that cleanup Zed had given me, I was still soaking.

Zed, Cass, and I made our way back out to the main entrance of the club, where multiple journalists still waited with their cameras at the ready to snap pictures of the rich and famous attending the grand opening.

"Darling," Chase purred when I descended the entry stairs to where my security had him detained. "What games are you playing tonight? I got your invitation." He held up the thick linen invitation that had been sent to all my guests, only his stated a time that suited *my* dramatic timing for once.

"How's your arm, Chase?" I replied with a feral grin. In the corner of my eye, I spotted Lucas jogging out to join us, still in the process of buttoning up his shirt. Good. It felt right that all three of my guys were here for this.

Chase's single eye flashed with anger and desire. Sick fuck probably got off on the fact that I'd shot him. "Did you invite me here tonight just to turn me away? Seems a bit weak. I burnt down your whole empire, and this is how you hit back?" He shook his head, mocking. "I'm disappointed. I thought we were having fun, escalating each time. That article today was *weak* too."

I smiled brighter as a familiar face approached from behind Chase. "Nonsense, Chasey baby, you just aren't seeing the bigger picture. I do *so* appreciate you taking the bait, though. It makes this so much easier."

His eye narrowed. "Darling—"

"Oh, I don't believe you've met my good friend Eric, have you?" I cut him off, holding a hand out to the gray-haired gentleman in a tux approaching.

Chase only looked confused for a moment, then he must have recognized *my friend Eric.*

"Maybe you have met," I murmured with a throaty laugh. "Nevertheless, Eric brought a few guests along for you to get acquainted with, didn't you, old friend?"

The police chief gave me an amused smile and nodded. "I sure did. Ms. Wolff, you look dazzling." He raised his hand, giving a signal, and all of a sudden there were a dozen guns aimed at Chase. "Ah, Mr. Lockhart. Back from the dead and up to his eyeball in trouble. You really picked the wrong target here, fella. You're going away for a long, long time."

Chase blanched, a disbelieving smile on his lips. "I'm sure you're confused, Eric," he replied with a smooth chuckle. "Chase Lockhart died five years ago. I'm—"

"Masquerading as an FBI agent under the assumed name of Wenton Dibbs, who *you* killed? Yes, we're well aware. Ms. Wolff has been more than generous with the evidence she's collected and compiled on your crimes. You are one sick fuck, you know that?" Eric nodded to one of his officers, who pulled out a pair of handcuffs and set about arresting Chase.

"Isn't this poetic?" I purred as he glared at me with pure fury. "You really should have seen this one coming, Chasey baby. You didn't *seriously* think you were keeping the upper hand this whole time?" He said nothing, and I gave a sharp laugh. "Oh, honey, you did? That's precious. Have a nice stay in lockup, though. I hear they're expecting you."

His lip curled in a sneer as he prepared to spew some threat or other at me, but he was swiftly silenced by Zed's fist smacking straight into his mouth. Blood sprayed across the pavement, along with a tooth, and Chase slumped unconscious in the grip of his arresting officer.

"Sorry," Zed muttered to the police chief.

Eric grinned. "I saw nothing. Good to see you again, De Rosa. When can we expect you back at the poker tables?"

Zed nodded to Timber. "Come on in now. I'll take all your money off your hands."

Eric let out a loud laugh. "You're on. I didn't get all dressed up not to play a few hands with you. Cassiel, are you in?"

Cass shook his head. "Nah, I'm going to get a drink with my woman." Lucas smacked him on the arm, and Cass rolled his eyes. "And this little prick. Good show, Gumdrop."

They headed inside, but I stayed out there a while longer, watching the unmarked police cars driving away into the night with an unconscious Chase Lockhart secured within. Only when they were finally out of sight did I draw a deep breath, feeling like I could breathe again for the first time in *years*.

The snare had caught its prey at last. Now it would be a test of our months of preparation to see that the rabbit never shook loose.

CHAPTER 62

Timber's opening-night party wasn't just playing host to the rich and famous within the Timberwolf territory. It was also studded with acquaintances of mine, allies who'd provided me enough security to pull off a ballsy move like I'd just done. Inviting Chase to his own arrest...not even he could have seen that coming, even though it was an imitation of my own "arrest" just two months earlier.

Striding back into my club, I scanned the crowd, picking out all my carefully placed players. Vega and his new second—a woman, to my delight—were over near the roulette wheel. Ezekiel was sipping soda water at the bar. Roach and a scrubbed-up crew of Reapers were on the dance floor. And there were my boys, Cass and Lucas, on their way up to the VIP lounge, where I'd already spotted Seph's guys chatting with Archer and Co.

I took a moment to soak it all in. To appreciate how far I'd come. Only six months ago, I'd have rather shot myself in the foot than admit I needed help.

Across the room, Zed caught my eye and shot me a wink, raising his glass in a silent toast as he headed for the basement poker tables with our chief of police, the new deputy mayor, and the special agent in charge of the regional FBI field office. As far as the bureau was concerned, Chase was nothing more than a con artist they were happy to wash their hands of.

I smiled to myself and made my way up to VIP to celebrate the first of what I hoped to be many wins against Chase fucking Lockhart. Everyone up there was in high spirits, full party mode, and despite my newly jubilant mood, I shied away from joining them completely. Instead, I headed straight to the bar and ordered an Aviation from Katie, the bartender.

"You made that victory look effortless," Archer commented, leaning on the bar beside me.

I scoffed. "Nothing about this was *effortless*, D'Ath. Trust me on that. It's not won, yet, either. But after all the work we've put into making it fail-safe, it'd fucking better work. The damage we had to suffer while waiting this out has made it all somewhat less than satisfying."

Archer nodded, running a hand over his bearded cheek. "I don't doubt it. Cass's fake death?"

He was asking how Cass being "dead" had played into my end game—what he'd been getting up to while out of the line of sight for so long. I gave him a sly smile. "A magician never reveals her tricks, D'Ath. You'll see soon enough."

He gave a husky laugh. "Fair enough. I never apologized for our fuckup in Italy."

"No, you didn't." I gave him a level stare as Katie put my drink down in front of me and poured a beer for Archer.

"I hope you know I'd never intentionally put Seph in danger. It never crossed my mind that she'd—"

"I know," I cut him off. "Seph…made some mistakes. We all did. What's important is that we don't repeat them." I arched a brow, driving my point home. "Ever. Second chances are hard to come by in these parts."

A smile crossed Archer's lips, and he dipped his head in acknowledgment. "Understood, sir."

For a moment, we just stood there in somewhat companionable silence, drinking our drinks and watching our *friends* partying together. That seemed like an unfamiliar word for me to use, but I couldn't think of any better way to describe them. Especially when Maxine and Hannah joined the group a few minutes later.

"Copper Wolf Distillery was leveled, huh?" Archer asked after a while.

I nodded. "The buildings, yes. The brand? Hell no. It'll be back up and running in no time."

He smiled slyly. "You'll need new advertising images when you relaunch." His gaze slid back to where Madison Kate was seated on a couch between his friends. Steele's arm was around her waist, and Kody played with her fingers as she chatted with my sister. They were so in love it almost made me gag.

Almost.

"Hey, babe, you don't wanna join us?" Lucas asked, coming over with his empty glass in hand. His cheeks already held the flush of intoxication, but I knew he would stop before getting drunk. We were all still too paranoid to lose control in public.

He and Archer exchanged a friendly handshake, and Lucas leaned in to kiss me, not even hesitating for a second. After all, we were among friends here.

"I'm fine here," I replied, leaning into his embrace as his arm looped around me. "You go back and have fun, though. You've earned it."

He gave me a curious look, but sensed I wasn't going to be pushed. So he took his refill from Katie and kissed me again before heading back over to where he'd been chatting with Ford and Kody.

Cass looked over when Lucas sat back down, then made his excuses to Rex and headed over to us.

"Don't tell me you're enjoying being social, Saint," Archer teased, sipping his beer like he had as much intention of joining the group as I did.

Cass quirked one brow. "Don't you have a fight coming up, D'Ath? All that beer won't be good for your fitness."

Archer gave a low laugh. "Nah, I canceled it. Kate's got some meetings in Pretoria she can't miss."

I reached for my drink, then chuckled when my ring caught the light. Suddenly it made a shitload more sense where Zed had gotten his hands on red diamonds. Madison Kate owned one of the world's biggest diamond mines.

"I was going to head downstairs and take Zed's money on the poker tables," Cass told me. "Wanna come sit on my lap and act as a distraction?" I raised one very unimpressed brow, and Cass gave a husky laugh. "Kidding. Of course."

"Well, I'm game. Let's take money from the rich bastards I invited, though. We need to pay for a whole lot of rebuilds." I finished my cocktail and took Cass's offered hand. "You coming, D'Ath?"

He drained his beer and put the glass back on the bar. "Fleecing rich pricks? Hell yeah."

The three of us made our way down to the basement gaming rooms and located Zed at a table with his politically powerful friends. They were laughing uproariously about something, and when I drew close, he dragged me into his lap with an impulsive movement.

He kissed me like we were totally alone in the room, then whispered in my ear about what he wanted to do when the club closed for the night. After all, we'd made a pact to christen our bars together.

From there on out, I was just counting the minutes until the party would end and the high-spirited guests cleared out. Last to leave were my sister and her bodyguards. After several hours of sipping on cocktails, I had a decent buzz going—enough that I voluntarily hugged her tight and told her I loved her.

Zed and Cass were joking and swearing as they lifted some

of the velvet couches up onto the stage, and I gave Lucas a confused look.

He shrugged. "They've got a plan, babe, just roll with it."

I smiled but didn't argue, instead heading to the bar where
Katie had left a bottle of whiskey out for us with some crystal
glasses. I collected them all up and made my way over to the stage
while Zed jumped down to lock up all the doors. The last thing we
needed was to be interrupted while we were all…relaxed.

"This is cute," I murmured, sitting down on one of the couches
beside Cass. They'd positioned it so that we had a full view of the
club. My mini-empire, until the rest could be revived.

"Zed wanted to make this part just for the two of you," Cass
confessed with a smirk, "but Lucas and I overruled him. We're a
fucking team, and we should celebrate the victories together."

"*If* that's okay with you," Lucas added, shooting Cass a hard
look. "We know you and Zed had an agreement."

I grinned, feeling more at home on a couch in the middle of
a stage than ever before. "I don't see why we can't do both," I told
them, then looked at Zed as he hurried back from the security
office. "Are the cameras switched off?"

He nodded. "Damn right. No way in hell do I want one of the
new bouncers stumbling across this footage."

He didn't waste any time with foreplay; our whole fucking
night had been foreplay enough. He just sank straight to his knees
in front of the couch and lifted the buttery silk of my dress over
his head.

"Oh shit," I gasped as he yanked me closer with his hands on
my ass, his mouth finding my cunt like a starving man finding
water. Not that I was complaining. My back arched off the couch,
my hands gripping Zed's head through my dress and pulling him
closer. I'd been worked up and on edge ever since they'd made me
come while Lucas was stripping, so it wasn't going to be hard to
get me to climax again.

Cass grabbed my chin between his fingers, capturing my mouth in a bruising kiss while Lucas worked the clasps and zipper of my dress. It was the kind of gown that just hadn't leant itself to underwear. So a moment later, when Lucas coaxed me to my feet, my dress floated to the floor around Zed in a puddle of silk, leaving me totally naked.

"This is how we should end every night out," Lucas commented, his eyes drinking me in and his smile wide.

Cass huffed a laugh. "And every night in, too."

Zed had his mouth full, hooking one of my legs over his shoulder as he licked me harder. I wobbled and fell back into the couch with a laugh, but he wasn't deterred. Cass's lips found my breast, Lucas claimed my mouth, and I ticked off my second orgasm of the night all over Zed's face.

"Holy crap, that was good," I moaned, my hips still rolling as Zed licked his lips and stroked his fingers into my still-spasming cunt.

He gave a low chuckle. "Buckle up, baby. We've only just started."

"Mine," Lucas announced, grabbing my leg as Zed shifted back. With a smooth motion, he spun me horizontally on the couch, then hooked my leg up over the back of it. My other leg draped across the seat, my high-heeled foot still on the floor. I couldn't have been spread out wider if I'd tried.

"You three almost killed me earlier," Lucas informed us as he stripped out of his shirt and freed his huge, glistening erection from his suit pants. He didn't seem to be wearing underpants either. "You know how fucking *hard* it is, watching my girl fall to pieces while I'm getting naked onstage?"

He shot Zed and Cass accusing glares, but they just grinned back as he shifted closer, bringing the tip of his enormous dick to my aching core. I moaned as he started to push in far too slowly for my impatient mood.

"Come on, Gumdrop," Zed teased. Sitting back on his heels beside the couch, he cupped one of my breasts with his hand. "Show Dare just how hard it was for you."

Lucas muttered a curse, but when I lifted my hips to push him deeper, he gave a grunt and slammed into me. I screamed at the burn of pain that always happened when taking Lucas first, but it was a good kind of pain. The kind that made me thrash and pant and beg for more.

Zed sucked my nipple into his mouth, teasing it with his teeth, and Cass leaned down to kiss me upside down. And Lucas? He pinned my hips to the couch with his huge hands and fucked me so hard and fast I saw stars.

"Shit," Lucas cursed, moaning. "You've got to be kidding me. Fucking hell, Hayden, I'm going to come already."

I laughed into Cass's kiss and reached out to dig my fingernails into Lucas's hip, encouraging him because I was already *so damn close* myself. These guys were turning me into a goddamn orgasm machine, and I was going to guess they had a personal challenge to beat our highest number tonight.

Lucas's thrusts got deeper, slamming into me as he chased his release, and at the first hot jerk of his cock within me, I screamed my own climax. My spine arched and my toes curled inside my shoes, and I rode it out on Lucas's thick shaft until the tremors began to subside.

No sooner had Lucas pulled out of me, though, than I found myself flipped over onto all fours with Cass's dick in my face and Zed's hands massaging my ass.

"Open those pretty lips for me, Red," Cass urged, his hand going to my hair and nudging me closer to his tattooed erection. Not that I needed any encouragement. I eagerly swallowed him down, my head bobbing up and down his shaft as Zed prepared my ass with lube. I wasn't even shocked; Cass had told me earlier that they'd be bringing *supplies* along.

508

"Remember that little toy I brought back from my travels?" Cass asked, somewhat breathless as I sucked his cock. I wasn't pausing to answer, just hummed my *yes* against his flesh, and he gave a small laugh. "Well, this one is a little bigger."

My confusion only lasted a moment before Zed started pushing a new toy into my ass. I moaned as it slowly stretched me wider with every millimeter, but Cass's hand on my hair kept my focus split between the toy in my butt and his dick down my throat. In reality, it didn't feel *that* insane. It was roughly the size of Zed's dick, and I was well accustomed to taking that like a champ.

It was the slow way he fucked it into my ass that was driving me nuts. Pushing a little, then pulling out, then pushing a little more. Pure torture.

"Holy hell," Lucas murmured. He'd dragged one of the other chairs close enough that his knee brushed my hand where I gripped Cass's leg. "That's so damn hot."

"Are you gonna come again, Red?" Cass asked with a gasp as I sucked him harder. My hand moved to cup his balls, playing with them as I bobbed on his cock, and he cursed on an exhale. "Hmm, I bet Zed can help you get there, can't he?"

Zed gave a murmur of agreement. The toy found its resting place, and his lips brushed a kiss over my butt cheek. Then his fingers were back inside my pussy, fucking me roughly and making the plug shift inside my ass.

Yeah, Cass had known what he was talking about. It was no shock when I came again, but my screams were muffled as he gripped my hair tight, shoving his cock deep down my throat, his hips rising to fuck my mouth. My hand still cradled his nuts, and I slid a finger back to press the strip of flesh behind his balls. He came with a shout, filling my mouth with his cum and making me swallow quickly to avoid choking.

"Goddamn," he groaned when I surfaced, licking my lips. "Gonna be like that, huh?"

Chuckling, I sat back on my heels and felt the delicious fullness of the plug moving with me. "Damn right it is," I murmured, then looked behind me at Zed. "How do you want me?"

His eyes flared, and he maneuvered us all around until he was on his back against the couch with me straddling him. "Oh yeah," he breathed as his hands found my waist, lifting me up so his cock could find my pussy. "Yeah, like this."

I lowered onto him, my pussy already so drenched there was little resistance. Still, my lower belly clenched and fluttered, my walls hugging him tight as I braced my hands on the arm of the couch above his head. "Yeah?" I teased, moaning a little at the doubled-up sensations thanks to that plug. I'd have rather they filled me with something else, though.

For a few moments I rode Zed slowly making him suffer a bit as my breasts bounced above his face. Then Lucas shifted out of his chair and came to stand behind the arm of the couch, his dick hard and ready to go again.

I looked up, locking eyes with him and licking my lips.

"Take it slow," Cass rumbled, slouching back into the seat Lucas had vacated, his fist gripping his dick as he worked it over, coaxing it back up.

Lucas snickered and tugged my mouth open with his fingers on my chin. "Keep up, old man. Just don't give yourself arthritis in the process." He winked at me, full of mischief, then pushed his dick between my lips.

Cass shot back an insult but watched with an unblinking gaze as I took Lucas deeper into my mouth and bounced on Zed's cock. As amusing as I found their banter, I badly wanted *all* of their participation at the same time, so I obliged by taking things slow and giving Cass a chance to recover.

By the time he smirked and thumbed his hard tip, I was almost losing my mind from anticipation.

"Saint," I moaned, holding Lucas's dick with my fist and watching Cass slick lube all over his cock. "Hurry the hell up."

Lucas and Zed both chuckled at that, but Cass just took it as permission to go slower, stroking the lube up and down his dick and making me jealous of his hand. To distract myself, I licked down the length of Lucas's cock, then closed my mouth over his ball sac, sucking gently and making him gasp.

"That's playing dirty, Angel," Cass scolded as I opened my mouth wider, carefully taking both of Lucas's balls inside while my hand worked his shaft. Zed was growing impatient beneath me, though, and I knew I needed to back off before I accidentally nipped something precious.

"Oh yeah?" I retorted, my gaze following Cass as he moved around to the couch behind me. "What are you gonna do about it, Daddy Cass?"

Zed gave a strangled noise beneath me, his fingers gripping my hips tighter. "Oh shit," he laughed. "Dare…"

"Zeddy Bear," Cass rumbled, seeming to ignore my question as he settled himself behind me. "You're comfortable in your sexuality, aren't you?"

Zed scoffed. "Absolutely."

"Good," Cass replied in a darkly dangerous voice. Oh shit. "Because things are about to get…real snug."

My eyes widened, and I gave a startled gasp as he started to push his lubed-up dick into me. But he hadn't taken the plug out of my ass. Nope, he was going in right alongside Zed, inside my pussy.

"Cass!" I yelped, my hand tightening around Lucas's dick.

"Shhhh," he replied, grunting as he pushed in further. "I've seen you take Lucas's monster and beg for more, Angel, just relax."

He was right, I had. But what the *fuck*? I still had a dick-sized toy in my ass and now—

"Oh holy fuck," I gasped as my pussy stretched to accommodate two cocks at once. "Fuck, fuck, *fuck*."

"Want me to stop?" Cass asked, pausing and panting as his hand gripped my hip tighter.

I shook my head. "Hell no."

All three of them chuckled the *sexiest* damn sounds, and Cass pushed in deeper. I was just about as full as humanly possible and in goddamn heaven about it.

"Good," Cass grunted. "Now get Gumdrop's dick back down your throat and hold the fuck on. I wanna see you come at least three times before he blows his load on your face."

Jesus triple-dicking Christ. If dirty talk could make me come... Cass would be damn near getting close. I did as I was told, opening my mouth wide once more and lapping at Lucas's glistening, salty precum before sucking him deep.

My whole body was just a mass of hypersensitive, overused nerves, and I barely knew what was up or down as they fucked me breathless. It took a bit of wiggling around and muttered conversation between Cass and Zed, but soon they found their rhythm to fuck me together. By the time I'd come a second time in this new scenario, I was so strung out on endorphins I was seeing stars and my whole skin was buzzing.

"Come on, baby," Zed grunted from beneath me, "one more for us. Come one more time, and we'll give you a break."

Both he and Cass reached for my clit at the same time, and I detonated between them. I screamed so long and loud that Lucas slipped out of my mouth, and his own hand took over the job, jerking his dick furiously as I thrashed and moaned between Zed and Cass.

"That's a good girl," Cass purred, grabbing a handful of my hair and tilting my head back even as I still quaked with intense, soul-deep aftershocks. "Go for it, Gumdrop."

Lucas grunted, then a moment later, his hot, wet cum splattered across my face.

I had no chance to catch my breath as Zed and Cass fucked me harder and harder, then Zed started coming. Somehow, his release sparked Cass, and they filled my cunt with their combined ejaculation together. It was hot and filthy, and I was a fucking *fan*.

After they gently slipped out, cleaned my face up with a cloth, and moved me to rest on the couch between their sweaty bodies, I felt all kinds of empty. Even with the thick plug still snug in my ass. For a while, the only sound in the club was our rough panting. Then I started laughing.

"What's funny?" Zed mumbled from where his head rested on my breast.

"Mmm, not funny," I corrected. "But we're *definitely* doing that again. Holy crap."

Cass chuckled. "Insatiable."

"I'm game," Lucas told me with a smirk, his hand cupping his junk and a hungry look on his face. Yeah, he wasn't done yet. I could see him plotting how to pull me out from between Cass and Zed already.

I saved him the trouble, getting up to stand in front of him with a knowing smirk on my face. "What do you want, Lucas?" I asked him quietly, threading my fingers through his hair and tipping his head back so I could kiss him.

He moaned into my kiss, his dick rising in his hand once more. If I was insatiable, what the fuck was Lucas? Oh, right. Nineteen.

"I want your ass, babe," he whispered, raw desire burning in his eyes.

Zed and Cass both huffed exhausted laughs, and Zed reached out to stroke my butt cheek. "Good thing we got her warmed up for you, then," he teased, his fingers tugging on the plug. "We didn't want anyone getting hurt." He gave Lucas's huge dick a pointed look, and Lucas just grinned.

Cass tossed him a bottle of lube, and Lucas wasted no time slicking it all over his dick in preparation.

"Turn around, Angel," Cass ordered. "Give us the full show."

He'd get no objections from me on that one. Zed pulled the

plug free, and I spun around to give Lucas my back. He shifted back onto the couch, leaning against the arm of it as he guided me onto his cock.

"Shit," I hissed as the tip made it inside. I moaned, shaking my head. "I think you needed to find a bigger plug." I was joking. Sort of. But Lucas was *definitely* thicker than that plug had been.

"Take it slow, Gumdrop," Zed coached, his heated gaze locking with mine as I relaxed my body and let him sink deeper. "That's it. Nice and slow. Pull out and re-lube if you need to. We want plenty more playtime tonight."

I laughed at that, and Lucas's dick pushed deeper. Holy fuck, he surely wasn't getting that whole thing in there, was he? Then again, I'd have said the same about taking two dicks in my pussy an hour ago, and now look where we were.

He made it about halfway—it felt like a shitload more—when Cass ordered me to lean back against Lucas's chest. I obeyed without question, and Lucas shifted his hips, pushing another inch inside.

I moaned but relaxed into his sweaty chest as he pulled me down onto him the rest of the way.

Lucas's breathing was rough in my ear, his whispered curses dripping in desire, and when I turned to kiss him, I knew I wasn't going to have a hard time coming again. Maybe twice. Fuck, who knew. There was no limit, apparently.

"Holy shit, Hayden," he breathed against my kiss. "Holy shit. So fucking *tight*. I could come so quick like this."

Zed grinned, and Cass rolled his eyes. "Fucking amateur. Move a bit, kid. Get a feel for it."

Lucas groaned and did as he was told, fucking my ass with shallow thrusts that drove me wild. He kept that up for several minutes of pure torture, while Zed and Cass watched eagerly and offered advice and tips. Bastards were getting off on just spectating…not that I minded. They both had their dicks back in hand, and I watched with hooded eyes as they jerked off.

"How's that feeling, Angel?" Cass asked, a smirk on his lips.

My only response was a long moan as Lucas drew out a little further, then fucked straight back in. I was like putty in his hands.

"Want more?" Zed offered, ever the gentleman.

I nodded against Lucas's chest, groaning again. "Yes. Fuck yes. Give me more." Because clearly I was a masochist.

Taking me at my word, Zed shuffled forward on the couch and slammed into my soaking pussy in one strike.

I screamed, convulsing, and Lucas hissed a sharp breath. But they both paused a moment to let me adjust before pumping in and out of me again.

Cass stood and came to stand beside the couch, a satisfied look on his face as he gripped his dick. "You know what I want, Angel," he purred, and I laughed. A few minutes later, I was *very* careful not to bite down when I came with Cass's testicles in my mouth.

Hours later, when we finally staggered out of Timber and into the waiting limo, I made a mental note to have the couches reupholstered. Nothing was going to get that much cum out of the velvet.

CHAPTER 63

By the time Monday morning rolled around, I was officially walking funny. Every muscle in my body felt like it'd been through a spin cycle, and I was happier than I'd ever been in my entire cursed life. I "called in sick" to work, which was a moot point when we had no office to return to. The entire floor at Copper Wolf headquarters had needed to be gutted, but our construction crew were starting work on a new fit-out already.

Still, the world didn't stop turning just because I'd way overused my pussy and ass all weekend. By lunchtime my phone was blowing up enough that I had to pull on my big-girl panties and head out to oversee some of the repairs myself. With so many projects running at once, it was a lot for my team to handle. I was determined, though. My venues would be back up and running before Chase even made it to trial, just to slap him in the face with his own failure.

Hannah came to meet me at Nadia's, our temporary office for the day, and Zed accompanied me so we could run through the reopening plans for Anarchy, Club 22, and the newest gem in our collection, Malebolge.

Seeming relieved when we entered, Nadia ushered us over to a booth in the back of her café and sat down opposite us. Underneath the table, Zed's hand found mine, his thumb rubbing my ring in what had become an unconscious habit.

"I'm at my wit's end," Nadia confessed, glancing over her shoulder to make sure no one was listening in. "I've never met a more willful, defiant child—"

"Hades!" The child in question spotted me across the café and came barreling over to join us. "Did Nadia tell you already? She's letting me come live with you until the school year starts! Isn't that great? Cass is gonna teach me how to shoot a gun."

My brows shot up so high they practically disappeared into my hairline. "Uh...what?"

Nadia just gave me a flat fuck-it stare, then shrugged. "I did my best. Besides, you owe me for nearly getting me killed. And trashing my café."

"What?" I squeaked again in protest. "I *rebuilt* your café!" I waved a hand around us, demonstrating the fresh designer interior that I'd footed the bill for.

Nadia just shrugged again. "It's only for two weeks, and it'll be a hell of a lot safer than the little devil sneaking off in the middle of the night in a taxi." She rolled her eyes skyward. "Besides, I'm an old woman and I don't have the energy for all of this."

Diana grinned like it'd been her plan all along to wear Nadia down with sheer eight-year-old energy. "It's gonna be *so* fun," she enthused.

I scowled. I severely didn't appreciate being pushed into a corner by a child. But Nadia was also Cass's grandmother, and I was a little bit intimidated by the old battle-ax, so I couldn't just tell her *no* outright. "Two problems," I snapped. "One is that we don't actually have anywhere to live right now. It'll be the better part of a year before our house is rebuilt."

Zed squeezed my fingers when I said *our* house. But that's what it was, now. It was *ours*. His, mine, Lucas's, and Cass's.

"Cassiel told me you're looking at renting the old D'Ath mansion in the interim to get you out of the hotel," Nadia said with a smug smile. "There's more than enough space there for all of you. And like I said, it's *only for two weeks*"—this was aimed pointedly at Diana—"until the school term starts, then Diana goes into the boarding school at Shadow Prep."

"What's the other thing, Boss?" Diana asked, mimicking the way Zed called me that. Little shit.

I rolled my eyes. "I don't like children."

The little girl scoffed. "You adore me, but nice try."

Zed laughed, not even bothering to cover his amusement at the sassy little asshole dictating our living arrangements.

"Oh, while I remember," I muttered, reaching into my purse to pull out a folded newspaper clipping from a small-town gazette six states away. I opened it up and slid it across the table to Diana. "I always keep my word, kid."

She read the headline on the article, then burst out crying. It made me stiffen for a moment, second-guessing whether I should have shown her that, but then she launched at me in a massive hug.

"Happy tears," Zed whispered, and I flipped him off behind Diana's back. I wasn't *that* clueless; her hug had given it away.

"I'll have her things all packed up for you to pick up tomorrow," Nadia told us *so* helpfully, patting Zed's hand. "Now. Cake and coffee for two?"

"Three," Zed replied. "Hannah is on her way."

"Thank you, Hades," Diana whispered as she continued hugging me. "Thank you so much."

As much as I wanted to harden myself against this little kid, I couldn't. I'd been her. I'd suffered similar abuses at her age. I simply couldn't shut her out...especially now. Her whole family was dead. We were all she had.

I sighed. "Go and help Nadia. We'll figure something out tonight."

Diana released me with a wide, teary smile, then launched at Zed with an equally tight hug. "You guys are the best."

"Diana!" Nadia barked from the kitchen, and the kid scurried back to work. Nadia wasn't using her as child labor or anything dastardly like that; she was just keeping a bored, mischievous eight-year-old busy and out of trouble.

"Did we just adopt a child?" Zed murmured with heavy amusement, retrieving my hand to link our fingers together once more.

I snorted. "No fucking way. It's two weeks, then she goes to boarding school."

He smiled but leaned in to kiss me instead of pushing the subject any further. Good. It'd already been pushed way too far as it was.

"Bosses!" Hannah exclaimed, making Zed pull away from my lips with a sigh. "Sorry, did I interrupt?"

Nadia bustled back over with a tray of coffee and cakes, and Hannah cooed over how good it all looked while taking a seat opposite Zed and me.

"Okay," she announced, eyeing the both of us. "I have business crap to run through with both of you, mostly about your schedules for the next month, but first I need to know...was Chase Lockhart *actually* arrested on Friday night?"

I bit back a smile. "He was."

She frowned. "You let that happen?"

"I *made* that happen," I corrected her. "Why?"

"I'm just...surprised. I didn't think you'd be happy to just have him arrested like a normal criminal, especially knowing how corrupt all the law enforcement in these parts are. How do you know he won't just get out again? He could already be out." She seemed genuinely concerned, so I pulled up my favorite new app on my phone to show her the time-stamped footage of Chase inside his holding cell, sporting a massive black eye.

"He's not," I assured her. "If not this, what did you expect?"

Hannah shrugged, still frowning. "I don't really know, sir. Maybe that you'd have killed him? Having him arrested and charged like a *person* seems so... I dunno. Anticlimactic?"

"Does it?" I challenged her. "Or does it just seem that way because you never saw the months of plotting, planning, blackmailing, and killing that went into setting this up? Maybe because you never witnessed everything I lost along the way, everything I had to grit my teeth and bear, knowing that if I was patient enough, my plan would come to fruition." I sipped my coffee, letting that sink in a bit.

"Besides," I continued, "death is so very final. Chase wouldn't have killed me, so I'm simply treating him with the same courtesy."

Hannah blew out a breath, shaking her head. "You're a bigger person than me, Hades. I'd have just shot him in the head a long time ago."

I gave a hollow laugh in response. "I tried that once, it didn't stick. This time I'm being smarter."

Hannah didn't have a reply for that, so she just changed the subject to the business affairs she'd come to discuss with us. Zed leaned in close, kissing my neck as Hannah chatted away, and I leaned in to his touch—his unwavering strength and support. He knew better than anyone what my victory over Chase had cost and why it was the *only* real win.

An eye for an eye...metaphorically speaking.

After we finished with Hannah, Zed drove me over to my physical therapy appointment. We arrived about ten minutes early, but I didn't think anything of it as we strode into the clinic. Mine was the last appointment of the day, all the other therapists already having closed up and gone home, but Misha's office lights were still on, the door ajar.

Zed and I were talking, so we didn't hear the warning signs until it was too late—until we walked right into the office and found Maxine bent over the therapy bed with her pants around her ankles and Misha fucking her like he was trying to win a prize.

Neither of them seemed to notice us standing there, and a moment later, Maxine moaned and thrashed with her release and Misha crossed the finish line with a satisfied roar.

Biting my lip to keep from laughing, I was tempted to just quietly back away. Zed, being a total prick, started clapping.

"Bravo!" he shouted, and Misha slipped out of Maxine—showing us why he'd made such good money working in porn—and dove for his pants. "Encore."

Maxine was way less embarrassed as she propped up on her elbow and turned to smirk at us. "Nothing you haven't seen before, Zayden."

I flipped off my friend, and she just waggled her naked rear at me with a laugh.

"Let's reschedule," I told Misha, grabbing Zed's arm and dragging him out of the office before Maxine could fucking proposition a four-way. She was the *worst*, but come to think of it, she and Misha were perfect for each other.

Zed and I grinned the whole way back to the car, then headed back to the hotel to break the news of our temporary house guest to the other guys. Emphasis on *temporary*.

CHAPTER 64

Chase was denied bail, shocker. But as badly as I wanted to leave him to rot in holding with anticipation hanging over his head, I still had my doubts on the security. No, I wouldn't feel safe until he was securely locked up in the prison I'd personally selected for him. So I pushed the timeline up with plenty of monetary lubricant, and his case went to trial in just three weeks.

Diana had been delivered to Shadow Prep boarding school a little over a week before, but considering how close the school was to our rented house, I wasn't shocked when she showed up on our doorstep at the end of the school week. She announced that since Zoya was allowed to spend weekends working in the cafe with Nadia, she should be allowed to spend them with us. Besides that, she had decided the other kids in the boarding school were all rich brats and if she was forced to spend the weekend there without Zoya, she'd stab someone.

I blamed Zed for that. He'd given the little feral a dagger as a starting-school gift, and she was probably sleeping with it.

So when Monday morning rolled around, I found myself doing the familiar Shadow Prep drop-off for Diana before heading to the Cloudcroft court where Chase's trial was being conducted.

Seph was waiting on the steps of the courthouse for me and gave a disbelieving laugh as I made my way up to her.

"Dare," she exclaimed, "you look... Are you feeling okay? Did you hit your head in the shower?" She reached out to feel my forehead, and I gave her a smirk, adjusting the string of pearls around my neck.

"I don't know what you're talking about, Persephone," I replied in my most innocent voice. "Corsets and leather didn't seem like appropriate trial attire."

She snickered, and her escort for the day, Lincoln, looked like his brain was short-circuiting as he took in my demure knee-length skirt, cream silk blouse, sheer pantyhose, and, of course, my pearls. I fully intended to clutch at them in horror as Chase's crimes were presented to the jury.

"You look like a sexy librarian," Lucas murmured in my ear, his hand touching the small of my back. "I'm gonna be hard every time I look at you today."

Cass grunted in amusement. "You're hard any time she breathes, Gumdrop. Besides, she'd need a pair of glasses to complete the sexy-librarian look."

I made a mental note to get some glasses for tomorrow.

Seph grabbed my hand as we entered the courthouse, and I shot her a grateful smile. For all my acting and bullshitting, this was still a huge deal. Yes, I was putting Chase through an actual legal trial to punish him further. Yes, I could have just had him killed at any point that he was in holding in the last three weeks. But a huge part of me *needed* this level of vindication. I needed his crimes to be aired out and for a court to condemn him for what he'd done. And not just what he'd done to the hundreds of people—children—he'd trafficked over the years, but to *me*. To make up for the years of abuse and the stains left on my soul.

This trial was about more than appearances. And Seph knew that. She knew deep down I wasn't a ruthless, coldhearted crime boss, lording my victory over my opponent to make him squirm. I was a victim seeking justice.

Of course, my guys understood that too, but it meant so damn much to have my sister there supporting me, especially after all the years she'd lived in ignorance, throwing my dark past at me as a weapon.

The first few days of the trial were harder than I'd expected them to be. I had to sit there and listen to all the evidence *I* had compiled against Chase. Stolen video footage, photos, recordings, testimonials. The hardest was when it came to my recent detainment. Chase had fucked up when he'd sent that video to Zed, trying to get a rise out of him. He'd sent it without any hacker available to delete it again, and even in my panic attack I had thought ahead. It was cut-and-dried evidence, and I wasn't so delicate not to use it.

After almost a full week of the prosecution's evidence, the defense for Chase took a scarce half hour. His attorney was a nervous, sweating man who stumbled over his words and all but told the jury he believed his client to be guilty. I smiled throughout the whole defense, quietly laughing to myself at the painfully substandard representation Chase had been able to acquire.

He was found guilty on *all* counts, to no one's surprise. The jury had barely even left the room before returning with a unanimous verdict.

Throughout it all, Chase never spoke a word. Not in his own defense or to hurl insults at me. He just sat there and *stared*, his single beady eye assessing me like he was trying to work out how in the hell I'd set him up so thoroughly. Trying and *failing* because despite several of the crimes I'd provided evidence on, I wasn't incriminated in any of them. Not once.

"All right," Demi said, coming over to me as Chase was led out of the courtroom in handcuffs. "Case is over. Spill."

I raised my brows. "On what?"

Her glare flattened. "You know what. How Chase fucking Lockhart ended up with what had to be the absolute *worst* defense attorney in the country? Or how you managed to even get your hands on half that evidence? Or, shit, how *you* aren't currently being charged alongside him?"

Cass and I exchanged a knowing look, both smiling. "Let's just say it took a whole lot of money, planning, research, blackmail, and…the occasional fatal accident. Eventually, though, we made sure not a single defense lawyer worth their salt would come within sixty miles of this case. Not if they valued their careers or lives." I kept my voice down, not wanting to be overheard by anyone as we made our way out of the courthouse and into the sunshine. Damn, it was a beautiful day. "As for how I'm walking away from it all? I didn't get to this position by leaving my ass uncovered, Demi. You know that. Chase put all his eggs in the wrong basket, thinking they were safe. I just drove a bulldozer over it."

She snorted a laugh. "And then some. What if he escapes?"

"He won't." I gave her a confident smile.

My aunt looked less convinced, raising her brows. "He's got seemingly bottomless pits of money, he could—"

"Not anymore, he doesn't." It was one of the first things I'd pulled the trigger on, before he was even arrested. I couldn't run the risk of him being granted bail, no matter how expensive. So I'd taken every damn cent in his name. The *entire* Lockhart fortune was now being bounced through accounts all around the world, cleaning any trace of its origin, and eventually it'd come back to me.

"Okay, but he still has connections," Demi pushed. "How can you be so sure he won't leverage one of them to escape and start this whole fucking game anew?"

I grinned wider. "He won't. His only allies of any concern are all dead." Either I'd killed them myself, like the six names on my list, or Cass had slipped into their homes like the ghost he'd been and provided them with an untimely end of "natural causes" during his stealth mission for me.

"I'm just saying he's resourceful." Demi frowned. She, like Hannah, couldn't understand why I hadn't killed him once and for all. They didn't understand, though. They didn't *understand* how death was a mercy Chase Lockhart didn't deserve. Not until he'd experienced just a fraction of what he'd put me through. What he *would* have put me through, if the scales of fate had tipped in his favor at any point.

I patted my aunt on the arm, reassuring her. "So am I, Demi. Trust me. Chase Lockhart is no longer a threat."

As I said this, the armored prison van carrying my nemesis pulled out of the loading dock behind the courthouse and turned into the street flanked by police cars. It slowed somewhat as it drew close to where I stood on the steps with my aunt, my guys just a couple of steps behind us.

I smiled a smug, satisfied smile and offered a small wave to the female driver with a long, silver-white ponytail looped through a uniform cap. She smirked, her blood-red lips curling up as she gave a finger wave back. Then she tipped the brim of her hat lower before accelerating the truck down the street, carrying Chase out of my cities…and my life.

Demi must have spotted her too, and gasped. "Was that who I think it was?"

I gave a low chuckle. "Yup. Told you he wasn't escaping."

Her eyes widened, and she nodded in understanding. "I thought you hated the Guild."

I shrugged and decided not to answer her question. "Come on, let's head home so I can take these ridiculous pearls off. We've got Seph's going-away party to plan too."

"Did I hear my name?" my sister asked, bouncing over to us with a huge smile on her face. "Congratulations, big sister," she told me, wrapping her arms around me in a tight hug.

"Thanks, brat," I murmured back, returning her hug.

She left with two of Rex's boys, and Demi gave me a kiss on the cheek before heading down the steps to her Uber. Then it was just me and my guys, standing in front of the Cloudcroft courthouse.

"So, how does it feel?" Lucas asked, his warm palm touching the small of my back. "It's all over."

I smiled, turning to face him, then my gaze shifted to Cass and Zed. "Is it?" I murmured. "It feels more like a new beginning."

Zed reached out, linking his fingers with mine, and rubbed his thumb over my ring, his love shining bright in his eyes. "Beginning of a new era. I like it."

Cass just grunted and loosened his tie. "I fucking love you, Red," he muttered. Then his eyes narrowed at Zed and Lucas. "You two aren't half-bad, either."

Zed snickered, but Lucas grinned and launched himself at Cass in a bear hug. "Grumpy Cat *looooves* us!"

Cass and Lucas joked and teased each other all the way back to the car, but Zed hung back and looped his arm around my waist as we walked. He didn't say anything, but he didn't need to. My turbulent soul was finally calm. Finally at peace.

For the first time in my whole life, I was completely *happy*.

CHAPTER 65

One Year Later

I'd said it before, and I'd say it again and again until the day I died. The absolute *best* way—scratch that, the *only* acceptable way—to be woken up at dawn was with a massive, hot, hard dick pushing into your sleepy cunt. Followed by multiple orgasms at the hands of your *three* legally wed husbands on the morning after your marriage in a temple in Tibet, of course.

Un-fucking-beatable.

When I'd told Cass that I would only get married if it were legal to marry all three of them, I hadn't known I was challenging him. He'd done his research, then one morning when Zed was tracing my spine tattoo and telling Lucas about our hike to base camp, it'd given him ideas.

It took the better part of a year for them to convince me, but here we were. I was helpless to refuse them anything when they put their minds to it. And with polyandry legal in Tibet, I had no real reasons to refuse. Fuck knew I loved them enough.

They woke me up at dawn, and we fucked like the newlyweds we were as the sun rose over snowy mountains. By the time we got around to cleaning up and putting on clothes to leave our room, it was lunchtime.

"Well, hey there, *Mrs. Timber*," Seph teased as we made our way into the main dining room of the luxury lodge we'd exclusively rented for the wedding party. "You look like you had an exhausting wedding night. You've got something here." She indicated to my neck where I knew full fucking well Cass had left a bite mark this morning. Fucking savage.

"Shut up, brat," I muttered, then yawned heavily as I sat down at the table. Rex was sitting with Demi and Stacey, and Diana was over at the buffet table filling her plate with as many sweets as she could get her paws on. Plenty of our other friends had made the trip to Tibet for the occasion, but for now it was just my guys and my sister at the table. Nadia had left us a note to say she was visiting a local family who would teach her how to milk a yak… or something.

Lucas draped his arm over the back of my chair and placed a soft kiss on my cheek before whispering one of the sexiest things on earth in my ear.

"I'll get you coffee, babe."

I turned to kiss his lips and murmured my thanks before he got up to deliver on his promise, leaving his seat vacant for Zed to steal.

"You guys are so loved up it makes me want to vomit," Seph told us with a smile. "Are you gonna talk to Little A today?"

I rolled my eyes. "Not you too."

Seph grinned harder. "What? I think it's cute. She totally suits Artemis, and it fits our theme."

"So does Diana," I muttered. But sometimes I could swear the feisty nine-year-old was even more stubborn than me. And that was saying something. She'd recently decided she wanted to be called Artemis because Diana is a *Roman* name, but Hades and Persephone are Greek. She'd gotten it into her head that she only fit in with our family if she swapped to the Greek goddess's name instead.

"We did say after the wedding," Zed reminded me.

I knew that; it was why I had brought the envelope down to breakfast with me. "Just wait until everyone is here," I said quietly as Diana headed back over to the table with a whole stacked-high pyramid of sweets on her plate.

"Hey, guys!" she greeted us enthusiastically. "The food here is *so good*, are you sure we have to leave tomorrow?"

"Yes," I replied with a soft glare. "You have to get back to school, and Seph needs to get back to her classes."

"And her *boyfriend*," Demi teased, poking Seph in the side and making my sister squirm.

Seph's cheeks pinked. "Shut up," she grumbled. It was a new thing for her, and she was all kinds of awkward when pressed for information about *Matthieu*. He was French-Canadian, a year older than her, and had turned out to be squeaky clean to the point of boring when I'd checked his background. Not that I'd ever admit it to Seph, but he was exactly the *nice* kind of guy I felt safe with her dating.

Also, I'd taken a quick day-trip to Michigan after their first date and had a chat with him myself. He wouldn't hurt her if he valued his balls.

Lucas returned with my coffee and a plate of food, and Cass slouched into the chair beside Diana, his own plate even more loaded than hers.

"'Sup, Big Man?" she greeted him with a nod.

He grunted a response around a huge bite of food.

Demi cleared her throat, then smiled at her wife. "Stacey, sweetheart, could you show Rex that gorgeous garden we discovered yesterday?"

Rex screwed his face up. "What the fuck do I wanna see a garden for?"

Demi rolled her eyes, and Stacey laughed as she nudged Rex out of his chair and herded him from the room, lecturing him on reading between the lines.

Diana gave me a suspicious look, her cheeks full of pastry. When I simply stared back at her, she chewed quickly and swallowed before putting her hands up defensively.

"If this is about that fight at school last week, I didn't start it."

I cocked a brow since that was the first I'd heard of any fights at school recently.

Cass rumbled with amusement. "Nah, but you finished it." He stuck his fist out, and Diana bumped knuckles with him. What the fuck?

I narrowed my eyes at Cass, and he shrugged.

"I took care of it with the school," he assured me, like *that* was the point. "They need a new wing added to the library anyway."

And he had the gall to question why we'd be shitty parents. The three of them had been subtly pushing *that* issue in the lead-up to our wedding, but eventually, after I'd explained my thoughts on the matter, they'd come around.

Simply put, I didn't want to mess up a kid with our lifestyle. We were killers, plain and simple. We ran illegal businesses, smuggled drugs and guns, and operated brothels inside our strip clubs. More than that, we would *always* have danger looming. The price of power was that someone would forever be trying to take what you had. Usually by force. One day, they might get lucky and actually kill one of us.

Unless we wanted to give that all up and move to the suburbs, we couldn't have kids of our own. I refused to raise a child in that world, and I was so deeply entrenched in it there was no possible way I could remove myself and start afresh. I'd end up shooting some bitch at a PTA meeting or something.

"This *wasn't* about that," I answered Diana. "But now I'm thinking it should be. Was anyone hurt?"

Diana scoffed. "Of course. Pretty sure I broke Carolyn's nose. The blood spray was *epic*."

Zed snickered, then covered it with a cough and hid behind his cup of coffee. Asshole.

I took a moment to sip my own coffee, then prayed for sanity in what I was about to do. But the guys and I had discussed it *at length*, as had Demi, Seph, and I. This seemed like the best solution.

Drawing a deep breath, I pulled the folded envelope from my pocket. "Diana—"

"Artemis," she quickly corrected. I glared, and she shot back an impish grin. "Continue."

I shifted my gaze to Lucas, silently asking if we were doing the right thing. His smile was pure encouragement, though, and Zed squeezed my knee under the table. Cass slouched back in his chair, extending his leg to press against mine, just like Zed used to do when I needed support.

"Fuck it," I muttered. "Here." I handed the envelope across the table to Diana.

She looked worried, biting her lip and frowning as she ripped it open and pulled the papers out from inside. That frown quickly faded as she read the first page, though.

"Is this…?" Her lips parted and her eyes went wide. Shit, her eyes went *watery*. "Hades, did you *adopt me*?" Her voice was all squeaky and shrill, and Seph winced, covering her ears.

I gave an uncomfortable shrug. "Figured it doesn't really change anything, you already spend every weekend at our house. But it will keep you safe if anyone ever wonders what happened to little Diana Manson."

Tears were rolling down Diana's face now, and she clutched the paper to her chest. "This changes *everything*."

"Oh my god, Little A," Seph snickered. "Be more dramatic."

Diana snapped a glare at Seph. "Fuck you."

Seph shot her a middle finger back, and I rolled my eyes. Again. I did that a lot when the two of them were in the same room together. At the end of the day, it hadn't been a hard decision to officially adopt Diana. She'd taken to showing up on our doorstep every Friday afternoon without fail, spending the weekend with us before going back to school Monday morning. Apparently when Zoya was home with Nadia, they spoke Russian all weekend and Diana didn't understand a word they were saying. Seemed like an excuse to me, but I also didn't call her out on it.

Cass had been teaching her to fight, Lucas had been training her in gymnastics—she was damn good at it too—and Zed, despite my scolding, had been quietly teaching her how to shoot a sniper rifle. She was a part of our family. When she'd asked to be called Artemis instead of Diana, it made us realize that although *we* thought of her as family, *she* still felt out of place.

I would never bring a defenseless child into my world. I *could* never knowingly raise an innocent child—whether biological or not—in such violence and danger. But Diana was already neck deep in it all and had adapted like it'd always been a part of her. I knew better. I knew from my own damage that her dark experiences had shaped her personality. It just so happened that we loved her, thorns and all.

"Does that mean I'm a Timber now, too?" Her smile was wide and hopeful, her wet eyes darting from Seph to Demi, then back to me.

"You sure are, kid," I told her. "It suits you."

Whatever else she might have said dissolved into incoherent babbling as she launched a hug at Cass, who was closest to her. Then she hopped up and went around the table hugging everyone, landing on me last.

"Does this mean I call you Mom?" she asked, sniffing back tears.

I peeled her away far enough to glare. "Call me 'Mom' and I'll sign you up for ballet classes." Diana gave a horrified gasp, and I laughed. "That's what I thought."

She grinned, then hugged me tight once more. Over her head, my guys all gave me soft smiles. We were a family, and now we had the legal paperwork to prove it.

CHAPTER 66

Two Years Later

A heavy clang echoed through the stone corridor, the metal gate open just long enough to allow me through before beginning to close once more. The security in this prison was staggeringly impressive, but it was for that very security that I'd been paying such a steep price for the last three years. For the security, and the extra-special personal attention my prisoner was getting from his jailers.

"It'll be a shame to see this one go," the scar-faced guard told me in a thick Scottish accent as I approached the isolation cell at the end of the corridor. He wore a leather apron, dark and stained with blood. *Guard* was a polite term for what he actually did within the prison.

I curved a cold smile. "Yeah?"

He grunted. "Aye. He lasted so much longer than the usual sheep I get tossed. Made it a real challenge to break him." He gave me a missing-toothed grin. "I won in the end, though. Always do."

"It's why I had him brought here," I murmured, eyeing the thick, locked door behind the guard. "I reviewed the recent footage. He definitely is broken now, hmm?"

The man dipped his head. "Oh, aye. All of this?" He tapped his head. "Gone. It happens to all of 'em sooner or later. Yer man was one of the longest."

I huffed a sharp laugh. "He lost his mind a long time before he came here. All right, let's get this done."

The guard nodded and cranked the heavy mechanical lock on the door, then hauled it open. "I'll wait out here, then. Knock when yer done."

My nose stung at the putrid smell inside the cell, but I stepped forward confidently and braced myself as the heavy door shut behind me. The light in the cell was harsh, leaving the broken heap of a man chained to the wall no place to hide.

"Your guards think you've finally broken, Chasey baby," I murmured, stepping closer and cringing at the smell. I'd watched *countless* hours of footage from this very room, but it was a different thing entirely to be there in person. "Is that true? Have you checked out?"

When I got close, I crouched down to his level. The way he slumped against the wall, his wrists bound and bloody, it'd be easy to believe he was dead already. A breath later, though, he raised his head and squinted at me with his one remaining eye. His eye patch was long gone, and the mess of scars on his face was in full view without the covering. But that stare…

"I thought as much," I murmured, holding his gaze.

"Darling," he croaked, giving a hacking laugh, "it's been forever. Miss me?"

I gave a tight smile. In the early days, when he was first *relocated* from his court-assigned prison, I'd taken an active hand in his torture. I'd drawn plenty of satisfaction returning his own methods of torture onto him threefold over. All except the rape, of course. I had *no* desire to touch him in that way…though the same couldn't be said for the guards within this very special prison.

But eventually, I'd had to face the fact that it was weighing on my soul too much. By continuing to return, I wasn't only torturing Chase. I was torturing *myself*. And if I ever truly wanted to be rid of him, I needed to walk away. So that's what I'd done. I handed his care over to the professionals and cleared him from my mind. Except, of course, for once a month when I logged into the secure server that showed me video documentation that he was still alive and still suffering.

"I think it's time, don't you?" I said softly, unlocking the shackles from his wrists. He dropped to the floor in a heap, like he lacked the strength to hold himself up anymore. Not that he'd need to. I was there for one reason, and it wasn't forgiveness. It was finality.

I stood up and nudged his shoulder with the toe of my shoe, rolling him over onto his back. A weak smile curved his cracked lips, and he looked up at me with resignation.

"You won, Darling," he admitted. "I underestimated you."

I tilted my head, smiling. "You really did." Not breaking his gaze, I pulled the Desert Eagle from my shoulder holster and aimed it at his face. "I hope you appreciate how poetic this ending will be for you, Chase. Almost like we've come full circle...except this time you won't be making a one-in-a-million recovery."

He hacked a laugh. "I don't doubt it. We had fun though, didn't we, Darling?"

I shook my head. "No, Chase. We really didn't. I hope you rot in hell for eternity." I wasn't religious in the least, but I liked the idea of eternal damnation for Chase fucking Lockhart.

My finger squeezed the trigger, and a bullet slammed home into Chase's face, right in the middle of his forehead. His one beady eye stared up at me, blank and lifeless, but I wasn't taking chances. Inhaling deeply, I squeezed the trigger over and over, emptying my clip into his head until nothing remained but a mess of blood, bone, and brain matter all over the stone floor.

If Chase had taught me anything, though, it was never to leave *any* doubts if you truly wanted someone dead and gone. So I calmly put my gun back in its holster and pulled the squeeze bottle of gasoline from my handbag. It was a quick job to douse the body with the pungent fluid.

Before lighting a match, I knocked on the door to ask the guard to open it. The last thing I needed was to accidentally blow myself up if the gasoline had been overkill.

The guard swung the door open, gave the body a long look, then nodded. "Thorough."

I smiled back. "I try."

Standing at the doorway, I retrieved the engraved silver lighter from my bag and flicked a flame to life. Then, as casual as feeding the ducks, I tossed the lighter onto Chase's remains and watched without blinking as his corpse went up in a whoosh of blue-orange flame.

"Gonna stay until he's ash?" the guard asked with zero judgment.

I nodded. "Sure am. He's risen from the dead once before… but never again."

The guard grunted a sound of respect. "I wish I could offer ye some marshmallows. Could had a wee celebration while you wait."

Reaching into my bag once more, I pulled out a bag of squishy pink treats I'd brought along just for the occasion. "Way ahead of you."

He gave a roaring laugh, shaking his head. "I'll leave ye to it."

The sound of his chuckles echoed along the corridor, and I made my way back into the cell now that the initial flames had died down to a less eyebrow-singeing level. I poked a marshmallow on the end of a dagger and toasted it over Chase's burning body, then snapped a selfie to send to the guys.

Their response was instant and unanimous.

We love you. Come home.

I smiled, because I could. I could finally go *home*, totally free of my demons, and into the arms of the men who loved me for *me*.

Chase Lockhart's hand had been wrapped around my throat for so long that I'd forgotten what it felt like to breathe freely. He'd tried everything to break me. He'd attempted to burn my whole empire to the ground; he'd even burned my Gumdrop. And in the end…it was Chase who wound up a pile of charred remains on a dirty, bloodstained prison floor.

Except this time, the only thing rising from ashes was my future.

I walked away with the sickly sweet taste of toasted marshmallow in my mouth and never looked back.

DISCOVER MORE BOOKS IN
THE SHADOW GROVE WORLD WITH
BOOK 1 IN THE MADISON KATE SERIES

CHAPTER 1

I shouldn't be here.

If my father knew…

But I would take those risks to witness this fight. This *fighter.*

Music boomed from the speaker beside me, and the crowd got louder. More frenzied and impatient. Adrenaline pulsed through my veins, pushing my own excitement to such a level that I could barely stay still. I started bouncing lightly on the balls of my feet just to keep from screaming or fainting or something.

A grin curled my lips, and I nodded my head to the familiar tune. "Clichéd choice but could have been worse," I muttered under my breath. "Bodies" by Drowning Pool continued to rage, and I pushed up on my toes, trying to catch a glimpse of one of the reasons we'd skipped out on our shitty Halloween party.

"MK, I don't get it," my best friend, Bree, whined from beside me. Her hands covered her ears, and her delicate face was screwed up like she was in physical pain. "Why are we even here? This is so far from our side of town, it's scary. Like, legit scary. Can we *go* already?"

"What?" I exclaimed, frowning at her and thinking I'd surely just heard her wrong. "We can't leave now; the fight hasn't even started yet!" I needed to yell for her to hear me, and she cringed again. She had reason to. In a crowd dominated mostly by men—big men—Bree and I stood zero chance of even seeing the octagon, let alone the fighters. Or if I was honest, one fighter in particular. So we'd climbed up onto one of the massive industrial generators to get a better view.

The one we'd picked just happened to also have a speaker sitting on it, and the volume of the music was just this side of deafening.

"Babe, we've been here for over an hour," Bree complained. "I'm tired and sober, my feet hurt, and I'm sweating like a bitch. Can we *please* go?" She tried to glare at me, but the whole effect was ruined by the fact that she still had a cat nose and whiskers drawn on her face—not to mention a fluffy tail strapped to her ass.

Not that I could judge. My costume was "sexy witch," but at least I'd been able to ditch my pointed hat. Now I was just wearing a skanky, black lace minidress and patent leather stiletto boots.

It was after midnight on October 31, and we were *supposed* to be at our friend Veronica's annual Halloween party. Yet Bree and I had decided that sneaking out of the party to attend a highly illegal mixed martial arts fight night would be a better idea. Even better still, it was being held in the big top of a long-abandoned amusement park called The Laughing Clown.

Like that wasn't an infinitely better way to spend the night than being hit on by a boy with a Rolex and then spending all of three minutes with him in the backseat of his Bentley.

Yeah, Veronica's parties all sort of ended the same way, and I, for one, was over it.

"Bree, I didn't force you to come with me," I replied, annoyed at her badgering. "You *wanted* to come. Remember?"

Her mouth dropped open in indignation. "Uh, yeah, so you wouldn't get robbed or murdered or something trying to hitchhike your way over the divide! MK, I saved your perky ass, and you know it."

I rolled my eyes at her dramatics. "I was going to Uber, not hitchhike. And West Shadow Grove is not exactly the seventh circle of hell."

Her eyes rounded as she looked out over the crowd gathered to watch the fights. "It may as well be. You know how many people get killed in West Shadow Grove *every day*?"

I narrowed my eyes and called her factual bluff. "I don't, actually. How many?"

"I don't know either," she admitted, "but it's a lot." She nodded at me like that made her statement more convincing, and I laughed.

Whatever else she'd planned to say to convince me to leave was drowned out by the fight commentator. My attention left Bree in a flash, and I strained to see the octagon. Even standing on the generator box for height, we were still far enough away that the view was shitty.

My excitement piqued, bubbling through me like champagne as I twisted my sweaty hands in the stretchy fabric of my dress. The commentator was listing his stats now.

Six foot four, two hundred and two pounds, twenty-three wins, zero draws, zero losses.

Zero losses. This guy was freaking born for MMA.

It wasn't an official fight—quite the opposite. So they didn't elaborate any more than that. There was no mention of his age, his hometown, his training gym…nothing. Not even his name. Only…

"Please give it up for"—the commentator gave a dramatic pause, whipping the crowd into a frenzy—"the mysterious, the undefeated, *The Archer!*" He bellowed the fighter's nickname, and the crowd freaking lost it. Myself included.

"Paranoid" by I Prevail poured from the speaker beside us, and by the time the tall, hooded figure had made his way through the crowd with his team tight around him, my throat was dry and scratchy from yelling. Even from this distance, I trembled with anticipation and randomly pictured what it'd be like to climb him like a tree. Except naked.

"I'm going to guess this is why we came?" Bree asked in a dry voice, wrinkling her nose and making her kitty whiskers twitch. Her costume wasn't as absurd as it could be, since most members of the crowd were in some form of Halloween costume. Even the fighters tonight wore full face masks, and the commentator was dressed as the Grim Reaper.

"You know it is," I shot back, not taking my gaze from the octagon for even a second. I hardly dared blink for fear of missing something.

One of his support team—a guy only a fraction shorter with a similar fighter's physique and a ball cap pulled low over his face—took the robe from his shoulders, and my breath caught in my throat. His back was to us, but every hard surface was decorated with ink. We were too far away to see details, but I knew—from my borderline obsessive stalking—that the biggest tattoo on his back was of a geometric stag shot with arrows. It was how he'd gotten his nickname. The stag represented his star sign: Sagittarius, the Archer.

"Ho-ly shit," Bree gasped, and I knew without looking at her she had suddenly discovered a love for MMA.

"They say he's being scouted for the UFC," I babbled to her, "except they said he has to stop all underground cage matches, and apparently he told them to shove it."

Bree made a sound of acknowledgment, but knowing her, she didn't even know what the UFC was, let alone understand what an incredible achievement that was for a young fighter.

"Shh," I said, even though she hadn't spoken. "It's starting."

In the makeshift octagon, the Archer and his opponent—both wearing nothing but shorts and a plain mask—tapped gloves, and the fight was officially on.

Totally enthralled by the potential of the main event fight, I

544

waited eagerly to see how it was all going to pan out. Would it be an even match of skills and strength, spanning all five rounds? Or would it be a total domination by one fighter? I could only cross my fingers and hope The Archer hadn't grown cocky with his recent successes and ended up KO'd in thirty seconds like Ronda Rousey.

The other guy struck first, impatient and impetuous. Watching the way The Archer blocked his attack, then struck back with a vicious jab to the face and knee to the side, I could already tell it would be over before the end of the first round.

"Damn, he's quick," I commented, while my fighter of choice dodged and weaved, not allowing any contact from his opponent. Each strike he blocked or evaded, he returned threefold, until eventually he had the other guy down on the bloodstained mat.

"Is it over?" Bree asked, gripping my arm.

I shook my head. "Not until one of them taps out or you know"—I shrugged—"gets knocked out."

"Brutal," she breathed, but there was a spark in her eyes that said she was having fun.

The Archer's opponent thrashed around like a fish on a hook, just barely holding back the arm threatening to get under his chin. Once the bigger, tattooed fighter got his forearm under there, it'd be all over for the guy whose nickname I hadn't even listened to.

"Come on, come on," I urged, bouncing slightly in my stupidly high heels. "Come on, Archer. Finish him!"

The struggle continued for a few more moments, and then some huge-headed asshole moved into my line of sight. Something happened, and the crowd roared. I could only imagine Archer had locked down his choke hold.

"Yes!" I exclaimed, craning my neck to try and to see. "Oh come on, *move!*" This was aimed at the guy blocking my view. Not that he could hear me.

The commentator started counting. It would all be over in ten seconds if the other guy didn't tap out before that.

"…three…four…five…"

Frustration clawed at me that I couldn't *see*.

"…six…seven…"

Bang!

Startled and confused, I jerked my attention to Bree at the loud noise. Had a car just backfired? Inside the big top? How the hell was that even possible?

"What was that?" I tried to ask but couldn't hear my own voice. My ears were ringing with a high-pitched sound, and everything else was on mute.

Bree was saying something and tugging on my arm, but I couldn't hear her.

What the fuck is going on?

"MK, come *on*!" Her words finally penetrated the ringing in my ears, and I stumbled as she dragged me down from our elevated position and into the chaos below.

I shook my head, still confused as fuck, until Bree's panicked yell sank in.

"Someone just got shot," she told me. "We need to get the hell out of here. Now."

Several more shots—because holy shit, she was right—rang out in the crowded space, and people scattered like bowling pins.

Bree and I clutched each other's hand as we crouched low and made our way as fast as possible to the exit, but we soon realized there was a whole lot more going on than a lone shooter. Between us and the door, an all-out brawl was happening, with at least thirty people swinging punches and kicks. Blood and fuck knew what else flew everywhere, I just barely dragged Bree out of the way when a burly guy in a leather jacket stumbled back from a punch to his face and would have knocked her over.

"We need to find another way out," I told her, stating the obvious as I searched around for another exit. It was a freaking big top, and there must been almost five hundred people spectating the illegal MMA fight night. The venue had to have loads of other exits. "This way!" I shouted, dragging her behind me as I ducked and weaved through the violent mob.

"MK," my friend exclaimed, tugging on my hand. "Look!"

I followed her shaking finger and saw a puddle of red across the polished concrete floor. A spill of pale-blond hair—the same color mine would be if I hadn't just dyed it hot pink for this costume—and a lifeless hand with chipped nail polish.

"Don't look," I snapped to Bree, yanking on her hand again to get her moving. One girl was already dead, and I sure as shit didn't want to join her.

It only took a few more minutes to get clear of the violent mess inside the big top. The night air held frost, and my teeth chattered as Bree and I hurried away through the dark amusement park.

"Th-that was…" Bree stammered over her words, and I slowed just enough to check that she was okay. Her eyes were wide and haunted, her face pale. She hadn't broken down into hysterical crying yet, so maybe shock was working on our side for once.

If nothing else, it'd hopefully keep her from mentioning why I was so seemingly unaffected by seeing a dead body and all that violence. All that bloodshed.

I locked down the memories of the last dead body I'd seen, stuffing them back into the tiny mental box they'd been in for exactly six years. Halloween was the anniversary of my mom's murder.

"Stay quiet," I whispered to her, my attention on the shadows around us. "We need to get back to your car and away from here."

My best friend, for all her amazing qualities, had zero clue how much danger we were in.

"What's going on, MK?" she demanded, her voice pitched way too loud for my liking.

"Shh!" I placed a hand over her mouth to emphasize my point. We were tucked into the shadows beside a dilapidated sideshow booth, and I frantically searched around us to check that we were alone. "Bree, you need to trust me. That was no random act of violence. Didn't you see the tattoos on those guys brawling? The patches on their jackets?" Her eyes grew even wider above my hand, and her breath came in jerky, panicked gasps. I nodded, confirming what she'd just guessed. "Yeah. Exactly. We're neck deep in the middle of a gang war, and if we don't get the fuck out of here soon…" I trailed off. She knew what I meant. If either gang—the Wraiths or the Reapers—caught us, the consequences didn't bear thinking about. Let's say death would be the easy way out. Bree would probably get ransomed back to her filthy-rich family, but I wouldn't be so lucky. Not because my father couldn't pay but because he'd somehow made an enemy of the Reapers' leader.

Voices came from nearby, laughing guys, and I pulled Bree farther into the shadows until they'd passed us.

"Let's go," I said softly when their chatter faded away.

Bree was right behind me as I started hurrying back toward where we'd parked. More and more people were spilling out of the big top now, so we kept our heads down and tried to blend with a group in costumes. It helped that Bree was still in her sexy-cat outfit and my waist-length hair was hot pink. We just looked like regular girls out for a Halloween party.

I almost let the tension drop from my shoulders around the time we made it halfway through the park, but we couldn't hide with the crowd forever. We'd parked Bree's car in a shed behind the south gate, and everyone else was flowing toward the west one.

Silently, I tugged her hand, and the two of us broke away from the crowd, immediately picking up our pace and hurrying past the broken-down bumper cars.

"This was a bad idea," Bree mumbled, but she stuck close behind me as we jogged—in heels—through the scary-as-fuck park. Why had it all seemed so damn exciting when we'd arrived?

Suddenly it was like we were stuck inside a horror movie and any minute now someone would jump out with a knife or chainsaw or something.

Adrenaline pumping through my veins, I rounded a corner without checking first and ran straight into the back of a guy in a full Beetlejuice costume.

"Shit, sorry," I exclaimed, catching my balance on my stripper-esque stiletto heels.

I made to move past him, but a huge hand circled my upper arm. He stopped me in my tracks at the same time as I saw the guy he'd been talking to…and the large, open bag of cash on the ground between them.

"Uh…" I licked my lips and flicked a look from Beetlejuice to the other man. "Sorry, we'll get out of your way."

I tugged on Bree's hand, ignoring Beetlejuice's grip on my arm as I urged her past me on the outside, away from Beetlejuice's leather jacket–wearing friend. It was dark enough that I couldn't make out what patch he wore, but it didn't really matter. They were both bad fucking news.

"What did you hear?" Beetlejuice demanded, shaking me a bit and getting up in my face. His friend just watched. Uncaring.

"Nothing," I snapped back at him. "We were just getting out of here. Some bad shit is going on in the big top."

Beetlejuice sneered, and the leather-jacketed dude snickered. Like they already knew and were happy about it.

"Let me go," I said, my voice firm. "We didn't see or hear anything, and we honestly don't care. There's already one dead girl in this park, and a whole ton of witnesses. This place will be crawling with cops any second now."

Beetlejuice narrowed his eyes at me, his gaze suspicious before jerking a nod. "You saw *nothing*," he snarled, the warning clear as he released me with a shove. "Dumb bitches." This was muttered to his friend as he dismissed us from his presence.

I walked a few paces, not wanting to run while they could see me, but gave Bree a look that practically screamed *hurry your ass up!*

"Wait." That one word hit me like a lightning bolt, and my whole body tensed, my foot frozen in the air. "Don't I know you?"

It was the other guy speaking, and his deep, *familiar* voice sent chills down my spine. He was closer now; I could feel his intimidating presence looming behind me. He was near enough that I could smell the leather of his jacket. He could simply reach out and break my neck if he wanted to.

Panicked, I made a snap decision.

"Bree, whatever you do, don't stop until you get to the car. I'll meet you there." I said this under my breath, but the glare I gave her silenced any protests she might have. "I mean it," I assured her. "Fucking *run*."

She gave me a tight nod, her eyes brimming with fear and determination, then kicked off her heels and disappeared into the night.

"Fuck this," Beetlejuice snapped, and his footsteps quickly faded in the opposite direction. But only his. My creepy shadow hadn't budged an inch.

"Yeah," he murmured, his breath stirring the hot-pink strands of my hair. "I thought I recognized that ass. Now what is a girl like you doing in West Shadow Grove, Madison Kate Danvers?"

I didn't run after Bree because I wasn't a fucking idiot. There was no way I'd outrun this guy in what I was wearing. And now that he knew who I was, he wouldn't just stand back while I took off either.

Instead, I did the only thing that came to my mind.

I spun around and punched him right in the face.

AUTHOR'S NOTE

Oh, hey, you! You MADE IT! Good work. Now…do you need a snack or some water or something? I know that one was a girthy bitch and I hope you stopped for pee breaks along the way.

You didn't *seriously* think we were just going to let Chase rot in jail forever, did you? I bet you're gonna be looking at marshmallows differently next time you go to toast one! I have it on good authority (from Hades) that they taste pretty fucking awful when toasted over a burning body. But I suppose victory tastes better than anything, so I'll let her get away with that.

Yes, I hear you, not everything got tied up in a nice, neat bow, *again*! You still have *questions*, dammit! And I feel for you. But my villains don't always play nice. They don't tend to leave video confessions or write their secrets in their diaries. Sometimes—like with Sandra—secrets simply go to the grave unheard. But if it makes you feel better, I know *all* the answers to your questions. I just didn't leave anyone alive to tell them on the page! Whoops-a-daisy.

Oh, Heather knows too. Does that help? No? Hmm.

Change of subject? Okay, good plan! I know you're still curious about a couple of characters that had little introductions throughout this series, but don't worry. Their day will come. Like Hades's tattoo says, *Everything happens for a reason*, and that couldn't be truer in this Shadow Grove–linked world.

A word of warning, though. Hades was a deeply damaged chick who dealt with her big feelings in bloodshed more often than not. But she's got nothing on this next heroine. Please proceed into the Guild with caution because they're *not* the good guys.

I need to express an enormous thank you to my content editor, sounding board, taskmistress, and general hand-holder Heather Long. This has been a goddamn *journey* but I think we just keep getting better with every conquest. Like I told you thirty-four books ago, you're the bestest editor who ever edited and yes, Zed is all yours (along with River, Zan, Beck, Rafe, Fucking-Kody, and you-know-who...*wink*).

To *you* my reader, thank you for sticking with Hades's story. I hope you enjoyed yourself. I also hope you'll come back to the Shadow Grove world again.